THE
DANCE
OF
VIPERS

A.K. NAIRN

Copyright © A. K. Nairn

All rights reserved.

No part of this publication may be altered, reproduced, distributed, or transmitted in any form, by any means, including, but not limited to, scanning, duplicating, uploading, hosting, distributing, or reselling, without the express prior written permission of the publisher, except in the case of reasonable quotations in features such as reviews, interviews, and certain other non-commercial uses currently permitted by copyright law.

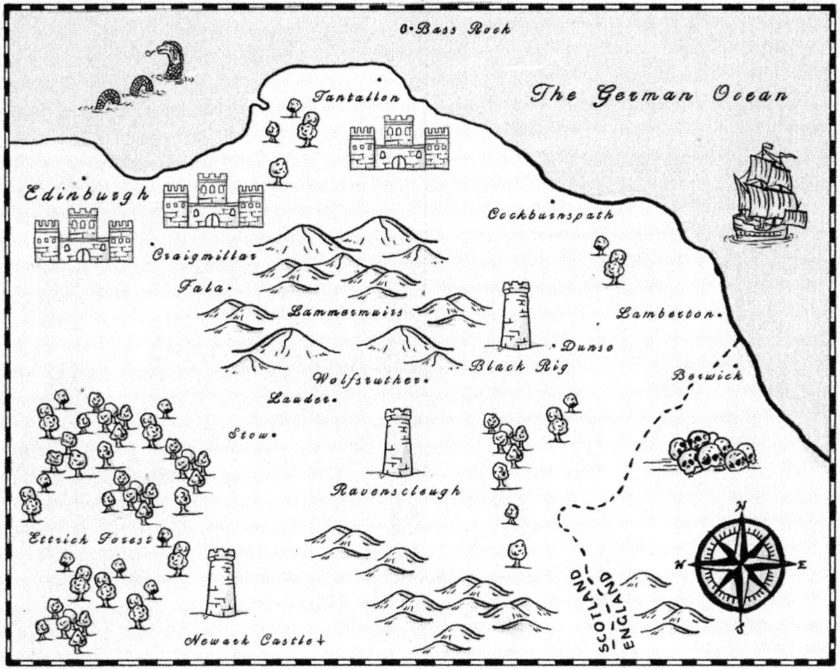
Bass Rock
The German Ocean
Tantallon
Edinburgh
Craigmillar
Cockburnspath
Fala
Lammermuirs
Lamberton
Dunse
Black Rig
Berwick
Wolfsruther
Lauder
Stow
Ravenscleugh
Ettrick Forest
Newark Castle
SCOTLAND
ENGLAND
N
W
E
S

Chapter 1

Antoine saw him first. The Frenchman had been scanning the horizon for their visitor when he noticed a slender figure on the edge of camp. The fellow was drifting through the tents, like a wisp of smoke from one of the smouldering fires. Occasionally, he would pause to look around, perhaps loosening his doublet or shifting his bonnet, by way of cover. Then he would move on to the next group of men, lingering for a while as they bantered over their ale. It had been a long, hot day, and they were exhausted from the march, but he did not raise a cup, did not share their jokes or join their games of dice.

He was doing his best to remain unnoticed, which is exactly what marked him out to Antoine.

"Watch that man," he said to Turnbull. His assistant took a moment to spot the fellow among the mass of Scottish soldiers gathered around them on the wild border at Lamberton. The sun was dipping, and the shadowy figures were difficult to distinguish against the purpling sky.

Finally, Turnbull had him. "Scraggy sort? Hook nose? Standing alone by the horses?"

Antoine nodded. "Yes, he's been weaving through the camp, like he's up to no good. I think he could be a spy."

Turnbull squinted. "Couldn't he just be a porter, on an errand for someone?"

"What, for the horses?" Antoine scoffed. For a clever lad, Turnbull sometimes said the silliest things. "I doubt it. And he's not one of the stable boys; he's a grown man. No, I think he's waiting for darkness to fall, before making a break across the heath."

They gazed again across the rough scrublands leading to the frontier line. Governor Albany had sent them here on this sweltering 14th day of June 1517, to welcome Margaret Tudor back from her exile in England. As the mother of Scotland's infant king, she had challenged Albany's authority to act as the child's regent, so her return was supposed to be an act of reconciliation. However, there had been no sign of the queen, and her absence had put everyone on edge, stirring up fears of double-dealing.

For a moment, Antoine wondered whether these fears were clouding his judgement. But as the remaining rays of light drained from the sky, his instincts were confirmed. The man crouched down, glanced around one last time, and then scuttled to a rocky outcrop shielded by a patch of gorse bushes, the final refuge before the open land.

Antoine nudged Turnbull's elbow and gestured for him to advance. They edged towards their prey, eyes fixed on the intruder as his head peeked through the thorns. The route meant skirting round the makeshift latrines, already stinking from a day's filth. Some spearmen squatted over a trench, emptying their bowels before wiping themselves with moss. Antoine gestured to a pair who had just finished. Together, they crept forward, getting so close to the fellow that they could almost count the freckles on his neck. Suddenly,

Turnbull's scabbard clanked against his leg. The man spun round, scrambled to his feet and took off.

The soldiers gave chase, with Turnbull pausing only to blow his horn and alert the rest of the camp. The fugitive sprinted towards a hut on the frontier line, from which a couple of English sentries were emerging, alarmed by the commotion. He was a fast runner and skipped through the long grass with ease. Antoine feared he might get away, but one of his troops successfully landed a spear ahead of the spy, disrupting his stride. The man swerved to his left but found himself running towards Turnbull. As he scrambled to find an alternative way through, another spear flew past him and blocked that path as well.

Now, in his hesitation, he was trapped. And he knew it. More men from the Scottish camp joined them and pressed around the escapee, who looked plaintively towards the English sentries in the distance. But they made no move to help him.

"Let's string him up," said the first spearman, licking his lips.

"Only once we've squeezed some news frae him," said the other.

Antoine frowned at them. "You'll do no such thing. Just get him tied and take him to my tent."

The soldiers grumbled but complied. As they led the prisoner back through the camp, some onlookers called out insults, while others watched with what appeared to be pity or even sympathy. This reminded Antoine that, for all the talk of reconciliation, even his own troops were bitterly divided. It reinforced his decision to leave his adopted country and its endless politicking as soon as this mission was over. But for now, there was work to be done.

Turnbull pulled back the tent flap and ushered them inside.

"Excuse the mess," said Antoine, gesturing around the dingy space. A couple of bedrolls, some stools and an oak chest stood on the bare earth, as there had been no time to gather rushes. "We wouldn't want you to report back to your master on our slovenly ways."

The prisoner remained impassive, as the Frenchman sat him down on a stool and sent the spearmen outside.

"Speaking of which," said Turnbull, "who *is* your master?"

The man still gave nothing away. Instead, he tilted his head back and gave a thin smile. Antoine recognised the expression from his many years as a diplomat: the posturing, the use of silence to convey strength. It was clear he was dealing with a skilled operator, not some novice who would crack at the first sign of pressure.

"You know, there are men out there who are less patient than I am. Should I hand you over, so they can deal with you?"

This time, the prisoner looked up to the roof of the tent, where an evening breeze was rippling the canvas. The sounds of camp filled the silence – men laughing, pots clanking, the German Ocean crashing in the distance. He bit his lip. "I presume you are de Lissieu?" he asked in a clipped English accent.

Antoine nodded.

"I have heard of you. We're all surprised that you're still here."

The Frenchman flushed, for his thoughts immediately went to his plans to return home – a fact he had not yet shared with Turnbull. Albany had foisted the lad on him when he had appointed Antoine the Warden of the Eastern Marches the previous winter. Although raw and excitable, the boy had proved to be a useful guide in this savage frontier region. Antoine had grown fond of him and did not relish the idea of telling him he was leaving. He felt relieved when the spy explained that he meant something else.

"We thought you might be in a ditch by now. The locals do not take kindly to strangers, do they?"

"I've been here almost as long as the hills," Antoine replied, as he always did when his foreign origins were remarked upon. "But thank you for your concern." He took a seat at the chest and steepled his fingers. "Now, my friend, tell me who you are and what brings you here. As you may know, we were expecting someone of a rather higher station."

"Very well. I am Robin Fortingale, equerry to the queen," the prisoner said smugly. He noticed Antoine's surprise. "That's right, an attendant of the royal household. Even considering Her Grace's recent change in circumstances, you are bound to grant me safe conduct. So perhaps you would be so kind as to undo these ropes and let me on my way."

Antoine grimaced. "Not so fast. First, we will need proof of your identity. Then I would like to know why you are here – and why your mistress is not."

"Hmmph. It is as Her Grace says: you're a stickler for the facts. An unusual trait up here. My documents are in my purse, but I cannot reach them right now." Fortingale raised his wrists to show a leather pouch on his belt. Turnbull cautiously reached in to unfasten the clip and pulled out a tightly folded wad of papers. While he inspected them, the prisoner continued, "As for my presence, I am here to scout for Her Grace. She has stopped awhile in Berwick, for she is disturbed that she might walk into a trap."

Antoine furrowed his brow. Governor Albany's secretaries had been in correspondence with the English court for months, and he had thought everything had been taken care of. "Nothing could be further from the truth," he said. "We are here to welcome the queen back and ensure her safety, that's all. You have Lord Albany's word on this."

"I'm afraid we do not always have great faith in the governor's word. We are told that he's in France, but for all we know, he could be waiting for us here."

Antoine put a hand across his heart. "I swear it's true. He sailed a week ago and will be in Rouen these next three months. In any case, he has left instructions for Her Grace to be treated with friendship and respect."

"Some say she is to be called 'the king's mother' instead of 'the queen', and 'Her Lady' instead of 'Her Grace'."

"Have you heard me do so?" Antoine asked. Inside he cursed, for he had urged against such pettiness, only for others to shout him down.

"No, sir, but can we trust Lord Albany's other counsellors to be so courtly?"

"I cannot choose others' words for them. But as long as Her Grace does not disturb the peace while our governor is away, she should have nothing to fear."

Turnbull finished checking the documents and nodded towards Antoine, signalling that the papers were in order. He placed them back in the prisoner's purse, and Fortingale secured them before proffering his hands. Antoine gestured for Turnbull to untie him, and the lad began to pick at the ropes with his dagger.

"There's also the small matter of Her Grace's upkeep," said Fortingale, inspecting the red marks around his wrists.

"Yes, yes," said Antoine impatiently. "I believe her jewels and wardrobe have already been returned to her."

"And her rental incomes? They've dried up like a stream in summer while the queen has been away – almost as if someone is trying to swindle her…"

Antoine had heard reports that such monies had been diverted, but he didn't know who was responsible. He decided to make it someone else's problem. "Not my area. But I'm sure the comptroller will straighten it out."

"Then it seems I can reassure Her Grace," Fortingale said as he moved toward the tent's entrance. Turnbull pulled back the canvas, but the Englishman lingered for a moment, before turning to give Antoine a hard stare. "There's just one final matter: What about the little king?"

Antoine flinched; the queen's access to her five-year-old son had been the most hotly contested point of the negotiations. It was not surprising, as her hopes for power, like everyone else's, hinged on him. He met Fortingale's gaze. "Everything is in order. She may visit him at Edinburgh Castle, according to the conditions we have laid down." He counted off the rules on his fingers. "With a maximum of four attendants, never overnight, and all subject to the final discretion of the captain of the castle."

Fortingale nodded slowly. "Well, let us hope that the captain uses his discretion wisely. We all know what mischief can arise when little princes are locked in towers."

Antoine did not answer, as he was weary of the rumours swirling around the boy. The competing claims for his custody, the threats, the plots, the scare-mongering – God's blood, the adults who swarmed around him were more childish than the child himself.

He watched as the spy walked back towards the border

and melted into the inky sky. All was black, save the sparks of the campfires behind them and the glow from the English sentries' hut ahead.

From the gloaming, Fortingale's voice rang out again. "Mark my words, sir. That boy needs his mother."

Yes, and that mother needs her boy, thought Antoine. The problem is, she is not the only one.

Chapter 2

Antoine had a restless night in the tent and was already awake when the birds began to trill. Sleeping on the flinty ground did not help, but he knew from long experience that his troubles were more of the mind than of the body. Doubt. Fear. Guilt. He had thought he had shaken off these demons, but still they visited him at times like this, when the world seemed to spin with change and uncertainty.

It had been four years since Scotland's disastrous defeat at Flodden. Two great factions had emerged from the carnage: one in favour of maintaining the long-standing alliance with France, the other arguing that it was time for the country to throw in its lot with England. The former camp had prevailed for now, leaving Albany to govern for the little king. But Margaret Tudor remained a potent threat. So why had Albany invited her back now, while he was away? Antoine's mind swirled with the incongruity of it all.

He roused Turnbull, and together they joined the troops as they prepared for the day. According to their orders, they were to escort the queen to Edinburgh, where they would oversee a visit with her beloved son. Then they were to return to the Marches, to keep guard on a bandit – or a "reiver", as they called them here. The authorities had been rounding up known troublemakers to reduce the likelihood of mischief while Lord Albany was away. At least *that* part of the mission made sense.

"Remind me of our prisoner's name," Antoine said as he scanned the horizon.

"Will Baird," replied Turnbull. "He runs a gang out of Ettrick Forest, so he's being held in a tower near Lauder."

"A killer, I assume?"

"Not according to Albany's secretary, although he emphasised we should not set great store by that. Any lack of blood on Baird's hands is simply down to his skill at robbing folk before they can draw a blade. He's a charmer. A magician. As crafty as Beelzebub, they say."

"Is that so? Then perhaps he could help us find the queen, as the Devil only knows where she's got to."

It was not until noon that a blast of trumpets heralded a small band at the frontier. The newcomers and their horses were clad in dazzling white damask cloth with gold accents that glimmered in the midday sun.

"It seems Her Grace is not lacking in income after all," said Turnbull.

"Let's not leap to judge her," said Antoine. "She simply reminds us of her status."

"Aye, and of England's power in comparison to our own."

Antoine surveyed the crowd of men gathered about them, more of an army than a welcoming party. "We play the same sport," he said wearily. "Well, let the games begin."

He enlisted a couple of clerks, and they walked slowly towards the border. As they went, Antoine could not ignore the echoes of a previous visit to this very spot. Fifteen years ago, as a relatively junior diplomat fresh off the boat, he had witnessed Margaret Tudor's arrival as a child bride for James IV. He recalled the euphoric atmosphere that had pervaded that occasion, the hope for peace and prosperity. He contrasted that mood with the slaughter that had followed and the tension he felt now. How the wheel of time turns, he thought, creating perfect circles while churning up lives and dreams along the way.

At the border, they were greeted by the familiar, bejewelled figure of Lord Douglas. The queen had married him less than a year after the old king's death at the hands of her countrymen, and it had not helped her cause. The young aristocrat was undeniably handsome, but he had the air of one who knew it, and his lust for power was the talk of the Scottish court. True to his haughty reputation, he made a show of yawning as Antoine approached.

"At last, de Lissieu. I trust all is in order and that you're ready to welcome Her Grace?"

"We were ready yesterday," Antoine said curtly. "But yes, everything is in order. I hope the queen is also prepared so that we can proceed, as agreed?"

Douglas nodded. "We are reassured that there's no trickery."

He smiled, as if enjoying a private joke, and instructed some men to bring forward a grand carriage. It was beautifully carved, with symbols of the Tudor rose entwined with Scotland's thistle. Its four horses plodded across the hardened summer mud, flanked by two foot soldiers on either side. When the vehicle was level with the border stone, it came to a halt, and the door opened.

The round, tightly coiffed head of Margaret Tudor

peeked out, her lips pursed with a severity that belied her twenty-eight years.

"Welcome back, Your Grace," Antoine said, bowing deeply. "It will be an honour to escort you home."

"Home?" Margaret said, looking around at the rugged landscape. She let out a deep sigh. "No more than it is yours, I fear."

Antoine felt a pang of fellow feeling for her. Despite their opposing loyalties, he had always enjoyed cordial relations with her at court and knew that she too had suffered from the recent conflict. Regardless of her finery and royal blood, she looked tired and anxious – almost downtrodden.

"Let us take you back over, Your Grace," he said, mustering as much kindness as he could. "You may resettle quicker than you think."

The Scottish clerks moved forward and began to check off the queen's party, one by one. There were twenty-four attendants, as agreed, including Robin Fortingale. If Antoine had not caught him the previous evening, he might not have noticed the spy at all, but now he found him quite intriguing. He observed his carefully crafted ordinariness and listened to the bland answers he gave to the clerks' questions. Antoine thought of his own guarded nature and wondered if espionage might have been an alternative career for him, had diplomacy not called.

While he indulged this fancy, he noticed that Lord Douglas had stepped up onto the footplate of the carriage. Leaning in through the window, he was speaking to the queen in hushed tones. Margaret detected Antoine's gaze and tapped her husband's elbow, prompting him to turn and step down. Without any explanation, he hurried off to the back of the group and beckoned to a couple of men.

Antoine felt uneasy but tried not to show it. "All well, Your Grace?" he asked brightly.

"All well," said the queen, although her face tightened a fraction.

"Then we are ready to cross?"

"Almost. Just let me get out of this wretched carriage."

She gestured behind her, and Antoine turned to see two ostlers leading a beautiful white palfrey by its reins. Like the rest of the party, the horse was resplendent in cloth of gold, complemented by crimson and black velvet trims. A page ran alongside, placing a mounting block by the carriage to assist the queen in stepping up into the side saddle and securing herself, while two ladies-in-waiting smoothed her dress.

Once they were satisfied, the queen straightened her back and took the reins. She glanced at Douglas, who nodded his approval. And no wonder – for at a stroke, she had been transformed from a pitiful refugee sneaking back into the country under the cover of a carriage into a proud queen returning to her people. The English escorts bid their final farewells and waved them off towards the other side, where the Scottish soldiers stood in a line, watching intently.

As they departed, Antoine wondered how many of his men secretly hoped they were welcoming back their new ruler, rather than just a special guest. He reflected on his earlier feelings of sympathy for the queen and found them wanting. Perhaps it was not she who was walking into a trap, but instead, he who was bringing in a Trojan horse.

The party made good progress on the coastal trail and reached Cockburnspath before sunset. The queen complained of a weak stomach – one of many maladies she seemed to suffer from these days – so they decided to stay at a tower for two nights, while her physician attended her. Her discomfort only heightened her ill humour. She pressed Antoine again about her income, her properties, and, most of all, her son. He was relieved when they finally moved on to Tantallon.

Lord Douglas's home was a great red sandstone fortress rising directly from the cliffs. The castle was surrounded on three sides by the ocean, which crashed against the rocks, sending ribbons of spray over their heads as they approached. The remaining wall was bedecked with the family arms – depicting a heart and three stars – either side of an arched entrance. In the background, about a mile offshore, loomed the bleached mass of the Bass Rock. It seemed to have a life of its own, for thousands of gannets and puffins clung to every ledge, writhing and screeching as dusk descended.

"Now you are *truly* home," Douglas said to his wife, though she still appeared unconvinced. Undeterred, he swept her up in his arms and hugged her tightly by the waist. Antoine found the gesture unduly coarse, but after so long without the company of a woman, he could hardly recall what was deemed appropriate these days. He waited for Douglas to acknowledge him, but he was busy whispering in his wife's ear, just as he had done at the border.

It was only after the head steward had led the queen and her entourage away that Antoine managed to catch his host's attention with a cough. This time, Douglas turned round, wearing a mocking expression.

"I fear our air does not agree with you, de Lissieu. You sound as if you're for the grave."

"Not yet, my lord. I'm afraid you'll have to tolerate me a little longer."

"Perhaps," said Douglas, stroking his beard to its

fashionable point. "Now, if you will excuse me, I must retire for the evening. My wife and I have much to discuss – privately, of course."

With that, Douglas turned his back, leaving Antoine to search for a porter to take them to their room.

"Well, mixing with the high and mighty is not all I thought it would be," said Turnbull, picking at some bread and cheese they had brought from Lamberton. They had been billeted in a small chamber in the East Tower and had been informed that there would be no feast.

"Perhaps it's better that we don't have to witness Douglas pawing at the queen," Antoine replied.

"Still, I would pay good money to learn what they are scheming about."

Antoine nodded in agreement. He believed that the queen's concern for her son was genuine, but something about Douglas's behaviour felt insincere. The extravagant embrace, the whispering, the request for privacy – it all seemed too obvious, even for a preening popinjay like him. Were they trying to present this as a lovers' reunion, rather than a meeting of political allies? Or was he overthinking things? If so, it would not be the first time.

The Frenchman set his bread aside and moved to the window. As he looked out over the German Ocean, he wondered if he would sail across these waters soon. Perhaps it was time to share his plans with Turnbull. He rehearsed the argument in his mind: his gratitude for the lad's support over the last year, his pride in what they had achieved together, but also the need for him to return to his own country, before it was too late for his career. After all, he was now forty. The silver flecks in his beard had turned into streaks, and the lines round his eyes were becoming more pronounced.

Turnbull approached before Antoine could gather his thoughts. With his lanky frame, short hair and bare chin, he resembled an overgrown child, his face brimming with curiosity and adventure, the way Antoine's had once been.

"That's a prison," the lad said, gesturing to a low stone structure on the Bass Rock. Two fires burned at either end, creating the appearance of demonic eyes, in a giant skull. "It's supposed to be a right hellhole."

"I can imagine," Antoine replied with a shudder. "Being cooped up with the noise and stink of all those birds. A pity for the inmates, rogues though they may be."

"The jailers won't have it much better. That will be us in a few days, I suppose – guarding this fellow Baird in some dark tower. I only hope it's not too boring."

"That would not be the worst outcome," Antoine said as he prepared for bed.

Chapter 3

The journey to Edinburgh was long but uneventful. The summer had come hot and early this year and the fields were full of peasants making hay. They paused to watch the procession, but their expressions reflected subdued curiosity rather than celebration. It was as if they too could not fathom the governor's intentions in inviting Margaret Tudor to return, nor the motives of the queen.

Upon arrival in the capital, the party stopped at the Palace of Holyrood to unload the baggage train. Lord Albany's weaselly secretary, Pentland, greeted them at the gate. It was he who had sent them their orders to guard Baird and who had also assured Antoine that it would be his last mission in the country. But for now, he appeared reluctant to talk about any of that. Instead, he slithered about with his quill and parchment, checking off the household members and their belongings. His manner seemed overly officious, as if he were deliberately wasting time.

After a while, Lord Douglas marched over to Pentland, eyes blazing. The secretary was supervising a team of stewards as they placed tapestries, gold cups and plates, bolts of silk and taffeta into a fleet of handcarts. He flinched, as a dog might when awaiting a beating from its master.

"Christ's wounds," Douglas exclaimed, ripping the parchment from Pentland's hand and throwing it to the ground. "Are we to stand here all day, while you scratch away with that quill?"

"I'm sorry, my lord," Pentland replied, reddening as he bowed his head. "Lord Albany is simply eager to ensure that all Her Lady's possessions are accounted for."

Douglas gripped him by the collar. "Lord Albany cares not a jot for my wife. And less of this 'Her Lady' if you know what's good for you, you odious little scribbler."

Though Antoine had little love for Pentland, he had even less for bullies. More to the point, he couldn't allow his master's secretary to be treated this way. He stepped forward, lowering his hands in a calming gesture.

"Gentlemen, gentlemen. It has been a long, hot day. Let's not allow a few formalities to get the better of us."

Douglas glowered at the Frenchman, before removing his hands from Pentland's throat. The secretary straightened his collar and picked up his parchment.

"I'm sure Master Pentland will be finished soon," Antoine continued. "And any further paperwork can be completed at the castle."

The queen nodded enthusiastically. "That's all I want, monsieur. To see my son and check that he is well. I have presents for him, gifts from his loving uncle too."

It was a clever move to involve King Henry, a subtle reminder that, despite Margaret Tudor's currently reduced status, she remained the sister of the most powerful man on this island. But for all Pentland's cowardice, he was not one to be distracted from his orders. Clenching his fists by his side, he finally revealed the news that he had been hoarding.

"About your son... I am afraid... you will be unable to see him today."

The queen gasped, and for a moment, Antoine thought she might faint.

"What do you mean?" growled Douglas, jabbing a finger in Pentland's face. "This has been agreed upon for months."

"De Lissieu confirmed it only a few days ago," added the queen, casting a desperate look in Antoine's direction, but he was as puzzled as any present.

Pentland clasped his hands together. "It is simply a precaution. As you know, all access to the king is at the discretion of the castle's captain."

"And?" Douglas demanded, his cheeks flushed and eyes wide with fury.

"And there are fears that a plague is coming from London. Since the king's mother has recently arrived from there, the captain believes it would be prudent to wait a week or so, before she pays a visit."

"Fie!" cried the queen. "This is surely some cruel jest. There has been sickness in London, as there has been in many places, but I left there almost a month ago."

"We understand," said Pentland. His voice hardened, and he spoke quickly and precisely, as if reciting a prepared text. "But we also hear that you fell ill at Doncaster and again at Cockburnspath, My Lady. While we are glad to see you are recovered, we must err on the side of caution. Lord Douglas can go to the castle now, with de Lissieu, to reassure you that your son is well. Meanwhile, we have prepared your old chambers here, with all the comforts you'll remember."

The queen looked to her husband for support, but for all his evident fury, he remained silent. With a jerk of his head, he signalled for her to do likewise. She then turned and bustled off into the palace, slapping away the hands of her ladies-in-waiting as they tried to assist her with her dress.

Half an hour later, Antoine rode up the High Street alongside Lord Douglas. The queen's husband was still seething, and they spent the journey in icy silence. Turnbull had stayed at the palace to receive further instructions from Pentland, so there was not even his chirruping to lighten the mood. Without conversation, every other noise became a thousand times louder: the clacks of the horses' hooves on the cobblestones, the haggling of goodwives at the weighing beam, the warning shouts from the tops of the tenements as folk threw out their filth. As the men steered through the squalid booths that spilled out around the Kirk of St Giles, the sounds merged into one ferocious roar.

Only once they had reached the castle, high on its vast rock, did they finally escape the city's din. A pair of pikemen met them and escorted them through various passageways to the huge keep known as David's Tower. Their path was frequently blocked by studded doors that sentries on the other side had to unlock. Soldiers were stationed at every side passage and on the landings of the spiral staircase that took them deep into the heart of the building. They climbed four or five flights in dizzying succession, and Antoine couldn't help but wonder where they were headed.

Eventually, the staircase came to a dead end. Antoine turned to the guards, confused, while Douglas looked equally perplexed. The interior walls were panelled but led nowhere. Instead, they faced an open window that offered a vertiginous view of the city below. For a brief moment, a terrible thought crossed Antoine's mind: had the governor used him as bait for a trap? Was the plan to throw Douglas out the window, dashing him on the rocks below? It did not seem like Albany's way, but it would not be the first time the castle had been used for such purposes.

He edged away from his fellow visitor, who seemed oblivious to the impending threat. One of the sentries handed his pike to the other, perhaps so the guard could launch himself at his victim. However, instead of attacking, the guard tapped on the panelling, and the wall slid open to reveal a large, vaulted room. Inside, a distinguished-looking man in a mulberry hat and gown was seated at a chessboard, opposite an impeccably dressed little boy.

"What in damnation are you doing here?" spat Douglas as he burst into the room.

The man turned round, and Antoine recognised him as Lord Hamilton, a sworn enemy of the Douglases. Hamilton had recently made his own bid for power but had since thrown in his lot with Lord Albany. Of all the great men of state, Antoine knew the least about him, for he often spent time abroad as the head of the navy. Nevertheless, by reputation, he was a shrewd, somewhat slippery fellow.

"I assume that you mean me and not His Grace?" said Hamilton, gesturing to the boy.

The visitors realised their lapse in etiquette and walked backwards to the doorway. There, they bowed deeply and waited for the little king to bid them in. It took a while for the child to dispense his regal favour, but eventually, like a trained puppy, he made the appropriate gesture.

"I am always happy to see my stepson," said Douglas, although Antoine noticed that the feeling did not appear to be mutual. They both came closer. "What I want to know is what you're doing with him?"

Hamilton was clearly enjoying his rival's discomfort and did not bother to get up. "No need to tie your hose in knots, sir. Governor Albany is simply keen for His Grace to have some adult company. Teach him the ways of statecraft, help him to become a great prince." He reached across the chessboard and picked up the ivory king. "These are dangerous times, and we must all do what we can, to protect our little leader."

"The child has no greater protector than his mother," said Douglas, narrowing his eyes. "And he needs a father figure, not some clapped-out sailor."

Lord Hamilton laughed. "Well, unlike you, I'm a blood relative, so clapped out or otherwise, I have only his best interests at heart. That's why I've supported the captain of the castle, in taking some sensible precautions."

Douglas looked like he might explode. So, it was Hamilton who had prevented the queen from seeing her son. Antoine could not work out whether that had been at Albany's behest, or had been Hamilton's plan, to slight his rival. Frankly, he was not interested: it was precisely this kind of manoeuvring that made him want to leave this place. For now, he reminded himself that he had his own captive to guard, and the sooner he could get on with that, the better.

Ignoring Douglas's incandescent presence by his side, he knelt by the king. The little boy had picked up some of the other chess pieces and was twirling them in his fingers. Antoine tried to make eye contact with him, but the boy kept his head down, his mop of auburn hair falling over his face.

"Apologies, Your Grace," said the Frenchman gently. "We are talking about boring grown-up things, when we should be asking how you are. Are you comfortable here? Is everything to your taste?"

The child did not look up, but Antoine saw his little fists tighten round the chess pieces. He moved to comfort him with his own hand, but then withdrew it, fearing it would be improper. Instead, he picked up a couple of chess pieces himself.

"Do you like this game, Your Grace? I'm afraid I've never mastered it."

Still no reply. Lord Douglas tutted, although it was unclear whether he was reprimanding the king for his taciturnity or Antoine for his indulgence. The Frenchman decided to give it one last try. "I only ask this to reassure your mother that you're well. She will see you in due course, but in the meantime, she wants to know that you are happy here."

The child's fists trembled so intensely that the whole board shook. In an instant, he hurled it to the floor, causing the pieces to scatter about the room. "I hate it here!" he screamed as he ran to a mullioned window, hauled himself onto a stone seat, and clutched a cloth toy to his chest. "I hate the castle, I hate the grown-ups, and I hate that stupid game!"

Lord Douglas muttered something about the child needing a father's rod, but Antoine waved him silent. He followed the boy to the window.

"I am sorry to hear that, Your Grace. But it will not be for long." As he said the words, he felt a stab of guilt, for he knew they were not true. "Meanwhile, tell us what we can do to help you. How can we make your stay more enjoyable?"

The boy looked out of the window. "I want to go outside," he pouted. He turned his toy around, to reveal that it was a horse. "I want to ride my pony. Go hunting. Catch something."

Antoine smiled at him. "I'm sure you are a fine horseman, Your Grace. One day, you will have the finest charger in the land and take part in grand chases, just like your late father." The boy wiped a tear from his cheek and hugged his toy horse closer. "In the meantime, I will ask the keeper if you can practise riding in the courtyard. And we'll find you a toy sword, if the chess is not to your liking."

Antoine rose and put a hand through the child's hair, not worrying about the etiquette this time. He left him at the window and returned to Hamilton and Douglas, who were facing off against each other, like roosters at a cockfight.

"I think His Grace needs a little freedom," Antoine said, with barely disguised disgust at the two men's antics. "And some friends of his own age. My Lord Hamilton, I beseech you to find some, from the children of the garrison. And pray tell the captain not to thwart the queen for too long. Lord Douglas, we should return to the palace and tell Her Grace she has nothing to be worried about. It will be better for us all if she's becalmed."

The two aristocrats shifted their fiery glares from each other to the Frenchman. Antoine knew these great men would not like to take counsel from one such as him. But he felt secure enough in Lord Albany's support to knock their heads together. That was how his master had always used him: as a stranger who could rise above the locals' squabbles.

What still did not make sense was why Albany would invite such troublemakers into his camp in the first place. Especially while he was abroad. As Antoine accompanied a fuming Douglas back to the palace, he was reminded of that old French saying: "When the cat is away, the mice will dance." It seemed fitting here. Except this country swirled with far more dangerous creatures than mice.

This was a dance of vipers, and if he wanted to get home alive, he must do everything possible to stay out of its twists and turns.

Chapter 4

Turnbull listened to Antoine's account with disquiet, as they stole out of the palace at first light. However, he knew his master was prone to ill humours and sometimes painted things darker than they truly were. For his own part, he felt his mood lift as they passed through the Netherbow Gate, that great portal between city and countryside. The sun was rising. The rolling hills of the Lothians opened up ahead. This was a new day, a new mission, a new start. Hopefully an opportunity for adventure too.

"I must tell you of our prisoner," he said brightly.

"Yes, I suppose you must. What kind of reprobate is he?"

"Well, he's thirty-five years of age. Never married. No family either. He grew up an orphan, and reiving is all he knows."

Antoine furrowed his brow. "He has no other work? No farmstead of his own?"

"No, he has no interest in tending the beasts he steals. He sells them on as soon as he can. Sometimes, at no great price either. It's as if he takes pleasure from the crime itself."

As he spoke, Turnbull instinctively placed a hand on the hilt of his sword. They had left the city and were riding over a rough heath, where thieves were known to lurk.

Fortunately, the track was deserted, save for a miserable trickle of paupers, heading towards the sea. The poor were always the first to be evicted when rumours of the plague were rife. Some even claimed that beggars deliberately spread the disease, so that they might find work as a result. But as they trudged along the muddy way, their possessions bagged upon their backs, these poor souls did not look to be profiting greatly from it.

"What of Baird's politics?" the Frenchman asked, as they gave the paupers a wide berth. "I presume he is for Douglas and the queen, otherwise why lock him up?"

"His only allegiance is to himself," Turnbull replied, with a wry smile. "As for locking him up, he surrendered voluntarily, like most of the reivers in the Marches. We've promised them a full pardon for past offences when Albany gets back, in return for some peace and quiet now."

"That sounds like a good deal."

"It is for most. But I cannot see our lords and masters honouring it with Baird. He has tweaked the noses of too many powerful men; they will surely do away with him."

Antoine gave a little snort. "Ah, Scottish justice at its finest. Well, at least Baird and his gang have good reason to behave for now. We just need to keep him secure, until Lord Albany returns."

After a few hours, they climbed into the Lammermuirs, the wild hills that marked the beginning of the Marches. As clouds passed over the rugged dales, Turnbull's own mood darkened somewhat. He had grown up in this region, but it was a long time since he had felt like a native. At thirteen, he had been sent to study at St Andrews, and while he had returned briefly to help his mother with the farm, he had felt compelled to leave again soon after. Now, his thirst for new adventures mingled with the taste of old troubles.

His discomfort was increased by his master's sudden interest in his background. "This is your native heath, isn't it?" the Frenchman said, as they forded a meltwater river.

Turnbull nodded. "A little further on, past Lauder."

"How strange that we've been in the Marches all this time and never made it here."

"We've been busy, sir. There hasn't been the reason."

"Still, we should visit your mother while we're over this way. I would like to tell her what a fine boy she's raised, what we've achieved together. We should say these things while we can, you know."

On the contrary, Turnbull knew he must avoid this if he could. Compliments aside, he was not ready for his past and present to collide just yet. And why was his master talking so wistfully, as if hinting at some hidden meaning? He recalled that the Frenchman felt guilty about leaving his own parents at an early age, so perhaps that was it. Still, as he continued to gabble about the importance of home and a man returning to his roots, Turnbull met his homilies with silence.

Eventually, his master gave up on whatever point he had been building towards, and, for a while, the only sounds were the rustle of the long grass and the buzz of the mayflies darting about the marshes.

As the light faded, Turnbull pointed across the moor. "Let's head towards those woods. If my memory serves me right, there's an inn where we can stop for the night."

The Boar's Head was a popular establishment, frequented by

merchants and tradesmen to break the journey between Edinburgh and the border abbeys. It was a warm evening, and the open shutters allowed a raucous chorus of laughter, shouting and singing to spill from the windows. The smell of ale wafted out and mixed with the heather-scented air of the moor.

It would be Midsummer in a few days, but the patrons were starting their celebrations early. Few noticed Antoine and Turnbull as they pushed open the oak door and walked into the taproom.

"Good evening, gentlemen!" said the innkeeper, a great sweaty fellow whose face seemed to consist mainly of chins. "What can I get ye on this fine night?"

Turnbull ordered two bowls of pottage and some ale, before enquiring about a room.

"Ye're in luck," the innkeeper said. "Two monks left this morning, so there's a wee space in the courtyard. Now settle yerselves down and tell us what brings ye here."

Antoine frowned at Turnbull to signal that they must be careful, so he let his master take the lead.

"There's little to tell. We have some business in Lauder, that's all."

"Ah, ye're French?" said the man, hearing his accent. "We dinnae get many o' you round here. Plenty in Edinburgh, o' course. They say Governor Albany has brought thousands o' ye over."

"Not quite," said Antoine, but Turnbull saw him cover the ring Albany had given him – a handsome gold band with the insignia of the warden's office etched into it. "Well, please excuse us. We have other matters to discuss."

The serving girl placed the ale and pottage on a tray and found them a place at a long trestle table. At the other end, some young men were carousing with the local harlots. Closer to them, a merchant was well into his cups. They turned their backs to him, but after a few minutes, he tapped Antoine on the shoulder.

"Did I hear ye've come frae Edinburgh, gentlemen?"

Antoine began to say that they'd said no such thing, but the man was not listening.

"Ye did well to get out, afore the plague," he slurred. "They say that Tudor woman's brought it up frae London." The man took a great swig of ale, then spilled almost as much again, trying to replace his mug on the table. He wiped the mess with his sleeve. "Why Albany's invited her back, I dinnae ken. Perhaps he means to bed her."

Turnbull rolled his eyes at his master, for this was the latest preposterous rumour to be travelling the taverns. Last year it had been that the queen was dead. The year before, it was claimed that the old king was still alive. However, such stories were usually whispered, not noised as brazenly as this. As the merchant continued to mouth off about Albany's bawdy desires, others leant in, their faces a mixture of grins and scowls.

"My brother here could tell ye a thing or two about the governor," said a man with a scar across his cheek. "Used to deliver victuals to the palace, didn't ye?" He shook the fellow next to him, who was slumped forwards and could not be roused.

"Your brother's wise to hold his tongue," said a man in a blue bonnet. "And if you have any sense, ye'll do the same."

Scar Face frowned and tilted his head back. "Why? Ye going to run off to France and get the governor ontae me?"

"Nae need for that," said Blue Bonnet, standing up.

"There are plenty of us here who are for Albany. So keep your poxy mouth shut or we'll rip another hole in it."

The inn fell quiet, as men across the room put down their drinks. Some got to their feet and gathered behind Blue Bonnet, others by Scar Face. While they sized each other up, Turnbull reached for his sword under the table. He had not been much of a fighter when he first joined Antoine last year, but he had learned how to handle himself since then. He began to unsheathe his blade, only to stop when he saw the innkeeper emerging from a backroom, wielding a cudgel.

"No politicking in my house," he growled. "Either keep your thoughts to yerselves or take your quarrels outside."

Blue Bonnet stared at Scar Face for a moment, as if weighing up the merits of a good fight or more drink. He seemed to choose the latter, grimacing as he retook his place. His supporters did likewise, drifting back to their seats, after patting him on the shoulder. Scar Face gave his brother another shake, and the fellow's eyes rolled open long enough for him to get to his feet and for the two of them to stagger to the door.

"I think we should go abed too," Antoine whispered to Turnbull. The lad was disappointed to miss out on the possibility of further excitement but downed the last of his ale. They pushed aside their pottage, which had gone cold during the argument, and edged the bench back from the table. Then they motioned to the innkeeper, who was still prowling about the main room, ensuring that no more fights broke out.

"I'm sorry. It's no' usually as bad as this," he said, giving them a heavy iron key, with instructions to use the back door and take the room to the right of the stables.

"Difficult times," murmured Antoine, before following the directions and stepping out into the fresh air.

This side of the building was much quieter, as none of the inn's windows looked out onto the courtyard, and the breeze carried the drunken noise off into the hills. It was getting dark, but the nickering of horses and the smell of dung guided them to the stables on the far side. To the left there was a strongroom, where the merchants stored their wares. Turnbull unlocked the door to the right and peered into a gloomy cell. The rushes stank and the room was stuffy, so he crossed the floor to let some air in.

But as the lad drew the shutters, he saw something which made him jump back from the window and fall to the ground. "Sweet Mary!" he exclaimed, as he picked himself off the floor.

Chapter 5

"What is it?" said Antoine, rushing over.

"A man," said Turnbull, still catching his breath. "Look, that's him over there."

A figure was running along the side of the wall, only to disappear round the corner.

"Did you get a look at him?" said Antoine, leaning out over the sill, to check that nobody else was there. As he pulled himself back in, he double-checked behind him.

"No, it was too dark, and he was already off. But I think he was waiting for us."

Antoine furrowed his brow. The lad was always dreaming up such stories. He really hoped that he was not going to turn this final mission into some hare-brained caper.

"More likely one of those tavern topers, taking a piss against the wall."

But he reminded himself that they were back in the Marches, that strange border region where nothing was as it seemed. He made sure to close the shutters again, and they went abed in the hot, stale fug that had been left by the monks.

They questioned the innkeeper about the incident as they prepared to set off the next day, but he claimed to know nothing about any intruder. Instead, he tried to win them over by giving them a plague bag each, for the journey. They were of the usual kind – muslin sachets filled with lavender – save that the material had been stamped with a boar's head. The innkeeper proudly explained that this emblem was a mark of quality in these parts and assured them they would come to no harm if they kept the bags close.

Armed with their talismans, they rode back out across the moor. Skylarks whirred around them, piping their songs as they cut through the air, which was scented by thyme and myrtle. The sun was already beating down, and Antoine wiped a bead of sweat from his brow.

"What a day," he said.

"Aye," replied Turnbull. "And what a night."

Antoine sighed as he sensed the lad's eagerness to pick events apart.

"You know, I've been thinking," Turnbull continued. "I cannot see how our visitor was simply a toper from the tavern. If he was just having a piss, why run away like that?"

"Who knows?" said Antoine. "But he can't have been waiting to attack us. If that had been his aim, he'd have found a way inside."

"Perhaps we disturbed him by coming back early? He might have been trying the window when we returned."

"I saw no signs around the window frame," said Antoine. It was a white lie, as he had not checked. He just wanted Turnbull to let the matter go.

"Then perhaps he was there to spy on us. Listen to what we were up to."

Antoine tutted. "That head of yours will fall off if it spins any further. We're not in the world of kings and queens anymore, thank God. So he'd have got few secrets from us save the fact that you snore and I talk in my sleep. Now let's forget about it and attend to where we're going."

Turnbull fell into a sulk, making the next few hours heavy going. They rode through deep valleys, dotted with long-haired cattle, grazing on the summer pastures. On the hillsides, there were many tiny cabins, which the folk used for minding their beasts over these warmer months. These *sheilings* were miserable dwellings, made of turf and the odd slab of stone. Wisps of smoke rose from their roofs, and the clattering of milk pails and cowbells drifted over on the breeze. They stopped to buy some fresh cheese from a peasant family, and the eating of it seemed to put Turnbull in better humour.

"Not long to go before we reach our tower," he said. "It'll be good to meet our prisoner, see what he's made of."

"Yes, and the keeper," said Antoine. "Did Pentland have anything to say about him?"

"Only that he was a rare beast – I think those were his words – and would not let us down."

Antoine stroked his beard. "Well, it's not like Pentland to be so positive. A good sign, I suppose. But come, let's get back on our way, and we can judge for ourselves."

Presently, they came across a river, which they deduced to be a tributary of the Tweed. After following it for a few miles, they picked their way through a dense birch forest. The thick canopy was oppressive, and they were relieved to emerge into the light on the other side, where an ugly square tower stood, surrounded by a high wall.

"Ravenscleugh," announced Turnbull.

They nudged the horses forward, only to find that the

road had been designed to veer to the right, no doubt affording the tower's archers a better shot at attackers. Deep ditches flanked the path, forcing them to stick to the road. Then, just as they seemed to be approaching the perimeter wall, the track unexpectedly curved back to the left. It was a clever way to slow visitors down, but how irritating for the inhabitants!

Eventually, the road straightened out and pointed them to the outer gate. It was shut, so Antoine looked for a face at the grille, but there was none. Neither were there any sentries on the battlements to appeal to. He was about to send Turnbull round the other side to look for another entrance when he heard a woman's voice. She was berating someone, only to stop and call more clearly: "What's your business, stranger?"

Antoine took a moment to collect himself before replying. "I am the warden, de Lissieu, and this is my aide, Turnbull. The keeper is expecting us."

"Ye can identify yourselves?" she called.

"Of course."

There was a long pause. "Very well," said the woman. "I'll be with ye shortly."

They heard more muffled sounds, then nothing for a while – until the gate slowly swung open. It revealed a stout woman, about fifty years old, wearing a plain russet gown. She had a heavy brow that could have been hewn from stone.

"Thank you, goodwife," said Antoine, giving her a flash of his warden's ring. "Now, if you would be so kind as to fetch the keeper, I will explain why we are here."

"That won't be necessary," said the woman. "I already know why ye're here."

Antoine was bemused. "I hardly think so. Just fetch the keeper, and we will say our piece to him."

"Him?" The woman scoffed. "There is no him. I am Mary Scrimgeour, the keeper of this castle and the current gaoler of Will Baird."

Wait, the keeper was a woman? Antoine stared at her in astonishment as Pentland's words came rushing back to him. The secretary had meant it as a sly jest, but in a way, he had spoken the truth: as gaolers went, this was a rare beast indeed.

―

Once they had recovered from their surprise, Antoine and Turnbull dismounted and accompanied Scrimgeour into the courtyard. A stocky fellow with a scraggly tawny beard came running, and the keeper barked at him to close the gate. As he passed them, Antoine noticed that he stank of ale.

"Our sentry, Moffat," said Scrimgeour, through gritted teeth. "He will be punished for his slackness."

Antoine had only just met the woman, but he did not doubt her threat. She seemed to bristle with hostility, and perhaps not just towards the guard.

He adopted his most charming smile. "It's a fine castle you have here, madame. That twisting path is a clever trick, although it must make it difficult when you leave this place."

Scrimgeour curled her lip, as if he had said the most foolish thing imaginable. "This is a gaol. We dinnae leave, sir. Nor would I advise you to, now that ye're here."

Christ, she was a tough one. Antoine was about to ask her what she meant when Moffat returned to take the horses. The Frenchman wondered where the stable boys were but handed over Carbonel, while Turnbull did the same with Fogo. They were left holding their panniers, but once again, nobody came to assist them. So, they took the panniers with them and followed Scrimgeour as she marched off into the tower itself.

"The storeroom," she said, as they entered a barrel-vaulted cellar. "We are provisioned by Mungo Bell frae the town. Every Monday at sunrise, he brings our order to the gate. We take it in, check it in the courtyard. Once we are satisfied that it contains nothing untoward, we keep it here."

Antoine nodded appreciatively. At least she knew what she was doing, even if her manner was surly.

"You trust this Bell fellow, then?"

"He has never failed me."

"That's good. Although, of course, we'll want to visit him ourselves." He noted Scrimgeour's scowl as he continued. "What about other deliveries?"

"There are none. Unlike most gaols, we dinnae allow packages frae friends or kinsfolk. A strict rule, since my late husband's passing." The woman moved her lips, as if to say more, but quickly pursed them again and turned toward the corner of the room, where she began to climb a spiral staircase set into the wall.

Antoine and Turnbull exchanged nervous glances but followed her up the winding passage into a dining area. There was little to it: a single trestle table, two benches and a plain fireplace. A girl was stirring a pot on the hearth. She was about eighteen, young enough to wear her fair hair long and without a coif. She had a sad countenance, Antoine thought, although he had a habit of finding his own melancholy in others' faces.

"My daughter Elspeth," said Scrimgeour, and the girl gave an awkward curtsey, before turning back to her work. The mother dropped her voice. "She handles a' the cooking, the cleaning and the washing. But if ye need anything o' that sort, ye must speak to me, ye understand? Lassies o' her age can be silly things, and it's better if she's no' distracted."

Antoine thought those last words had been directed at

Turnbull, but the lad's mind was already elsewhere. "Are all the windows like this?" he said, pulling at the iron yett that barred the only point of light in the room.

"Aye, all strong. Samson himself couldnae move them if he tried." Scrimgeour allowed herself a smile of satisfaction, as if there was nothing these men could think of that she had not already anticipated. She ushered them upstairs again, past a rudimentary garderobe, into another open chamber, where a handful of straw mattresses littered the floor. A man lay curled up on one, wheezing rhythmically.

"Crichton is our other guard," said Scrimgeour. "When he wakes, he'll change places wi' that fool Moffat. Ye can grab a mattress each as well."

Antoine furrowed his brow. "We all sleep together?"

"All except my daughter and the prisoner. I'll show ye their quarters presently. Why? Were ye expecting some fancy chamber o' your own, sir?"

The Frenchman bit his tongue. He *had* expected a more comfortable arrangement, but this was not his primary concern. "Not at all. I am troubled by the numbers though. There are only five beds here, and it sounds like they're all accounted for. In which case – where do the rest of your soldiers sleep?"

"There are nae other soldiers, sir. It's just us. We will be six now you have joined."

"Six to run the whole tower?!" Antoine went to the window and looked out over the courtyard. There was no sign of life, except Moffat, slumped beside the gate.

"We have thirty men at Black Rig," said Turnbull. "And even then, we often find ourselves light-handed."

"Ravenscleugh is no' Black Rig," said Scrimgeour sharply. "And while ye might ken how to run a garrison, ye clearly ken little o' running a gaol. Ye've checked the windows, asked about the path, talked about the provisioning. They're all in order, o' course. But the biggest risk to any prison is the folk who work there. If ye cannae trust them, a' the rest is for naught. So over many years, we've learnt that the fewer we have, the safer we are."

Antoine scratched his head in disbelief. "Doesn't it drive you to madness, locking yourself up in this place, with no other company all day?"

"It doesnae suit everybody," said Scrimgeour. Her face went blank for a moment before she regained her attention and turned for the stairs again. "But some o' us are made o' stronger stuff. Now, enough o' this gabbling. Let's show ye what ye're here for."

As they wound their way up the final flight of stairs, Antoine wondered what had made this woman so hard-hearted. What had happened to her husband? How did she survive? But she was right – he was not here for any of that. He was here to keep watch over this prisoner. If he could guard him safely, until Albany returned, he would be free from his own shackles. And if this strange creature could help him in any way, then so much the better.

Chapter 6

They arrived at the top floor: a gloomy attic built out of the eaves. The central landing was cramped and contained nothing but a bucket of water. Three doors led off from this area: two were closed, one was open.

"This is my daughter's room," said Scrimgeour, pointing to the open door on the left. Antoine peered inside and was disturbed to see that it looked more like a prison cell. There was a tiny box bed and bench, but nothing more – no personal possessions or fancies as one might expect of a young girl's room. He thought of her melancholic face again.

"What about that one?" said Turnbull, nodding to the middle door.

"No longer in use," said Scrimgeour. "It's locked, and the key is gone."

"You're quite sure?" said Antoine, for this woman did not seem the type to lose anything, let alone a key.

"Quite sure," she said, with a note of bitterness. "It used to lead onto some outside stairs and thence to an old postern gate, but that was years ago."

Antoine examined it. It was firmly secured, so he turned to the final door.

"And this is Baird's cell?"

"Aye. Now you can see what ye're dealing with. And why ye'd be better to leave his care to me."

Scrimgeour pulled back a shutter in the door and peered through a little hatch. She craned her neck for a better view and nodded for Antoine to take a look once she was satisfied that all was in order. When he put his head to the hatch, he saw a cell, just like the one used by the daughter, except for a piss-pot in the corner and a plate and cup on the floor. A man sat on the bench, although his features were hard to make out in the dim light afforded by the tiny, barred window.

"Looks like we'll need a candle," said Antoine.

"He's no' allowed one," said Scrimgeour. "No flames, no oil, no flints. Nothing that could be turned to rope either. And above all, nothing sharp. You must remember that this is a most dangerous fellae. Are ye sure ye still want to see him?"

They nodded, so Scrimgeour took their swords and carefully unlocked the door. It opened with a creak, and the men stepped in. They breathed the foul air, a ripe concoction of piss and ordure, mildew and sweat. Then the door closed with a heavy clunk.

Antoine felt his heart race. He had been a prisoner himself in another life, and the feelings of confinement always left him unsettled. In contrast, Baird seemed perfectly calm. One half of his face was still shrouded in darkness, while the other was illuminated like a crescent moon. He had piercing blue eyes, a fine nose and long dark hair. Only his unkempt beard gave any indication of his current status.

"Good evening, Baird. I'm the Warden de Lissieu, here to oversee your time at Ravenscleugh. This is my assistant, Turnbull."

"A pleasure, gentlemen," replied the prisoner, with a

gleaming smile. "It'll be good to have some company. As ye can see, it's a wee bit lacking at the moment."

He gave a slow wave about the empty cell. The movement was graceful, almost like a dancer's in its elegance. No, that wasn't it. Antoine had it now – like one of those conjurers who toured the village fairs. He reminded himself not to be taken in by the fellow's charm. "I'm surprised our paths haven't crossed before," he said bluntly.

"Perhaps they have, monsieur. In our line o' work, we're often busy in the night, are we no'? Who kens if we've passed each other on some dark moor or other. It's part o' the thrill for me. Not knowing who's chasing me, who I'm up against. Perhaps it is for you too?"

Baird licked his lips as he waited for an answer, but Antoine did not give him the satisfaction. Instead, he instructed Turnbull to look about the room, and the lad started to nose about the corners, checking the state of the window and the walls.

"Aye, there's no place like those moors," Baird continued. "The open space, the smell o' heather, wolves calling in the night. I look forward to roaming there again, when ye've set me free."

As the reiver spoke these last words, he gave Antoine a probing look. Had he guessed that he was unlikely to be pardoned along with the other prisoners? The idea that they might be keeping the man under false pretences had sat ill with Antoine ever since Turnbull mentioned it on their way here. But if he were to be more honest with Baird about his prospects, it would remove his incentive to behave.

He tried not to give anything away. "We're simply here to guard you. When Lord Albany returns, someone else will decide your fate."

Baird nodded thoughtfully, as if this simple statement told him everything he needed to know. He ran his hand through his hair only to stop and furrow his brow. He tutted, rummaged about again and picked out a louse. Then he held it between his thumb and forefinger, as it tried to wriggle free. "That's the way wi' fate, monsieur. In the end, it's decided by others."

He closed the louse in his fist, clenched it and threw it on the floor. "But these are strange times. Those others can change quickly, if ye get my meaning?"

"I've no time for riddles," said Antoine, although he felt strangely compelled to find out what the rogue was implying.

"Forgive me. I mean only that masters come and go. Kings and queens, even. And when they change, so can the fortunes of humbler creatures, like you or I."

Baird gave another flamboyant twist of his hand, to reveal that the louse was still there, alive in his palm. He let it crawl along his finger and then onto the wall, where it escaped into the gloom.

Antoine felt disturbed, not just by the man's dexterity but by his penetrating gaze, his aura of omniscience, his talk of kings and queens. He was quite unlike any other reiver he had ever met – more daunting, yet more fascinating too.

The Frenchman nudged Turnbull, and they returned to the door. "Philosophy is not my strong suit, Baird. Just make sure to cause me no trouble, and I'll do the same for you."

"Well, what did ye think to him?" said Scrimgeour, once she'd let them out and locked the door again.

"He was just as you described," said Antoine, who was keen to win her over. "Charming, but a dangerous man, no doubt."

"Aye, now ye see," she said with a smile of vindication. "Well, it's getting late, so let us have some supper afore putting ourselves abed."

They went down to the dining hall, where Elspeth had prepared a dish of saltfish and summer beets. Crichton joined them after waking from his slumbers. The sentry seemed a cheerful young fellow, which was just as well, as Scrimgeour and her daughter said little throughout the meal. He was enthralled by Antoine's experience of the world and pressed him for stories about the countries he had visited. What did people eat? How did they live? What was the weather like? The Frenchman fielded the questions as best he could but began to feel uneasy as they strayed into enquiries about his homeland. He was relieved when Scrimgeour motioned for her man to stop.

"Enough trittle-trattling, Crichton. It's time for ye to relieve that wretch Moffat on the gate. And for me to take my daughter to her room. Gentlemen, I will see ye presently."

They were now alone in the tower, for the first time. Antoine went to the garderobe to relieve himself. As he expected, it was a primitive affair, opening onto a cesspit far below. The filth looked – and smelled – like it had not been cleared for years, and he held his nose as he did his business. He finished as quickly as he could, before returning to the hall.

"Christ, those jakes are something to behold," he said to Turnbull. "You wouldn't think so few people could make such a mess!"

The lad laughed. "I'll let you complain to the keeper, sir."

Antoine smiled. "Yes, she is a dragon, isn't she? I fear she is not happy about us being here."

They took off their boots and climbed into their beds. The mattresses were lumpy, and they each had to shift around to find a comfortable position. Eventually, they ended up facing each other in the stillness of the room, the only movement coming from the flickering torches on the wall. Antoine closed his eyes but felt the familiar sensation of Turnbull watching him. He was an inquisitive soul, and nothing much got past him. It had made him a useful assistant this past year, but his intense scrutiny could sometimes be unnerving.

"Why *are* we here, sir?" Turnbull said at last. "To guard the prisoner, of course. But why us, when Widow Scrimgeour seems to have it all in hand? And what will happen to us afterwards?"

Antoine felt a shiver of guilt run through him, but he was too tired to talk of his future plans tonight. "Let's just concentrate on the task at hand," he murmured as he turned over. "As Baird said, these are times of change, so who knows what will happen to any of us next."

"Of course," said Turnbull quietly.

Chapter 7

In the morning, Antoine met Scrimgeour by the stables. He explained that they would be going into Lauder, to announce their presence to the townsfolk and tell them to stay away from the tower. It had been Pentland's final instruction and seemed like a sensible idea to the Frenchman, but Scrimgeour disagreed.

"I've telt ye, we have our ways," she said, wagging a finger at him as if he were a child. "And one o' them is that we stay here at all times. The minute ye go into that town, ye invite danger back wi' ye."

Antoine tried to appease her as he took Carbonel's reins from Crichton. "I understand your concerns, and we will be cautious, I promise. However, I am the warden of these parts, and it would look ill for us to hide away. We must make our presence known, show we are in command."

"And what of me? What will your presence say of *my* command? That I cannot be trusted to do what my husband and I…" She stopped and corrected herself. "…what *I* have done for years?"

So that was it. Her pride was hurt. Perhaps she was not so cold after all.

Antoine lifted himself into the saddle. "We will make sure to tell folk that we are merely visiting. And that we have the highest respect for you. Now let us be off, for the sooner we can do this, the sooner we'll be back."

Scrimgeour shook her head and returned to the tower, stopping briefly to scold Elspeth for the time she'd taken to fetch some water. The girl protested, which earned her a slap for her impertinence, causing her to spill the pail and start all over again. As she trudged back to the well in the courtyard, Antoine noticed Crichton give her a look of sympathy, but she did not respond.

Lauder was a small town, but it was surrounded by high walls, which might have been the envy of a larger burgh, were they not so dilapidated from years of war. Antoine and Turnbull entered through a gate known as the East Port. Inside, there was really only one long street, which was crammed tightly with wattle cottages, trade booths, food stalls and a couple of inns.

Halfway along the street, it opened onto a square, with the mercat cross at its centre. A small crowd milled around it, and Antoine stepped onto the octagonal plinth to address them.

"Men and women of Lauder, I am your warden, the representative of Lord Albany." He scanned the faces to gauge where their loyalties lay, but nobody gave anything away. "As you may know, our governor is abroad right now, and it is important that we keep the peace in his absence. So he has sent us here to watch over one of your neighbours – a reiver known as Will Baird." This time there were a few nods of recognition, some sideways glances to acquaintances. "We are keeping him at Ravenscleugh and would urge you to stay away from the tower, if you do not have good reason.

Anybody who is seen approaching will be considered hostile and—"

Just then, a bell tolled. Antoine looked at Turnbull for an explanation, but the lad merely shrugged. The villagers began to mutter to one another as another dolorous chime rang out. Then another, soon after: a distinctive, muffled sound. There could be no mistaking it now; this was a death knell—and for a man, judging by the three strokes. Antoine tried to conclude his speech, but the villagers were no longer listening. They started to move off in groups. As they separated, a scruffy young fellow hurried over, wringing his hands.

"Monsieur Warden?" the man said. His hair was very fair and crudely cut, like straw. Antoine nodded and bade him forwards.

"I am Dewar, sir," he panted. "Servant of Joseph Walkerburn, the bailie. My master's just died, and I hope ye might take a look at him."

Antoine put his hand on the man's shoulder, in an attempt to calm him. "To look at him? How so? Do you mean that he's been killed?"

"No' killed, sir, no. Well, no' by another's hand." Dewar looked around at the remnants of the crowd. Some of the departing villagers had stopped to find out what was going on. He lowered his voice. "He has… taken his own life, poor man. Now he'll be damned for all eternity, and his house will be ruined."

An outbreak of whispers among the onlookers suggested that he had not been successful in concealing his news. As for Antoine, he was still unsure what he was expected to do.

He leant in. "That's a terrible thing, no doubt. But if it truly was self-murder, then I'm afraid I cannot help. We're here on some very particular business and cannot be distracted."

"I beg ye, sir. Just take a look, see if ye can help us make sense o' it. Perhaps my master left some explanation, some clue as to why he did it."

Antoine scratched his head. He would rather not get involved with such a sorry tale, but the man was insistent, and he felt he had no choice. Perhaps it would be helpful to win some friends in the village, should they need a favour in return. He sighed and told the servant to lead the way.

Dewar was lavish in his thanks and hurried Antoine and Turnbull up the street, towards the far end of town. Some of the villagers followed them, and they were met by another group gathered outside a sizeable, whitewashed house with a steep thatched roof. All the shutters were closed, as if to hide the shameful secret that lay inside. Dewar growled at the onlookers to be gone and ushered Antoine and Turnbull in.

The main room was dark, but some tallow candles had been lit in the corners, to give off a smoky glow. A thin, whey-faced woman stood in the middle, staring straight ahead. Antoine followed her gaze and saw a man's body, laid out on a table. His eyes were red and swollen, like a bull's balls. Otherwise, his face was drained of colour, his neck disfigured by a deep, fleshy groove, soon explained by the noose lying beside him on the table.

"Mother of Christ," said Antoine quietly as he crossed himself.

"My husband is beyond prayer, I fear."

"Yes," said Antoine. "But I hope God gives you succour." He struggled to find more words and felt relieved when Dewar came to his aid.

"I was just telling the warden that my master might have

left an explanation," the servant said, craning over the top of the body. He seemed agitated. "That's strange. I was sure there were some papers or suchlike here."

"No, nothing," said the woman blankly, waving her hand. "You can see for yourselves."

Antoine took a candle and leant over the corpse. She was right, there was nothing there. He drew closer to the body. The man's lips were thin and dry, his cheeks stiff and cold to the touch.

"When exactly did you find your master, Dewar?"

The servant continued hunting around the other side of the body. "At daybreak," he said distractedly. "I'm always the first up, o' course. I came frae my quarters out the back and was surprised to see his shadow on the wall, as I came through the study. I feared he was waiting for me, to chide me for some matter. But no, he was dangling frae that rafter."

"And yourself, goodwife?"

"I was attending my sister's lying-in all night. She gave birth in the early hours, so I am just returned."

Christ, what a world this is, thought Antoine. Beginnings and endings, with so little joy in between. He looked at the man's face again, trying to imagine what he had been like in life. What could have driven him to commit such a terrible act, a mortal sin that would see him burn forever? Perhaps it was better not to know.

While he pondered this, Turnbull walked around the table and picked up the noose. "You're sure he did this to himself?" he said, turning the rope over in his hand. Antoine scowled at him, for he thought it improper to ask such questions in front of the wife. However, she seemed lost in her own world, her eyes empty of emotion.

"Who else could have done it?" Dewar replied, rubbing

his forehead as if he, too, were no longer sure where he was. "Ye ken, now that I think of it, I'm sure I saw a letter, lying on a book..."

Antoine sighed. "Well, as your mistress said, it's not there now." He cast an eye around the room, noting that nothing appeared out of the ordinary. He checked the dead man's hands and found them similarly unremarkable, albeit a little inky, as you'd expect from a bailie whose job involved keeping records of all kinds. Mindful of a case from last year where he had been deceived by a dead body, Antoine asked if he might inspect the fellow's chest, but again, it revealed nothing suspicious. They should never have embarked on this fool's errand.

"I think we are finished here," he said. Dewar tried to persuade him to have a look in the study, but Antoine made some excuse about needing to get back to Ravenscleugh. He extended his condolences to the bailie's wife and stooped to pass through the low front door, back into the street, where the neighbours had gathered again, to gossip and to judge.

As they returned to the mercat cross to fetch the horses, Antoine tried to maintain a respectful silence, but Turnbull would not let up with his chattering. Had the bailie really done that to himself? Might a robber have been to blame instead? What about that letter the servant claimed to have seen? There was just something about the whole piece that did not quite make sense.

Eventually, Antoine hushed him. "You're desperate for us to investigate this, aren't you? But there's nothing to suggest it was a murder. There was no sign of an intruder or a struggle. The servant was the one who alerted us, and the wife was away all night. As for that letter, if it ever existed, I'd put money on her removing it, to spare herself. Perhaps even to secure a proper burial for her man."

Turnbull's mouth fell open.

"There you go," said Antoine. "You hadn't thought of that, had you? As long as we keep our beaks out of it, that poor woman can pay a priest to turn a blind eye and secure him a grave in the churchyard. In the meantime, stop willing this to be something that it's not."

Turnbull flushed. "It is not a case of willing anything, sir. It is just a sense I had. I think you had it too."

Chapter 8

Turnbull loved his master like a father. No, more so, for his own father had not been so kind. But Hell's teeth, the Frenchman could be infuriating at times. He would overthink the slightest detail, yet dismiss an idea with more meat to it, if it did not suit his purpose. Not that he always revealed his purpose. Sometimes working with him felt like groping in the dark.

They arrived back at the mercat cross in silence. Good, the horses were still there – always a concern in a place like this. Turnbull remembered the time his two brothers had their nags stolen from outside a tavern in Hawick. Davie and Edward spent a week tracking down the culprit. Then they ambushed the thief on his way home from church and recovered their beasts, at the cost of a few cuts and bruises. Their celebrations were wild, but just two weeks later, they were dead in an English field. These memories of family pricked him.

"Perhaps this is the moment for me to visit my mother," he said as he climbed onto Fogo.

His master gave him a curious look. "Then I'll come too. As I've said, I would dearly like to meet her."

Turnbull's stomach lurched, for he was still not ready for this. When he didn't answer, the Frenchman's voice hardened. "You're not using her as an excuse to sneak about, asking questions about this Walkerburn, are you?"

The lad scowled, although this thought had crossed his mind. "No, just to see how she fares. But she's a strange fish. And it has been a long time. Let me see how her humours lie, and then I will introduce you. Meanwhile, I trust you can find your way home?"

His master nodded, and they agreed to meet at the tower before dusk.

Turnbull rode out through the West Port, with the afternoon sun in his eyes. As he went, he thought about what might lie in store. As the youngest of three brothers, he had always been his mother's pet: the sensitive student to Davie and Edward's wild warriors. Her affection had only increased when those two had fallen with their father at Flodden. For a while, Turnbull had welcomed the outpouring of love, found solace in their mutual grief, practical support in running the farmstead. But his mother's attentions had become overbearing, and he had enlisted with the governor by way of escape. She had taken it badly at the time – would she feel the same way now?

He splashed through a burn and continued up the hill to their farmstead. The ground here was marshy, and while he had done his best to drain the bog, it had clearly reverted to its soggy state. The drystane dyke had fallen into ruin too, perhaps raided by the neighbours. At least the house was still intact, although the reed thatch looked like it needed replacing. In the yard, a woman was cutting thistles with a long scythe. She watched him approach but did not stop what she was doing.

"Is that you?" she said as he finally came close, her voice so hoarse that he could hardly hear it above the swish of her blade and the rush of the summer wind.

"Aye, Mother," said Turnbull. He was shocked by how she had aged. Her hair was greyer, her cheeks raw. When he clambered off Fogo and went to embrace her, he noticed that she was thinner too. He took care not to press too tightly on her bird-like frame. "I am come to see you, as I said I would."

"Aye ye did," she said, holding him back again at arm's length. "Although, I didnae think it'd take this long. And now look at ye, a grown man. Ye must be what...?"

"Twenty-one, Mother."

"Twenty-one," she murmured. "My ain wee Dod. No' that ye sound like ye're frae here any mair."

"I'll always be frae here," he said, although the vowels felt false in his mouth. He reverted to the accent he had learnt at St Andrews and polished in Edinburgh. "Now, I hope you have some of your broth on the boil and we can talk of old times?"

His mother nodded and led him inside. Turnbull was pleased to see that she did indeed have a little pot bubbling away, even if the brew was a little more watery than he remembered. As they supped, he told his mother of his time in Lord Albany's service, recounting how he had met the governor himself, along with great men like Lord Douglas. How, just a few days ago, he had even come close enough to touch the queen herself.

His mother listened intently, as if he were speaking a foreign tongue. "It's a great shame for that lady," she said at last, dabbing her lips. Her words surprised Turnbull, for when he had last been home, she had blamed Margaret Tudor for their family's troubles. After all, wasn't it the queen's countrymen who had bathed in their folk's blood? Surely, his mother could not have switched sides now.

"It's not like you to speak up for the English party," he said.

"I speak for no party, only the woman herself. Kept away from her own son by your master, Albany. It seems to be a favourite trick o' his."

Turnbull saw what she was getting at and tried to change the subject. "And yourself, Mother. How goes it here? I hope the crops are flourishing in this fine weather?"

"It's too hot," she said, waving a hand. "Everything is spoiling."

"The beasts then, they keep well?"

"How would I ken? They're up on the summer pastures, being tended by your uncle. I have to pay him for the privilege, so it's hardly worth the bother." She took his hand and pressed it. "Listen, Dod. I cannae run this farmstead on my ain. It's too much work. There are reivers who would take what little I have, in a single night. I need a man about the place."

Turnbull sighed. "You know I cannot stay here, Mother. I'm sworn to serve Lord Albany and my master, the warden, too. He's a good man, and I will rise with him."

"Or he'll rise on your back. That's usually the way wi' such folk." Although she stroked his cheek, there was a bitterness to her voice, and he was glad that he had not brought his master here to witness it. "I beg ye to think about this, Dod. Give up on this Frenchman, before he gives up on you. Come back here and we'll make it like the old days."

Turnbull finished his broth and put the bowl aside. He had no intention of returning to the old days, for he was a young man with the world in front of him. However, he felt guilty all the same. He gave her a hug, more fulsome this time, and said he would return soon.

"See that ye do," said his mother, her eyes brimming. She straightened his collar, smoothed down a lock of stray hair. "By the way, your horse's tail looks patchy," she said, as he climbed onto Fogo. "That looks like pinworm to me. If ye stay awhile, I'll see to it."

"Thank you," said Turnbull, but he knew that he must go, before he felt the heaviness that had driven him away in the first place.

There were still two hours to dusk, and Turnbull was not looking forward to returning to Ravenscleugh. If his mother was overbearing, she was as nothing compared to Widow Scrimgeour. And what was his master keeping from him, which rendered him so tense? The idea of being cooped up in that tower with the two of them – and that strange prisoner – did not fill him with joy. As he came back through Lauder, he decided to stop for an ale.

The Red Lion was busy as a tooth-puller had been in town, and his customers were now dousing their poor gums to numb the pain of his ministrations. Turnbull took a stool in the corner and listened to them as they regaled others about the excruciating treatment. With each telling, the pliers became bigger, the pincers sharper. One woman, her jaw grotesquely swollen, held up her bloody tooth and said that expelling it had been more painful than birthing any of her seven children – but at least it would give her no more trouble, unlike them!

The others chortled, but as the laughter faded, a small fellow leant into the group, a serious look upon his face. "My pain was hellish too," he said with an exaggerated whisper. "But as ye say, it's come and gone. Unlike the torments Bailie Walkerburn will have to suffer."

Turnbull's ears pricked up. He remembered his master's instructions not to investigate this matter, but he couldn't help listening to what these folk had to say. Surely that was permissible? He drew his bonnet over his head.

"Aye, they say he near jerked his own heid off," said another toper. "Must have been something terrible to drive the fellow to it."

"It was his gambling," said the little fellow, who looked pleased to have all eyes upon him. "Lost a' his money to that stranger who passed through. The fellae must have been a vagabond once, for he had a V burnt into his foreheid. Well, a vagabond he is nae mair, for he bought everybody in here a drink to celebrate his win."

"Must have been a hell o' a purse."

"Aye, and a hell o' a curse… for Walkerburn!"

The drinkers went back to moaning about their teeth, and Turnbull hastily finished up his ale. He was intrigued by the story of the bailie and the vagabond, the way that men's fortunes could spin on a ha'penny these days. It reminded him of what Baird had said the previous night, about these times of change. It made him think, too, that his master had been right to call this a self-killing: Walkerburn had clearly lost his wager and then lost his wits, to boot. He resolved to be more cheerful with Antoine when he returned, although of course he would have to be careful about explaining where his fresh intelligence had come from.

Turnbull had hoped to be back in time for supper, but when

he entered the hall, he found it empty, apart from Elspeth. The girl was scraping some chicken bones into a pot for the next day. He gave her a nod of recognition, but she immediately turned away. As she did so, he caught a blue mark on her cheek, where she had been slapped that morning.

He went upstairs and was glad to find his master on his own. He gave a penitent bow and lit a candle from the wall torch.

"So, how was your mother?" said Antoine. There was a tetchiness to his voice, which Turnbull quickly sought to dispel.

"Oh, in fine spirits," he lied. "She would be glad to meet you at some point."

"That is good to hear. And you have let go of that Walkerburn business?"

"Yes," Turnbull said, more truthfully this time. "I think that you are right, sir. In fact, as I passed through town, I heard something that just about confirms it."

He told the Frenchman about Walkerburn's wager, presenting it as something he had heard while watering his horse, rather than eavesdropping in the tavern.

"Well, I'm glad that you've seen sense," his master said, although he still eyed him suspiciously. "But I cannot say the same for Widow Scrimgeour. When I told her of Master Walkerburn's self-killing, she looked like she might spew."

"Strange. Did she know him?"

"Apparently not. But she turned puce and hurried off. At any rate, she's in a dark mood, so let's stay out of her way. Baird is safe – I checked on him earlier. And that's all that we should care about."

Chapter 9

The next day, they set off to interview the provisioner. After all, this Bell fellow was the only other person with access to the tower, and they needed to ensure that he was trustworthy.

It was a bright day, and Antoine was glad to feel a little warmth in his bones. He had never got used to the weather here – the icy wind that could chill a man to his marrow, the mist, the constant rain. So today he savoured the sun on his skin and imagined the same rays beating down on him as he surveyed some golden vineyard back home. If the next few weeks went well, he might even make the final picking. Then he could raise a glass to his time here, and it would all have been worth it.

He was still swirling the claret in his mind when a bell rang out. It was the same muffled toll as yesterday – the parish church lay near the East Port, which they had just passed – except this time, there were only two chimes. A woman had died, it seemed. Antoine raised an eyebrow to Turnbull and suggested they must press on to find the provisioner, before they were collared by any more grieving families. However, as they reached the mercat cross, they were engulfed in a commotion.

"It's Walkerburn's wife!" cried a woman as she rushed past them, clutching a child. "Murdered in cold blood!"

Antoine's stomach tightened, but he didn't want to encourage any more of Turnbull's fancies, so he agreed they would make a brief diversion to the bailie's house, to investigate.

As with the day before, a crowd was milling about the door, but this time, the servant was not there to drive them away.

"Make room for the warden," said Turnbull, clearing a way to the front. He opened the front door of the cottage, and they stepped back into the dingy room they had visited yesterday. The bailie's corpse was still laid out on the table, just as it had been, although a foul smell now rose from it. Meanwhile, the wife's body was slumped on a chair in the corner, her hands tied behind the wooden frame. Her head lolled to the side, her matted hair obscuring her face. Her white kirtle was drenched in blood from half a dozen stabs to the abdomen, and the floor rushes underneath her were so darkly stained that they looked burnt.

"Sweet mercy," said Antoine, turning away. He had seen his fair share of dead men over the years, but never a woman butchered like this. As he tried to control his stomach, he noticed a skinny fellow at the door. Through the dim light, Antoine saw that the man's hands were bloody, and his wadmol smock was covered in rusty smears.

"I didnae do it," said the man, as if he could read the warden's mind. "I'm just the one who found her. I came round to check on her after her husband's... passing... and then saw her like this. Sorry, I forget myself – I'm the neighbour, Erskine."

The fellow rubbed his hands across his smock in a

desperate attempt to cleanse them, but it was no good. Antoine tried to calm him with some simple questions.

"What time was this, Master Erskine?"

"No' long ago. I didnae want to disturb her first thing, given she was grieving."

"Of course. And she is exactly how you found her?"

"Aye, I tried to undo the ropes, but the arms were too stiff. The gore was all over me. Her face in my face. Eventually, I gave up as I couldnae bear to be so close…"

"I can imagine." Antoine did not want to examine the woman either, but he knew that he must. He bent over her and used a clump of clotted hair to lift her head. The goodwife's face was fixed in a terrifying grimace. The Frenchman let the head drop gently and stepped away.

"Very well. I believe you are telling the truth, Master Erskine. So just a few more questions. Did you see anybody enter the house or behave suspiciously beforehand?"

"No," spluttered the man. He clasped his hands, as if to thank God that he was not under suspicion. "Many folk came round yesterday afternoon, to pay their respects for Bailie Walkerburn, but I saw nobody peculiar."

"Did you hear anything untoward?"

"Just my neighbour crying. I thought little of it, as she'd just lost her man. By the time night fell, all was quiet."

"And the servant? Dewar?"

"Naewhere to be seen, sir," said Erskine, shaking his head. "I fear he's done for her, then made off into the night."

Antoine was ashamed to feel a twinge of relief, as it seemed that the killing was a simple domestic affair. A horrible one, for sure, but nothing so very unusual for this wild place. More importantly, nothing requiring their time. He said as much to Turnbull when Erskine went back outside.

However, the lad's face told him that he was not done with the case yet.

"Shouldn't we check the rest of the house, sir?"

"What for? It seems perfectly clear what has happened."

"Not necessarily. What if Dewar's been kidnapped? It's common enough round here."

"Men are only kidnapped when they're worth something," said Antoine irritably. "Not the likes of a common servant."

"It's just that he seemed a decent enough fellow yesterday."

"Mayhap he was, until he realised that his master's death put him out of a job. Then he decided to take whatever he could."

Antoine sighed and moved into the study. Papers and ledger books lay strewn on the floor, as if to confirm the place had been ransacked: another finger pointing at Dewar. Still, the Frenchman knew Turnbull well enough to realise that if he did not humour him, he would be like a dog with a bone. "Very well, have a quick look in the servant's quarters, and I'll go upstairs. But whatever we find, we cannot chase after this fugitive, when we have a proper villain to look after."

Turnbull took the back door, towards Dewar's lodging, while Antoine headed up the stairs. Like the study, the Walkerburns' bedroom was in a state of disarray. The mattress had been sliced open and the straw thrown all over the room. A dresser lay on its side, a handful of clothes spilling out. On the floor, there was a hexagonal wooden box, with painted sides. Antoine picked it up, and the lid fell off. All that remained inside was a sad collection of cheap brooches, clasps and pins.

He came back downstairs and met Turnbull returning from the yard.

"Well?"

"Nothing, sir. Dewar's room was stripped bare."

"While all the others have been rummaged through."

"Yes," said Turnbull meekly. "It looks like Dewar's our man, as you say."

"No, for the last time, *Baird's* our man. This is a distraction. Now, let's get back to our business and find this provisioner Scrimgeour mentioned."

They pushed their way back through the crowd and gave Erskine a coin to get the place cleaned up. In this heat, the bodies should be buried as soon as possible. Someone should tell the relatives and persuade the priest to lay both souls to rest together. They would return the next day, to make sure that all was well. And then that would be that.

The provisioner, Mungo Bell, was a squat little man with crinkly eyes and a well-worn smile. He greeted them in his ramshackle office, at the back of a bakery. The smell of fresh bread filled the air, mixed with the tang of brewing from a side room. A chicken pecked about the floor before flapping off to join its brethren in the yard.

"You're a man of many parts," said Antoine, introducing himself and Turnbull.

"Aye, it's wise to keep your fingers in lots of pies these days."

The Frenchman explained their mission at Ravenscleugh, and Bell confirmed the system that Scrimgeour had described, whereby the tower's supplies were deposited outside, every Monday. The provisioner's voice was firm and his gaze steady, an encouraging sign in a place where so many dissembled. Antoine could see why Scrimgeour might favour him and was about to finish the interview when the man threw out a question of his own.

"So what do ye think o' the Walkerburns, sir?"

The Frenchman was taken aback, before quickly recovering. "It is perhaps as you have heard. The bailie seems to have died by his own hand. Then the servant panicked and killed the wife. The house is robbed and the culprit gone."

"Aye, that's what they are saying," said Bell. "But perchance, there is more to it than that." His eyes flickered, and Antoine felt the man was judging him, as much as the other way round. "Ye see, one o' my carters was coming back wi' a load frae Selkirk last night and saw Dewar on the road. Guess who he was talking to?"

Antoine shrugged.

"One o' your prisoner's gang. A reiver known as Cottar Craig."

"What?" said Turnbull. "The servant was conversing with one of Baird's men?"

"More than that, I think. Dewar seemed to be showing Baird's man a bag. My carter couldnae say much more, for he jigged the horse and got out o' the way afore he came to any harm. But he swears that's how it looked."

Bell fixed his smile, as if awaiting further questions, but Antoine was still trying to process the news. He rubbed his temples, before piecing together his thoughts.

"Do you know if Baird had any dealings with the Walkerburns?"

"None that I ken of, sir."

"Did he know their servant?"

"I cannae see it, no."

"And Widow Scrimgeour? Could she have known any of

them? She seemed to flinch when she heard of Walkerburn's death yestere'en."

"I dinnae think so," said Bell, his voice less solid than before. A queasiness came over Antoine. He felt Turnbull itching to ask more – and indeed, he had plenty more questions of his own. But he saw the provisioner's face harden, as if he already regretted sharing his news and would not cough up more. It occurred to him that the man's evidence was second-hand in any case and that they might have better luck with Baird himself – if any of this business could be remotely described as lucky.

They hurried back to Ravenscleugh and were relieved to find there were no signs of mischief. Moffat opened the gate with his usual casual greeting. Scrimgeour was also of a calm demeanour, even as they described the terrible scene they had discovered. She was adamant that she did not know the Walkerburns or their servant. It was only when Antoine mentioned the provisioner's story, about Dewar conversing with one of Baird's men, that she became agitated.

"That's too much o' a coincidence. He must be up to something."

Moffat shrugged. "Well, at least he cannae be planning an escape. He kens he just has to stay here awhile, to be pardoned for his crimes."

"Unless he suspects he won't be released," Scrimgeour murmured. She turned to Antoine. "Did ye say something to unsettle him?"

"Of course not," said Antoine, although he recalled the probing look that Baird had given him that first night. Had his face betrayed his discomfort, at the idea of guarding someone under false pretences? He could not be sure, but perhaps another conversation would settle it.

They took the winding staircase to the prisoner's room. Scrimgeour let them in, before locking the door behind them, as she had done the other day. But this time, she stayed at the hatch, peering in to find out what was afoot.

"Ah, my new friends," said Baird smoothly. "To what do I owe the pleasure?"

"We have some questions," said Antoine, watching him carefully. "Questions relating to some folk in Lauder: Bailie Walkerburn, his wife and their servant Dewar."

The prisoner shrugged. "The names mean nothing to me. But if ye'd like to introduce me to them, I'd be happy to make their acquaintance."

"That won't be possible," said Turnbull sharply. "Walkerburn and his wife are dead, his servant gone. We think he may have robbed them, before selling their goods to one of your men."

"I see. Well, as ye may have heard, my men dinnae kill. And only the very worst o' reivers would ever harm a woman."

"The servant was seen talking to one of your men on the road to Selkirk," said Antoine. "A rogue called Cottar Craig. So if you know more than you're letting on, you'd better spill it out."

A glint came into Baird's eye. "If anybody kens more than they're letting on, it's you, monsieur. Perhaps one day ye'll be straight wi' me, and I'll see if it's worth helping ye. In the meantime, good luck wi' your wee puzzle."

Chapter 10

Baird's words danced round Antoine's head that night, as he lay awake in the hall. It was his hour of watch, the moment between his first and second sleeps. Normally, he would spend the time setting his thoughts to paper, but the prisoner's jibe had thrown him. He did not like the way Baird turned every interrogation into a questioning of himself. He remembered the way that the prisoner had talked of enjoying the chase, for the thrill of it alone, and wondered whether he might be getting some kind of dark pleasure from their conversations too.

As he lay in this restless state, he could not stop his mind returning to the terrible things he had witnessed these past few days. Could Bailie Walkerburn have been murdered, after all, then his body staged like a self-killing? There had been no signs of foul play, but perhaps Antoine had not looked hard enough, in his desire to be free of the case. Could the wife have been involved in some intrigue, only to fall victim to it later? And what of the servant? Had he committed both crimes? Or neither? Oh, for goodness sake, this was ridiculous; he was chasing after shadows.

Once more, he reminded himself that he must focus on Baird and on Baird alone. Those were his orders, the instructions that he must follow to ensure his own release. As he stared up at the dark crannies of the ceiling, an idea began to form.

A few hours later, they were on the road to Lauder. The sky was completely clear, as if the sun had risen early to sweep away all the cobwebs of the night, but not for the first time, Turnbull found his mind befogged by his master's intentions. Only when they reached the East Port did the Frenchman start to explain himself.

"So, Turnbull, why do you think we're here?"

The lad scratched his head. He didn't like it when his master tested him this way, but he knew that the habit had sharpened his wits over their time together.

"To interview the carter who saw Dewar with Baird's man?" he essayed.

"No, it sounded like he told Master Bell all he saw. But you are close."

"To visit the place they met then?"

Antoine shook his head. "I doubt there will be anything by the roadside. No, go back a little. What did the carter say Dewar was showing Baird's man?"

"A bag."

"Correct. And what might that bag contain? What would the Bairds want from a fellow like Dewar? A man who – if we are right – had just ransacked his master's house?"

Turnbull shrugged. "Jewellery? Gold?"

"I don't think so. The bailie was of middling rank but hardly rich. And Baird's men are supposed to be keeping their noses clean. They would not risk their master's neck for the sake of a few coins or baubles. No, I think Dewar must have brought Baird's gang something of uncommon value." He paused to raise a finger. "I don't know what that might be yet. But I think we should revisit Walkerburn's house and see if it tells us anything."

With that, they quickened their pace and pushed their way through the crowds gathered about the mercat cross. It was Midsummer's Eve, and traders were putting up stalls in preparation for the festivities that would go on long into the night. Girls threaded flowers through their hair while boys eyed them from a safe distance. The mood was light, and for a moment, Turnbull, who was a lad of sanguine temperament, felt his spirits lift like the ribbons that fluttered in the cool breeze. It was only when they arrived at the Walkerburns' house that he remembered the grave purpose of their visit.

"Cleaners," said a burly man, pushing past them on his way out of the house. Three others followed him, clutching buckets, brooms and mops. "I'd leave it a few minutes, gentlemen. We've splashed some vinegar about, and it'll sting your eyes."

They followed the workman's advice before nudging the door open. Sure enough, the smell of death mingled with the equally pungent smell of cleanliness. Yet, the house did not seem greatly tidier.

"No wonder they asked us to wait," said Turnbull, shaking his head. "They wanted to be long gone by the time we discovered their shoddy work."

"Yes, I fear the neighbour took our coin and just got his friends to do the job. Still, let's take a proper look and see if anything leaps out. Of course, whatever Dewar stole will not be here, but if we know the kinds of items the bailie kept, we may be able to guess what's been taken. Then work out why Baird might want it."

They started at the table, where Walkerburn's wife had

been laid out alongside her husband. Both were covered by a fraying mortcloth, so Antoine quickly pulled it back to ensure they were as they should be. Yes, their eyelids and mouths had been closed, their arms folded. But nobody had bothered to conceal their wounds. Turnbull tutted and moved to the other side of the room. The blackened rushes had been swept into a corner, but the chair had not been wiped; bloody stripes still marked where the woman's arms had been bound.

Turnbull went out through the back yard, to check on the servant's lodging. It was just as he had left it, yielding no further clues. When he returned to the house, his master was coming down the stairs. He shook his head, as if to confirm that his own search had also been unsuccessful. They then progressed to the study, which, of all the rooms, was in the greatest disorder. While most of the papers had been cleared from the floor, they had simply been stacked in rough piles on the settle. The bookcases were in disarray as well, with leather-bound tomes left this way and that — some spines facing outwards, others inwards.

"What a midden," said Antoine, picking out a thick ledger and leafing through its pages. "Those cleaners have left it worse than they found it. We'll have to sift through everything and see if anything leaps out."

"That could take all day," said Turnbull, glancing around at the jumble of despatch boxes, scrolls, envelopes and books. "What exactly are we looking for, anyway?"

"That's the thing: we won't know until we find it. Let's go through what we have and then determine if anything relates to Baird."

There were two bookcases, one on either side of the room. They each took one and began to work through the despatch boxes, one at a time. It was heavy going, as most of the papers within were written in a tiny, spidery ink – Walkerburn's own hand, presumably – and related to tedious legal matters. After an hour, Turnbull mused that he had gained an intimate knowledge of every mill, dovecote and coney warren in the valley, but had gleaned nothing about their prisoner.

Next, they moved on to the ledgers.

"These look like rent books," said Turnbull. "Look, there are lots of numbers, arranged by what seem to be the names of farms."

"They're unlikely to help us then, as we know Baird owns no land. But have a look at this." Antoine held up a scroll with some kind of diagram etched on it, and Turnbull peered over his shoulder.

"A map?"

"Almost. It's a building plan. It relates to works at Melrose Abbey, if I'm not mistaken."

Turnbull's eyes lit up. "I doubt Baird has much interest in churches. But what if there are maps of other places here? Places he might wish to raid? Or even a plan of Ravenscleugh? There might be sewer systems or tunnels that we don't know about – ways for him to escape."

"Let's not jump to wild conclusions," said Antoine, much to Turnbull's annoyance, as it was his master who had pointed out the diagram in the first place. "But yes, we should see if there are others like this, in case we're onto something."

With this in mind, they put the ledgers to one side and concentrated on the scrolls. While not all of them were maps, there were enough to indicate that the bailie had a keen interest in architecture and cartography. They found designs of battlements, floorplans of towers, charts showing secret paths through marshes, and fording places across rivers. The room resembled a robbers' library.

Antoine stroked his beard, as he spread the papers out on the floor. "In truth, we can only guess what Baird has taken from this house. But whatever it is, it seems he has a plan, at least in the general sense." He paused. "And he would only need a plan if he does not believe in our promise of a pardon."

Turnbull tilted his head as he thought this through. "If he were confident of being released, his men would be lying low, not trading in nefarious papers."

"Exactly."

"So whatever Baird's men have discovered must lead them to believe it will somehow free their master?"

"And Baird must think he has nothing to lose. This means we need to be more wary of him than ever. But first, let's finish this job."

Turnbull looked about the room. They had searched both bookcases thoroughly, and now only the settle remained. He raised the lid and reached inside, pulling out a handful of loose papers. Antoine did the same, and they spent a while sifting through them. However, these documents seemed to be of little interest, as they mostly contained local ordinances concerning issues such as the town watch, common grazing rights and observance of the curfew. After reviewing his stack, Turnbull set it down and was about to close the lid when his master let out a dry chuckle.

"Well, well," he said, waving a large piece of folded paper. It was one of those printed pamphlets which had started to circulate in recent times. "I fear this will not help us with Baird, but it shines a light on Walkerburn."

Turnbull was intrigued and helped his master straighten

the broadsheet out. It was dominated by a crude woodcut of a nobleman holding a knife, looming over a cowering woman.

"Yet another slur on Albany," said the Frenchman. "Some story that he has only invited the queen back so that he can kill her."

Turnbull shook his head. "So Walkerburn was for the English party then?"

"It seems so. Not that it helps us much today, other than to say he was a gull to believe such nonsense."

They leant over the pamphlet and took a moment to read the text. It was a stream of slanders and conjectures.

"One wonders at the minds of those who write such things," said Turnbull, folding the paper up again. He was about to replace it in the settle when Antoine stopped him.

"No, we should not let such a lie remain in circulation. You keep it for now and we can destroy it later. Meanwhile, let's see the neighbour and get him to fetch those cleaners again."

They left the Walkerburn's house and went next door. Although Erskine no longer had bloody hands or clothes, he still looked shaken. His jaw trembled as he wished them good morrow. "Ye've been back to the house, gentlemen?"

"Yes, we wanted to conduct another search. Just in case we missed anything the first time round."

Erskine gulped. "Of course. And did ye find aught?"

"Nothing obvious. But we think our prisoner may be involved somehow. Would you know anything about that?"

"No, sir, I swear to ye."

"Could Baird have known Walkerburn?"

The neighbour was confused. "Not to my knowledge. One is an outlaw, the other the local bailie."

"That counts for little round here," said Antoine. "Well, we will continue to investigate this matter until we understand Master Baird's role, if any. In the meantime, have your friends come back to finish off their cleaning."

Erskine frowned for a moment, then his eyes widened in fear. "What friends?" he said. "I only invited some women to come in, as ye instructed. But they're no' due here for another hour."

Chapter 11

"**G**od's blood, it's we who are the gulls," exclaimed Antoine. "Those buckets and mops were just a cover."

"Aye," said Turnbull. "And whatever was in that house is surely gone now. Do you think they were Baird's men?"

"I imagine so. Still, let's not be despondent. Their visit confirms that we are right to follow this trail. There was something valuable in that house. Dewar took it to Baird's gang, and they likely returned for more. Or perhaps to destroy some remaining clue. If we're to keep our prisoner secure, we must find out what he's up to."

Antoine was suddenly conscious of Erskine standing there, hanging onto every word, his eyes occasionally flitting to the pamphlet in Turnbull's hand. The Frenchman felt that it was unlikely that such a lily-livered fellow had anything to do with the Walkerburns' deaths or Baird's intriguing, but he might secretly sympathise with the English party. If so, perhaps he might be turned to good use.

"Master Erskine, you seem unduly bothered by this broadsheet we have found."

The man started to stammer a half-hearted denial, but Antoine was sure he had hit the mark. He waved him silent. "Of course, with this new printing business, this filthy slander sheet might not be the only one around. So I am half-minded to search all the houses on this street, round up anyone in possession of it, for treason. We could start with your home if you like, or I could give you some time to destroy any such material that you know of, in return for you listening out for gossip about Dewar and Baird."

Erskine took Antoine's hand and shook it vigorously, between desperate professions of innocence and gratitude. The Frenchman felt sorry for him but thought it was a good moment to turn the screw. "You have two days to find us something. And do not think of deceiving us."

While Antoine hoped that the neighbour might be able to winkle something from the other townsfolk, he did not want to put all his eggs in that basket. Instead, he decided to take Turnbull to The Red Lion to see what they could discover for themselves. The tavern was bustling with Midsummer revellers. Many had spent the day gathering herbs to ward off malign spirits, and the room was filled with the delightful aroma of their endeavours. In one corner, a band of minstrels sang of the coming solstice, while some of the topers looked like they might not make it to that hour. The Frenchman spotted a man sitting alone, well into his ale, and thought he would make a good place to start.

"It shapes to be a goodly night, friend."

"Aye, it does," said the man, a baxter, judging by his flour-covered smock and hair. "Although I fear I've drank away my coins too early."

"An easy mistake in this hot weather," said Antoine, clapping him on the back. "Still, we may be able to stand you another ale or two, if you can help us with some questions."

The baxter narrowed his eyes. "You're the warden, aren't ye, sir? I saw ye speak at the mercat cross. I wish ye well, for unlike some round here, I'm all for Albany. But I prefer no' to get involved in politicking."

"No need to worry about that. It's not politicking we're interested in, but rather this business at the Walkerburns."

"Of course, a terrible thing, but I ken little o' it."

Antoine slid a groat across the table. "We think the servant Dewar is behind it. Perhaps in service of our prisoner, Will Baird. Can you think of any connection twixt the two?"

The baxter shrugged. "I really couldnae say. I've made it my business to keep out o' the Bairds' way, and I only met Dewar when he came in for his master's order. A quiet man, he was."

"Did he have family nearby? Somewhere he might run to, after committing a crime like this?"

"I dinnae think so. He was frae Fife, if I recall. He's probably flitted there."

Damnation. Fife was days away and no good to them at all. Antoine moved the coin back towards himself, and it seemed to pull a lever within the thirsty fellow's mind. He raised a hand. "No, wait, I ken where he might go. The Sanctuary of Stow."

"St Mary's?" asked Turnbull, intrigued. Turning to his master, he added, "It's a strange place, just past my mother's. Unlike a typical sanctuary, it stretches on for miles."

"Aye, there are plenty of reivers holed up there," said the baxter. "If your man Dewar is serving the Bairds, I'll warrant they've hidden him there for now and will smuggle him out when the time is right."

Antoine tossed the coin into the man's greedy paw and stepped outside with Turnbull. Despite the late hour, the sun was just beginning to set behind the West Port, casting a golden glow down the High Street and illuminating the faces of the revellers. Some monks from Melrose had placed a statue of St John the Baptist by the mercat cross, as if to remind the godless locals that it was the eve of his feast too. However, the rays of light enveloped the wooden figure, causing his eyes to sparkle and his teeth to gleam in a most unholy fashion. The effect stirred a memory deep within Antoine, but he could not quite place it.

He took Turnbull's arm, and they walked towards the West Port with the great ball of fire looming behind it. Along the way, they tried to engage people about Dewar and the Bairds but found few in the mood to answer questions. Not for the first time in the Marches, Antoine felt that the locals would rather draw a veil over their troubles than let a stranger in.

They were about to give up when Turnbull whispered, "Don't turn round, but I think we're being followed."

Antoine kept his head locked forwards and reached for the hilt of his sword. "Are you sure? The crowds are so thick it must be hard to tell."

"As sure as I can be. A little fellow in a blue hood keeps bobbing up behind us, but whenever I turn round, he disappears."

"Did you get a good look at him?"

"No, he's kept himself well covered. But the hood is not hard to spot on a warm night like this."

"Then let's split up and see if we can catch him. Why don't you tarry here, while I head through the gate."

Antoine shuffled forward with the rest of the crowd, who were advancing towards a clearing, just beyond the West Port. Three fire pits were being lit, in accordance with

The Dance of Vipers

tradition: one of bone, one of wood and one a mixture of both materials. The crowd cheered as the flames took hold and the smoke rose on the summer breeze, like some pagan incense. Antoine recalled the smile on the saint's face again and wondered why this ceremony felt both strange and familiar. Then it struck him; it reminded him of the bonfire from last All Hallows' E'en, when he and Turnbull had been attacked. He tightened his grip on the hilt of his sword and peered through the swirling smoke.

Antoine spotted him: the man in the blue hood. But as soon as he laid eyes on him, he was off again, into the throng. The Frenchman tried to push towards him, but a group of jugglers blocked his path. Looking around for Turnbull, he hoped the lad might intercept their stalker at the gate. However, the fellow seemed to sense the threat and spun off to the side, the blue hood flashing in and out of view, like a kingfisher down a riverbank. By the time Antoine reached the West Port, there was no sign of him, and there was nothing left to do but fetch Turnbull and inform him of the near miss.

"Ach, he must have slipped past me, by that fortune teller's stall," said the lad. "Did you see any more of him?"

"No, as you say, he seemed determined to hide his face."

"How strange. Do you think it could be the same fellow we disturbed at The Boar's Head?"

Antoine had not considered this. He had to admit it was a possibility but was loathe to encourage Turnbull's fancies beyond the specific task at hand. As was often the case, he suggested a middle path between the lad's taste for adventure and his own caution.

"Well, if it is him, then he must be quite determined, for that was days ago and miles away. But let's add him to our list of questions and see if he might lead us to Dewar or Baird."

They continued to quiz the revellers, but it was tough going, as many of them were fox-drunk by now and unable to make much sense. Others had gathered round the fire pits, where local youths were taking turns jumping over the flames. They were there to burn off their primitive energies before getting back to the hard work of the harvest, and they did not take kindly to some strangers interrupting their fun.

Antoine was about to bring the night to a close when Turnbull pointed to two groups of men arguing on the far side of the fires. The figures were in silhouette, but there were two or three of them on each side, pushing and jostling, while the other revellers moved out of their way.

"Look at them, sir. They look more the sort who would know the likes of Dewar or Baird. What say we go over there and see if they can help us?"

Antoine hesitated. Again, he could see the truth in Turnbull's words but feared they might be stepping into someone else's battle. "Help us or slay us?" he said.

As if to make his point, a blade flashed in the firelight.

"Most likely that's just for show, sir. But we've had no joy with these merry-makers. Perchance we'll fare better with the rougher end of town?"

The Frenchman thought about how close he was to going home, how important it was to close this thing with Baird down. He nodded reluctantly, and they edged their way round the fires.

The heat from the three pits was fierce, forcing Antoine to shield his face from the flames. As he turned away, he saw one of the brawlers draw back his arm and bring a cudgel down on his foe. The victim's friends sprang to his defence, and there was another flash of silver. A scream suggested that it had found its mark. So much for the blade being just for show! What sacrilege this was, to draw blood on a feast day.

The crowd parted, as the violence sent the bystanders into a panic. Antoine tried to push through, but the surge of people fleeing the fight made it impossible. In the commotion, one group managed to get on their horses, their figures clear above the melee but still shrouded in shadow. By the time Antoine and Turnbull managed to break the ranks, the riders were off, leaving the others still scrambling for their mounts.

"Stay where you are!" Antoine shouted to them.

Three brawlers looked to their right as a young lad approached with their horses – he looked no older than twelve. Panicked, he dropped the reins, before darting back into the crowd.

"I said stay where you are!"

The men unleashed a torrent of oaths. One of them kicked over a set of chicken spits, sending hot meat and metal skewers flying through the air. They used their swords to cut a path through the screaming bystanders, before disappearing into the darkness. Within a few seconds, it was all over, and Antoine found himself trying to calm the three horses to prevent them from crashing into the crowd.

"Who were those men?" Turnbull asked one of the few onlookers who remained.

"They werenae frae the town," slurred the fellow, as he stooped to pick up a half-cooked chicken breast from the ground. He brushed off some dirt and took a bite. "But I think some o' them belonged to that gang frae Ettrick Forest. What's their name? Oh, aye. Baird's Bairns."

Baird stretched back on his bed, as if he cared little for their report, but Antoine felt it was an affectation, that he was listening more carefully than ever.

"So if I have this right, ye're saying my men might have paid some servant to kill his mistress and perhaps his master too, but ye've found nothing to link us? You think they might have stolen something from the bailie's house as well, but ye cannae tell me what or why? Oh, and my lads might have been in a fight, but ye dinnae ken wi' who?"

"Don't be clever, Baird. We know you're up to something."

"Well, I wish I kent what it was! But no, I'm stuck in here, while you have your Midsummer revels." He smiled, not in a wicked way, but almost with conspiratorial warmth. "Perhaps if ye let me out awhile, I could help ye wi' your sleuthing?"

Antoine stifled a laugh. He had to hand it to the fellow; he had a fine sense of humour. In another world, he might even have made an entertaining friend. But in this world, jests could be dangerous, and he was not going to be the butt of one.

Chapter 12

Antoine woke early, to the sound of some strange clanging. For a moment, he feared it might be those funeral bells again and dreaded to discover who Death had visited next. But as he came to his senses, he realised that the noise was sharper and much closer. Was it swords clashing? His pulse raced as he scrambled to his feet. That lazy carl Moffat was curled in a ball and did not respond to Antoine's attempts to rouse him. But soon, Turnbull was rubbing the sleep from his eyes and joining him at the window. They both looked out onto the courtyard, from which the noise seemed to emanate. Nobody was abroad at this hour, but an ominous orange glow poured from the stables.

Grabbing their weapons, they sprinted downstairs and headed for the main door of the tower. If they could secure that, they could gain a better sense of what was going on. They clattered round the corner of the stairwell and into the storeroom, swerving to avoid a pile of old crates left against the wall. As they reached the door, Antoine felt that something was off. What the hell could it be? When he attempted to draw the bolts, he saw it: someone had removed the iron bars.

He nodded to Turnbull, feeling a surge of concern. Their main line of defence was undone. Were they under attack from within? He flung the door open, and they raced across the courtyard towards the stables. The orange glow was now unmistakably a fire, the clanging louder than ever. His mind flashed back to last night's fight – the flames, the blades, the blood. As he leapt inside, he half expected to see the brawlers again, come to retrieve their horses. Instead, Crichton stood at a blacksmith's forge, hammering an iron bar in the furnace. Scrimgeour was watching over him, standing just out of reach of the blaze.

"Crichton telt me about the state you arrived in last night," said the keeper, motioning for the guard to stop his din. "So I decided to strengthen the bars on our door."

Antoine breathed a sigh of relief and returned his sword to its scabbard. "That's a good idea. I just wish that you had told me."

"I telt ye that if ye went into town, ye'd bring danger back wi' ye, and now it seems ye have." Scrimgeour flicked her head towards the brawlers' horses.

"On the contrary, we're doing our best to keep all of us safe and sound. Now, if you excuse us, we're off to the sanctuary at Stow, to look for a fugitive. Make sure those bars are back in place by the time we are returned."

They took Carbonel and Fogo from the stalls and saddled them up, while Crichton resumed his banging and Scrimgeour's face burned brighter than the furnace. They were leading the horses out of the stable when Elspeth entered, carrying a basket of apples. Her mother looked her up and down, as if searching for something to complain about. Eventually, she found it.

"Get out of here wi' those aipples, ye'll have these strangers' horses spoilt afore they've been here a day. And clean the mud off your clogs while ye're at it, ye filthy wee besom!"

On the way to the sanctuary, Antoine insisted on stopping off to see Turnbull's mother. The lad tried to dissuade him, by stressing the urgent need to track down their fugitive, but the Frenchman would not be put off. Turnbull hoped that he did not have some hidden plan in mind. He remembered how wistfully his master had spoken of their time together, as they had crossed the Lammermuirs, and he felt this visit smacked of the same flavour, like a settling of accounts, a tying up of loose ends. A farewell, even. Or was that simply the way he himself felt, about visiting his mother?

When they arrived, she was in the yard, still cutting those thistles.

"Good morrow!" said the Frenchman, in a voice that was uncommonly ebullient for him. "What a pleasure it is, to meet the mother of the great Dod Turnbull."

"Good morrow, sir," Turnbull's mother answered coldly. "You must be his master, then, the warden?"

"I am. We're on business at the sanctuary, and I persuaded your son to stop here, so that I could tell you what a fine lad he is."

"Ah, he needed persuading, did he?"

"Not at all, he has oft spoken of this place. He is very proud of it, as you should be of him."

Turnbull found his master's high praise as unsettling as his mother's sullen welcome. He shifted awkwardly in his saddle and hoped that they could cut the visit short, but the Frenchman was already dismounting.

"I also wanted to give you a token of my gratitude, for raising him so well."

Wait, what was this? His master was bringing out a purse.

"I dinnae wish your charity," said his mother, with a shake of her scythe.

"Of course, I apologise, madame. Don't think of it as charity. More as recompense for lending me your boy."

She waved the purse away. "When ye lend something, it is customary for ye to get it back. But I see no prospect of that wi' you and Dod. Unless ye're here to say ye're finished wi' him?"

Turnbull did not like his master's hesitant response to this and jumped in for him.

"Mother, I have told you before; we are on an important mission for the governor and cannot give up now. He's charged us with bringing peace to the Marches, and we've already made a little progress. Progress that will help all the people here, including yourself. But there is still much to do. Indeed, we're on our way to the sanctuary right now, in search of a murderer. So if you cannot summon up the manners which you've long drummed into me, then we will take our leave."

His mother straightened up and laid down her scythe. Taking a corner of her apron, she wiped a tear from her eye. "I am sorry, sir. My son is right. I should be grateful for your words. And more so for your kind gift. It's just that life is desperate enough out here, wi'out being on my ain."

Turnbull climbed down from Fogo and put an arm around her. "I know it is, Mother. And I hate to see you struggle so. Why don't we go inside and we will see if there's anything we can do to help?"

She nodded and turned to go back into the house, leaving the two men to follow on.

"Thank you for this," Turnbull whispered, as he took the purse from his master. "I will make sure she takes it and that her pride does not undo her." But in his heart, he wished the Frenchman had told him of his plan. It made him wonder what other intentions he was keeping to himself.

They entered the farmstead, and Turnbull's mother ladled them up some broth, which, as ever, was sitting on the smouldering hearth. The men sat down on a cracket bench, while she took up a stool and tried to compose herself.

"Apologies if it's a wee bit thin, sir. It always is, at this time o' year, wi' the beasts away and the harvest not yet in."

"It is delicious, madame. Now, tell me how we might help you, beyond my clumsy gift."

To Turnbull's dismay, the question seemed to irk her again. "Can ye make the rain come, sir?"

"Alas, no. Although I've rarely found it lacking here."

"Can ye make my lambs fatter, or my hens lay more?"

"Again, I wish I could."

"Then can ye spare my only son frae death? Spare him frae the fate his father and brothers met at Flodden?"

"That's enough," said Turnbull sharply. He put his bowl on the floor and reached for her hand.

"No, don't worry," said his master, though his voice had also hardened. "I understand how difficult these last few years must have been for you, madame. I, too, have lost loved ones on the battlefield. But we are at peace with England now, partly thanks to your son's good work."

"What kind of peace is it, when reivers roam the land?"

"We are turning our minds to them right now. That's why we're on the road today."

His mother laughed bitterly. "Ye'll never get rid of the reivers, sir."

"Perhaps not, but we can help control them. And protect you while you're here."

"I doubt it. And in any case, I already have protection. Every quarter, I pay my dues, so that some bandit doesnae torch my house or steal my beasts. I dinnae need more strangers to protect me, I just need my son."

Turnbull felt his stomach lurch. He had explained this local custom – known as 'blackmail' – to his master last year but had never thought that his own mother might be a victim of it. While he was put out by her tone, he felt ashamed of his own naivety.

"Who is it that's taxing you, Mother? We can have a word with them."

"I dinnae ken. They send a factor to pick up their dues, while they stay in the shadows."

"Then we could visit him, tell him to leave you be."

"He willnae listen. Besides, he's no' been round awhile."

"Tell us a name or where he bides. We will track him down."

"Very well," she said. "I dinnae ken his name, but I ken where ye can find him. He bides down in Lauder. I believe he is the bailie there."

Chapter 13

They rode swiftly to the sanctuary, urgently discussing this latest revelation and how it might help them discover what Baird was up to. They now knew that Walkerburn had been collecting protection money for some unknown party. Could Baird be that shadowy figure? If so, did the bailie lose his paymaster's gold in his wager with that vagabond? This might explain why he'd taken his own life and why his servant had sought out the gang to make amends. Whatever he brought them had clearly not been enough, which is likely why he had alerted them to something else of great value in his master's house. That's why they returned the next day.

But what were they after? Antoine felt that this was the last piece of the puzzle, as they drew up to the sanctuary's palisade.

A rotund priest met them at the gate. His face was mottled, and his bulbous nose perforated like a sponge, as if he were too fond of the communion wine. He smeared a strand of greasy hair across his ruddy face and gestured for the men to dismount.

"Greetings, gentlemen, and welcome to the Sanctuary of Stow. How can I help you on this fine summer's day?"

"I'm the Warden of the Eastern Marches," said Antoine,

showing his ring. "We are searching for a house servant named Dewar, who may have killed his mistress a few days ago."

"I see. Well, we've had no arrivals this past week, so I fear your trip is wasted. And before you ask, you may not just walk in and ask others of him, either."

"Even as the warden?" Antoine asked, exasperated.

"*Especially* as the warden," replied the priest, positioning his great bulk in the centre of the path.

"God's nails," said Turnbull. "It seems your holy sanctuary is open to everyone save the very ones who seek to uphold Our Lord's commandments."

"And yet you just broke the third of them," said the priest, breaking into a throaty laugh. "Which may solve both our problems."

Antoine and Turnbull exchanged blank looks as the cleric continued merrily. "You just committed the sin of blasphemy, a crime in law as well. Which means that I can now grant you entry. For the appropriate donation, of course."

They shook their heads at the clergyman's blatant corruption but crossed his sweaty palm with silver anyway and continued through the gate. As Turnbull had explained at the tavern, the sanctuary was enormous, stretching far beyond the village of Stow itself. At its centre stood the Church of St Mary's, where lines of pilgrims waited to visit the holy well. However, the priest ushered them past these worshippers, down a narrow street lined with guesthouses and trinket stalls, leading them to an altogether less godly quarter, crammed with makeshift shacks. Gaunt faces peeped out from within, watching the newcomers with suspicion. Hands slipped out of sight, possibly to secure weapons or hide looted treasure. Everywhere, the reek of destitution and criminality hung in the air.

"This place is as rough as a badger's arse," said Turnbull warily.

"We do not judge," said the priest, ushering them to a little square, where a group of hard-faced men were swigging wine from a jug. "Although having said that, these fellows might be the very sort to help you."

He deposited them with the outlaws, leaving them to make their own introductions. Antoine skipped over the pleasantries.

"Good morrow, gentlemen. Some of you might know me as your warden, so I apologise if I am not the most welcome of visitors. But I care not why you're here or what dealings we may have had in the past. I'm interested in something quite specific: the whereabouts of a man named Dewar, who was Bailie Walkerburn's servant down in Lauder."

The men stared at Antoine with expressions of utter contempt, so he decided to change tack.

"I believe this fellow – and possibly his master – may have had some dealings with Will Baird's gang in Ettrick Forest. Some of you may have come across these reivers yourselves, you may even be at feud with them. So if you wish to have revenge, this may be your chance."

The suggestion only inflamed the criminal assembly. "Whatever any o' us may think o' Will Baird, we willnae sell him out," said a muscular man whose head looked as though it had been put through a washing mangle. "So why don't ye take your questions and shove them up your arse?"

The others laughed and chimed in with their own insults. Antoine felt like saying he would lock up every one of these miscreants the minute they stepped out of the sanctuary, but he knew he must not deviate from his purpose. He racked his brain for what to say next. All at once, he remembered what Baird had told him about the harming of women. Frankly, he had been in the Marches long enough to know that reivers were perfectly willing to do this when it suited them, but they also liked the idea of a code of honour.

"Then let's talk about this Dewar. He is not like you. We suspect he slaughtered his mistress, while she was grieving for her husband. I know what you must think of a coward like that, so if you know anything of him, tell us and we'll be gone."

The men muttered their disapproval but still seemed reluctant or unable to help – until a tall man in a red shirt stood up. He rummaged in a knapsack and took out a short length of rope, which he threw to Antoine.

"I hear the woman-killer is hiding up at the tannery on the edge o' Lauder. There, ye can use this to string him up, on behalf o' all o' us."

It took another hour to leave the sanctuary. Once they had parted ways with the first group of men, a trickle of less hardened criminals approached, whispering offers of help. Antoine and Turnbull listened to everyone who came forward but soon realised that these wretched inmates had little real intelligence to offer; their suggestions were merely thinly disguised pleas for coin or clemency.

They could smell the tannery long before they reached it, with the stench of piss, shit and decaying flesh hanging in the hot air, like the breath of some foul dragon.

"Urgh, this is worse than the jakes at Ravenscleugh," said Turnbull.

"Yes, it's a clever place to hide, although he surely can't plan to stay here long. Let's hope we find him before he moves on to his next den. Meanwhile, let's protect ourselves from the miasma."

They took out the nosegays they'd been given at The Boar's Head and clutched them to their faces as they rode up to the entrance of the tannery. The first building they encountered was a gatehouse, where fleshers could deposit their hides, but there was nobody on duty when they approached. A cart stood in the yard, half unloaded, yet its owner was nowhere to be found. The skins in the back were crawling with flies as they baked in the afternoon sun.

"Strange," said Antoine. "You'd think the place would be in full flow at this hour."

"Perhaps it's closed for St John's Day?" ventured Turnbull. "Or the workers are sleeping off their Midsummer ale heads?"

"No, the gate is open. And look, there are tools lying about over there. It's as if a storm has blown through and carried everyone away."

"Damn it. If the people here were protecting Dewar, they might have seen us coming and made off. Let's have a quick look and see if they've left anything behind."

They tethered the horses and entered the first building. It was an enormous warehouse, full of hides on tables, stretching devices and rope pulleys. These hides had not been treated yet, so bits of hair and fat still clung to the skin. Antoine recalled how Walkerburn's wife had been butchered and mused that it would be fitting to catch her killer in this factory of death.

They passed into the second room and gagged as they were confronted by a mixing vat, full of dogshit. A pair of gloves and a spade lay on the floor nearby, another sign that someone had left in a hurry. Beyond it, there were more vats, of bark, ash and what looked like hot water, judging from the steam still rising from it. Further still were the leeching pits, used to burn off the last slivers of flesh from the hides, in the hellish liquid known as lye.

"Surely nobody could bear to hide in here," said Turnbull, edging round the pits.

"A man will do anything to save his life," said Antoine as he, too, took care to keep his balance on the wooden boardwalk.

As he spoke, a muffled banging sound came from a room at the end of the chamber. They drew their swords and cautiously crept forwards. The noise came again, as if someone was knocking from inside. Antoine's pulse raced. He turned round, lest they be attacked from behind, while Turnbull examined the door.

"It's locked," he said. "But whatever's in there is hellish hot. I can hardly touch the handle."

There was another clunking knock followed by a man's voice. "Help! Whoever ye are, please help us!"

Turnbull pressed his mouth to the door. "Who is this? What's going on?"

"Urquhart, the tanner, sir. He's locked us in the drying room. It's like a bloody oven in here!"

"Who did this? Dewar? One of Baird's men? Is that person still here?"

He strained for a reply, but before the man could answer, there was an almighty thud. A crossbow bolt quivered in the door, just inches from Turnbull's head.

"Christ's blood," said Antoine, falling to his knees. His assistant followed suit, a look of terror on his face. They both crawled along the boardwalk, to take refuge behind a vat of some foul liquid, as the captive tanner screamed through the door.

"What goes on? Let us out, let us out afore we die!"

Antoine put his nosegay away while he thought their position through. Whoever their assailant was, he was probably alone, otherwise his accomplice would have fired another bolt by now. But he would be reloaded at any moment.

"We need to rush him somehow, in between shots. Let's see if we can draw his fire."

Antoine took his bonnet off and put it on the tip of his sword. Then, after counting to five, he poked it round the corner of the vat. He braced himself for another blow, but either the fellow was too clever, or he had already gone, for no arrow came. As he plotted his next move, the screaming from the drying room became more intense.

"Let us out of here! We cannae breathe!"

What a hellish way to die, thought Antoine. And we will perish with them in this stinking hellhole if we don't do something quickly. He cast about for inspiration, but nothing came to mind. His throat and nostrils filled with the noxious fumes in the stygian chamber, and he began to scramble for his nosegay. But before he could locate it, he broke into a cough. The noise triggered another bolt, which flew past his ear and embedded itself in the door jamb.

"What's that?!" screamed the tanner, joined by other wails from the locked room.

Antoine clutched his chest, as if to check he was still alive. Finding that he was, he got to his feet and started running to the back of the room. The attacker's face was obscured by the fumes rising from the leaching pools, but Antoine could see him fitting another bolt into his crossbow.

Then, thinking better of it, he cast the bow aside and drew a dagger from his belt before ducking behind a pillar. Antoine glanced at Turnbull, who was running alongside him. The odds were now more favourable: two against one, with swords against a knife.

He reached the far end of the room, ready to clash steel with his hidden enemy. But as he stifled another cough, he saw two hands emerge from the thick, noisome vapours. The hands scooped a bucket through the pit of lye and cast it into the air. Antoine quickly pushed Turnbull to safety, as the scalding liquid cascaded over him. In that moment, he felt as if he were on fire. Then everything went black.

Chapter 14

As Turnbull watched over his master the next day, he marvelled at how close they had both come to death. If his master had not pushed him, if the attacker had been more accurate with his throw, if God had willed it otherwise. If, if, if. As it was, the lye had missed his master's face but burnt through his left arm and sent him into shock. Turnbull had managed to free the terrified tannery workers just in time, then borrow one of their carts to get him back to the tower. He was only just reviving.

"Argh. Am I aflame? What is going on?"

"Stay calm, sir. You are survived, but you must not over-excite yourself."

"That's you, Turnbull?" Antoine's eyes blinked open, only to close immediately. "Praise God, you're safe."

"Thanks to your quick thinking, sir. The workers are released as well, but our attacker managed to escape."

"Damn him. Was it Dewar, do you think?"

"Not from the tanner's description. I fear we were tricked by the fellow at the sanctuary. He sent us here, then used others to delay us, before tipping off someone to ambush us."

"Of course. We were stupid there."

"Or we're up against someone very clever," said Turnbull. "Whether that's Baird or someone else, they clearly have a great secret, one they're determined we don't uncover. We won't catch them on our own, especially now you're injured."

Antoine began to protest that he would soon be back on his feet, but as he tried to sit up on his pallet, he winced and clutched his arm. Elspeth had wrapped it as best she could, but the bandages were already coming loose.

"Urgh, you're right, of course. Send a message to Pentland and see if he can spare some men from Edinburgh. As for me, perhaps Mistress Gray could help."

"Who, Catherine?" said Turnbull, thinking his master's injury had left him confused. Catherine Gray was a healing woman whom they had befriended the previous year. He knew the Frenchman had stronger feelings for her too, but they had been unrequited, and they had not seen her in some months.

"Yes Catherine," said his master, grimacing. "Don't worry, I will not make a fool of myself again. My cheeks might burn a little, but the embarrassment will be worth it if she can make this bloody fire leave my arm."

Turnbull saw the anxiety on Mungo Bell's face as he entered the provisioner's office. It was as if the man had seen a ghost.

"By God, I didnae expect to see you here again," he said, jumping up from his desk. He ushered the lad in and made sure that nobody had followed him through the bakery, before shutting the door. "I heard ye were attacked at the tannery and that your master might no' even have made it."

"He lives still," said Turnbull. "But it was a close-run thing. Now we need your help so that we can catch whoever's after us."

"I see," said Bell, slumping back into his chair. "And why me, for pity's sake? What do ye need doing?"

"Two messages sending. One to Edinburgh, one to a friend near Dunse. I thought you could handle them. You said before that you had your fingers in many pies?"

"Aye, but I'll have nae fingers left if I'm no' careful."

Turnbull took out two sealed letters from his satchel and laid them on Bell's table. He placed a silver coin on each, but the provisioner did not move for them. Instead, his eyes flitted to the door.

"Listen, son, I've done this long enough to ken when something big is afoot. I can feel it in the air, see it in the faces o' my customers, smell it when I step out o' this room. It's the spread o' fear. Like when a monster's coming."

"What do you mean?"

"Everyone is running. They had the Walkerburns' funerals yesterday, but there was naebody frae the family. Then ye mind that carter o' mine who saw the servant talking wi' Baird's man? He's gone too – telt me he'd made a mistake and was off to work on the fishing boats. Even that neighbour ye spoke to, Erskine: away wi'out a word. Naebody wants to talk about any o' this. And even less, do they want to talk to you."

Turnbull shook his head. The news about Erskine was particularly galling, as he had seemed to have more to tell. He started to take the money back from the table. "So you won't send our messages?"

"I didnae say that," said Bell, gripping the lad's hands. "I'm saying fear comes at a price. So if ye double those coins, I'll find two willing riders. But this is the last time. After that, please dinnae visit here again."

Turnbull reluctantly agreed to the deal and left by the

back door, at Bell's request. He climbed over the turf dyke at the far end of the yard, before picking his way across a series of allotments, chicken runs and middens and re-emerging by a side-wynd to the mercat cross. He was just about to untether Fogo when a wiry man emerged from behind a flesher's stall and stayed his hand.

"Hello, friend. Fine horse ye've got there."

Turnbull was disturbed as the man had a tight hold of him, and his neighbourly words were laced with menace. "Can I help you, sir?"

"I hope so. Ye see, me and my friends have been victims o' a crime."

The lad sighed. Perhaps this was an innocent approach, after all. "I'm sorry to hear that, but as you may have heard, the warden and I are already occupied with this Walkerburn business."

"I dinnae ken anything about your business," said the man sharply, before forcing a smile. As he bared his teeth, Turnbull was disgusted to see that they were practically green. "But you already ken something o' mine. Me and my friends were attacked by those cur-faced Bairds, on Midsummer's Eve. That's our horses that ye've got. Well, now we want them back."

Turnbull's eyes widened. "It was you fighting the Bairds? Before we talk of horses, tell me what you were arguing over."

"The usual Midsummer nonsense," said Green Teeth, with a shrug. "Some lassie we all had eyes on. A bonny wee thing, but no' worth losing three nags over."

Turnbull thought about this for a moment. He was sure there was more to this fellow than he was making out, but perhaps they could strike a bargain. "Well, I can hardly give you the horses back without knowing who you are and what you know of the Bairds. Why don't we go to the tavern and share an ale? Then I could discuss this with my master later."

"I'm no' in the mood for ale, laddie. I'm in the mood for horses. As for your master, I wouldnae mention it to him if I was you. A Frenchie willnae understand how things work round here. But you're a local boy, aren't ye? You ken what it's like." He licked his lips. "Your mother keeps a farm on the Stow road, I think? It must be hard up there. All alone, wi' no man to protect her."

"Wait. Are you threatening my mother? Because if you—"

Green Teeth waved his hand. "I'm no' threatening anybody. Give us our horses back and a' will be fine. Come find me, once ye've had time to think about it."

Turnbull jerked his arm away from the man and watched him disappear into the shacks and stalls of the town square. This was the last thing he needed right now. He already felt guilty enough about his mother, without some brute stirring him up. He told himself to forget about it, that this fellow was just trying his luck. And besides, hadn't his mother said that she had protection put in place? Mind you, it had been Walkerburn whom she'd been paying for it, so perhaps she was not covered now? He felt he should check on her, just to be sure.

He wheeled Fogo around and headed for the West Port, instead of the East. Was it his imagination, or was the town much quieter than usual? He passed the Walkerburns' house, but for once, there were no crowds outside. Erskine's place, next door, was similarly devoid of life. There were no watchmen on the gate as he passed through. Even the air was uncommonly still, the birds quiet. He remembered Bell's words about a great fear spreading, a monster coming, and he quickened his pace.

He was halfway to his mother's house when he had that feeling of being followed again. There had been that fellow outside the window at The Boar's Head, the hooded figure at Midsummer, and their attacker at the tannery. Was it the same person? And were they on his trail now? Could it even be that green-toothed rogue, showing that he knew where his mother lived?

Turnbull glanced over his shoulder. There was nobody else on the road, but he thought he saw a sudden movement in the woods.

Damnation. He had been a fool to come here, when all the signs were ill. Perhaps he should turn back – but no, that would take him past those woods again. Or he could burst onwards in a gallop – but he was miles from anywhere secure. After weighing his options, he decided his best bet was to go into hiding and see what he was up against.

A little further on, the path went through a copse of oak trees. From his childhood, he remembered there was a dip in the land just beyond it, formed by a fast-flowing burn. He and his brothers used to go there, to catch trout with their hands, and he knew the tumbling water would conceal Fogo's nickering. He guided the horse there to slake its thirst. Then he went back to the woods and cast about for a lookout point. As he did so, he noticed a rider approaching, the man's head bobbing as if he were searching for someone. So he had been right – he was being followed! He quickly clambered up the nearest tree and positioned himself across an overhanging branch.

The rider entered the woods, and Turnbull strained to see whether he came accompanied. It didn't seem so. That was good! But how big was he? How well-armed? He should check that first, before deciding whether to take him on.

The fellow was almost upon him, seemingly oblivious to Turnbull's presence overhead. From this angle, it was impossible to see his face, only the top of his bonnet as he looked around. Yet, there was something familiar about him. He did not have the stealthy posture of a hunter; instead, he had the hunched shoulders of someone who was scared. Who the hell was it? In an instant, he had it: it was Erskine, Walkerburn's neighbour.

As he passed underneath, Turnbull leapt off his branch and knocked the fellow from his horse.

"God preserve me!" the man screamed, as they rolled on the ground. As Turnbull had hoped, Erskine was not much of a fighter, and was soon pinned down by his wrists, begging for mercy.

"Never mind God," said Turnbull. "Why the Devil are you following me? You were supposed to be bringing us intelligence, and yet you disappeared from town and have been on my back for miles."

"But that's just it, I beg of ye. I left town because I heard something. Something ye might find interesting. I was only following ye to tell ye of it."

Turnbull looked at the man beneath him, who appeared genuinely terrified. "Go on, then, what's your story?"

"Ye promise ye willnae hurt me?"

"I promise I *will* hurt you if you don't come out with it."

"Very well," said the man, nearly in tears. "Some friends o' mine have found another body. Somebody's been stabbed near Ettrick Forest."

"Good Lord. Was this dead man connected to the Bairds or Walkerburn? We can't chase every killing."

"I dinnae ken, sir. But there was something peculiar about him – something I thought ye'd want to ken about."

"What's that?"

"He wasnae frae round here. Oh please, promise ye won't harm me."

"Just get on with it. If he's not local, then he's unlikely to be of interest."

Erskine snivelled. "Very well, sir. He was an Englishman, an equerry to the queen, no less. His name was Robin Fortingale."

Chapter 15

Antoine woke with a start, to the feeling of hands around his windpipe. He was still weak from the attack at the tannery and had slept through into the afternoon. But this strange pressure on his throat made him jerk upright. He threw his arms out, only to feel searing pain down his left side.

"I'm sorry," said Elspeth, jumping back from his bed. "I'd just changed your bandages and was fastening your shirt."

Antoine breathed a great sigh of relief. "Forgive me, mistress. My head is clouded."

The girl remained standing, watching him as if she were not sure what to say or do next. As if she were afraid of him. Or of the world in general. He patted his right hand on the mattress, and gingerly, she resumed her place.

"Thank you for looking after me, Elspeth. You've done well to preserve me. And do not worry, you will not have to nurse me long, for a healing woman should arrive tomorrow."

The girl kept her head down as she continued with his shirt, but he saw her eyes widen with alarm. "Does my mother ken?" she said quietly.

"Not unless Master Turnbull has told her. So if you see her first, tell her it will only be for a while."

Elspeth shook her head. "She willnae like it."

"I fear that there's little of life that your mother likes," said Antoine. He screwed up his face, as he tried to sit up and get a better look at her. "Why is she so hard on you? What has made her this way?"

The girl turned her back on him, supposedly to wet a cloth in a bowl of water. Her shoulders shook, and it was some time before she managed to whisper a reply.

"She's no harder on me than life has been on her."

She swivelled round again and pressed the cloth to his forehead. They were now face to face, and he could see that the bruise on her cheek was turning green. He wondered how many blows she had suffered over the years and whether she would ever have someone to care for her, as she now did for him.

"Life is not some demon that you should be afraid of, Elspeth. There is a world outside these walls, and one day you will see it."

A smile formed on the girl's lips, but she immediately controlled it. "That's what Master Baird says. That birds should not live in cages, whether they be me or him, or even the little king himself."

"You speak to Baird?" gasped Antoine. Christ, the mother would have a fit if she knew this – and he was not best pleased himself.

"No, he speaks to me," the girl replied. Her voice was stronger, more defiant than he had heard it before. "He whispers frae his cell at night. Tells me stories. Makes jests. Sometimes, he even shows me tricks."

Antoine remembered the sleight of hand that Baird had shown in their first meeting, how he had caused the louse to vanish and then appear again. He felt sure the reiver was up to something, with this ill-loved girl. "You must not listen to him," he said, pressing her hand. "He pretends to be your friend, but I fear he hides his purpose."

"As ye wish," said Elspeth, sullenly. "But I think ye have him wrong. I find him a kind man. Good-hearted. He even wishes you well, sir, although ye are his captor." She paused. "Ye ken, he has an idea o' your attacker at the tannery, if only ye would listen."

She looked like she might say more, but just at that moment, her mother shouted up the stairs, screeching that she must leave Antoine alone and take the prisoner his supper. The girl flustered and sprang up. In an instant, she had shrivelled back into her normal, hunched posture. She made to beetle off, but the Frenchman took her arm.

"Take me with you, when you visit him. If Baird knows something of my attack, I want to hear what he says."

Elspeth's hand trembled as she pushed Baird's bowl through the hatch. She waited until the prisoner had taken it to the other side of the room, then quickly unlocked the door and let Antoine in, before securing it again. The Frenchman was exhausted just from climbing the stairs and decided to get to the point.

"I hear you have some intelligence for me, about my attackers at the tannery. Let me guess: it was not your men?"

Baird smiled. "Your powers of divination are intact, sir. Even if your arm isnae."

"Then what is it you've got to say to me?"

"Can we no' just converse a while?"

"I've told you before, I don't have time for your games," sighed Antoine. "So whatever it is, just spit it out. You might be able to impress the girl with your magic, but my old eyes are less easily fooled."

Baird nodded and gestured for the Frenchman to sit down opposite him. As he did so, the prisoner reached for his bowl and took a spoonful of pottage. It looked like a mess of foul slops to Antoine, but Baird swirled it around his mouth, as if he were savouring the moment.

"Very well. Last night, your lad came in to question me. I fear I was nae help, for being locked in here makes it hard to ken what's going on outside. But overnight, I had a wee idea. He telt me that the fellow who splashed ye wi' the lye first attacked ye wi' a crossbow..."

Antoine frowned. "And so?"

"Crossbows are a rare thing these days, are they no'?"

The Frenchman shrugged. "The arquebus is coming in its place. But it will be a while before it reaches these parts, thank God. In the meantime, people will use whatever comes to hand."

"Perhaps so. But then longbows are more easily found – and half the cost."

"So what's your point?"

"Only that this weapon may belong to someone of a greater rank than a humble thief like me. Have ye ever thought o' that? Someone who hunts for pleasure – or has enough coin to pay a marksman. Why, a weapon like that would be worthless in my trade, as ye'd never load it frae a horse."

Antoine was struck by this argument; after all, the reivers depended on speed and agility to do their business. But surely this idea of some great man being involved was a distraction. And didn't the locals sometimes use a smaller crossbow that could be fired from the saddle: the *latch*, he seemed to recall? He realised that Baird might be testing him, waiting for

Turnbull to be away to see whether this foolish Frenchman knew his way around the Marches. Well, he would show he was no naive foreigner.

"That's a very good point. True as an arrow, you might say. But now you remind me that I must fly." He gave the prisoner a knowing glance as he called over his shoulder. "Mistress Scrimgeour, see to the latch!"

Baird smiled at the clever wordplay. "I'm glad to have hit the mark, sir. I look forward to more target practice with you soon."

That evening, the pain in Antoine's arm grew even worse. He prayed that Catherine would arrive the next day, with one of her remedies, or at the very least, with her gentle touch. In the meantime, he was visited by the rather less kindly Widow Scrimgeour.

"What's this I hear about a friend o' yours?" she barked as she stormed into the hall.

"Ah, you've spoken to your daughter," said Antoine. "Yes, a healing woman we know is coming to tend to my arm. She's a good person; you will like her."

"I've telt ye already what I think o' new arrivals. The fewer, the better. As for a healing woman, who's to say she's no' a witch?"

Antoine flinched; after all, Catherine had been accused of this very thing last year, even though she was innocent. He chose to bypass the comment.

"Widow Scrimgeour, I beg you to make her welcome. We must all work together if we're to prevent Baird's mischief-making, which you have so wisely warned us about."

"Dinnae try your honeyed words on me."

"Then think of your daughter. Mistress Gray can take some of Elspeth's load awhile. You work her too hard as it is."

Scrimgeour leant over his bed. "Spare the rod, spoil the child. But then what would you ken about that?"

Even in his weakened state, Antoine was enraged by her impertinence. He recalled Lord Douglas saying something similar about the little king at the castle and was affronted that she would touch on his own failure to produce an heir.

"Widow Scrimgeour! I may not wield a rod, but I am still your master."

"Aye, but sometimes the mistress of a house kens better than the man," said Scrimgeour, jabbing a finger at him. "Twenty years my John and I lived here, twenty years and no' a single prisoner escaped. That was down to me, no' him. My ways, no' his. Then one day, he went against me – let a family send a parcel to their son. And what was in it? A knife."

Antoine felt a sense of dread building in him. "He slew your husband with it?"

"No, you fool. But he took John's keys, got through that door I showed you and escaped through the postern gate. My husband couldnae handle the shame, so he followed the prisoner out onto the self-same passage and threw himself off the wall."

So that's why Scrimgeour had been so upset when she heard of Walkerburn's self-killing. Why she was so particular about her rules. And so keen to keep the outside world at bay. All at once, he could see the fragility of her own tower, the wall she had built around herself. Her face crumbled, and she wiped a tear from her eye before composing herself.

"Afterwards, my daughter found the keys where the prisoner had thrown them, and we locked the door and the postern gate. Then we flung the keys into Crichton's furnace. I watched them melt. Now, we must never speak o' this again."

Chapter 16

Turnbull's mind raced as he rode towards Ettrick Forest with a still-shaking Erskine. What on earth could Fortingale have been doing here, so far from the palace and the queen? Was he scouting for something, as he had been that day on the border? Could his death be connected to the Walkerburns'? More importantly, was he himself riding into a trap right now? He eyed the dark strip of trees on the horizon and imagined who might be lying in wait for him.

Presently, they came to a bastle house on the edge of the forest. Like most such dwellings, it was a squat building, with arrow slits for windows and a reinforced door.

"For protection only," said Erskine, catching Turnbull's disquiet. "My friends are no' reivers, but staying out here, they are forced to live like them." He dismounted and tethered his horse, fumbling with the reins as if his hands were made of clay. Then he advanced to the door and knocked in a distinctive way. *Rat-tat. Rat-tat-tat-tat.* Turnbull watched from the safety of his saddle as the heavy door opened to reveal a man's face. He was dressed in black so that his head appeared to float in the gloom of the bastle's interior.

"This is my friend, Barty Veitch. It's him that found the body. Or rather, the body found him."

The host stepped into the light. With his dark suit, pink face and blinking eyes, he resembled a mole, popping out of its burrow. Back bent, hands clasped, he seemed wracked with worry and not in the least threatening. Unless he was being used as bait, of course. Turnbull peered into the black of the bastle house, but it was quite impossible to see who else might be lurking there. He nudged Fogo to the side of the building, where there were no arrow slits.

"Come over here, both of you," he said, and Erskine and Veitch did as they were told. But they moved stiffly, their bodies tense, their eyes radiating fear. Yes, there was something not quite right about this, as if they were the guilty parties, not the informants.

He gestured to the house. "Are we alone?"

Veitch put his hand on his heart. "I swear it, sir. I moved my wife and bairns out this morning, and they'll bide wi' friends until this trouble passes."

"That is good. And the body?"

"Round the back. I can take ye there now if ye like?"

Turnbull eyed the men carefully. "No, I will attend to that presently. But for now, I'm more concerned by how he got there. And what you're holding from me."

Veitch put his hand to his mouth, as if to confirm the accusation, while Erskine fell to his knees. "Sir, when we last spoke, ye telt me your interest was only in your prisoner, Baird?"

"That's right," said Turnbull. "You were to look out for any ties twixt him and your neighbour. Or with his servant, Dewar."

"And that promise still holds good? As long as we speak the truth, ye have nae care for politicking, or which camp we be for?"

"It is no business of ours, unless you make it so."

Erskine rose and gripped his friend's arm. "There, I telt ye we could trust these gentlemen. Now tell him how this came about, Barty. Just like ye set it out to me."

Veitch closed his eyes and took a deep breath before beginning. "I am a cloth mercer by trade, sir. But it has been hard labour these past years. All this fighting is bad for business. So like any man with mouths to feed, I must look for other ways to turn a coin."

It was a familiar story, so Turnbull gestured for him to go on.

"Last Candlemas, a man stopped at our door and asked whether we might give him a bed for the night. The snow was falling thick, and he might perish if he pressed on to Lauder, so we considered it our Christian duty to agree. But there was something about him that unsettled us. So instead o' letting him into our bastle, we put him up round the back. There are some old stables there, and he seemed happy enough wi' this arrangement as long as he was out o' the cold. Anyway, the night passed wi'out trouble, and in the morning, he paid us a pretty penny for our trouble. Then, as he left, he said that we could make more coin, if we would do the same for his friends."

Turnbull frowned. "What friends were these?"

"That was the thing. We were no' to ask their names or business. This fellae said he preferred to keep himself to himself, rather than announce his presence to the world at some crowded inn. He said that there were others like him, who would pay good money for the same, and if we gave him the nod, he would send them our way."

"I see. And what did you take from that?"

"Just that there was good coin to be made."

"You must have wondered why, though?"

"Forgive me, sir, but wondering doesnae feed my bairns. I took the coin and said we'd do it." Veitch bowed his head. "And so time passed. Every now and again, a man would come to stay. Never more than one at a time. Always for a short while only. They paid us well, as the first man had done, and we asked nothing of them, as we had been telt, although…"

"Yes?"

Veitch hesitated and looked at Erskine, as if asking for permission to go on. His friend nodded, although the gesture was one of resignation rather than encouragement. "Sometimes, they let slip a word or two. And when they did, we noticed that they spoke like strangers. English folk, to be precise."

Turnbull jerked his head back. "English folk? Then you've been entertaining spies all this time? And Fortingale is just one of many? No wonder you do not wish to talk of politicking. It sounds like you've kept quite the nest of serpents here."

Erskine threw his hands out. "I swear to ye, it's no' what ye think. My friend saw a way to make some coin, that's all. But neither o' us care a hoot for the English or the queen." He corrected himself. "I mean, for that lady. The mother o' the king."

Turnbull saw the desperation in the men's faces. They were like common thieves, pleading at the gallows. "That may be so," he said, dismounting. "But it still leaves the small matter of an English spy lying dead, in your backyard. So move on to how you found him, then let's have a look at him."

"As ye wish," said Barty Veitch. He took Fogo's reins and helped to tether him, as if that might help him untangle the knots in his own mind. "So, this latest fellae arrived last week. Four days afore Midsummer, as I recall. He was the same as the others. Had an English accent, said he'd be staying a few days, paid us upfront. Apart from that, we saw little o' him. He left early each morning and came back at dusk."

"You have no clue how he spent his time?"

"No, sir. We left him be, as we'd been instructed. Then yestere'en, he staggered in, as if he'd been on the ale, save that his horse was gone and he was clutching his side. When he moved his hand to beckon me, I saw his doublet was drenched in blood. Well, of course, I ran to help him, thinking he'd been robbed, but before I reached him, he fell ontae his knees. More blood spewed out, this time frae his nose and mouth, and he rolled ontae his back. His eyes were gone, his face like snow. But as I called for my wife, something stirred in him, and he managed a few words."

Turnbull gripped his elbow. "Come on then, man, what did he say?"

Veitch swallowed hard. "'Tell the queen she must beware.' Then his eyes flickered, and he was gone."

Veitch had laid the body across some bales of hay in one of the stables. Identity papers lay at the corpse's side, but Turnbull did not need them to confirm that it was indeed the spy they had caught on the border. As he surveyed Fortingale's curled lip, he mused that this proud man might have enjoyed the riddle that he had left behind. Why was he here, and what had those final words meant – if indeed they were not just the final babblings of a man whose mind was drunk on death?

He returned to the original purpose of his visit. "It sounds like Fortingale arrived around the same time as this business with the Walkerburns. Do you think he could have been in communion with them, or their wretched servant Dewar?"

"I dinnae think so," said Erskine. "I'd have noticed if a stranger like that visited my neighbour."

"What about the Bairds?"

"Perhaps. They bide close to here, after all. But I cannae think why an equerry to the queen – I beg your pardon, to the king's mother – would consort wi' reivers such as them."

No, neither can I, thought Turnbull. God, how he wished his master were here, to help make sense of this. He moved to the other side of the body, where the man's bonnet and other personal artefacts had been neatly placed on the bale. Among them was a duck whistle, likely used for signalling to confederates, a small mirror, no doubt for the same purpose, a silver-plated drinking flask, a quill and ink bottle, and some parchment. And what was that? A muslin bag? Turnbull picked it up and turned it over. To his astonishment, it was a nosegay bearing the mark of The Boar's Head, just like the one they had received from the innkeeper.

He took out his own nosegay and confirmed they were identical. "Where did you find this, Veitch?" he asked.

"In his purse, sir, same as all the other stuff. They dole them out at an inn on the moors."

"Yes, I know. We passed through there ourselves – and were watched by someone." He scratched his head, trying to recall what the intruder at The Boar's Head had looked like. He had only seen him from behind, but Fortingale's slender frame would fit the bill. Was this the person who had been following them all the way from Edinburgh? "What about Midsummer's Eve? Could your guest have attended the festivities in Lauder that night?"

Veitch shrugged. "I suppose. He came in afore dusk, as usual, but he could have slipped out again quite easily."

"And yesterday as well? Could he have been at the tannery on the edge of town?"

"Again, it is possible. Although he did not reek of that place."

No, thought Turnbull. Yet he begins to reek now. And something else stinks about this whole story too.

The foul miasma lingered in the stable, even as Veitch and Erskine buried the spy in the woods. It was too dangerous to get back to Ravenscleugh at this hour, so Turnbull made himself a bed in the hay and tried to settle down for the night. But he could not sleep. He was no longer afraid that his hosts might be hoodwinking him, but his own mind seemed determined to play games with him.

What on earth could Baird's gang have found at the bailie's house, that would also be of interest to an English spy? Turnbull reflected on the papers they had leafed through in the study. He found little meaning in any of those rent books, maps and legal papers, so he was left with the pamphlet that had accused Albany of wishing to kill the queen. At the time, they had dismissed it as the latest slander, cooked up by the rumour-mongers in some squalid ale-pit. But a sickening thought came to him. What if the governor really did mean to do away with his great rival, as the scuttle-sheet had suggested? If their prisoner had found firm evidence of this plot, he might intend to take it to the queen, in return for his release. In which case, perhaps Albany had sent them down here to ensure Baird did not reach her.

"Tell the queen she must beware," Fortingale had said.

But it was Turnbull who now tensed. He was no great admirer of Margaret Tudor, but surely he and his master could not be the unwitting enablers of her murder.

Chapter 17

Antoine recognised Catherine Gray's scent before she entered the room. He was never sure whether the sweet fragrance of rosewater, ambergris and cloves was just the result of her work as a healing woman or some potion she had prepared for herself. But as he breathed it in, it instantly reminded him of her tender nature, her touch. He looked forward to her dimpled smile, but when Crichton showed her in, her expression was pained. As she came forward, it turned into a scowl.

"There ye are, ye silly man. The way Turnbull's letter described your wounds, I thought ye might have left us."

"I'm sorry to disappoint you," Antoine said, sitting up in his pallet. "Still, now that you are here, I hope you can repair this arm of mine so I can put it to further mischief."

Catherine frowned at his jest, but he thought he caught a glint in her deep green eyes as she knelt down beside him and delved into her haversack. She took out a flask of some tincture or other and gently began to unwrap Antoine's bandages. She tutted. "The last time we met, ye said ye would soon be leaving all this behind ye."

"The last time we met, we both said many things," said Antoine softly. She kept her head down as she soaked a piece of lint with the tincture and dabbed at his burns. He winced at the pain and reminded himself of that age-old wisdom about not opening up old wounds. "At any rate, I'm glad that you are here. We're grappling with an uncommon evil and could do with another friend by our side."

"Then here's to friendship," said Catherine as she wound a fresh bandage round his arm. "Now tell me what all this is about. How have ye ended up in this dark tower, and who's done this to ye?"

Antoine was relieved that there seemed to be little awkwardness between them and took her through the events of the last week. How they had been sent down here to watch over Baird but had then been dragged into this business at the Walkerburns' and attacked by some stranger at the tannery. He had hoped that all the different threads might come together in the telling of the story, but as he related each twist and turn, he saw that they made less sense than ever.

Catherine listened intently, as she always did; that was her great skill, beyond her medicinal powers, he had come to realise. So when her face lit up, those dimples of hers finally flashing, he thought she might have some fresh wisdom to share. But her expression quickly faltered. Her gaze drifted over his shoulder, so Antoine turned to see what had caught her eye. Turnbull was standing in the doorway, his face clearly troubled. Without exchanging greetings, the lad stumbled into the room.

―

When Turnbull had finished his account, Antoine gave a deep sigh. The news of Fortingale's murder certainly complicated matters, but the lad's misgivings about Lord Albany seemed plain mad.

"I've known the governor for years. He is many things, but not a murderer."

Turnbull raised an eyebrow. "With respect, sir, we have both seen his temper at close quarters."

"Our master has a hot head, that is true. But we're not talking about a moment of anger here. Inviting the queen back, for the sole purpose of killing her, would be a premeditated act. One that would break with all his recent policy."

"Perhaps he considers the result to outweigh the risk? With him out of the country, he could deny all responsibility."

"No," said Antoine sharply. He tried to wave his hand, but a burst of pain shot through his arm. "Our master is no fool. He knows that if he were to harm a hair on Margaret Tudor's head, her brother would burn this country to the ground. That's why he ordered us to welcome her back with kindness in the first place. So whatever danger the queen may be in, it is not from our side."

"Then who, sir? Certainly not the English party, for she is their leader."

Antoine furrowed his brow. "A new faction, perhaps. But whoever it is, they will find it hard to touch her. For as long as she stays in Edinburgh, she is well protected by her own bodyguards, the Douglases and the city watch."

He meant the words to calm the others, but in truth, he was disturbed by these latest developments. They had been ordered to ease the queen's return and keep Baird out of trouble. Was it possible that they might fail at both tasks? And worse, that the two matters might be connected? If so, he could forget about a return to France. Indeed, between Lord Albany's wrath and King Henry's rage, he would be lucky to keep his head off the block.

He felt his melancholy rising, when Catherine broke the silence.

"Forgive me, sir, but what if the plot requires no touch?" Both men looked at her in bemusement as she continued. "You describe this prisoner Baird as an illusionist. Could he be using some kind of trickery, to make the queen afeart?"

Antoine rubbed his beard. "Hmmm, you could be right. If Baird can make the queen *believe* that Albany plots against her, she might favour him, whether it be true or not."

"You think he created those slander sheets?" said Turnbull.

"No, I highly doubt it. But mayhap he didn't need to. Such papers circulate in our towns; it is the new way. Suffice for his men to place one in Walkerburn's house and then let us spread the word that anyone in possession of the same would be charged with treason."

"Those so-called cleaners were putting it there, not taking something away?"

Antoine warmed to his theory. "It could be. A man like Baird would know how rumours spread round here. On their own, the pamphlets would count for little. But when we two loudmouths put the word out that we would not tolerate them, the stories would grow legs. Then if one of the queen's spies were killed while investigating such a plot, it would all but confirm it."

"Step forward Baird, to warn Her Grace."

"Exactly. The queen, in her gratitude, would agitate for our prisoner to walk free. No doubt with a bag of gold into the bargain."

Catherine nodded, and, not for the first time, Antoine had the uncomfortable sensation that she had reached this conclusion a little while before. "Well, I'll leave you men to your deliberations," she said, packing up her haversack again.

He felt another twinge of pain, though whether it was physical or due to her departure, he did not know.

"Wait," he said impulsively. "I'd like to introduce you to Master Baird, for I have an idea how we might catch him out, and the more eyes on him, the better."

As Antoine expected, Widow Scrimgeour was outraged at the thought of it.

"Dinner wi' a prisoner? I have never heard a more foolish thing."

Given her distress over her husband the previous night, Antoine was patient with her. But he was sure that a little wine might loosen Baird's tongue and insisted that she prepare the hall accordingly. After much protest, Scrimgeour called Crichton to fetch some leg irons and roused Moffat from his slumber, to help bring the prisoner down.

"There! We greatly outnumber him," said Antoine as everyone took their places.

"Aye, so said the sheep when the wolf came for dinner," replied Scrimgeour.

Just then, Baird shuffled into the room, his chains clanking with each step. His two guards deposited him at the table, before going to stand by the stairwell. Antoine checked that there were no knives present, only spoons. Turnbull poured wine into wooden cups, and Elspeth ladled out meat stew onto four bread trenchers, before taking the pot away and joining her mother at the hearth.

"Well, this is an unexpected treat," said Baird, with a twinkle in his eye. He took a surnap and made to place it on his lap, but in an instant, it was gone. Before Antoine could tell him to desist from his trickery, it had reappeared across his own thighs. The reiver smiled. "A present, Monsieur Warden. Ye seem to have a habit o' making a mess o' things."

Antoine took a sip of wine. "That's very kind. But I'm afraid it's you who's in danger of leaving a trail of crumbs for us. We've swept up most of them already and will turn to the others presently, but for now, let me introduce you to Mistress Gray of Cheeklaw, here to mend my arm."

"Ah, a healing woman!" said Baird, bowing courteously. "I could have done with you three days ago."

Catherine fidgeted with her kirtle, as she did when she was discomfited. "Oh aye, and why would that be, sir?"

"I hear that if ye harvest fern seeds at midnight on Midsummer's Eve, they can make a man invisible?"

Antoine expected Catherine to dismiss the notion as a fairy tale, so he was surprised when she seemed charmed by the rogue's interest. The two of them spent some time on the subject, with Baird explaining that he had often tried to collect the seeds, only to find them too tiny to gather. Catherine confessed that she had only succeeded once, with the powder lying at home, untested.

"Perhaps I'll visit ye, to try it," said Baird with a wink. "If the warden will ever set me free, that is."

Antoine was irritated by the prisoner's flirtatious manner, as if he were trying to win Catherine as an ally. And surely that last jibe confirmed that Baird knew he would not receive a pardon. It was infuriating to be taunted in this way. Still, he was not ready to interrogate the rogue just yet. Instead, he topped up everyone's cups and let the small talk continue. As they ate and drank, they mused on the uncommonly hot weather and what it might mean for this year's harvest. They talked of horses and the art of training them. They covered card games, fishing, hounds and taverns – everything except English spies or queens. The Frenchman watched for signs of impatience in Baird, but the reiver seemed happy to indulge their idle chatter. Indeed, he seemed to store away every word, as if it might hold some secret treasure.

Eventually, once they had finished their second jug of wine, Antoine made his move.

"Well, I must admit that I have enjoyed our converse tonight. It is just a pity that we may not have another."

"And why would that be, sir?" asked Baird.

Antoine dabbed his lips. "You were placed in this tower to secure your good behaviour – and that of your people. But your gang seem to run amok, with fresh outrages every day. Under the terms of your confinement, we would be entitled to string you up."

"And yet you do not," said Baird. "Which suggests that ye're a decent man. Or ye cannae back your charges. Or that I have something ye desire. Perhaps all three."

Antoine frowned. The man could be as impudent as he was charming, when he wanted. And the wine did not seem to have made him drop his guard as he had hoped. He decided to be more pointed.

"We know what you are up to, Baird. It would suit you to have Lord Albany deposed. Or at least for you to have his name blackened and to win favour with the queen. You said as much on our first night, didn't you? That we live in a time of great tumult and that when masters change, there is hope for others to improve their fortunes. That's why you're spreading wicked tales about the governor."

Baird listened, intensely as ever, those bright eyes glinting as he formulated his response.

"I honestly dinnae ken what ye talk of, sir. Ye'll have to be mair specific."

"I will be when it suits me. But until then, cease this act of innocence."

"There is no act. Why, even if I wanted to make mischief, how on earth would I do it frae in here? How would I convey my orders – or marshal my men?" Baird raised his eyes, like a choirboy at evensong. "The thing is madness, unless ye think I have a little bird to whisper to."

Chapter 18

Antoine could not sleep, so he used his hour of watch to sketch out his thoughts. Baird did seem to be up to something, he was sure of it. But was this notion of a grand deception itself an illusion? A trick within a trick? Had the shameless cozener even helped them to construct the idea, to distract them from his true designs? As Antoine pinched the candle, he resolved to be more wary of the magician's smoke trails from now on.

They rode out at daybreak. Widow Scrimgeour made her usual grumblings about the dangers of leaving the tower. Catherine protested that Antoine's arm was in no shape for the journey. Even Turnbull seemed less cocksure these days, for some reason. He mumbled something about waiting for reinforcements, but they had heard nothing from Edinburgh, and Antoine felt they could not tarry.

"Baird is a clever fellow," he said as they approached the walls of Lauder. "But one thing is certain: he cannot be acting alone. Somebody out here must know what he has in mind. It is just a matter of finding them."

"I don't know about that," said Turnbull. "The provisioner told me that there's not a soul in Lauder who's prepared to talk to us in good faith."

"Which is why we must look elsewhere," said Antoine, wheeling off to the south. "The townsfolk may be scared, but the countryfolk are desperate. Your mother said as much."

"Yes, she did," said Turnbull, and he nudged Fogo to follow on.

They left the mud track for the open hills. The heather was in bloom, turning the slopes purple, the air fragrant. They could see for miles: over a sea of cottongrass, ridges and ravines, countless burns and sikes to the sheilings of Gala Water and beyond. But their eyes were fixed on one thing: the dark green mass of Ettrick Forest, which spread out across the horizon and reached into the landscape like a giant's grasping fingers.

"We're surely not going into the forest itself?" said Turnbull as they cantered down a steep brae.

"No, but let's ask some folk around the edges. If anybody knows what the Bairds are up to, it will be them. This is where the rascals lurk, after all."

They paused to let the horses drink at a valley spring, before steering towards a plume of bluish smoke. As they came over the brow of the hill, they expected to find some cottages but were met instead by a smouldering mound of branches and turf, in a freshly cleared patch of heathland. A charcoal burner's stack. And judging by the way the owner jumped up at the sight of them, not a legal one either. Perfect, thought Antoine.

"At ease," the Frenchman called, choking back the acrid smell. "I am the warden, just here to ask some simple questions. If you answer them well, we'll be on our way. If not, we may need to poke about your business."

The man scrambled down from his stack, on a rickety ladder. His face was black, which only accentuated the fear in his wide white eyes. "Begging your pardon, my lord. I think I may have strayed here, by mistake."

Antoine smiled at the pitiful excuse. "As I say, that is not my concern for now. I'm more interested in your neighbours. The folk you share the forest with. The Bairds."

The charcoal burner put a hand over his heart. "I have nought to do wi' them, sir. I swear upon the Holy Rood."

"I don't doubt that. But you must see all sorts come and go here."

"I try to keep my neb out of it. If ye want to ken more about that lot, ye should ask Stumpy Watt, at the top o' yonder hill. He used to ride wi' them, until he lost his hand."

Antoine raised an eyebrow. "That sounds like an excellent idea. But for now, let's stick with you. Have you seen anything of this gang recently?"

"I promise ye, I havenae. They tend to ride out in the winter."

"Quite so. But they have visited Lauder of late. Did you see them pass on Midsummer's Eve, for instance?"

"No. It's been quiet as a grave."

"Then have you seen anything else out of the ordinary? Remember what I said: if you help us, we will get on our way. But if you give us nothing—"

"Wait. There was one thing," said the man. "Ye're no' the first stranger to pass this way recently. He said nothing o' the Bairds, but he was a strange one a' the same. Asked a lot o' questions that I couldnae answer, then headed up the valley."

"Go on," said Antoine, narrowing his eyes.

"The fellae was looking for some servant, named Dewar.

And yet he was the last person ye'd think would be looking for a runaway, for he was commoner than me. A vagabond he was, wi' a great mark on his face, like this…"

The charcoal burner traced a V shape on his sooty forehead, then furrowed it in confusion as Antoine and Turnbull spurred their horses and cantered up the valley.

―――

"I had forgotten all about the vagabond," said Turnbull, as they rode. "We know he won a tidy sum from Bailie Walkerburn – there were witnesses to his celebrations. So why would he be looking for Dewar afterwards?"

"Perhaps he only received a downpayment on the night, and the servant stole the rest?"

"I suppose. Only a fool would accept credit in these parts though."

Antoine pondered this as they came to a lonely cottage at the top of the hill. "This must be Baird's old comrade's house. Perhaps he can shed some light on it."

They dismounted and knocked at the door. A giant of a man came to greet them, his menace not diminished by the absence of one hand. He pointed the stump at Antoine's bandaged arm and laughed. "Who are you, stranger? My long-lost twin?"

"Alas, no. But we do have some other things in common. And if you can help us, we'll make it worth your while."

They introduced themselves properly, and Stumpy Watt grudgingly allowed them into his hovel. The timbers were in a poor state, the plaster peeling from the walls. A woman was sitting on a battered apple crate, darning a pair of hose, while three little girls tugged at her skirts.

She frowned at the visitors. "I hope ye're no' inveigling

this one into trouble. Watt wants to put his reiving days behind him."

"Want has little to do wi' it," muttered her husband. "I'm little use to anyone now, as ye can see for yerselves."

"That might be where you're wrong. You used to be in Will Baird's gang, didn't you? We're guarding him at Ravenscleugh and would like to know more about him."

Stumpy raised his chin defiantly. "I've no' ridden wi' Will for three years now. And in any case, I willnae betray him."

"We're not asking you to betray him, just to tell us of his character."

"Ye have him as your captive, why don't ye study him yerselves?"

"Because, as I'm sure you know, he is a shape-shifter, who wears a masque when he is watched. You've seen him in his natural state."

The reiver rolled his shoulders, as if wrestling with the dilemma, only for his wife to put her darning aside. "Ye'll pay for this?" she asked. When Turnbull confirmed it, she continued. "Then get on wi' it, Watt, as it may be the only coin we see this summer."

Her husband glowered at her but gave a sigh of resignation. "Very well. I'd say that Will is the cleverest man I've ever met. But he has a good heart too. When I had this accident in his company, he paid a barber-surgeon to fix me up, then visited us wi' a small purse to tide us over."

His wife tutted, but Antoine ignored her and continued. "That speaks highly of him – and of you, for he must have appreciated your service. But what of his other men, the ones still in the forest? Do they stick to the same high standards?"

"They do as Will says too."

"Even now he's in our custody?"

"They ken Will's rule: if ye steal well, there's nae need to kill."

"And yet we're investigating a number of murders, which seem to contradict that."

"Perhaps new men have joined the gang?" suggested Turnbull. "Men who do not know the rules – or do not stick to them. Somebody has mentioned a vagabond, for instance, a fellow with a branded face."

"New men join a' the time," said Stumpy scornfully. "But the rules dinnae change. As for a vagabond, that wouldnae be Will's style, let alone one whose face is marked. The fellae would draw too much attention, be too easy to catch."

Like a one-handed man, thought Antoine. Yes, for once, this had the ring of truth to it. He could hear the regret in Stumpy's voice, the sadness of one who had been forced to trade a life of excitement and relative reward for a desperate existence on this hillside. "Well, some of Baird's men are certainly up to something, and mark our words, we will catch them. So this is your last chance to tell us what you know."

Turnbull took out his purse and let it jingle, as a fisherman might dangle a fly. Stumpy moved his head slightly but did not reach for the money. "I've telt ye already, I'm no longer in their circle."

"Have you seen something of them, though? I can tell you're holding back."

"That man was good to me. I willnae give him up."

Antoine was about to tell Turnbull that they should go when Stumpy's wife stood up. "God's blood, ye stubborn man. Are ye determined to starve us all?" She brushed away her children. "While my husband mopes about this place, one o' us has to earn us a living. So here ye are: two days ago, while I was picking cabbages on our pitiful scrap o' land, I saw three men chase a fellow up the brae. Him on foot, them on horses. He made it to the ridge afore they caught him, jumped off and set about him. Then they rode off again. There. Is that enough for ye?"

"Were they the Bairds?"

"We dinnae ken for sure," said Stumpy feebly.

But his wife leapt up and shoved him aside. "Who else would they be round here?" she said, as she snatched the purse from Turnbull's hand. "And if ye get yerselves up that ridge, ye can find out who the other one was as well."

A dozen red kites were swooping about the top of the hill, as if to point the way. As Antoine and Turnbull drew near, they scattered, only to regroup and dive ever more furiously at a point just over the brow. The Frenchman recalled Christ's teaching that the flocking of vultures would presage the Day of Judgement and hoped the same might apply in the world of mortal justice too.

They reached the ridge. The kites were quite frantic now. A couple of them fell upon the new arrivals, as if trying to drive them from the scene. The horses grew uneasy, and the men had to dismount and leave them under a great sycamore tree, where they could not be mobbed. They advanced the last few yards on foot. As they did so, the wind changed, and their nostrils filled with the awful stench of a rotting body. There it was, spread out in the long grass, pink holes showing where the forest beasts had ripped at it. The eyes had been pecked out by the birds, and there were maggots in the cavities, but the straw-like hair provided all the identification Antoine needed.

"Dewar," he said, and Turnbull nodded gravely. Covering his mouth, he knelt down and checked the body, while his assistant poked about the long grass.

"Urgh," said Antoine, blenching at the putrid flesh. "It's a good job we found him today, as he will not last long here. Not in this heat. As it is, it's hard to make out which wounds are made by men and which by beasts." He stood up, in search of cleaner air, and scratched his head. "You know, it's strange that the Bairds – if that is who they were – climbed off their horses to slay him. If they simply wished to kill him, they would have found it easier from the saddle."

"It suggests they meant to question him first."

"Yes, you could be right. Well, we have another murder on our hands. But otherwise, I fear there's nothing more to learn here."

Antoine was heading back to the horses when Turnbull raised a hand. "Hold, sir, do not speak so soon." He bent down and picked up something from the long grass. A tiny piece of silver glinted in the sunlight. "What do you make of this?"

Chapter 19

Antoine took the piece of jewellery from Turnbull. It was in the shape of a heart, although some fragments on the sides suggested it had once been part of a bigger piece, such as a brooch or a necklace. Could it be a lover's token? The notion seemed ridiculous, in this desolate spot, yards away from a rotting body. Yet, what else could it be? As Antoine wracked his brain, he felt he had seen this design before but could not recall where – or on whom. Turnbull stored the piece in his purse, and they rode back to Lauder.

"We may have won somebody's heart, but this case gets unlovelier by the day," he murmured as they neared the town. "That's three bodies we have now. Four, if you include Bailie Walkerburn's self-killing. All seemingly connected to some plot of the Bairds, to make the queen afraid. I feel it's time to warn her."

Turnbull frowned. "Even if it's all a trick?"

"I think so, yes. To do nothing would be treason – she is still the king's mother, after all. We should press her on the need to stay in Edinburgh. Then we can untangle what Baird is up to, and whether there be true danger to her at all."

They entered the town through the West Port and made for Mungo Bell's. Turnbull reminded his master that the provisioner was reluctant to carry any more messages, but Antoine argued that he would surely make an exception for the queen. They tied up the horses outside the bakery, and Turnbull stood guard on the door as Antoine went in to beg one last favour.

The bakery was dark and deserted. "Hello?" called Antoine, as he waited for his eyes to adjust to the gloom. There was no reply, so he stepped into the kitchen. The ovens lay cold and empty, like tombs. "Hello?" he called again. Once more, there was no answer save the echo of his own voice. However, he had the sense that he was not alone. He drew his sword and advanced to the back office. The door was very slightly ajar, so he pushed it open and waited. Still nothing. From this position, he could see most of the room – but not all of it. It appeared to be empty, but a half-eaten trencher of bread and cheese sat on the provisioner's desk. Antoine took another step forward, just as a hen launched itself from a barrel and landed, with much flapping and screeching, on the other side of the desk.

"Jesu!" a voice exclaimed, and Mungo Bell tumbled into view. He had evidently been hiding behind the desk but had been knocked off his hunkers by the hen's attentions.

"Well, well," said Antoine, shaking his head at the man's undignified state. "I thought you had gone."

"I might as well have," said Bell as he got up and brushed himself down. "For a' the business that there is these days. Didn't your laddie tell ye? I cannae help ye anymore."

"I understand your position. But this time, I come on a matter of great import: the queen's life may depend on it."

"Christ's bones," muttered Bell. "What are ye dragging me into now?"

"We do not know yet. It may be nothing. But we need

you to send a letter to Her Grace, advising her to stay in Edinburgh. Do this one thing and we will leave you, I swear on the Holy Book."

The provisioner shook his head. "Honest to God, I cannae help ye this time."

"You must, sir. This might be treason that we talk of."

"No, I mean I cannae help ye for your task is impossible. The queen has already left Edinburgh and is just a few miles away from us. In Ettrick Forest, of all places. If ye mean to keep her frae these parts, I'm afraid ye've come too late."

It was another hot afternoon, and Turnbull was dripping with sweat, even though he was standing under the bakery's awning. He wondered what was taking his master so long. Was Bell proving obstinate? Or had he vanished, like so many other townsfolk, in the wake of these crimes? He thought about going in to offer his master support when a figure appeared. It was Green Teeth, the man who had threatened him the other day.

"We meet again, Master Turnbull. Brave of ye to be on the streets, when so many others have fled."

"I'm waiting for my master," said the lad coldly. "You'd best begone, before he catches you."

"Oh, I winnae be long, dinnae ye worry. I'm just here about our nags. Have ye had time to think about them? We're impatient to get them back."

Turnbull glowered at him. "I've told you, the horses stay with us, until you tell me who you are – and why you were arguing with the Bairds."

"And I've telt ye, I cannae do that. So we seem to have a problem." The man cracked his knuckles, then spread his hands in a gesture of conciliation. "Look, all we want is our nags. And all you want is your dear mother to be safe. So let's be practical. How about we come to the tower some night, pick up the horses, and we'll leave the auld girl alone?"

Turnbull stroked his chin. He didn't like the fellow one little bit, but he understood how folk prized their horses here. He was worried about his mother too. Perhaps there was a deal to be struck? "You'll have to do better than that. Never mind who you are. Just tell me something about the Bairds and I may be able to return your nags. But you cannot come to the tower; I'd have to come to you."

"Ye drive a hard bargain for a young laddie," said the man, with a smile. He looked about himself. "Let me think about your offer and come back to ye. But we must reach agreement soon, so dinnae go disappearing. Remember, your mother depends on ye."

With another furtive glance around, he skipped off down a shadowy side-wynd, just as Antoine came out of the bakery.

"Who was that?" asked the Frenchman.

"Just some rogue, pestering me for money," said Turnbull. He did not like to keep things from his master, but he remembered Green Teeth's warning. In any case, Antoine did not pursue the matter.

"Well, we have bigger worries than that, I'm afraid. Margaret Tudor has already left Edinburgh and is staying at her castle in Newark, with Lord Douglas."

"What? In the middle of Ettrick Forest?" spluttered Turnbull.

"I'm afraid so. What's worse is that some malcontents appear to be planning an attack on her. Who knows how it relates to Baird, but the plot seems to be quite real after all."

They scrambled back on their horses and made off for Ravenscleugh at pace, with Antoine trying to explain his conversation with the provisioner along the way. Apparently, one of Bell's men had overheard a conversation in a tavern. A group of watchmen were saying that Douglas and the queen had passed through Ettrick Forest in the dead of night, on their way to Newark Castle. Bell's man had surmised that the watchmen must be supporters of the French party, as they referred to the queen as "that lady" rather than by her royal title. But more worryingly, they had then traded knowing comments that "Margaret Tudor had better watch out" for she was "in for a nasty surprise".

"Sweet Mary," said Turnbull as they reached the twisting approach to Ravenscleugh. "What do you make of it? It's true, the queen owns most of Ettrick Forest – perhaps she is simply here to take the fresh air, especially if the plague has worsened?"

"As warden, I would have been notified if that were the case. There are formalities for these things, even here."

"Then she and Douglas are up to something? You remember, we thought as much at Tantallon?"

"Quite possibly. But if they are planning their own attack, surely they would launch it from the capital? That is where the king is – and all other power besides. Why come to this godawful place? And who's arranged this nasty surprise for her?"

They were now at Ravenscleugh's outer wall. The gate opened, and Moffat let them in, with a lazy wave of his hand. He reeked of alcohol again, laced with a repulsive body odour. As they hurried past him, they looked up to the tower. Baird was at his window, his face rendered golden by the dipping sun. A flash of white betrayed a smile.

"By Christ, I'd like to wipe that grin off his face," said Turnbull as they climbed the spiral staircase.

"Which one of his faces? That's the problem," said Antoine.

———

They contemplated interviewing Baird again, but decided it would be of little use, given his love of dissembling. Instead, they gathered Catherine from the hall and took her back down to a quiet corner of the courtyard, where the three of them could talk discreetly.

"It seems I was wrong," said Catherine, flushing. "There is a real plot against the queen, and it is on our very doorstep."

"On Baird's doorstep, more like," said Turnbull.

"Exactly," said Antoine. "I still can't fathom what he's up to. But I'm sure Lord Albany is not involved. He was quite adamant that we should treat the queen well. So if Baird is conspiring with some higher power, it cannot be our master." He looked up and saw the prisoner was still at his window, although he was now just a black shape. "Whoever it is, I think we need to tell Her Grace," he continued.

"Yes, but Bell will not take any more messages for us."

"Which is why we must take the news to her ourselves."

Catherine put her hand to her head. "With your arm? And this young lad? Ye wouldnae last an hour in that forest afore the Bairds set upon ye."

Turnbull, too, looked sick with worry. "Mistress Gray is right, sir. Surely we should wait for the reinforcements to arrive."

Antoine was surprised by the lad's reticence. Normally, he had to hold him back from such adventure, but he seemed to have been stirred up by something recently. Whatever it was, he could not let the boy's queasiness get in the way. For if the plot were real and they were found to have done nothing, their heads would roll, not just their stomachs.

"We have no idea when they'll be here."

"I sent the message two days ago. They could be on their way already."

"And if they're not? What if something happens in the meantime?"

Catherine shook her head. "Why must ye always be so pig-headed, sir? It will be the death o' ye – and Turnbull as well."

By God, she knew which strings to pull with him. Still, she was right, he must not put the boy in danger. Antoine set his jaw and replied stiffly, as if to put the matter to rest. "We do not both have to go. In fact, it may be wise for Turnbull to remain here and make sure the tower stays safe. If I strike out at dawn, I will get through the forest before those lazy bandits have had their breakfast. Or, at the very worst, I'll find out the truth behind their boast that they do not believe in bloodshed."

Chapter 20

True to his word, Antoine set off with the rising sun. He went over the hills rather than by the main road and found the land deserted, although he was wary of every rock and thicket that he passed. The ground was hard, and he had to be careful not to ride Carbonel too fast, lest he did them both an injury. He had borrowed an old brigandine jacket from Crichton, so that he might appear as an ordinary traveller, but it was too small, and the leather rubbed against his wounded arm. Perhaps Catherine was right, that this was a foolish mission to undertake, but it was too late to turn back.

After a few hours, he came to the ditch that marked the edge of Ettrick Forest. Now the task was finding a way in. The woodland was vast, and he had arrived at a different spot to the one he and Turnbull had visited yesterday. The ground was rougher, the trees denser. He wished the lad were here – he was still puzzled by his desire to stay at Ravenscleugh – but, in his absence, he tried to scout a suitable entrance. Eventually, he met a tinker who pointed him towards a pair of great oak trees, which leant into each other, like a couple of drunken men.

He passed through this natural archway, into the greenery. It was slow going at first, as there were so many overhanging branches and roots to beware of, but after a while, the woods thinned out into a succession of deer pastures, coney warrens and heathlands. As Antoine dismounted to let Carbonel drink from a fishpond, he mused that he was in a place which had been specifically designed for hunting: a wild place but one where human eyes were never far away. He remembered Baird's words about enjoying the thrill of the chase and wondered whether he was the stalker or the prey right now.

After a few more hours in the forest, Antoine began to adjust to its strange patterns of shade and light, the sudden scrabblings in the undergrowth, the musty air. As his breathing settled into a steady rhythm, he found himself daydreaming of Catherine. Had her care for him last night been more than friendship? Had her mention of Turnbull's safety even been designed to hide her true concern? He realised that these were foolish thoughts, but he let his mind wander down such unlikely paths, safe in the knowledge that he would never put them to the test.

Presently, his reverie was broken by the sound of water in the distance: a good sign, as he knew that Newark Castle was on the Yarrow River. He put his fantasies aside and headed towards the low burble. The way took him through a wildflower meadow, the air scented by bladder campion and pansies. A roe deer poked its head above the long grass, its eyes locking onto his, as it decided whether to flee or not. It was enough to distract him for a moment, and by the time he spotted the two men lurking in the bracken, they were already pointing their crossbows at him.

"Do not move," said a thickset fellow with a fuzzy beard.

"My fingers are itchy wi' a' this meadow seed, and I may shoot my bolt if I am startled."

Antoine did as he was told, for he was well within range and would not be able to spur Carbonel quickly enough in this long grass. He affected a smile, although his body was stiff with apprehension. "I am sorry if I disturb your chase, gentlemen. As you may hear, I am not from these parts and have wandered here by mistake. If you can point me to Newark Castle, I will be on my way again."

The men eyed him suspiciously, their weapons still aimed directly at his chest. The first one sucked his teeth. "Why would a stranger be creeping about here? And what business do ye have in Newark?"

Antoine was encouraged by the questioning, for if they meant to kill him, they would surely have struck out by now. Still, the crossbows disturbed him, as he recalled the attack at the tannery. He tried to be evasive. "That's for me to discuss when I get there."

"There are rewards for catching foreign spies," the first man muttered to his friend.

His companion licked his lips. "Aye, there are." He nodded to Antoine. "So, tell us who ye are, afore we put a bolt through ye and take ye for some coin."

The Frenchman sighed. Perhaps he needed to impress his status on them after all. He spread his shoulders. "Very well. I am the Warden of the Eastern Marches, and I'm on my way to Newark Castle, with an important message for the queen."

The men responded with momentary deference, only for the first one to break into a chuckle. "Hark at him. He wears that tatty brigandine but says he is the warden."

"And thinks the queen is at Newark," said his friend. "Perhaps this hot weather has addled his mind, Swinney!"

Antoine had had enough of this. "Be careful, gentlemen, for I can prove my identity, more easily than you can prove that you're not poachers." He thought about showing his ring but did not want to provide another excuse to rob him, so he pulled out his papers instead. "I am visiting the queen to warn her that she may be in great danger. As will you be if you prevent me from reaching her."

His captors whispered to each other, then the one named Swinney gave a slight flick of his head. "Very well. Norrie, take those papers to our mistress and see what she says. As for you, monsieur, dinnae make a move."

As Norrie scurried off, Antoine tried to make sense of his situation. His pulse still raced at the sight of Swinney's crossbow, but the fact that the leader of this group seemed to be a woman offered further encouragement, as that surely ruled out Baird's band – or indeed any gang of reivers? He tried to ease some more information from Swinney, but the fellow gave nothing away until his friend returned, with orders to take him to their leader.

Now his captors treated him with great courtesy, as they led him across the meadow and through a thicket of gorse, to yet another deer pasture. Dogs barked at their arrival and were calmed by a houndmaster. A dozen or so armed men stood staring. Behind them, lads loaded animal carcasses onto a cart. And in front of all of them was a young woman, in a smart riding coat and hood.

"Monsieur Warden," she said, beckoning him forward. She could only have been twenty or so, but she had the high bearing of a rich lady. "I am so sorry that my men have detained you, but as you can imagine, we are wary of strangers in the forest."

Antoine was encouraged by her polite manner, but was

there also an edge of mockery to her voice? He bowed. "Of course. I understand. But as I was telling your men, I am on an important mission. One that I would press on with, if you'll allow me."

"Yes, I hear you are on royal business," the girl said, to sniggers from her men. "But I'm afraid you have been sore misled. For the queen is not at Newark. My brother has left her at the palace, so that she can be near His Grace, The King."

Antoine furrowed his brow, and she smiled at his confusion. "Forgive me, I should introduce myself: I am Lady Janet, Lord Douglas's sister. It was I he accompanied back to Newark two days ago."

All at once, the Frenchman saw his mistake. Those watchmen who had talked of Douglas bringing "that lady" to the forest had meant this proud young woman. Antoine had never met her before, but he knew she had a reputation at court, for being something of a malapert: the very sort that would attract the tavern gossips. He cursed his error, although he remembered that this still left the prophecy that Margaret Tudor was about to receive "a nasty surprise" – and Fortingale's message that "the queen must beware".

Ignoring her self-satisfied smirk, he attempted a recovery. "Well, it is delightful to meet you, Lady Janet. But whether Her Grace be nearby or not, I still have important information regarding her safety. So perhaps I could continue to Newark, so that I can take it to your brother?"

The young woman considered this, only to give a coquettish giggle. "No. I have a better idea. We have finished with our sport, so we will take you there ourselves."

It was late afternoon before they arrived at Newark. The castle lay deep in the heart of the forest, surrounded by ancient pine trees, oaks and yews. Although it was built around a great tower block, the thick foliage muffled all sense of human presence until the final approach. It was the perfect place to keep a secret, thought Antoine – but perhaps it might hold the key to unlock one too?

As he waited in the barmekin while Lady Janet went to fetch her brother, the Frenchman remembered how hostile Douglas had been a fortnight ago. However, when the young aristocrat arrived, the arrogance was no more. He put a hand on Antoine's shoulder and guided him into the tower with the solicitousness of a long-lost friend.

"Thank you for coming, de Lissieu. My sister has explained why you are here. Forgive her silliness, she is only a young girl. But I am vexed by your news about my wife. Come tell me what you've learnt."

Douglas took him up a spiral staircase to an anteroom where they could talk privately. He closed the door and drew up two chairs by a diamond-paned window. Antoine sat down opposite him and looked up to the panelled ceiling, as he ordered his thoughts. Then he cleared his throat and tried to summarise what they had discovered in the last week.

He began by explaining how he had been charged with guarding a notorious reiver, at Ravenscleugh. This Will Baird was a man of uncommon cunning. He seemed to be trying to orchestrate his escape, using some unknown documents, stolen from the house of the local bailie. At first, Antoine had thought Baird was simply trying to scare the queen, but the murders and Fortingale's dying words had convinced him that the threat was real.

Douglas listened to the Frenchman's story with great

interest, probing certain facts and asking him to repeat things which were not clear. Then, when he had finished, he sat back in his chair. "This is a foul thing and no mistake. You have done well to bring it to me." He steepled his fingers. "Although why you have come forward is a mystery. We are enemies, after all?"

Antoine smiled, for he himself had wrestled with this question all the way from Ravenscleugh. He gave the answer that he had used to convince himself. "I'm a diplomat by trade. I try not to think of enemies. I simply think of my master's interest. And in this case, it is clearly in my master's interest – not to say the whole country's – that the queen is protected."

"You don't worry that Albany himself is implicated?"

"I cannot believe that, sir. When he left for France, he was adamant that we must look after Her Grace."

"Yes, he voiced that desire most noisily, didn't he? The perfect cover, if anything were to happen."

"I swear my master's intentions are as he states them."

Douglas tapped a finger on his lips and then nodded, as if Antoine had passed some secret test. "Yes, I think you're right. Albany is a clever man. He knows better than to touch Her Grace. So we are left with a riddle. What did Fortingale mean by his warning? And who must we beware of?"

Antoine was tired from the long ride, and his arm still throbbed from the attack at the tannery. He was struggling to keep up with his own account, let alone answer Douglas's questions, so he was relieved when the young man changed tack. "You know, I think my wife may be safe after all. She is determined to stay in Edinburgh, that she might see her son. And as long as she remains there, surrounded by her guards, my men and the palace troops, she has little reason to fear for herself."

"Then Fortingale was mistaken?"

"I would be surprised if he were entirely duped. That man could smell a rat before a kitchen cat. But perhaps we have misread him?"

"How so?"

Douglas leant forward and gripped Antoine's arm. "I fear the threat lies not to the queen, but to the little king. Think about it. My wife's death would benefit nobody – it would merely provoke her brother's ire. But if her son were to pass – well, that would clear a path to the throne for someone."

Antoine gasped. "My master would never hurt that boy. The idea is quite unthinkable."

"I said nothing of your master," replied Douglas. "I believe this points to that blaggard Hamilton."

Chapter 21

Turnbull felt guilty about letting his master go to Newark alone. But he had been churned up by these threats to his mother and was mindful of the need to stay nearby, as that cursed bandit had instructed him. Now, as he folded up the message which had just arrived from Edinburgh, he breathed a sigh of relief. The reinforcements they had requested would be arriving in two days, and not just any old reinforcements – a party led by Lord Hamilton himself.

Safe in the knowledge that he had done one thing right, he set out for town to get his blackmailer off his back.

Lauder's square was deserted when he arrived, save for some crows hopping about the mercat cross. Turnbull tied Fogo outside Mungo's Bell's place and peered inside, but the bakery was closed. He crossed over to the opposite side, to escape the midday sun, but it was similarly devoid of life. As he turned to head for the West Port, Green Teeth appeared from a tailor's doorway.

"Back so soon," the man said. "Good. That means ye're here to parlay. Let's get this bargain struck and leave each other be."

It irked Turnbull that the man had read him so well: he

was here to parlay, of course, but he must not appear to be an easy touch. "First, you tell me something about the Bairds," he said. "Then we'll see about any bargain."

"As ye wish. But keep your voice down. As ye'll ken, folk dinnae like loose tongues round here."

Green Teeth gestured for Turnbull to accompany him down a wynd, between a butcher's and a fishmonger's. The lad was uncertain whether to join him at first. There was a stack of old herring barrels halfway down the passage and a blind corner at the end. Did the fellow have confederates waiting? No, that would not make sense: the man wanted those precious horses back and would not touch him, while he had them. The knowledge strengthened Turnbull's resolve, and he stepped into the alley's shadows.

"Right," said Green Teeth, glancing about himself, as if he too were wary of an attack. "I have done my best to find out what the Bairds are up to. I must say it's no' easy, as they keep their cards devilish tight to their chests. But the local nashgabs say they plan to spring their master and boast that they'll leave nobody alive in pursuit o' it."

So their suspicions were confirmed: Baird did mean to escape. However, this sounded like a more brutal plan than the subtle intrigue they'd imagined. Turnbull frowned. "I thought they didn't believe in shedding blood?"

"They dinnae believe in getting caught for it. But they do it, a' the same. Why, I've heard they've killed two men by Ettrick Forest, in the last few days alone."

That must be Fortingale and Dewar, thought Turnbull, although he wanted to make sure. "Tell me more about them."

"That's all I ken," said Green Teeth.

"Then you have brought me very little. Certainly not enough to get your horses back."

The man's face darkened for a moment, before breaking into an ingratiating smile. "Wait, I've left the most important detail to last."

"Go on."

"There's talk that the Bairds will make their move upon the next full moon. That's just four days from now. So ye dinnae have much time – and neither do we."

Turnbull's eyes widened. Hamilton would be here in two days, but how many troops would he bring? "You're sure of this?"

"Aye. That's the one thing that everybody agrees on. But it presents us wi' a challenge, does it no'?" Green Teeth's voice hardened. "We will come for our horses in three days' time, afore Baird and his gang ride off wi' them."

Turnbull thought about this. Although this rogue had brought some useful intelligence, he did not want him near the tower. "As I've said before, I'll bring them to you. We can meet here if you like."

"No, I dinnae like. I dinnae like one wee bit. A young laddie like you, wi' three horses, would be robbed o' them afore ye'd gone a mile. So here's what we'll do instead. There'll be three o' us. We'll come to the main gate at dusk. Make sure ye're there alone and the nags are a' saddled and ready to go. When we tell ye, open the gate, and we'll be gone in a minute."

The arrangements seemed quite impossible to Turnbull. How would he replace Moffat or Crichton on the gate? How would he assemble the horses without arousing suspicion? More to the point, how would he explain the animals' absence afterwards? He began to protest, but the man waved a hand.

"The time for bargaining is over, laddie. Any problems

are yours to deal wi'. But make sure ye do, otherwise ye ken what will happen to your mother."

Turnbull pondered his predicament all the way back to Ravenscleugh. The more he thought about it, the more he felt he should tell Antoine when he was back from Newark. After all, Green Teeth would never know, and things would be easier to arrange with his master's approval. The trick would be to prepare all the groundwork so that the Frenchman did not view it as a great trouble.

By the time he had arrived, Turnbull had the beginnings of a plan. "Lord Hamilton will be bringing reinforcements in a few days," he told Moffat, who was slouched at the gate, as ever. "It's likely that we won't have enough room in the stables, for his horses. So see if you can build a temporary rail and shelter over here, and we'll move a few of our nags out."

"As you wish, sir," sighed the sentry. "Might no' be a bad thing in any case, as yours looks like it has pinworm. We wouldnae want it to spread."

Turnbull looked at Fogo's tail and saw that it had indeed lost much of its hair – just as his mother had observed a few days ago. He made a note to ask Catherine whether she might prepare a treatment for it, but meanwhile, he turned his mind to Baird's escape.

Instead of entering the tower straight away, he walked around the courtyard's inner wall, looking for any weaknesses in the masonry, but all was in order. Next, he checked the new bars which Crichton had fitted to the main door: they, too, seemed strong. In the hall, he asked Elspeth whether there had been any change in the prisoner's behaviour, but she replied that there had not. He began to relax. Whatever he felt about Widow Scrimgeour, he had to admit that she kept a tight gaol. Feeling her hawk-like eyes upon him, he said as much.

"Aye, it would be tighter still, if ye would get out of my way!" she said. "When you are out merrymaking wi' your master, I check these things a' the time. Yesterday, it was the roof and stairwell. Today, the window bars, the brickwork, locks and bolts. Tomorrow, I will patrol the outer wall. When will ye trust me to do my bloody job?"

Turnbull was struck by the mounting fury in the keeper's voice. It was as if the act of sharing her secret, about her husband's death, had unlocked a sluice gate that now let torrents of anger pour forth, from deep within. He decided not to enrage her further, with talk of Baird's treachery. "We trust you greatly. The same cannot be said for our friend upstairs, that's all."

Elspeth took this as her signal to go to bed, flashing an anxious look to Crichton as she went. Turnbull and Catherine readied themselves for sleep as well. Meanwhile, Scrimgeour stomped down to the kitchen and clattered pots about. When she returned, her cheeks were raw. She snuffed the candles and took her place in the straw. After some more tossing and turning, the room fell quiet.

As he lay in the gloom, Turnbull wondered when his master would return. He still felt guilty, that he had let him visit the forest on his own, but there was no stopping that man when he had a bee in his bonnet. And besides, if both of them had gone to Newark, Turnbull would not have discovered the timing of Baird's plan. He had made himself useful. He had not been selfish. He would make amends when this business with the horses was done, his master had returned and Hamilton's reinforcements had arrived. Over and again, he tried to tell himself that he had done nothing wrong. And yet he found himself unconvinced.

As he fought with his mind, his body nagged him to empty his bladder. Christ, he was never going to rest tonight! He got up and picked his way through the sleeping bodies. A wall torch on the stairwell guided him towards the jakes. He pulled down his hose. But just as he prepared to piss, he heard what sounded like a whisper. He looked over his shoulder, thinking that someone had followed him in, but there was nobody there. He did himself up again and went back to the stairwell, but it too was empty. Perhaps he had imagined it?

Except there it was again: a low muttering, as if someone were right beside him. He returned to the tiny room, looked to either side, then up to the ceiling and down to the floor. Still nothing. But as he rubbed his ears, in case they were playing tricks on him, he saw a flash of light from the jakes itself. What in Hell's name? He peered down through the hole, towards the cesspit. To his astonishment, somebody seemed to be standing on the thin path between the cesspit and the castle wall. They were moving back and forth, illuminated by the mean orange glow of an oil lamp.

From this vantage point, Turnbull could see only the figure's silhouette and the top of their head. They were pacing about, with an urgency that did not bode well. Every now and again, they would stop, bend over, then move out of sight again. But at one point, they brought the lamp nearer to their head and allowed Turnbull to see that they were wearing a blue hood. Just like the fellow who had followed them at the Midsummer's festivities!

Turnbull forgot about his bladder, but his heart began to quicken. What was anybody doing outside the castle at this time of night? He thought of calling to them but realised that would simply send them running. Instead, he knelt down by the garderobe's wooden seat and, doing his best to ignore the stench, took a closer look through the hole.

The prowler had stopped right under the privy shaft. They put their hands to their head, as if in a gesture of despair, confusion or anger. Then they lifted their chin and mumbled something to themselves. As they did so, Turnbull got a brief glimpse of their face. It was difficult to make out in the dark, but as they turned into the dim glow of their lamp, a shiver ran down his spine. Was that Elspeth Scrimgeour?

In truth, he couldn't be sure whether it was the keeper's daughter, but he felt certain it was a woman. He tried to get a better view of her, but she disappeared again. When, after a few moments, she did not return, he ran back into the stairwell. He paused, not knowing which way to run. The hall, to raise the alarm? The main gate, to see if he could catch whoever it was? Or Elspeth's room, to rule her out? All at once, he was struck by a bolt of clarity: he must check that Baird was still in place.

He raced up the stairs to the top floor. Everything was eerily quiet. But thank God, the prisoner was still in his cell. Turnbull looked through the hatch and saw him quite clearly, in the moonlight. An eye twinkled. "Everything all right, sir?" Baird said impudently, without raising his head.

Ignoring him, Turnbull checked the girl's room. He was relieved to see her curled up in bed, her long, fair hair spilling over the blankets of her pallet. Next, he tried the handle of the middle door, the one which had been locked since Scrimgeour's husband killed himself. It was fastened tight.

Satisfied that any danger might yet be averted, he prepared to return downstairs, to enlist the others' help, when something told him to revisit Elspeth. He peered through the hatch again. She had not moved. He watched her for a few moments, and she remained absolutely still. He listened for the sound of breathing, but there was none. How strange. He rapped gently on the door.

"Elspeth, are you alright?"

She did not reply, so he knocked a little louder.

"Elspeth, can you hear me? I need you to get up."

Once more, she did not stir. Turnbull felt sick as he turned the handle and entered her room. He was relieved to find that there was no sign of anything untoward. The girl seemed fast asleep, her head turned to the wall. She did not move a muscle as he approached her bed and bent over. He said her name one last time. When she did not answer, he put a hand on her shoulder to rouse her. But what was this? Her body was completely soft.

Pulling back the blankets, he was confronted by a pile of clothes, arranged in the shape of a body. And as for the flaxen tresses which had lain across the pillow, he now held them in his hands and saw them for what they really were: a handful of long hairs which had been cut from a horse's tail.

Chapter 22

The Great Hall of Newark was small compared to those of the grander castles of the land, but impressive for such a remote location. It was decorated with beautiful tapestries, each representing a hunting scene. The top table had been set with pewter plates and wine glasses, fit for a palace. As Lord Douglas offered him a place at his right-hand side, Antoine once more contrasted his courtesy with the lack of hospitality he had shown previously.

It was as if the young aristocrat were wooing him. But for all his charm, it made the Frenchman feel uncomfortable.

Lady Janet – now changed from her riding coat into a beautiful primrose gown – sat to her brother's left with a lady-in-waiting. Other lieutenants and their womenfolk joined the side tables. Then a servant sounded a horn, and a team of servers brought forth the messes: a selection of plates straight from the day's hunt.

Douglas began by making light conversation with his sister and her attendant, before angling his back, to talk privately with Antoine.

"So, have you chewed on what I told you earlier?" he said. "About Lord Hamilton and his designs on my stepson?"

Antoine helped himself to a portion of tender partridge

breast, while he formulated his response. When Douglas had first made the accusation, he had seen it as a vindictive slur on a political rival. But in the absence of any other explanation, perhaps he should not reject it so lightly. If there were even a grain of truth to it and the king were imperilled by his inaction, he would never forgive himself. And neither would the great powers of the land.

"As I said this afternoon, I will do anything I can to protect His Grace. I simply struggle to see how Hamilton could benefit from harming him."

"Because Albany is next in line for the throne? In theory, perhaps. But if the king passed in unnatural circumstances, all would be up in the air."

Antoine shifted in his seat. Even to talk of the succession could be considered treason, but Douglas appeared to have no such qualms.

"Your master would be suspected of foul play, whether he was innocent or not. But my wife and I would not benefit either, for without the king, we have no claim of our own. If Hamilton played it right, he could destroy all his rivals with one blow."

"What do you mean, 'if he played it right'?"

Douglas sighed. "If the death were murky enough to taint Albany but not so egregious for King Henry to invade, Hamilton could present himself as the obvious compromise for all parties, French and English. The man's a fiend. My wife will die of shock when she hears of this."

Antoine thought about the queen's great love for her son, Fortingale's warning that she must beware and the tavern gossips' prediction that Margaret Tudor was in for a nasty surprise. He recalled Hamilton's calculating manner at Edinburgh Castle too – and the fact that he had been Albany's foe not so long ago. He had to admit, it started to make terrible sense.

"If all this be true, then what role does my prisoner Baird play?" said Antoine hoarsely. He took a hefty draught of wine.

"I don't know yet," said Douglas, stroking the point of his beard. "You said he might have some documents or other. Perhaps he has found evidence of the plot and hopes to sell it, for his freedom?"

Antoine frowned. "If so, wouldn't he have offered it to us?"

"Unless he aims to sell it to Hamilton, so that he may destroy it," said Douglas, thumping his fist on the table. "Tell me, how secure is this tower of yours? How large is the garrison? How strong the defences?"

Antoine gave a brief explanation of the arrangements at Ravenscleugh and tried to reassure his lordship that there was no way Baird could escape or even communicate with his gang.

"That is good to hear," murmured Douglas. He turned briefly to his sister and raised his glass before continuing with Antoine. "Thank you for your help, monsieur. I will deal with Baird's friends in the forest. Meanwhile, just make sure you keep him absolutely secure."

Turnbull ran out of Elspeth's room, still clutching the bundle of Fogo's hair. What fools they had been, to be deceived by that girl. But what was the purpose of her ruse? Surely she was not the "little bird" that Baird had jested of, as being his messenger? Turnbull glanced at the reiver's cell again and saw that he was standing at the door, his face pressed to the hatch. The wall torches flickered in his eyes as he flashed a sly grin.

"I telt ye that we live in strange times, sir. But even I didnae imagine one o' my gaolers escaping!"

Turnbull cursed him as he raced downstairs to raise the alarm. In his haste, he crashed into Crichton, hurrying in the other direction. The collision took the lad's breath away, so that he was left bent over, his hands on his knees. The guard put an arm round his shoulder.

"Sorry, sir," he whispered. "I heard some noise upstairs. Is everything in order?"

"No," said Turnbull, holding up the strands of horsehair. "Elspeth has tricked us. She's escaped from her room somehow and is skulking about outside the walls."

Crichton frowned. "Ye're sure o' that?"

"Yes, I saw her through the jakes, of all places. I fear she's helping Baird."

"It won't be that. Is he secure?"

"Still in his cell, thank Christ. But for how much longer, I do not know. Quick, let's tell the others and catch the girl, so we can find out what this is all about."

Turnbull made to pass the sentry on the stairs but was surprised when the fellow blocked his way. He was looking at him in a strange way, his usual friendly countenance replaced by a serious expression. "Let's not be hasty, sir. Why don't ye come wi' me?"

God's nails. Was Crichton up to something too? Turnbull made to cry out, but the sentry placed a hand across his mouth. His eyes bore into him. "Dinnae worry, I willnae hurt ye, sir. But come wi' me, and ye'll see that it's no' what ye think."

Crichton relaxed his grip on him and slowly moved his hand away. The sentry nodded, in recognition of his cooperation, then gestured for them both to go upstairs.

Turnbull followed obediently, although his heart pounded with every step. Could he trust this man? Or should he shout out, while he had the chance? He watched the fellow's sword swing in its scabbard as they went and cursed the fact that he had left his own sword by his bed.

When they reached the landing, he saw Baird still waiting at his hatch. "Ah, there's more of you?" the prisoner laughed. "This becomes like a mummers' play!"

"Get back to your bed," said Crichton. "And keep your yapping down. I swear if ye say one more word, ye'll no' leave that cell alive."

Turnbull was reassured by the sentry's harsh tone with the prisoner. But his head still spun with what this was about, as he allowed himself to be guided into Elspeth's room. Crichton motioned for him to sit on the bed, while he himself stood behind the door. Then they waited in the gloom. Several times, Turnbull made to ask for some explanation, but the sentry put his finger to his lips. Just when his patience had almost run out, he heard the faint sound of steps. They did not sound like they came from the landing or the staircase, but from further away. Crichton gestured for him to remain calm. A metallic click sounded, the noise of a key turning in a lock. A door creaked and was carefully closed. Another click. A few more footsteps, much closer. Then the door to their room opened, and Elspeth Scrimgeour stepped in.

"By Jesu!" she gasped at the sight of Turnbull on her bed, but before she could say anything more, Crichton had leapt on her and covered her mouth. For a moment, he simply held her, as she thrashed about in his arms, her eyes wide with terror. Then she recognised him and began to calm down. "Easy," said Crichton gently. "It's just me and Master

Turnbull. I need ye to tell him what this is a' about. Tell him everything, mind you. But dinnae take too long, or the others will be up."

This last warning sent the girl into another fit of panic. She took the weight off her legs so that she fell out of Crichton's grasp and onto the floor. Shaking her head, she clasped her hands in front of her. "Please," she whispered. "Dinnae tell my mother."

"We'll see about that," said Turnbull. "Now be quick, like Crichton says."

"Very well," said Elspeth. She lifted her chin and looked up to the ceiling, as if to collect her thoughts. It was the same gesture that had caused him to recognise her before. "It's like this. Ye ken the story, I think, about how my father met his end?"

Turnbull nodded. "Yes, your mother told my master of it, a few days ago."

"Then ye'll have heard her talk o' the key to that door. The key the prisoner used to escape. The night my father... did away wi' himself."

"That's right. Your mother explained how you locked the door and the postern gate afterwards and melted the key in the furnace, so that it could never be used again."

"Aye, except we didnae do that, did we?" Elspeth said to Crichton. She trembled as she placed her hand in the sentry's palm. Wait. They were a couple, then? That would explain the furtive looks and the sentry's desire to protect her. How had they not noticed this before?

"No," the sentry said dolefully. "I had an idea that it might be useful to keep a secret key, as it's a hard old life in here. So I melted another one instead and hid the real one in the stables."

Elspeth opened her hand to reveal an iron key. "My mother didnae notice it, in her grief, but I did. And ever since, we have talked of running off together."

Turnbull tried to take this news in. "So you have been coming and going by the postern gate, all this time?"

"No, not at all," said Crichton. "It proved one thing to have a key, but quite another to slip out unnoticed. The widow likes to keep an eye on everybody, as ye may have seen…"

Yes, thought Turnbull, especially her daughter.

"So we dared not use it for some time," Crichton continued. "Until you arrived with your horse, that is, and we saw how its flaxen hair might help."

"It was Midsummer, and I wanted to see the festivities for myself." Elspeth gestured at her blue cloak. "I put this on so that I might pass unrecognised, although I fear ye might have seen me by the West Port? Anyway, I had a taste o' freedom, smelled the flowers and the bonfires, watched the dancing. Felt alive. Then I returned to this cursed prison. It was only when my mother said that she'd be patrolling the walls the morn that I became afeart, for she might see my footprints by the gate and remember chiding me for my mucky clogs. I went to remove my tracks tonight."

"Mercy me," said Turnbull, "Do you realise what might have happened if one of Baird's men had caught you and taken the key?"

"They would have no reason to suspect I had one," Elspeth said defensively.

"Did you speak to anyone while you were in town? Or could anyone have seen you leave?"

"No, I was careful to come and go like a shadow. Crichton telt me how."

"I'm sorry, sir," said the guard. "This is my fault. I

shouldnae have encouraged her in her fancies. Nor indulged my own through her."

"Well, you have been exceptionally foolish, both of you. Let me consider what I must do with this. Meanwhile, give me that blasted key and get back to your beds."

When Elspeth handed him the offending article, he noted that her hands were not trembling anymore. Indeed, she almost seemed relieved to have shared her secret. "Please dinnae tell my mother, Master Turnbull. But if ye do, so be it. For those sweet hours o' freedom were worth anything that she may visit on me now."

Chapter 23

The next morning, Antoine rode hard from Newark and arrived back at Ravenscleugh by noon. He raced up the stairs of the tower to tell Turnbull and Catherine of his time in the forest. They were deep in conversation in the hall and looked troubled. Well, whatever their woes, he was just about to add to them. He gave a rushed account of his encounter with Lady Janet in the forest, the absence of the queen, and Douglas's suspicions about Hamilton.

"Lord Hamilton?" said Turnbull, putting his hands to his head. "But that's who's bringing our reinforcements."

Antoine felt sick. "Do you know how many men he'll have?"

"The messenger didn't say. Only that he's due tomorrow. And I have heard from other sources that Baird aims to escape on the full moon. That's just two days away."

"Sweet Mary. He may not even need to free himself, if his Lordship holds the door open."

"Or someone else does," said Turnbull, holding up a large iron key. "I was just telling Mistress Gray that I caught the Scrimgeour girl escaping by the postern gate last night. I do not think she's guilty of anything, beyond stupidity. But it shows this tower may not be as secure as we thought."

Antoine's mind whirled. He had just assured Lord Douglas that Ravenscleugh was in good order. What would he say if he knew that his greatest enemy was about to pay a visit – and that the prison was as leaky as a pauper's roof? He wondered if he should go back to Newark and raise the alarm, but there was no time. He needed to think as if his life depended on it. Which, he reflected miserably, it probably did.

"You can explain that one to me later," he said, rubbing his temples. "Now, is there anything else you need to tell me?"

Turnbull started to say something about the confiscated horses, but the Frenchman waved him down. "I mean anything important to the safety of this tower. God's sake, lad, first you send me off to the forest on my own, and then you do not even take care of matters here." The boy scowled at Antoine as he continued. "It is possible that our prisoner is working with Lord Hamilton, to do some injury to the king. If that happens on our watch, then we can all forget about our horses and start worrying for our heads!"

The Frenchman got up and walked to the window. He looked through the slit, to the courtyard below. Scrimgeour was berating Elspeth, as usual. Crichton and Moffat were larking about at the gatehouse. Their garrison looked more threadbare than ever. He felt bad for snapping at Turnbull, but before he could say anything, Catherine had spoken up.

"Are you sure about all this, sir? Two days ago, ye believed that any danger was to the queen, not the little king?"

"Yes, but Douglas is right," said Antoine, turning round. "Nobody gains anything by harming the queen. It's the king who matters. And only Hamilton might benefit from his demise."

"Would he go so low as to kill a bairn, though? His own flesh and blood?"

"With respect, you have not mixed with folk like this. You do not know them as I do."

"What, because I am some stupid healing woman?"

Now it was Catherine's turn to glare at him. God, he was making enemies of the very ones he loved the most. The ones he needed by his side. He should really apologise to both of them and encourage them to make a plan together, but instead, he returned to the window. "I need to be alone," he said.

There was an awkward mood at the dinner table. Antoine tried to cajole Turnbull and Catherine, but they maintained a sullen alliance against him. Elspeth and Crichton exchanged worried looks, no doubt fretting that their trysting might be revealed. Scrimgeour looked as if she were keeping the lid on a pot of rage, that was bubbling up from the very core of her being. How Baird would enjoy the discord that he had helped to sow! Antoine mused that this might be the fellow's last night of incarceration. And his own last night of freedom. He resolved to question him one more time, before their fortunes were reversed.

Elspeth trembled as she escorted Antoine upstairs, but he was too focused on interviewing Baird to chide her about last night's misdemeanour. She bundled him into the cell and slammed the door before scuttling off.

"Forgive me," said Baird. The prisoner was lying on the floor of his cell, with his arms and legs stretched out. "It does me good to loosen my bones. I cannae be hobbling out o' here when the moment comes."

Antoine ignored his supercilious grin. "Do not worry.

You might only need to climb the scaffold, if what I hear is true."

The man continued to stretch. "Oh aye? And what is that?"

"Our latest evidence suggests you're involved in a deadly plot."

Baird laughed, as he performed another exercise on the floor. "Last time ye just charged me wi' spreading rumours. My wickedness seems to increase by the hour!"

"This jesting ill becomes you, Baird. We also know that your men – or some powerful others – plan to spring you on the full moon."

The prisoner raised an eyebrow. "I appreciate the warning and will make a note of it. Although, of course, it would only make sense for me to escape, if you had no intention of granting me a pardon."

Antoine jabbed a finger. "That promise was dependant on your good behaviour. But everywhere we look, it seems your hands are bloody."

Baird performed a final stretch before sitting up. "Then perhaps your eyes deceive you. For if I wanted to escape, I would already be gone. And if I wanted bloody hands, I would not need to leave this room."

With this, he waved his right hand in the air, while opening his left one to reveal a dagger. Antoine gasped, as he realised it was his own. In Elspeth's anxiety, she had forgotten to take it off him when entering the cell, and Baird had clearly found a way to pluck it as he stretched. Antoine braced himself for an attack. But instead of leaping on him, the prisoner flipped the dagger round and offered it hilt-first.

"Good luck wi' your investigations, sir. And see ye on the full moon."

Antoine was now more confused than ever. Was Baird involved in some plot, or was the prisoner groping about in the dark, like the rest of them? If there was a plot, did it threaten the king – and if so, how? And was Hamilton the mastermind of all this – or was Douglas simply casting rocks at his sworn enemy? Antoine wished that he could mull these questions with his friends, but when he returned to the hall, Turnbull was not there, and Catherine was packing her haversack.

"What's this?" he said, as she bundled up some phials in a muslin cloth and put them in her bag.

"I'm leaving in the morning," she replied, without lifting her head. "If ye're right that trouble's coming, I would rather be away."

"Ah, do not say that, Mistress Gray. I need your counsel here."

Catherine fastened the haversack's buckle and stood up. "You? Listen to my counsel? I sincerely doubt it."

He came towards her, arms spread in a profession of innocence. "I care greatly what you think. More than you will ever know."

Catherine shook her head. "Ye said it yerself. What could I possibly ken about the great folk who rule us?"

"I simply meant that the men we're dealing with are not of the common run. They are difficult to fathom."

"Says the man who is more unfathomable than any! Who kens what ye think, let alone what ye feel, half the time?"

The words struck him to the core, for even he sometimes found himself impossible to read. But right now, he knew he wanted Catherine to stay. He came closer and put his hands lightly on her shoulders.

"I've put forth my feelings for you before," he said awkwardly. "You made it clear they were not requited. I told you about my desire to return to France as well. If you are saying there is a chance—"

"No, I don't mean that," Catherine said. She flushed, and he took his hands away. "Ye are a dear friend, as I telt ye afore. And I ken why ye want to return hame, even though I wish ye wouldnae. I am talking about Turnbull. He must be devastated by the news of your departure, and yet ye treat him harshly sometimes."

Antoine shifted uneasily. "About my news and Turnbull…"

"Oh, don't say ye havenae telt the lad?"

"Told me what?" said Turnbull, appearing at the door.

Chapter 24

Turnbull didn't believe his master's excuse that his news related to Mistress Gray's departure. The two of them had looked guilty, as if they were hiding something from him. As the lad waved Catherine off the next morning, he felt as if he had swallowed an anvil. But the heaviness did not just come from the leaving of a friend; it was from a sense of loneliness and betrayal. It made him think that he would not tell the Frenchman about these horses after all. For why share a secret with one who concealed so much himself?

His mood was further darkened when he found that wastrel Moffat had not finished the new tethering rail. He was berating him when Antoine wandered over.

"Turnbull, we need to talk."

"I'm afraid I'm busy with the horses," said the lad.

"Well, forget them for a moment. Hamilton will be here soon, and we need to agree how we will deal with him."

It was a fair point, thought Turnbull grudgingly. They could hardly accuse such a powerful man of plotting to kill the king. Especially if he had brought a great army with him. But they would have to explain what they had done over the last fortnight and why they had sent for help. What must they say and what should they leave out?

"I'm sure you'll think of something, sir."

"Oh, do not be a martyr, boy. Otherwise, you might end up like one. This is treason we are talking of, remember. We must tread carefully."

Turnbull pondered this. "Then we let him take the lead. See what he knows – and where his interests lie. Keep our own answers vague. If he is truly plotting against the king, his questions may reveal it."

The Frenchman clapped him on the back. "That's more like it. If we stick together, we may come out of this in one piece."

Turnbull nodded but reflected that it was hard to stick together without trust. Until that was restored between them, he must see to himself.

Antoine spent the rest of the morning with Scrimgeour, trying to work out the logistics of housing the new arrivals. Accommodation was one thing – there was plenty of room in the hall, and tents could be put up in the courtyard if necessary – but food supplies were running low, especially as Mungo Bell had not made yesterday's delivery.

"This is a' your fault," said Scrimgeour, as she made an inventory of the cellar. "Ye've scared off our provisioner, then invited more hungry mouths to feed. If ye'd only listened to me, we'd no be in this place."

"Let us hope that Hamilton's men bring some victuals of their own then," said Antoine tetchily. "And if not, they will have to get out foraging. It will not be the first time an army has had to catch its own dinner."

As it happened, when Moffat called to say that Hamilton was approaching, he did not speak of an army but of five men. Antoine and Turnbull raced to the gatehouse to get a better look. The sentry appeared to be correct. Hamilton was at the front, his mulberry gown recognisable from a distance. Four lancers in steel bonnets followed him, their breastplates glinting in the sun. As they wound their way up the castle's twisting approach, they resembled a silver snake, slithering towards its prey.

"Presumably, this is just an advance party," said Turnbull, squinting through the gatehouse slit. "Otherwise, we are not much better defended than before."

"Perhaps defending us is not what they have in mind," said Antoine, as Moffat opened the gate and the men rode in.

No sooner were they inside than Hamilton leapt off his horse. Scrimgeour glowered as he pushed past her and beckoned for Antoine and Turnbull to join him in the far corner of the courtyard.

"What the hell have you two been playing at?" he said when they were out of earshot. Gone was the calm, calculating politician from Edinburgh Castle. "From what I gather, the local bailie is dead by his own hand, his wife and servant murdered, and an English spy killed as well. You were supposed to be calming the region, not inflaming it!"

"There are dark forces working against us," said Antoine vaguely, as he and Turnbull had agreed. "We were attacked ourselves, at a tannery in Lauder."

"And have you found out who these forces are, what these attacks are all about?"

"Not yet, my lord. But we have made some progress."

"Did you find anything in the bailie's house? Any papers that might shed light on things?"

"No, we searched the house, but there was nothing," said Turnbull.

Hamilton furrowed his brow. "How hard did you look?"

"We made a thorough search," the lad said. He hesitated. "But it's possible that someone got there just before us and spirited something away. Perhaps someone working for our prisoner."

Just then, Antoine caught sight of Baird, at his window. The reiver put his hands around the bars, as if he were willing them to disappear. Frankly, Antoine would not be surprised if he possessed such a power, amongst his many gifts. Hamilton followed his eye and gave a mean smile. "Well, I think it's time I spoke to this prisoner of yours, don't you? In the meantime, you really have no sense of what these documents might pertain to, or where they might be held?"

"No," said Antoine. "We were hoping you might help us. Perhaps when the other troops arrive, we can make a plan together?"

Hamilton snorted. "We can talk of the other troops at dinner. As for making a plan together, I fear you've done enough damage already. Now get that sour-faced witch to take me to Baird's cell."

Antoine was infuriated by the man's tone. He was ordering him about as if he were already on the throne. The Frenchman beckoned for Scrimgeour to fetch the keys, but as he tried to join them on the stairs, Hamilton made it clear that he wished to conduct the interview alone. Antoine thought of protesting but feared this might raise his visitor's suspicions, so he acquiesced meekly and went back to the gatehouse.

"Well, what do you think?" he said to Turnbull. Moffat had just finished that new rail and the lad was tethering the three horses they had confiscated at Midsummer. It irked Antoine that he was so focused on such trivia, but he was conscious of the need to go easy on him, after last night.

Turnbull sighed. "Hamilton seems to be uptight about something. He is greatly interested in the Walkerburns, in particular. As if he knows what lay in that house."

"Or at least he fears what it might be: something that incriminates him." Antoine looked over at Hamilton's troops, who were gathered closely in the yard. "At any rate, keep an eye on those men. If you see anything untoward, come straight to me."

Given the shortage of table space and food, Hamilton declared that he must eat first, with Antoine and Turnbull. Then everyone else could do with the leftovers. The decision infuriated Scrimgeour, and she glared at the men as they took their places. "I am the keeper of this tower," she muttered, as she helped Elspeth bring out the messes. "Not some skivvy in a country tavern."

In contrast, Hamilton seemed to be in better fettle after his conversation with Baird. As he took his place, he declared himself quite satisfied that the prisoner was not involved in the Walkerburn business. Indeed, the more he thought about it, he doubted whether those killings should be of any concern to them at all.

"What if we find fresh evidence?" said Antoine, reaching for the rabbit stew, which Elspeth had placed in a tureen, in the middle.

"Bring it to me, by all means," said Hamilton. "But there's no need to go looking for it. We have bigger matters to contend with now."

Antoine flashed Turnbull a quick glance, as it seemed strange that their visitor had dropped his interest in the Walkerburns so easily. And what were these bigger matters to which he referred?

"I hope all is well in Edinburgh?" the Frenchman asked airily.

"Things are never well in Edinburgh," said Hamilton, taking a sip of wine. "The city is a cesspit of treason and conspiracy. With Lord Albany away, Margaret Tudor back, and the king still a child, bad men lurk in the shadows, ready to pounce when the time is right."

Yes, thought Antoine, and you might be at their forefront. He reminded himself to play the innocent for now. "Albany will be back, before too long. When he returns, he will settle things."

"I would not be so sure of that," said Hamilton.

"How so?"

"The talks in France go slowly. Albany may be delayed. Meanwhile, the plague sweeps our land. It brings chaos, fear, unreason. Those who might otherwise bide their time are made impetuous. Why, there are even rumours that the king himself may be in danger."

As Hamilton said these words, he locked eyes with Antoine. The Frenchman felt he was looking for a reaction, checking what he knew of any plot. He made sure to stay stony-faced.

Eventually, Turnbull broke the silence. "That is terrible news, my lord. Do you know who might be behind such an outrage?"

"It is not hard to fathom. Whose desire for power outstrips all others in this kingdom? Whose every move is driven by greed and ambition? Whose only hope relies on possession of the king? That popinjay, Lord Douglas, of course! He has no royal blood of his own, and his wife does not have the position he hoped for. So he must contrive a way to seize the king. That's the only way the other lords will support him."

Antoine shuddered as he recalled his encounter with Douglas two days ago. Was it possible that the young aristocrat had invented that story about Hamilton's plot, to cover his own tracks? Or was it the other way round, and Hamilton was now slandering his rival to conceal his treason? Either way, he must say nothing of his visit to Newark.

"Surely the queen would not support this. She may be desperate to see her son, but she would not wish him to be taken violently?"

Hamilton shrugged. "She grows impatient. She's now been in Edinburgh for almost two weeks, without sight of His Grace."

"Then we must reassure her, that this is temporary. That she will have all the access she desires, as soon as the plague has passed."

"Forget that lady for a moment!" said Hamilton sharply. "It's Douglas who is driving this. He sees Albany away, his wife's power diminished, the country divided and distracted. This is his chance to strike, and I fear he will not waste it."

"Then how can we help?" said Turnbull. "Perhaps when our reinforcements arrive, we could divert some to investigate?"

"Reinforcements? Don't you understand? There will be no more troops for you. We need every man we can lay our hands on, back in Edinburgh. That's why I have brought so few down today. Only to find that your prisoner has nothing to do with all this, anyway."

"But my lord," protested Antoine. "Even if Baird is not involved in this great treason that you speak of, he is clearly up to something. And we have intelligence that he plans to escape in two days' time!"

Hamilton thumped the table. "For the last time! Your prisoner is a nobody. Get rid of him for all I care. But do it on your own. We will be leaving in the morning."

Chapter 25

Hamilton woke early and stomped about the hall, complaining about his bed. It forced the others to get up. Elspeth managed to scrape together some bannock crusts for breakfast, but Hamilton declined his share, saying he would rather leave it for the tower's rats. He gathered his men in the courtyard and called for a mounting block. As he waited for Moffat to fetch it, he took Antoine aside.

"It will be good to see the back of you, de Lissieu. I was told that you could be relied upon, but by Jesu, you have caused nothing but trouble so far."

Antoine could bear his regal tone no longer. "Perhaps our paths will cross sooner than you think. Great men can find themselves in trouble too. Some even seek it out."

Hamilton's face darkened. "That is true. But truly great men are too clever to be caught. So make sure you do not pick fights above your station. Know your place, monsieur. Know your place."

Turnbull spent the day wrapped up in worry. He was supposed to be forming a plan to guard against Baird's supposed escape tomorrow, but all he could think about was Green Teeth's visit tonight. He tried to calm himself. The three horses were at the rail. He had promised Moffat that he could slip off for an extra ale at sundown. When the men came, he would release the nags and slam the gate. And if his master ever asked where the horses had gone, he would simply reply that he had attended to business, as he had instructed him.

He rehearsed the argument again and again. They paid informants all the time. Indeed, this was scarcely even a payment; he was simply returning goods to their original owners. He had tried to tell his master, but he had shut him down. Oh, why did this sit so ill with him? He must overcome these foolish worries: he must do whatever it took, to protect his mother, then get on with securing the tower, as he had been ordered.

It took an age for dusk to fall. As the birds settled down for the night, Turnbull's stomach was no more becalmed. He shunned his master's attempts to make small talk and said that he wished to sharpen his sword on the whetstone, in preparation for the next day. Clenching his fists, he went downstairs, entered the courtyard and approached the main gate. Moffat was waiting for him, as they had agreed. Turnbull clapped him on the shoulder, and the sentry scurried off, to take his sneaky ale.

The lad was now alone. The moon hung low in the sky, not quite full yet, but in its final stage of ripening. Turnbull was momentarily distracted by its wonder. At St Andrews he had used a lunary to plot its phases, had mapped its dark spots and learnt how it governed the seas and women's flowering. But there was something magical about it too, that could not be explained by dusty parchments. As he gazed at its pitted surface, he wondered what portents it held for him, how it might be pulling at the tides of his own life.

A rough voice interrupted his thoughts. "Are ye there, Master Turnbull?"

He pulled back the hatch of the gate and came eyeball to eyeball with Green Teeth. Turnbull jerked his head back. "Christ's nails, but you are stealthy!"

The visitor gave a sly chuckle. "Silence is a virtue. My only one, some say. But come, we dinnae have much time. Have ye got our nags?"

"Yes, they're all ready to go."

Turnbull moved his head, so that Green Teeth could see the horses behind him. But as he did so, he caught a glimpse of two other men, lurking to the left of the gate. They slunk back out of view. "Wait, who else is with you?"

"My friends," said Green Teeth, frowning. "As we agreed. Three o' us, one for each nag. Now hurry up and open the gate before your master hears. Ye dinnae want that, do ye?"

Turnbull scrutinised his face, its rough features bathed by the glow of the moon. He began to feel uneasy. "Tell your friends to step out of the shadows, where I can see them. Then I will open the gate."

"Christ's sake, we dinnae have time for a' this, just get it opened and we'll be gone."

"If you don't show yourselves, I—"

Just then, Moffat came back, earlier than expected. "Scrimgeour caught me toping on the stairs," he said, with a scowl. "Hold, what's going on here?"

Turnbull cursed under his breath. "Just some travellers. I am dealing with them."

"Travellers at this hour?" Moffat creased his brow and approached the gate for a better look. Turnbull tried to block his path, but the sentry peered over his shoulder and then, spying Green Teeth, pushed the lad out of the way, to come right up to the hatch. His mouth opened, as he processed what was happening. But before he could say anything, a dagger pushed through the slit and struck him in the eye with great force. He staggered backwards, the blade still protruding from his skull, and fell to the ground.

Now all was mayhem. Moffat thrashed in the mud. Steel hissed from scabbards. Green Teeth banged on the door and shouted for Turnbull to open up or get the same. When two loud clangs rang out to his left, Turnbull spun round to see a pair of grappling hooks clamping the wall, like a monster's claws. God's wounds, they were under attack! And it was all his fault.

He bent over Moffat, weighing the chances of dragging him back to the tower, but he already looked too far gone. Blood bubbled around the man's eye socket and trickled down his chin. The sentry gripped Turnbull's wrist as he tried to remove the blade. But it wouldn't budge, it was jammed deep in the bone. As the lad continued to tug, a head rose behind one of the grappling hooks. A man hauled himself up, boots scraping stone. Turnbull froze. Then he tore Moffat's fingers free and ran.

Turnbull reached the tower's entrance, just as two men scrambled over the wall and dropped to the ground. For a moment, he thought they might take the horses and be done, but instead, they ignored the beasts and headed straight back for the main gate. They undid the bolts and opened it, allowing a horde of men – perhaps as many as twenty – to rush in. As they poured through, Turnbull jumped inside the tower, to be met by Scrimgeour and Antoine, their faces ashen.

"What the hell is happening?" said the Frenchman.

"We're being attacked," Turnbull spluttered. "Moffat is down, and I think he may be done for. They've scaled the walls and are coming for us."

"I knew it!" said Scrimgeour. She began to ram the door's iron bars into their brackets. The speed at which she worked was remarkable, but as she secured the last bolt, something struck the woodwork with an enormous thud. There was a brief pause, followed by another terrifying impact, which seemed to shake the entire tower to its foundations.

"A battering ram," said Antoine, putting his hands to his head. "Sweet mercy, we cannot stay here and be flattened. Our only hope is to go upstairs and fight them from above."

"You run if ye like," said Scrimgeour. Her eyes were wild, her mouth flecked with spit. "But I'm the keeper o' this tower. It's no' just my hame, it's my whole bloody life. And if anybody wants to take it from me, they'll have to step over my deid body!"

Turnbull watched as she pressed herself against the door, only to flinch with the latest blow. To his astonishment, she was smiling, even as her body shook. He realised that she would not be gainsaid, so he joined his master and raced upstairs. Crichton and Elspeth met them in the hall, and they explained what was going on.

"That bastard Baird," said Crichton.

"No," said Turnbull nervously. "I do not think it's his gang. I think they may be his enemies."

"What? How do you know that?" said Antoine.

The lad hesitated. This was no time to admit his error, in trusting Green Teeth's word. Perhaps that time would never come. Instead, he claimed that the men had shouted threats to Baird as they had stormed the gate.

"Are you sure?" said the Frenchman. "It could be another of his tricks."

"Completely sure. I fear they're here to kill him. And us too, if we're not quick." He despaired about the disaster he had brought upon all of them but forced himself to think. His master was right, there was no way that they could defend themselves in the cellar. The stairwell might be easier, but even there they would soon be overrun by a larger force. They were trapped, then. Or were they? "What about the postern gate?" He rummaged in his purse and pulled out the key he had confiscated from Elspeth. "If we move now, we can escape by that secret passage and take Baird with us!"

His master looked sceptical, but did not offer an alternative. The banging from downstairs grew louder and more terrifying. Elspeth began to cry, prompting Crichton to put an arm around her, his other hand gripping his sword. God's sake, they were all going to die if his master did not make up his mind soon. As the tower shook again and Scrimgeour let out a shriek of demented laughter, Antoine nodded and ushered them to the stairs.

They ran up to the top floor, Elspeth now wailing about going back for her mother, the others insisting that she could not be saved. Baird stood at his door, his face pressed to the hatch. For once, that supercilious grin was gone, replaced by an intense and calculating countenance.

"What happens here?" he urged. "Have my boys come to pay a visit?"

"No," said Turnbull. "I think it is your foes, rather than your friends."

Baird's eyes swept the room for inspiration only to return dejected. He tutted, with the resignation of one who has run out of cards. "Then I suppose ye're off and ye've come to say farewell."

"Not so," said Antoine. "Our orders are to keep you secure, so we will take you with us. Don't try anything foolish though. Are you clear on that?"

The fellow brightened. "As clear as day. But how do ye propose we escape?"

"By the postern gate," said Turnbull. He jerked his head. "That door will take us there. Hurry up, before they're upon us."

Elspeth fumbled for the key to the cell, and all three men readied themselves to receive the prisoner. But as the door swung open, they found Baird peering out of his window. What was this scoundrel up to now?

"It's as I thought," Baird said miserably. "They have men round the back too. We are doomed unless we find another way."

Turnbull's heart sank. Was this it, then? The end of it all? He beckoned Baird forward, so that they were all on the landing together. He put the postern key back in his purse, as if hiding one idea might reveal another. Then it hit him.

"Downstairs!" he shouted. His companions looked perplexed but followed him as he hurtled back down the spiral staircase. He leapt down the steps two at a time, colliding with Baird at one point before picking himself back up. There was more banging from downstairs. Thank God Crichton had strengthened those bars; they surely wouldn't hold out much longer though.

Turnbull stopped at the first floor and tumbled into the garderobe.

"Is this some kind of joke?" his master said.

"No, look." The lad knelt down and peered through the

privy hole, just as he had when he spotted Elspeth three nights ago. "The shaft is just big enough for us to pass through. And if there's anywhere they won't be guarding, it's surely the cesspit!"

Turnbull realised that his companions were looking at him as if he were mad. Baird laughed. "Well, at least it will be a soft landing. And it seems to be our only hope, so if naebody else wants to try it, I will."

He pushed himself to the front and put a boot on the edge of the privy.

"Oh no, you don't," said Antoine, barring his way. "You'll be the last one out. Otherwise, you'll be off into the night. Crichton, you go first. Then see if you can break Elspeth's fall. We will follow you, but do not wait for us."

The sentry sheathed his sword and climbed into the privy shaft. Even in his state of urgency, he winced at the stench that surrounded him. Then he let go of the edge and plummeted to the ground. He landed in the cesspit with a splash, and Turnbull was relieved when he picked himself up and whispered that all was clear. Blenching from the smell, Crichton turned for Elspeth. The girl lowered herself into the hole. She moaned again about wanting to go back for her mother, but as Scrimgeour's ravings rose up the stairwell, Elspeth seemed to accept that was impossible. She let herself go and was gathered up by Crichton. He took her hand and, with a brief glance back at the others, they ran off into the night.

"Right, who's next?" Baird asked, a hint of urgency in his voice now. There was a sound of wood smashing downstairs. Turnbull really wanted to be the next one to escape, but he knew he couldn't – not after what he had done.

"You go, sir," he said.

Antoine frowned. "What, and leave you here, with him?"

"He has nowhere else to go; they'll kill him if they catch him. Now hurry, and I'll follow."

"Very well, but be quick yourself. Then we'll both get him to the woods."

The Frenchman entered the privy shaft, grimacing as the rough stone grazed his burnt arm. He plunged to the ground, stood up, and took his sword out again.

Back in the tower, there was more shattering of wood. Metal breaking. Turnbull wondered if he should let Baird go first, but his guilt did not extend that far. He squeezed into the stinking hole and instantly let go, hurtling through the fresh night air only to land with a squelch in the dark filth of the cesspit. By God, it was disgusting. He held his breath as he gazed back up to the privy and prepared to secure the prisoner again.

But instead of lowering his feet, Baird pushed his face into the hole. "See to yerselves, gentlemen. I've had a change o' plan."

Chapter 26

Antoine tried to ignore the stench that enveloped him, the wet, cloying feel of his clothes, as he stared back at Baird.

"I'm sorry to leave ye in the shit," the prisoner laughed. "But I think the postern gate is free after all."

He held up the key, and Antoine groaned: the reiver must have lifted it from Turnbull, when they collided on the stairs. Had this raid been a ruse, after all? And yet, Baird's tone did not seem to have the malice of an enemy who had dealt a deadly blow. It was more like that of a child who had played a trick on his friends.

"The postern is just round the corner," Antoine protested weakly. "We'll pick you up there, when you land."

"No ye won't," said Baird and he disappeared from the privy hatch, just as a tremendous crash echoed from within the tower. Men began to cheer. Scrimgeour let out a series of dreadful screams, before stopping abruptly. Horses whinnied, no doubt terrified by the chaos unfolding around them. Antoine wished that he could see through the walls, but it was clear that the tower had been taken. They needed to escape – and recover their prisoner if they could.

He took Turnbull's elbow, and they raced off towards the postern. They would surely get there first, for Baird would have to climb a flight of stairs, just to reach the inner door, then unlock it, negotiate the outside stairs in the dark and descend through the side return to the gate.

Sure enough, as they came round the corner, Baird was still edging his way down the side of the tower. The great stone mass blocked the moonlight from this angle, meaning that he would have been invisible in the shadows, were they not looking for him. He lowered his head as if he were watching them too. Then he resumed his slow progress – only to freeze and push himself against the brickwork, so that he practically disappeared. Was he having second thoughts? Either way, the hesitation meant that they should be able to catch him.

Antoine nudged Turnbull to follow him to the gate. But the lad was not paying attention to the tower. He was looking beyond, towards the far corner of the outer wall. Three men were running their way. To Antoine's horror, the men were pointing at them – rather than at the dark figure who had melted into the face of the tower. So that was why Baird had stopped.

Turnbull drew his sword and readied himself for the fight. Antoine began to do the same. But when a third man appeared, his silhouette suggesting he was wielding a poleaxe, the Frenchman realised this was a battle they could not win. He thought of distracting them, by alerting them to Baird's presence overhead. But that would be to condemn the man to certain death. Despite the rogue's myriad of deceptions, he did not deserve that fate. There was only one thing left to do.

"Run!" Antoine shouted as he replaced his sword in its scabbard and spun off towards the woods. They went as fast as they could, but it was difficult in this dim light. The ground was rough, and their feet skidded on the loose stones.

In twenty yards, they would be out of the tower's shadow and into the moonlight, but for now, they must avoid tripping over hidden bushes or boulders. Antoine began to tire. His burnt arm was still not fully healed, and it hurt every time he pumped it forwards. He turned his head to see if their pursuers were still with them and was dismayed to see that they had closed the gap.

All at once, there was a scream, and one of the chasers disappeared from sight. The others pulled to a halt and looked down. Antoine and Turnbull took this as their chance to catch their breath and watch. It seemed that the fellow with the poleaxe had fallen into one of Scrimgeour's ditches and mutilated himself with his own weapon. The others climbed in to help him as he howled in agony.

Satisfied that they were safe, at least for now, Antoine gestured for Turnbull to keep going towards the woods. As he looked back to Ravenscleugh, he saw men on the battlements, setting the tower on fire. Below the walls, a figure was running in the opposite direction; it was Baird, who had used their pursuit to make his own break for it, slipping away unnoticed. As Antoine and Turnbull finally emerged into the moonlight, the prisoner turned towards them, and, like a player leaving the stage to rapturous applause, he waved.

They groped their way through the woods, until they were quite sure that they were not being followed. They stank of shit, from landing in the cesspit, but their nostrils were also filled with the dank, fungal smells of the forest and the acrid tang of burning. As they trudged through the undergrowth, Antoine reflected that he had lost everything: his prisoner, his tower, and most of all, his hope.

As he felt his melancholy growing, his assistant broke the silence. "Sir, this is my fault. I've brought this disaster on us."

Antoine saw some truth in this but saw little point in stating it. "You weren't to know Baird would take the key, any more than I foresaw him stealing my dagger the other night."

"It's not just the key, sir. Those men would never have been at the tower without me."

It was a strange thing to say, but the Frenchman was too tired to pursue it. He sighed. "We have all made mistakes. Baird has outwitted us. As for those men, we have no clue who they might be."

"But sir—"

"No, let's not beat our own backs, lad. Let's just focus on staying alive. What do we do when we come out of these woods? Where do we go? Where are we to stay the night?"

Turnbull put a hand on his master's shoulder, to dip him under a low-hanging branch. "I've been thinking about that," he said carefully. "We need to find a shelter as soon as possible, otherwise we'll be easily spotted. But it can't be just any place, since those attackers might scour the taverns for us. It must be somewhere completely secure."

"You mean the sanctuary at Stow? I'm not sure we'd be safe there, given the way we were tricked the last time."

"No, a little closer than that." He hesitated. "I think we should go to my mother's."

"Your mother's?"

"Yes, think about it. Even on foot, we can make it in a couple of hours. If we can trust anybody, it's her. Indeed, she'll be glad of the company. We can eat, make a plan. Most of all, we can borrow some horses." He paused, and his voice cracked. "Do you think Carbonel and Fogo will be alright, sir?"

Antoine groaned at the thought that they would not see their faithful friends again: yet another loss. But he reassured Turnbull that reivers would not let good horses burn. And inside, he was pleased that the lad seemed to be himself again. Likewise, he had exorcised his own guilt about returning to France, for there was no chance of that now. As they reached the edge of the woods, he found comfort in the idea that, whatever happened next, there would be no more secrets between them.

Turnbull breathed a sigh of relief that his master had accepted his story about seeking sanctuary with his mother. In truth, he was not going there to seek protection, but to give it.

He was terrified by what Green Teeth's friends might do to her, now that he had thwarted their plot to seize Baird. So whatever other plans he and his master might need to make, they had to get to her farmstead first. He quickened his pace, as they climbed into the moors.

It was difficult to navigate at this hour, even with the moon's assistance. The towns and villages had extinguished their fires for the curfew, making the hills blend into the black. It was as if somebody had smeared the whole valley with molten pitch. Only Ravenscleugh's tower of fire stood out on the horizon behind them. As Turnbull gazed back at it, he was sickened by the thought that, even if the horses had survived, the flames would be consuming Scrimgeour and Moffat, thanks to his recklessness. He could only pray that they had already died from their wounds, before the blaze took hold. Now he must turn his back on them and look after the living.

"I wish I knew who we were up against," said his master as they crept along a grassy ridge. They were taking care not to crest it, lest their silhouettes gave them away. "My fear is that it's Hamilton. Perhaps Baird let something slip when they spoke alone, so he sent his men back to silence him."

"Hamilton's men are from the West," said Turnbull uneasily. "I think these men were local." He hesitated while he wrestled with how much more to say. "Perhaps they're from the gang that fought the Bairds at Midsummer?"

"Well, whoever it is, we need to stay out of their way until we know what we are doing."

Turnbull agreed, even though he knew they might be hurtling towards their attackers at that very moment.

After another hour of tramping through the hills, they came to the burn where Turnbull had fished as a child – and where he had ambushed Erskine a week ago. He could work out the rest of the way from here. They followed the burn upstream, before cutting across those marshes that he had once tried to drain. The ground was reassuringly sticky underfoot. It took them to the drystane dyke, which ran all the way to the farmstead. Trailing a hand on the wall's mossy stones, he led his master up the hill to the yard. They were almost there. Turnbull's heart pounded with anxiety but also the hope that they were not too late.

The moon passed behind a cloud as they came upon the house. All was deadly quiet, as it should be at this hour. The shutters were closed. But to Turnbull's horror, the door was slightly ajar. A little light crept through the gap. It was just enough to illuminate a stranger's horse.

Chapter 27

Antoine gripped Turnbull's arm as the lad made to run towards the house. Silently, he gestured for him to stay calm. After all, couldn't there be an innocent explanation for this visitor? A neighbour checking on a lonely widow? A traveller, who had lost his way? No, the boy was right to be alarmed. Nobody would come all the way up here at this time of night without good reason. Unless, of course, they had a bad reason.

"Can you see anybody else?" Antoine whispered.

"I don't think so," said Turnbull, his breath heavy as if he had run all the way from Ravenscleugh.

"Is there another door?"

"No, just that one."

"Then let's get either side of it, without making a sound."

Antoine let go of him and peeled off to the left, creeping as if on broken glass. He could just make out Turnbull on the other side, his jaw clenched, eyes fixed on the open door. He eased his sword out of its scabbard, allowing enough noise to prompt the lad to do the same, without alerting whoever was in the house.

Only a few more steps to go. He felt something scratch at his legs: the thistles that Turnbull's mother had been cutting the other day. He used his sword to brush them aside. In the process, he hit something metal – a pail or churn, perhaps? – but escaped with the lightest of taps. The horse turned to stare at him, its eyes aglow, but it did not make a sound.

They were either side of the door now. Antoine stopped again, craning his neck towards the gap. All he could see was the flicker of a low fire. He heard a log spit and crackle. Then, as he inched closer, he felt his foot stick, as if he had stood in wet paint. He lowered his eyes and saw that a pool of dark liquid had gathered on the threshold.

Unable to help himself, Antoine took a deep intake of breath. The sudden noise caused the horse to stamp a hoof. Turnbull's eyes caught up with the cause of the commotion, and he, too, gasped. The lad threw the door open, and they burst into the room. In front of them lay a man, whose throat had been cut from ear to ear. And on the other side of the hearth stood his mother, holding her scythe. The curved blade glistened in the firelight.

"You took your time," she said blankly. Then, wrinkling her nose, she added: "And what the hell's that smell?"

Turnbull ran to his mother to embrace her, but she held him at arm's length. It was not just the state of their clothes, Antoine thought, although, by God, they stank. Her face was curiously free of emotion, her body rigid, her mind elsewhere. The Frenchman had seen this expression before, on the battlefield. It was the look of someone who had killed for the first time. He gently removed the scythe from her hand and set it against the wall, before guiding her onto a stool.

"What happened? Did he hurt you?" said Turnbull, as soon as she had sat down, but Antoine told him to wait a moment. He went to the cauldron and doled out a bowl of broth. Giving it to Turnbull's mother, he proceeded to tell her their own story, as she cupped her hands and let the liquid warm her bones. He took his time, made their situation sound less perilous than it was and even made light of their "baptism" in the cesspit. Only when he had seen a little life return to her eyes did he encourage her to say her own piece.

"He came about an hour ago," she said, nodding to the man on the ground. "I was already abed when I heard a horse come up the hill. I've no' been a good sleeper since your father died, ye ken. Too many worries, nobody to share them wi'."

Turnbull bowed his head as she continued. "I thought it was a queer thing, for anyone to come at this hour. So I went to the windae. Through the crack in the shutters, I saw a young fellae tie up his horse, and make his way to the door."

"Did you recognise the man?" said Antoine.

"No," said the woman. "But he looked nervous. His hands were shaking by his sides, as if he wasnae looking forward to his visit." She turned to her son. "For a second, I feared it was a messenger, wi' some ill news o' ye, Dod. Some lackey o' Lord Albany, to say that ye'd been slain. But then I saw the fellae take out his sword, and I kent it was me that Death was after. Mair important, I kent I didnae want to go wi' him."

Turnbull squeezed her hand. "So what did you do?"

"I hid behind the door and held my breath awhile."

"And then?"

"When he pushed the door open, I hooked him wi' my scythe, as if *I* were the Grim Reaper and no' him."

Antoine went over to the body, while Turnbull attended to his mother. The man's legs were crossed at the ankles, lending him a curiously peaceful demeanour. His long, dark hair fanned out around his neck, becoming congealed with his blood and the rushes and the mud of the floor. He looked about the same age as Turnbull, a youth in grown-up garb. Perhaps he had been undone by thoughts of his own mother as he crept into the house. Or perhaps he had just been beaten by a widow's determination to survive.

Antoine peered at the corpse's face. "Did he say anything before he died?"

Turnbull's mother frowned. "The poor laddie had nae time. Went down like a sack o' turnips, then was gone in seconds."

"I see. Do you have any idea why he came here in the first place?"

"I have nae idea." She looked to her son, but he turned away. "Oh, monsieur. I'm no' going to be in trouble, am I?"

"No," said Antoine. At least not with us, he added to himself. He knelt down and felt around the dead man's body. It was still soft, as if he were just sleeping. A purse dangled from his belt, but it contained nothing of interest, beyond a couple of small coins. His clothes were unremarkable too: just a leather jack, wadmol shirt, dark hose and a rough wool cloak. Except, wait a moment, what was that brooch on his shoulder? It was a nicely wrought piece, consisting of three stars, but the bottom had been snapped off. It looked familiar somehow. Antoine racked his brain, trying to think of where he'd seen it before. Then he had it.

"Turnbull, where's your heart?"

The lad was offended. "I am caring for her the best I can, sir."

"No, not like that. I mean, where's the silver heart that you found beside Dewar's body?"

Turnbull remained perplexed as he rummaged about for the piece of jewellery and gave it to his master. Antoine unclipped the dead man's shoulder brooch and held both pieces together. It was as he'd thought: they fitted perfectly. Three stars above a heart: the very same design that they had seen fluttering on the banners at Tantallon Castle, two weeks ago. It made his own heart flutter.

"So much for being a love token," he said. "This is the Douglas coat of arms."

"Wait, then it is the Douglases who killed Dewar?"

"It looks like it. This bit must have snapped off as they fought on that hill. More importantly, this suggests they also raided Ravenscleugh tonight." Antoine stood up, still holding the two pieces of jewellery together. He shook his head in dismay. "I told Lord Douglas all about the tower's defences when I was at Newark. I practically invited him in."

Turnbull looked uneasy. "As you said, sir, let's not beat our own backs. But let me get this straight: do you think that everything Douglas told you is a pack of lies?"

"Not necessarily. He might be right that Hamilton is plotting to kill the king. But what's clear is that Douglas wants the evidence and will kill anybody who gets in his way."

"Including us?"

"I fear so. And even those we love."

Turnbull glanced at his mother. She was holding her bowl in her lap, while staring into the fire. He turned back to his master. "I should have been here to protect her from this."

"It is hardly your fault that they have visited her."

Turnbull's chin trembled. "She told me that she needed me."

"We're both here now, that's all that matters. Let's get her abed and make a plan. I say we sleep in shifts tonight, lest this man's confederates come looking for him. We can prepare some horses in the morning. Then perhaps we take her to your uncle's. She said he was up at the sheilings, didn't she?"

"Yes."

"Right. Let's get this fellow out of here. We can give him a decent burial tomorrow, but I don't want him stinking out the place. We are doing quite enough of that ourselves."

Chapter 28

It was a long night. Turnbull took the first watch, but Antoine found it difficult to sleep, after all that had happened that day. The wind was strong up on the hill, and each time the breeze caused the timbers of the house to groan, the Frenchman would wake up. By the time Turnbull roused him to change places, he felt like he had barely shut his eyes. Exhausted, he propped himself up by the door and kept himself alert by thinking out their next move.

If Lord Albany were here, they would surely make for Edinburgh, to warn him of Hamilton's suspected plot and Douglas's murderous response. But with their master in France, there was nobody to tell beyond his slimy secretary. That hen-heart Pentland would not wish to take on either of these great men, with such paltry evidence. For what did they really have beyond a broken brooch and some tavern gossip? No, if they were to make any accusations, they needed to be on firm ground, otherwise they themselves would be in grave danger. That meant recapturing Baird, to find out what he possessed.

But how could they find him, before Douglas or Hamilton did? An idea came to Antoine, just as the cockerel crowed for morning.

"Stumpy Watt?" said Turnbull, as he dumped the last shovelful of earth on the grave they had dug for last night's intruder. After Green Teeth's false deal – the rotten fruit of which he was burying right now – he was in no hurry to parlay with another reiver.

"Yes," said his master. "He rode with Baird for years, remember? If anybody can find him, it's him."

"But can we trust him? He was not keen to help, when last we visited."

"I fear we have no choice. Assuming Baird has returned to the forest – as I am sure he has – finding him will be nigh impossible. The place will be crawling with the Douglases by now – and Hamilton's men as well, perhaps. They'll be able to cover far more ground than us, but if we have a guide, we might yet outwit them."

Turnbull leant on the shovel as he thought about it. His master was right, of course: to foil this plot, they needed to get their hands on Baird. But that would mean leaving his mother again. As he saw her coming out of the house with a pail of well water, he felt his guilt return.

"Something to clean ye up," she said, putting the pail down and taking a scrubbing brush from her apron. Turnbull was relieved to see that she looked more like her old self. Indeed, she appeared strangely content.

"Thank you," said Antoine, as he began to scrub the filth from his hose. "I hope you're feeling better this morning?"

"Much better, monsieur. I was surprised last night, that's all."

"You were lucky," said Turnbull, taking the brush from his master. "Still, you're alive, and that's the main thing."

"Aye," she beamed. "And you're here too. Now we can look after each other again."

God's teeth, thought Turnbull. She thinks I will be staying. No wonder she's so happy: she's still in shock. "Mother," he said hesitantly. "This place is not safe for any of us now. It's better that we take you to Uncle John's, so he can look after you."

Her face crumpled. "What, ye're going then?"

"I'm afraid so. We must continue with our mission. There's talk the little king is threatened."

"Then let your master protect him, while you stay here wi' me."

For a moment, Turnbull flirted with the notion, but it was impossible. He had made his choice on this a long time ago. "I'm sorry. We have work to do. I beg you, come with us, and I'll make sure that you're safe."

Her face stiffened. "No, you go if ye like. But I willnae leave here. It's my hame, it's all I ken."

Turnbull was disturbed by the echo of Widow Scrimgeour's words before she perished in her tower. Why were folk so wedded to their land here? Such talk only pushed him out into a world where people came and went as they pleased. He set the pail of water aside and made one final plea. "If you really won't come with us, then let us leave you some money to hire help."

"I dinnae need your money, I telt ye that the last time," his mother said hotly. Then, something made her soften. "Listen, dinnae worry. I'll get some help in, when I find someone I can trust. Meanwhile, if last night has taught me anything, it's that I can look after myself." She turned to Antoine. "Just promise me this, monsieur. Whatever this mission of yours is, make sure it counts for something. Put an end to all this bloodshed, spare other mothers from their pain."

"We will do our best," said the Frenchman.

Turnbull agreed, but as he said farewell to her, he worried that he no longer knew what those words meant.

———

They took the intruder's horse and a nag from the stable and reached Stumpy Watt's farmstead by mid-morning. The reiver and his wife were outside, picking gooseberries. Their three scrawny girls filled baskets of their own, while singing a lullaby. It was a little early in the season to be harvesting this fruit, thought Antoine: a sign of hunger perhaps. He was ashamed to think it, but the family's desperation might help.

"Good morrow to you. I didn't think we'd meet again, but we may have further use of you."

Stumpy set his basket down, and Antoine felt he saw the man redden, as if he were embarrassed to be caught doing such lowly work. "Oh aye? And why would that be?"

"Your old master turned out to be just as clever as you suggested. Escaped from Ravenscleugh last night. Now we need someone to help us get him back."

Stumpy laughed. "That's Will for ye. But I've telt ye afore. I'll do nothing to betray him."

Turnbull came closer and took out his purse. "You wouldn't be betraying him. You would be saving him from certain death."

"What do ye mean?"

"Some very dangerous men are after him."

"Dangerous men?" said Stumpy's wife, gripping her husband's arm. "Then dinnae go wi' them, Watt. Ye owe nae favours to anybody, save me and the bairns."

The old reiver looked exasperated. "It was you that took their money last time."

"Aye, because all I had to do was pass on what I'd seen.

This is different. What happens if ye're killed? All the coins in Christendom willnae help us, then."

Stumpy bit his lip as he considered this. But there was a glint in his eye, as if some old flame had been reignited.

Antoine saw it and nodded to the purse. "We'll pay two times what we gave you last time, if you can take us to Baird's lair. Three times, if you deliver Baird himself."

"No, my wife is right. The reward must match the risk. So six times the coin, just to find the lair. Then catching Will is up to you."

By Christ, the man might be dressed in rags, but he was a better negotiator than many of those gold-chained fops that Antoine had known as a diplomat. The Frenchman moved to close the deal. "Four times, and that's our final offer. Not bad for doing your old friend a kindness."

Stumpy's wife shook her head. "Ye promised me ye wouldnae ride again."

"Aye," said her husband. "But I promised I'd provide for ye as well." He turned to the visitors. "Very well, I'll do it. But ye must tell me everything ye ken about Will and what he's up to. That's the way he taught us: 'A hunter must climb into the mind o' his prey.' Now it's time to climb inside *his* heid, for once."

It took the best part of an hour to explain all the goings on of the last two weeks. To Antoine's irritation, Stumpy asked questions about every tiny detail: how exactly did Baird escape, what was he wearing, what had his mood been like and much more besides. Antoine was beginning to doubt the wisdom of enlisting him, when he told his eldest daughter to fetch his horse.

"Right. I think we're ready to go," he said, pointing due west to a group of low, wooded hills. "If Will was coming straight from Ravenscleugh, he'd head for the nearest safe entrance to the forest, which would be exactly yonder. Any further south, and he might run into the Douglases, coming up frae Newark. Any further north and the woods become too thick for a horse."

"But the man escaped on foot," snapped Antoine. "How many times do I have to tell you?"

Stumpy smiled. "Will Baird might have *escaped* on foot, sir. But if I ken him right, he'll have stolen a nag frae the first farm he passed. He probably reached the forest last night, while you honest gentlemen were still puffing your way over the moors. Now, if ye want to catch up wi' him, think like thieves and follow me."

They set off at a gallop, over the mosses, with Stumpy leading the way. It was remarkable the way he guided his horse with just one hand. Antoine and Turnbull were still getting used to their new mounts and could barely keep up with him as he took them across foul-smelling marshes, scree-strewn hills and slippery-grassed valleys.

Eventually, they came to the foot of the hillocks that Stumpy had pointed out from his house. And yet, where was this forest entrance that he had spoken of? Had he been mistaken? Or could this even be a trick? It occurred to Antoine that the giant could easily have lured them to this lonely spot to rob them. Except the fellow looked as if he were in no mood to abandon their adventure just yet. After his initial reluctance, he now bore the countenance of someone in his element. Someone who could do more than pick gooseberries all day.

"I ken what ye're thinking," said Stumpy as they

approached the wall of green. "There's no way in here, is there? And for anyone save us, there isnae. But a few years ago, we created a set o' secret passages, so we could get our horses in and out o' the forest as we pleased."

Antoine and Turnbull watched as he padded over to a patch of hawthorns and dismounted. He peered through the tangle of branches, and then, apparently satisfied by what he found, he reached down to the base of the thicket and pulled at some thick stems. The bushes moved. They were not growing at all; they had been placed there as a covering! With a few more jerks, he had cleared away four or five huge pieces of vegetation, to reveal a gap which was just big enough for a horse to pass through.

"This way," he called. For once, he let Antoine and Turnbull go in front, so that he could replace the hawthorns and get back on his horse. The three of them continued down a long, dark corridor. Antoine had never seen anything like it before: a tunnel, fashioned from nature. Stumpy explained that the path was tended regularly, so that it could be traversed safely in the dark. The branches had even been cut to an exact specification, so that a local nag could pass, but not the larger horses that the authorities might use. Talk of this made Antoine miss Carbonel again. But in truth, his old friend would be of no use here.

They squeezed their way down the verdant passage, completely hidden from the outside world. After a few hundred yards, they came to a clearing, and Stumpy manoeuvred his horse to the front. He cast about on the ground, looking for tracks. There was a jumble of faded hoofprints to the left, as if a sizeable band had gathered there some time ago. But Stumpy pointed to a single set, leading off to the right. These marks were crisper, deeper, fresher.

The dew was undisturbed. Whoever this was had come through last night.

They picked up the trail, as it led round a ragged copse of birch trees and into a lush meadow. It reminded Antoine of the spot where he had met Lady Janet's hunters. He knew that place must be far away, but he was disturbed by the sensation of being watched. The ill feeling continued to dog him as they followed the trail across a heath, then around a collection of strange-shaped rocks from which a natural spring bubbled. The water made the ground muddy, and the tracks became deeper. The trail seemed to lead on, quite obviously, into some long grass. So why had Stumpy stopped?

The reiver wheeled his horse about and swore under his breath. "Urgh, this is a false trail. Will's used the mud to make it look like he's headed up that way, but I think he's doubled back over there, where the ground becomes harder and he becomes impossible to track." He pointed to a thin strip of stony ground branching off from the trail.

"Are you sure?" said Antoine.

Stumpy shrugged. "No, but it's a favourite trick o' his."

"So we abandon this path?"

"Not only that, but we go in the opposite direction. And quick, for we've wasted enough time on this already."

He spurred his horse, and they followed, exchanging nervous glances. As Stumpy had predicted, there were no more prints to follow from this point, so they had to rely on his intuition. He spotted a circle of stones where someone had made a fire, but the ashes were clearly old. He found a makeshift hut, only to discount it as a poacher's hide. However, when they came upon an open meadow, Stumpy became more animated.

"Ah, I remember this place," he said in a hushed voice. "Ye see those oak trees at the far end? They look like a mass o' trunks, but they're actually a hollow ring. We made camp in there many a time. I'll wager that's where Will is now. But watch, we need to be careful if we're to catch him."

He led them back a hundred yards, so that they could swing round from behind a rambling spinney of elms and blackthorns. Turnbull asked whether they should dismount, but Stumpy whispered that they would never catch Baird if they did so. Instead, they hunkered down in their saddles, leaning over their horses' shoulders to make themselves as small as possible. They got to within a hundred yards of the oak ring and saw a gap in the trees, through which a barrel was visible. A man was leaning against it, perhaps sleeping off last night's ale. Could it even be Baird himself? Maybe this would be easier than Antoine had thought.

It was almost time for the final run-in. Antoine eased himself up in his saddle, so that he would be ready to charge forwards. He gestured for Turnbull to do the same. But he noticed that Stumpy seemed preoccupied by the meadow to their left. The long grass lay as flat as floor rushes, so there could surely be nobody lurking there. Ah, hold on, he was looking at a pink face, just visible through some bushes on the side of the outlaws' camp. The fellow seemed to be staring back.

"Do you think he's spotted us?" whispered Antoine, distraught that they might have been foiled at the last.

"No, I think he's dead. And if we're no' careful, we will be too."

Chapter 29

In a matter of moments, all three men were at the entrance to the camp. Sure enough, the sentry was as dead as stone. The man by the barrel was not sleeping either. There was no sign of Baird, but at least three more bodies were sprawled about the clearing, all motionless, marinating in their own blood. One of them, draped over a mossy log, looked young enough to be a child.

"What a sight," said Antoine as they dismounted.

"I knew we were in trouble, when I saw that trampled grass," agreed Stumpy miserably. "It takes twenty horse or mair to make a mess like that. And only at a gallop."

They went over to the sentry. The man's eyes remained wide open, in an expression of eternal vigilance, but they now realised that he was only sitting upright because his head had slumped forwards, supported by the thorns. Stumpy lifted it back. "One o' Will's men, alright." He touched the man's skin and frowned. "Still warm as well. Whoever did this probably passed through in the last hour."

Antoine's heart quickened. "They might still be nearby, then."

"Aye, we'd better take a look about, then get gone while we can."

They hastily checked the bodies, although Antoine

doubted that they would yield anything useful. Whoever had attacked this place had known exactly what they were after and would not have left without it – or him. If only Stumpy had not wasted all that time with those questions – or by taking them on that false trail. On the other hand, perhaps the delay had been a Godsend. Otherwise, their bodies might have lain here too.

After inspecting the sentry and the fellow by the barrel, they came to two redheaded men lying on their backs. They were strikingly similar, their mutilated bodies arranged symmetrically, hands almost touching, as if they had become one in death. "Ah, the Petrie twins," said Stumpy sadly. "Will's deputies, these days. Brave lads and clever wi' it. What a world this is, what a terrible waste…"

As the old reiver mourned his former comrades, Antoine checked the rest of the camp. He had noticed that all the bodies had been wounded from above – with downward blows to their shoulders, necks and faces. That suggested the attackers had not dismounted. Perhaps there was the slimmest of chances that they had missed something on the ground. He started by picking through a stack of spears, but all it showed was that the attackers had come and gone quickly, otherwise they would have taken the weapons with them. A pile of blankets was similarly unhelpful. But as he turned his head from them, the Frenchman noticed something extraordinary.

The child's body was no longer draped across the log. It had moved a good four feet towards the outer ring of trees. Antoine scratched his head. Could the boy still be alive? No, he was lying spreadeagled, his face as bloody as a butcher's hands. So was he imagining this? Again, impossible: a dead child was always a horrible thing to behold, and he could remember exactly how this one had first appeared, even in the chaos of their arrival. There was something very strange going on, then.

Antoine took a couple of steps forward, his eyes not leaving the body. It remained exactly where it was. He came a little closer. Again, the child did not budge, but was that a new smear of blood leading from the log to the body's current position? And was that little chest moving, ever so slightly?

As he scrutinised the body, an eye opened. It met Antoine's. Both parties froze. Then the child was up and running as if he had never been more alive.

"Stop!" shouted the Frenchman, but the boy was as agile as a monkey. He leapt over the log that had been his grave until a few seconds ago. Turnbull came running to help, but the child escaped his flailing arms. Changing direction this way and that, the lad almost made it to the entrance of camp when he collided with the enormous figure of Stumpy Watt.

"Slow down, little fellae. We're no' here to hurt ye."

The child stared back at the reiver, a mixture of insolence and terror in his eyes. The others came over, still reeling from this discovery. As Antoine caught his breath, he saw how cleverly the boy had smeared himself with others' gore. He could only have been twelve years old, but he had the wit and cunning of the forest, alright.

"We're friends of Will. We want to save him and catch the folk who did this."

The boy frowned. "My master never mentioned a Frenchie friend."

"No, but perhaps he mentioned me?" said Stumpy. "Ye must be new, but afore the Petrie twins, God rest their souls, I was Will's right-hand man. Until fate played this wee joke on me."

He raised his right hand, and a look of awe came over the child. "Stumpy Watt?"

"Aye, wee man. Now tell us who ye are and what's gone on here this morning."

The child seemed reassured that the visitors were not hostile, so, with a deep breath, he launched into his story. "Very well. My name is Francis Bromfield, but most folk call me Fleabite. I was orphaned in an English raid, and when Will heard o' it, he took me under his wing. I've been wi' him ever since. As for this morning, most of our lads were out hunting, when this other lot attacked."

Stumpy shook his head. "And Will – was he even here at all?"

"Aye, ye've just missed him. He was off like a cannonball, before they could get their filthy hands on him."

"Did they take anything, these attackers?" urged Antoine.

"No, a couple raked about our stuff, just like you were doing earlier. But the rest chased after Will."

"And do you know who they were?"

"Of course. They were the Douglases. They've been on our tails for weeks."

Antoine looked carefully at the boy. There was a certain innocence to him, despite his feral appearance. He might be caked in dirt and blood, but his hazel eyes still sparkled. The Frenchman decided the child could be trusted. The question was whether he understood what he had witnessed.

"You're sure it was the Douglases?"

"Aye, sir. They cried their name as they charged in."

Antoine nodded. This was the custom in the Marches, but it could easily be abused. "They couldn't have been the Hamiltons in disguise?"

"I am sorry, sir. I've never heard o' them. Only the Douglases. The men have talked o' little else this month."

Antoine sighed. If the boy hadn't even heard of such a great family, it put his whole testimony in doubt. Still, it would be worth hearing what he *did* know, just in case. He told Fleabite to explain what all this "talk" had been about.

"Very well. Two weeks ago, one o' our men, Cottar Craig, met a manservant on the road to Selkirk. This servant was in a right state. Said that he was leaving town and needed money and shelter for a while. Claimed he had some goods that might help to spring Will and would we make a deal wi' him."

Turnbull leant in. "Did he say what these goods were?"

"That's the strange thing. All he had was some rotten letter and a book. The letter had been written by his master, who'd just killed himself. The book was some dusty old gubbins that belonged to him as well. Ye wouldnae think they'd fetch a bawbee at the market, but this servant said they'd something to do wi' the royal family, and Lord Douglas would pay handsomely for them. He said if we could get them to His Lordship, he might even set our master free."

"He mentioned Lord Douglas and Will specifically?"

"Aye."

"So what did your man do?"

"Well, Cottar cannae read, but he thought this sounded tasty, so he led this servant through the forest on the promise o' showing it to the others. But once he had him truly lost, he took the goods and sent him on his way. The servant argued and tried to get his things back, but Cottar is a big lad, so eventually, the man gave up and ran off into the hills."

"And Cottar brought the stuff back here."

"Aye. The Petries can read…" The boy broke off to

glance at the twins' bodies before correcting himself. "I mean, they *could* read, so they took the letter and the book away. Frae that point on, the two o' them acted like they were guarding the crown jewels. They wouldnae tell the rest o' us exactly what they'd found; they just said we were to lie low until they'd worked out what to do wi' it."

Turnbull creased his brow. "I imagine that did not sit well with some."

"No, there was a lot o' bitching amongst the men. We're no' supposed to have secrets frae each other. So on Midsummer's Eve, some o' the younger lads went off into town to search for the Douglases. They thought they could strike a bargain wi' them. The thing is, the Douglases are a haughty lot and said they wouldnae deal wi' forest folk. They attacked our lads, and later, we heard they'd killed the servant too. We've been fending them off ever since, while squabbling amongst ourselves."

"What a mess," said Stumpy. "Will wouldnae like to hear o' this."

No, thought Antoine. Unless he had known something all along? In the tower, Baird had switched between blissful ignorance of the outside world and dark hints of coming change. Had he been bluffing, or had he known more than he'd let on?

When asked, the boy was certain. "We've had no contact wi' him since he gave himself up, so I'm sure the first he heard o' it was last night. He telt us that some reivers had attacked Ravenscleugh, wi' the idea o' killing him, but that he'd escaped in the stramash. He thought he recognised them as Douglases, and we explained why that might be so. At first he was angry wi' how we'd handled things, but he changed once he'd read those precious bloody texts. He even slept wi' them last night, and when he rose, he talked o' taking them to Edinburgh. He was just saddling up when the Douglases attacked."

"So he took the book and letter with him?"

"Aye," said Fleabite. "I saw him put them in a bag. He shouted for me to run to him, but I was too afeart to move. He called again, but it was like my legs had turned to stone. So he spurred his horse and sped off, but as he went, he looked at me, and I was shocked by his countenance."

"What do you mean?" said Antoine.

"He didnae look his normal self. Nor even a proper grown-up. He looked worried. Scared. Alone." Fleabite's chin trembled. "He looked like he might cry."

Chapter 30

Stumpy comforted Fleabite as the boy was finally overcome by the horrors that he had witnessed that morning. Meanwhile, Turnbull drew Antoine aside.

"What do you think, then? Can we trust him?"

"Look at him," said the Frenchman, nodding backwards. "There's not a chance that a child could act out such a performance."

"Then it's the Douglases behind all this?"

"I think so. But perhaps only because the Hamiltons are plotting something even worse." Antoine stroked his beard. "I wonder if that's why Baird is on his way to Edinburgh now. If he has evidence that incriminates Lord Hamilton, he might hope to bring it to him, so that he can destroy it. Then that blaggard will grant Baird a pardon in return."

Turnbull groaned. "They probably stitched the bargain up, in their private meeting at Ravenscleugh."

"Perhaps. But then how did Hamilton know that Baird would soon be out, to secure the book and letter? Unless it was his men that stormed Ravenscleugh after all?"

Turnbull felt uneasy. If there was one thing he was sure of, it was that the Douglases were behind that attack. After all, it had been Green Teeth who had led the charge on the tower and Green Teeth who had sent a man to his mother's, wearing a Douglas brooch. The trouble was, he could not explain any of this to his master. He was relieved when Stumpy came over, with Fleabite under his arm.

"Well, gentlemen, have ye formed a plan?"

"By the sounds of it, we should be on the road to Edinburgh," said Turnbull cagily.

"Aye," said Stumpy. "That's what the boy says." He hesitated. "Ye promise ye'll treat my old master fairly, if ye find him?"

"We're his best chance," said Turnbull. He was not sure whether he believed that, given their suspicions about Baird's dealings with Hamilton, but he wanted to get going.

"In that case, I have one last thing that might help ye. Whatever the reason he's going to Edinburgh, he'll need to stop somewhere. There's an abandoned bothy house we've used on raids afore. In the moors above Fala, beside a grove of rowans. Ye could do worse than to head there. Just make sure ye get there afore the others."

Stumpy smiled awkwardly, and Turnbull realised that he was waiting for his payment. To be fair, the fellow had kept to his side of the bargain, in finding them the camp. Turnbull withdrew his purse and started counting out some coins.

"Wait," said Antoine. "Perhaps you could take us to this place? You've done well for us so far, and we could do with all the help we can get."

Stumpy scratched his nose. "I dinnae ken about that, sir. I should really be getting hame."

"You know Baird better than any of us."

"You ken him well enough by now. As I say, ye just need to climb into his mind."

"We would make it worth your while?"

Turnbull saw how Stumpy stared at the coins in his palm, but the giant seemed determined to resist temptation.

"No, this adventure has persuaded me that my wife is right: the quiet life is no' so bad," he said, with a rueful smile. He looked down at Fleabite. "And the wee man says the same. We'll let the others bury this lot when they get back frae their hunting. Meanwhile, I'll take him back to ours, and we'll see if we can make farmers o' each other."

With that, he sent the boy off to get the horses, watching him with an unmistakeable fondness, that seemed incongruous upon his craggy features.

Antoine and Turnbull rode all day across the hills, shunning the main paths and any settlements. It was difficult to avoid all human eyes, though, as it was the time of year when many folk were gathering hay, weeding crops, and damming streams to wash their sheep before the shearing. All they could do was slow down, to be less noticeable, then spur the horses again when they were out of sight.

By the time they got past Oxtoun, it was getting dark, and they realised they would not make it to the bothy that Stumpy had talked of. Instead, they needed to think of somewhere to stay themselves.

"What about The Boar's Head?" asked Antoine. "It can't be far from here."

Turnbull screwed up his face. "Might be a bit dangerous with all these Douglases around?"

"Not if there are twenty of them on Baird's tail, like the boy described to us. They'd never fit in a place like that. They'd more likely go to one of Douglas's towers nearby."

"Can we trust the innkeeper, though?"

"He didn't seem one for politicking."

"So he said. But I'm sure we were spied on last time, despite his protestations. Possibly by Fortingale. Remember, I found that nosegay on his body, with the tavern's mark?"

Antoine felt a shiver of guilt, as he had dismissed the notion of an eavesdropper when they had first visited the inn. If he had believed Turnbull back then, could they have somehow prevented these terrible events?

"Perhaps that's all the more reason to visit it," he mused. "It strikes me that Fortingale might hold the key to this. He's the only one Douglas surely can't have killed, since they're both on the same side."

"His wife's equerry."

"Exactly. It would make much more sense for Hamilton to have killed him. We know how agitated Fortingale was, about the safety of the little king: he talked of it when we caught him sneaking about on the border."

Turnbull's eyes lit up. "Perhaps the queen suspected foul play, when Hamilton would not let her see her son at the castle, so she sent Fortingale to spy on us? He followed us to The Boar's Head and on to Lauder, where this business with the Walkerburns was brewing. Then Hamilton had him killed when he got too close to the plot. That would explain his dying words, wouldn't it: 'Tell the queen she must beware.'"

"It might explain a lot more," said Antoine grimly. "Remember, we may be chasing Baird and the Douglases tonight, but if Hamilton means to harm the king, he must be our ultimate quarry. Let's see if we can squeeze anything from the innkeeper before we go abed."

As they approached The Boar's Head, they were greeted by the same raucous sounds as before. But this time, they did not enter the taproom, as they wished to interview the owner in private. Instead, they tied the horses round the back and found a side door that led into the brewery. They pressed the latch and let themselves in. The air was warm and malty, in contrast to their cold determination. The only light came from a tallow candle in the corner. As they picked their way through barrels, vats and mash tuns, Antoine remembered the attack at the tannery and put a hand on the hilt of his sword. There was a door on the far side of the room, which looked like it might lead to an office or suchlike, so they made for that. Turnbull was just about to open it, when a shadow fell upon them.

"Where do ye think ye're going?" said a gruff voice behind them.

They swung round to see the innkeeper, scowling at them. He was holding that cudgel of his with an unmistakeable menace.

"Easy, sir," said Antoine, spreading his arms. "We just wanted to converse with you, without all those topers about."

The innkeeper stared at them, as if trying to put the faces and the accent together. "Hold. You're the Frenchman who passed through a fortnight ago."

Antoine felt that there was a note of fear in the man's voice, as if his words were a statement of guilt as much as recognition. He decided to push on it, but not too hard. Not while that cudgel was an arm's length from his skull. He lifted his right hand slowly, so that the man could see his ring. "Yes, I should have said. I am in Lord Albany's service. I am the Warden of the Eastern Marches, and this is my assistant."

The innkeeper swallowed hard. "And what brings ye here? I telt ye last time, I try to keep a peaceful house."

"Quite so," said Antoine. He noted that the man's grip on his weapon had loosened. It was time to press his advantage. "But as we saw upon our last visit, many people are restless these days. We've come to investigate a plot that might touch upon your tavern."

"We talk of High Treason," said Turnbull. "Now, have you somewhere quiet to discuss this?"

The innkeeper's shoulders dropped, as the gravity of the situation dawned on him. He looked down at his cudgel, and Antoine briefly worried that he might attack them after all, but instead, he used it to rap against a wooden hatch and called for the barmaids to mind the taproom awhile. Gesturing for the visitors to go through the other door, he took the candle and left the weapon outside.

They entered a tiny room, less an office than a den. There was just enough space for three stools and a desk. Antoine quickly surveyed it and found no obvious danger, but he kept the door open and angled his seat in such a way that he could see if anybody tried to join them. The innkeeper took the stool on the far side of the desk, his fingers twiddling as he waited for the interrogation to begin.

"Ah, that's better," said Antoine, as he moved the candle to the centre of the desk. It revealed every worry line and bead of sweat on the innkeeper's jowly face. "This will not take long if you answer all our questions honestly. But please do not dissemble, or it will be the worse for you, you understand?"

The innkeeper nodded meekly.

"Good. Because I fear you may not have been so truthful with us last time. You remember, we thought we had been listened on, but you denied all knowledge of it? Well, since then, we've found the body of an English spy, with one of your nosegays on him. He's linked to a whole list of other murders and possibly to a plot against the king. So you had better tell us if you know aught of him."

The innkeeper clasped his hands. "Upon the Holy Rood, I dinnae. So many folk come here, I cannae remember all o' them."

At first Antoine took the man's movement as a simple plea for mercy, but on closer inspection, he saw that he had also positioned his elbows so that they covered a thin ledger on the desk. So he *was* hiding something. "Perhaps you have records that might prompt your memory?" said the Frenchman sharply.

The man shifted in his seat, his elbows inching forwards again. "Alas, nothing that would help ye here. Folk rarely give their name in places such as this. Especially if they're up to nae good."

"Of course," said Antoine. He narrowed his eyes. "But I'd like a little look at what you have, all the same."

He reached over to grip the edge of the ledger and jerked it from underneath the innkeeper's meaty arms. The man gulped as he passed the book to Turnbull, who wetted a finger and leafed through a few pages of dense handwriting.

"Interesting," said the lad, after a while. "The 19th of June. The evening we arrived. As you say, there are few names. But you've left descriptions, haven't you? Two monks departed that morning, along with some cloth merchants from Lasswade and a horse trader from Selkirk. Then two groups of pilgrims and a stone mason arrived." He smirked. "That last one pissed his bed, according to this."

Antoine tutted. "Never mind all that. Is there anything to interest us?"

Turnbull ran his finger back down the list. "Ah, here we are: 'a Frenchman and his guide.' And look: the very next one must be Fortingale. 'Englishman. Could be trouble.' So it looks like our man did follow us here. And you suspected him of something from the start."

The innkeeper put his head in his hands, while he reconsidered his position. "Ye ken, I think I do remember the fellae now. Slim, wi' a bent nose?" Antoine rolled his eyes at the miraculous return of the man's memory. "He arrived late and sent a stable boy in to fetch me, as he'd ridden all day and wanted to go straight abed. I went out and he complained about the price – that's all I meant by 'trouble'. But he paid up in the end and left afore first light."

"So why did you not tell us of him when we complained of our own trouble, in the morning?"

"He had already gone by then; I didnae see the point."

"The point of reporting an English spy?" said Antoine. "You'll find it on the end of an executioner's axe if you're not careful."

"There was nothing to suggest he was a spy," said the innkeeper desperately. "Why, as I recall, you dismissed the whole idea yerself." He paused to calm himself. "Look, sir, I swear to ye, I ken nothing about this Englishman apart frae the fact he stayed one night here and had a rude way about him. But give me till the morn and I'll find ye something on him. Do we have a bargain?"

Antoine stood up. "Bring us something and we'll see. Now, find us a room and make sure we are safe this time."

Chapter 31

Within minutes of the innkeeper calling on them the next morning, Antoine realised that he had no news. The fellow spent too long enquiring as to their sleep, pulled too many ingratiating smiles. But in a strange way, the lack of substance lent his story credibility. Overnight, Antoine had reminded himself how inconspicuous Fortingale had been: if the innkeeper had plucked a host of witnesses to the Englishman from nowhere, he would not have believed him. No need to let him off the hook just yet though.

"That's it?" said Antoine, with exaggerated dissatisfaction when the man had finished. "He had a chestnut mare and headed south in the morning? It's not exactly the detailed evidence we were after."

"I swear, I've asked everyone about him. The serving maids, the stable boys, my steward, my regulars. It seems the man came and went like a ghost."

"Then you are still in a hole. You knowingly sheltered an English troublemaker. Who is now dead amid talk of treason. At the very least, your inn will have to close. At worst, well, who knows what, these days…"

The innkeeper shook his head in disbelief at the injustice of it. But he had come prepared. His face hardened. "That's a shame. I have other information that might help ye. If I'm to be ruined, I may as well no' bother."

"Whatever you know, I'd give it up. We might be able to help you."

The man suppressed a snort. "Very well. While conducting my enquiries, I heard a tale that struck me sideways. Something unrelated to this Fortingale character, but much mair worrying if ye ask me." He paused to milk the moment. "Apparently, a group of plague cleaners passed through last week. Ye ken the sort. White wands and a' that. They'd been working in Edinburgh, to fend off this dreadful pestilence that sweeps the city."

Antoine nodded. "The rumours were just starting as we left."

"Aye, the rumours," said the innkeeper, with a wink. "They spread quicker than the malady itself, don't they? That's why my steward turned these men away, said they'd scare off our other customers. Anyway, they protested that they'd taken potions to protect themselves and would settle for getting merry in their own room. But again, my man was having none of it. He said their miasma would remain and afflict the next folk to stay. And that's when they shared their secret." Another pause. "There is no plague in Edinburgh. It is all a lie."

"What?" said Antoine and Turnbull together. The innkeeper smiled at their confusion.

"As I said, it is all a lie. They said they were each given fifteen pence a day – have ye ever heard the like? – to enter empty houses and pretend to clean them out. They were to be as obvious as possible. Smoke the places wi' burning heather. Board them up and put red crosses on them. They were even to cart away bundles o' rags, as if they were dead bodies."

"But why?" said Turnbull. "Nobody in their right mind would spread such a panic. And if they did, they would be straight for the block."

"Aye, unless their masters owned the block, if ye take my meaning? These cleaners hinted they'd been paid by someone o' great rank. They wouldnae say who it was; they said it would be the end o' them if they did, but they said someone grand was behind it. Someone that we would a' ken. My steward thought it sounded like a barrel-load o' nonsense, so he sent them on their way. But now ye've come with this talk o' treason, it's got me thinking. What if their story is true? What if this pestilence is all a show? What if *this* is the terrible plot ye're looking for, monsieur?"

The story took Antoine by surprise, and at first, he dismissed it as the usual tavern talk and unrelated to their quest. He told the innkeeper that he was safe for now but that he should send word if he learnt anything more about Fortingale. Meanwhile, if the man had any sense, he should dispose of that ledger.

It was only when they were halfway on the road to Fala that a terrible thought occurred. Could Hamilton have invented this pestilence, to keep the queen away from her son? Worse still, might he plan to use it to murder the little king, without arousing suspicion?

For what better way to kill a child, than under the cover of a plague?

―

The more they talked it through, the more cunning Hamilton's plan appeared. The king would be kept in isolation, away from prying eyes. His symptoms could easily be feigned, perhaps with the help of a friendly doctor. The body would be buried quickly, in order to protect others. No doubt the queen would be distraught, but Hamilton could point to all the public measures he had taken to protect the king. As Douglas had put it, it was a plot murky enough to discredit Albany but not egregious enough for the English to invade.

"It all starts to make sense now," said Antoine.

"Yes," said Turnbull. "And remember those men, who searched Walkerburn's house before us? They were dressed as cleaners too. That's surely too much of a coincidence."

"I agree. But without that book and letter, we can't prove a thing. We've got to catch Baird before he takes all the evidence to Hamilton and destroys it." Antoine spurred his horse. "Now let's find that blasted bothy house."

They arrived in Fala by mid-afternoon. The sun had been beating down all day, and they had ridden the horses hard, so they stopped to let them drink from a burn. As they did so, an old woman appeared. She was driving a dozen or so hefty-looking pigs with a stick and kept her head bowed as she approached. The pigs joined the horses in slaking their thirst, leaving the humans in an awkward silence. It occurred to Turnbull that the woman might be able to help them.

"Good morrow," he said, with a doff of his cap. "Your beasts seem to be fattening up nicely."

"Aye, sir," said the crone. "They eat better than we do these days." A glint came into her eye. "Ye can buy one if ye like? Or all o' them, if ye prefer."

He smiled. "Perhaps we'll come back at Martinmas, when they're good and ready.

Meanwhile, we're looking for a bothy house. A wooden

hut by a rowan grove. If you can point us there, there's a penny in it for you."

"Ah, that's an easy one. It's just over that hill, sir." She nodded towards a low, wooded knoll. "There's no' usually anyone around, but look, there's some smoke above the trees."

The men turned to the east, where a thin column of grey was rising into the buttermilk sky. It could only be half an hour away at most. If it were Baird, they should catch him before he moved on to Edinburgh. But they would need to be quick, for they were not the only ones looking for him. Turnbull pressed a coin into the woman's wrinkled palm and climbed back into the saddle. "Thank ye," she said, with a toothless smile. "And good luck to ye both."

She gave them a curious look – no doubt wondering what these two strangers wanted of some hut in the middle of nowhere – but there was no time for further explanation, as they raced towards the knoll.

They reached the woods in minutes, only to find that the greenery was too thick to pass through on horseback. Turnbull suggested skirting round the edge, but Antoine feared that they might be spotted, so they dismounted and found a sheltered spot where they could tether the beasts, unseen. Then they continued on foot, creeping towards the light that poked through the final tangle of branches and foliage. When they emerged on the other side of the woods, they could see a shack, by a grove of rowan trees, just as Stumpy had described. But they now realised that the smoke was coming from a bonfire in front of the house, not from the house itself.

"Odd," whispered Antoine, and he gestured for Turnbull to join him in a crouching run to a fold in the land.

As they lay there, peering over the edge of the natural ditch, Turnbull began to feel uneasy. Was this some kind of trap? Something wasn't right here. But before he could put a finger on it, the door of the house opened, and a figure emerged: Baird.

Turnbull's heart quickened, and he started to get up, but his master stayed him. "Wait. This may be our only chance to catch him. We mustn't charge in too soon."

The reiver looked about, causing them to duck down for a moment, before rising cautiously again. Seemingly satisfied that nobody was about, Baird picked up some logs from a stack and placed them on the fire. He watched as the flames built and the smoke thickened. A light wind had blown up, causing the clouds to drift to one side. He stood with his hands on his hips, before taking another look around and returning to the house.

"What do you think he's up to?" said Turnbull nervously.

"I don't know. It seems a strange time to light a fire. It's boiling hot out here, and he's supposed to be lying low."

"Yes, he's cleverer than that. All this is doing is slowing him down, when he could be getting off to Edinburgh."

"Then what?"

As Turnbull pondered this, Baird emerged with more logs. Putting them on the fire, he watched with apparent satisfaction, as great rolls of ash and cinder drifted off into the sky. The heavens darkened, as if a storm were coming. Turnbull made to stand up again, and this time, Antoine nodded his approval. But just as the lad straightened, he saw two other faces in the bushes, by the house. Someone else was watching Baird – and they were even closer to their target!

Turnbull flattened himself again and pointed out the

figures to his master. Antoine cursed under his breath. As they stared towards the hut, they could see more men lurking in the bushes. Baird had his back to them and seemed completely oblivious to any of his watchers' presence. He gave the fire a poke with his sword and then returned to the house. For a few moments, nobody moved a muscle. Antoine and Turnbull remained frozen, as it became clear that their rivals were much more numerous and nearer to their prize. The other men seemed undecided too. Then one of the watchers waved a hand and ran forwards, beckoning for the others to come.

"I recognise that fellow," whispered Antoine, as the leader positioned his accomplices in a semi-circle at the front of the house. Turnbull squinted at the man and agreed he looked familiar. It was only when he turned around that he realised it was Green Teeth. God, he hoped his master would not remember him speaking to that foul creature outside The Red Lion. But they had bigger things to worry about now. Green Teeth had reached into the fire and was taking out a log.

The scoundrel held it at arm's length, shielding his face from the intense heat. He gestured for others to do the same. Half a dozen men were soon standing by the front of the house, blazing weapons in their hands. They couldn't possibly mean to torch the house, with Baird still inside? That would make no sense, for if these were the Douglases – and Green Teeth's presence surely meant they were – they needed to recover the evidence against Hamilton in one piece. They must intend to smoke him out, then. Either way, Turnbull felt completely impotent to stop them, as they drew their arms back and let fly.

The first torch landed on the roof. Woosh! The wooden

shack was ablaze in seconds. The next missile bounced off but tumbled onto the ground, where the flames licked against the wall. One by one the men rained fire upon the hut, so that the building looked like something out of hell. The smoke was black and jagged at Turnbull's throat, reminding him of the acrid fumes which had chased them through the forest after that terrible night at Ravenscleugh. Surely Baird could not stay inside much longer? Surely the Douglases would not let him?

Except that as Turnbull watched the door, hoping that the reiver would stagger out, he saw that Green Teeth and his friends did not seem to care about Baird's fate, or this precious evidence they were all searching for. Rather, they were celebrating. The flames rose and the smoke billowed, dark and furious. There was a crash as the roof of the shack collapsed and the walls began to shake. Turnbull turned to his master, in a mixture of despair and terror, only to see that the Frenchman bore the same expression. They covered their faces, as a wave of fire seemed to wash over them.

"Hot, isn't it?" said a man behind them.

Chapter 32

Antoine stared at Baird. How the hell had he escaped, and why was he standing here right now? The reiver seemed to read his mind. "There's a back door," he said. "And that smoke made for a nice wee distraction, just as I had hoped. Now, I reckon we'll have an hour afore they realise I wasnae in there. So if ye want this treasure everyone's looking for, ye'd better come wi' me."

The Frenchman looked at Turnbull, unsure if this was yet another ruse. The lad frowned. "Are you saying you surrender?"

"Ah, now, let's no' be foolish. Ye ken me better than that, I think? No, I willnae give myself up – but I will give ye the goods frae Master Walkerburn's house."

Antoine was about to reply that he would not bargain with a common criminal – or an uncommon one, for that matter – when a terrible roar came from the hut. A section of the wall had collapsed, and an orange ball now ripped through the rest of the flimsy structure. The attackers, though still jubilant, were pushed back by the heat, and Antoine worried they might turn and spot them.

"Very well," he said. "Let's go somewhere we can talk. But first, why the change of plan? You know these goods could fetch a pretty price – one that we might not be able to match."

Baird looked unusually serious. "Plan? There's never been a plan. And as for payment, I'll give ye them for nothing, just to get the cursed things off my hands."

Baird had hidden his own horse a little further into the woods, but it was not long before they were all mounted and thundering back down the hill. They splashed across the burn where they had stopped earlier, before continuing over some common land and through a small orchard, brimming with plums and cherries. Tucked away behind these trees was a tiny cottage. In the yard, pigs were feeding at a trough, while a woman filled it with a bucket of swill. It was the old crone they had met earlier.

"Welcome back!" she called merrily. Antoine clasped his forehead. So she had been in on this from the start. He wondered if he could trust anybody – or anything – round here. "It's good to see ye're safe and sound," she continued. "Now, get yerselves inside while I see to these beasts."

The Frenchman looked at Turnbull to see what he thought, only for Baird to intercept the glance. "Peggy looks after the hut while we are away. Dinnae worry, ye'll be completely safe here."

Baird's promise was hardly reassuring, but they had little choice, so they tethered the horses and stooped to pass through the low door of the house. The room was dark but filled with the delicious aroma of a mutton stew, bubbling on the hearth. As Antoine breathed in the meaty fumes, he realised that they had not eaten properly for days. He was desperate to fill his belly but knew he must attend to business first. They took a stool each.

"So, Baird. You have us where you want us. Now bring

us these papers that your men stole from Master Dewar." He wanted to make clear that they knew some of this story already, and so would not easily be deceived. "The lad Fleabite told us all about the book and letter, when we found him at your camp."

The reiver took a sharp intake of breath. "Fleabite is alive?" He clasped his hands. "Oh, thank God. Thank God for that. I was sure those curs would slay him."

"Yes, he feigned his death and is now with a former confederate of yours, a certain Stumpy Watt."

"Wait. Fleabite is with Stumpy? How's that come about?"

Antoine watched Baird carefully for signs that this surprise might be an act. But something in the reiver's expression convinced him. Although the Frenchman wished they could get to the matter in hand, he realised that he might need to clear the man's mind of distractions first, so he quickly explained their travels since leaving Ravenscleugh. When he was finished, Baird shook his head.

"So it was a massacre, as I feared. But still, the boy's alive and that's a blessing. Ye ken, he was an orphan, just like me."

Antoine thought he saw Baird's eyes glisten in the flickering light of the hearth. He remembered how Fleabite had described his master being close to tears when he rode off from camp, and it struck him that Baird's distress that day might not have been for his own safety, but for the boy's – or perhaps due to some shared bond between them. He really was a curious fellow. But Antoine could not spend all day trying to fathom him. It was time to find out if they were right about this plot.

He cleared his throat. "About this evidence, then."

"Of course," said Baird absent-mindedly. He got up and

went to a heavy oak chest. Antoine expected him to open it, but instead, he wrapped his arms around it and heaved it to the side. A shallow pit revealed itself, just big enough to hide a ledger book and a folded piece of parchment. Baird bent down to gather them, before pushing the chest back into its place. He handed the documents to Antoine.

"Here ye are, sir. Frae Bailie Walkerburn's house. I'd start wi' the letter."

The Frenchman put the ledger on his lap and unfolded the parchment on top of it. It was written in the same spidery hand that they had seen when they had searched the bailie's study. But despite its ordinary appearance, just holding it made Antoine shiver. After all, it contained the last thoughts of a desperate man, before he committed the worst sin on God's earth. What darkness must have driven him to it?

The Frenchman began to read aloud.

My dearest Joan. Please forgive me for what I am about to do and for the brevity of this letter. I would rather have said a true farewell to you, my only love, but time does not allow it.

I have made a foolish mistake, wasted all our money on a wager, that cursed habit of which you have warned me so often. In truth, I have done worse than that, for the money I wasted belonged to our master. You know my Lord Douglas and how he will punish this. His rage and vengeance will be terrible, so I would rather take my fate into my own hands.

Antoine stopped to give Turnbull a meaningful look. "We knew Walkerburn collected illegal rents – your mother told us that. And we'd heard he might have lost some money in a wager. But this puts the two together."

"Yes, pilfering Douglas's coin was not a wise move. But what's this got to do with Hamilton and his plot against the king?"

Baird furrowed his brow. "I think ye have your ropes tangled, gentlemen. Keep going and ye'll see."

"Very well," said Antoine. He found his place again.

As for you, my darling, you must escape while you can. Destroy this letter once you have read it, but take the book, for it may be the only thing of value which I can bequeath to you.

Ah, thought Antoine, here was the meat of it: the bit where Walkerburn would tell his wife about Hamilton's plot and how she might turn a coin from it. The Frenchman scanned the next two lines. Hold on, what did that say? He stopped dead. He read the words to himself again, his mind whirling with confusion.

"What is it?" said Turnbull, leaning over his shoulder.

"Tell him," said Baird. He stood up abruptly, unable to contain himself. He paced about the hearth.

Antoine took a deep breath and bent over the letter. "Very well," he said, before continuing in a slow, deliberate voice, so that he did not mistake a single word.

The book shows how my Lord Douglas steals the rents from Ettrick Forest from under his good wife's nose. All so he can feather the nest of his concubine, that harlot from Traquair.

Jesu, this was madness. Douglas was working against the queen? Antoine was bursting with questions and could sense Turnbull's agitation growing beside him but kept going.

The queen does not suspect her husband, of course, but she has already sent spies looking for her revenues. They will pay well for this information. The trouble will be to find them. So take the book to your brother and see if he might help, but go quickly, for my master will come looking soon, and he will spare nobody to suppress this.

Once more, I beg your forgiveness, and I commend myself unto the infinite mercy of Our Father, God Almighty.

Your loving husband, Joseph.

Antoine turned the letter over, to make sure he hadn't missed anything, then replaced it on the book. A stunned Turnbull promptly took both documents to scrutinise for himself.

"So this secret is not about Hamilton at all, but Douglas?" said the lad as he leafed through the leather-bound ledger.

"That's right," said Baird. "He's been cheating the queen in mair ways than one. Now he tries to kill anyone who kens it."

"That's why his men were celebrating earlier. They thought they had destroyed you and all the evidence."

"Aye, they'll soon be disappointed."

Antoine felt like a keg of gunpowder had gone off in his head. He rubbed his temples. "That first day on the border, Fortingale said the queen was missing rental incomes. Naturally, he thought that we were swindling her – but it was Douglas all along."

"It seems so," said Turnbull. He ran his finger down a column in the ledger. "Look, here's a list of payments, relating to lands round Ettrick Forest: Newark Castle. Yarrowford. Dryhope. There are dozens of places listed. All granted to Margaret Tudor upon her marriage to the old king, but Douglas has been harvesting the profits without telling her. I wonder if that's why Fortingale was down here – to investigate? And why he was killed as well."

Antoine gave a hollow laugh. "Remember, we thought Douglas could not be to blame for that one because they were on the same side, but how little did we know! When Fortingale said that 'the queen must beware', he was talking of her husband."

Turnbull put the book aside and returned to the letter. He frowned. "What about this other accusation, that he has some mistress from Traquair?"

"Ah, I ken this one," said Baird. "Or at least my men explained at camp. It's his old sweetheart, Lady Janet Stewart of Traquair. Apparently, they have been living openly together at Newark, while the queen has been away. They may even have had a bairn together."

"Jesu," said Antoine hoarsely. "So when those gossips said that Douglas had 'that lady' down at Newark, this was who they meant. And the same for their jibe that the queen would 'soon receive a nasty surprise'. They were talking of her husband's treachery." He stopped to think this through. "Christ's sake. That woman I met on my way to Newark – I'll wager it was not Douglas's sister at all but this Stewart woman! This whole thing has been a deception. One lie after another, trick upon trick."

"Aye," said Baird. "What kind o' twisted mind would think o' such a thing?"

Chapter 33

Old Peggy came back in from the yard and attended to the stew. She doled the meaty broth into wooden bowls and gave one to each of the men. As Antoine waited for the liquid to cool, he mulled Baird's words. Was the reiver simply making a jest about his own love of a trick, or was there something more to his teasing? Sometimes, his meaning was as elusive as the steam that rose from this stew, twisting and turning, before vanishing in the air.

"I understand what Douglas has been up to now," Antoine said to Turnbull. "Even the excessively loving way he greeted his wife at Tantallon was no doubt intended to present them as a happy couple. But where does that leave Hamilton?"

"He must have caught a sniff of this scandal," said Turnbull. "Or at least heard that Walkerburn possessed something that incriminated Douglas. That's why he came down to Ravenscleugh and asked so many questions about the bailie."

"Yes, but he seemed to drop his interest after a while." Antoine paused to eat, then turned to Baird. "After speaking to you, in fact. We've never heard what you talked about, in that private meeting of yours."

The reiver took a spoonful of stew, then wiped his beard.

"He asked me many questions about the Walkerburns, just as you did. But as with you, I couldnae tell him anything."

"You're sure of that?"

"For the hundredth time, I was locked up while the whole business unfolded."

"How did Hamilton comport himself? Did he ask you to do anything? Try to strike a bargain? Make any promises?"

"No, and even if he had, I wouldnae have believed him."

"Did he talk of the outside world, then? The king, the queen, matters of state?"

Baird shrugged. "No' really. He pushed me on Lord Douglas, that's all. He seemed convinced that I was working for him, but I kept telling him I wasnae."

As Antoine stirred his stew, his mind swirled with the day's many revelations. He tapped Turnbull's elbow. "That tallies with how Hamilton appeared when he came downstairs. He seemed content that Baird and Walkerburn were not connected with his investigation."

"Yes," said Turnbull. "But he was still agitated by Douglas. Do you remember, he accused him of meaning to seize the king? We paid him little heed, for we thought he was trying to cover his own tracks, but it sounds like he was right all along. This letter and book do not touch on it directly, but they reveal great division in the land. That was Hamilton's worry, was it not? That Douglas would exploit the chaos that grows around us, to get his hands on His Grace?"

Antoine felt his skin prickle. "Not just any chaos. Hamilton made specific mention of the pestilence, remember? How it spread fear and confusion through the land – conditions which Douglas could exploit. Perhaps Hamilton was not *behind* this fraudulent plague but was *investigating* it."

Turnbull put his bowl aside. "God, perhaps that's how these things come together. Douglas has deceived the queen and fears he may be found out. He tries to kill anyone who knows of his treachery but sees his power slipping away. Possession of the king is his only hope, so he fabricates this plague to steal the little king. Hamilton is onto him but cannot pin him down."

Antoine suddenly became aware of how intently Baird was listening. The reiver reminded him of a cat, crouching in the long grass, before pouncing. They should really get going and talk about this in private.

"You have done well to come to us," the Frenchman said, as he stood up, the book and letter in his arms. "But you would do better still to forget what we've just talked of. This matter could be more dangerous than any of us imagine."

"Why do ye think I've brought these things to ye?" said Baird. "I just want shot of them afore they kill me. My only request is that, whatever ye do wi' them, ye put in a good word for me. If they're as valuable as ye say, perhaps I will be pardoned after all?"

Antoine hesitated. The reiver had surely made too many enemies now, for that to be a possibility. After weeks of dancing round the subject, it was time to be truthful. "I will make sure your contribution is known to all, but I fear there will be little rest for you in Scotland."

Baird nodded. "I thought as much. Indeed, I have suspected it from the beginning. I must find another way to save my skin, then."

"I'm afraid so," said Antoine. As they walked to the door of the cottage, he was surprised to catch himself hoping that the rogue would escape. Perhaps he could jump on a ship to Denmark or join the rush to Polonia as so many enterprising souls were doing these days. Either way, Baird might just have saved their own skins. For while they would still need to report the ignominy of losing their prisoner, they now possessed something which might be of far greater value. If they could get to Edinburgh in time, that was.

They shook Baird's hand heartily, thanked the old woman, and made off.

The sun was just starting to sink as they came back over the final stretch of moors. The hills were wild here, the land unforgiving. This was where they were most vulnerable, for there was nowhere to run and nobody to help them. Antoine kept his eyes on the jagged outline of the city on the horizon – the castle on its rock, the crags of Arthur's Seat, the spires – and told himself that they just needed to get to the walls before dusk and they would be safe. Only the more he thought of it, the more dangerous he feared Edinburgh itself might be.

After all, they were about to accuse one of the most powerful men in the land of being an adulterer, a fraudster, a murderer and a traitor. If others believed them, they would be heroes in their own camp, for the revelations would rip the English party asunder and could even bring the queen to their side. But if their claims did not stand up, they might soon be trading this book and letter for their own death warrants.

They needed to play this carefully. They would tell Pentland first, for slippery though Albany's secretary was, he was assuredly on their side and was clever in such matters. If he found the evidence compelling, they would tell the city guard to call an end to this fraudulent plague and warn the captain of the castle to increase the guard on the king. Next they would inform the queen of her husband's treachery – although God knows how she would react to that. Finally, they would enlist Hamilton: Antoine still resented the haughty way he had behaved at Ravenscleugh, but they would need his troops to fend off Douglas, if he tried to take the city.

The Frenchman thought about how long that might take in practice. Another two hours to reach the gates before they closed for the night? Three more to secure the city, the king, the queen and Hamilton? Five hours in total, then, to save his life or lose it. He watched the sun dip another fraction over the heather-clad moors and spurred his horse onwards.

Eventually, the hills began to soften, the landscape to open. They came to a ridge above the main road, between Edinburgh and the coast. A stream of people was moving seawards, driven on by the city bells. The constant pealing – a sure sign that the pestilence was in town, whether it was real or not – gave the exodus an added urgency.

Antoine and Turnbull rode down the brae and nosed into the crowd. As they pushed against the flow, a tide of human misery engulfed them. Women and children cried out that the markets had been closed and raised their hands for something to eat. Hawkers pestered them to buy posies, charms and herbal cures. Men swore at them for going in the wrong direction: were they completely mad, did they want to die? No, thought Antoine, but if the rest of their journey was as slow as this, they might well do. He gestured to Turnbull, to steer the horses off the road and onto a bridle path.

This trail allowed them to pass more freely, and they made good time before they had to rejoin the road. They were almost at the city gates, but the crowds here were particularly thick, and there was an appalling stink, the like of which they'd never smelt before. Somebody explained that an order had gone out to clear the middens and dump the filth in the high tide. A cart carrying a load of steaming ordure blocked their way. It had stopped because a peasant was berating the driver.

"That's my dog on there," he shouted, pointing to a mangy corpse on the side of the dung heap. The animal's throat had been cut, and its head hung from its neck, creating a grotesque second mouth.

"All strays are to be killed," shrugged the cartman. "That's my orders."

"It was no stray," spat the peasant. "I tell ye, it was mine. And now ye must pay me for him."

Antoine craned over their heads to see if there was another way through, but they were hemmed in by a ditch on one side and a wall on the other. The peasant continued to shout at the carter. All the while, the sky darkened. The Frenchman began to despair of making it to the gates in time when a sturdy constable arrived and swiped the peasant with a stick.

"Ignore this cur," he shouted, as the fellow begged for mercy. "He's been trying this trick all day. Now the rest o' ye shift your arses, unless ye want a taste o' this as well."

Antoine mused that the peasant's fraud was further proof that even a plague could be exploited by a cunning mind. But it was small beer compared to the plot that they must foil. He pushed past the tail-end of the cart and through the throng of wretched families, towards the city wall. He could see the gates now. Good. They were still open, although nobody was entering them. More importantly, fires could be seen within: the curfew had not been called yet.

They rode up to the gates and approached the nearest sentry. "Good evening, sir. We have urgent business in the city."

The man moved his halberd to bar their way. "Naebody's allowed in, especially no' strangers. Now move along like everybody else."

"I'm the Warden of the Eastern Marches," said Antoine firmly. "This is a matter of national import. I must get to the castle and the palace before nightfall." The sentry looked him up and down, and the Frenchman realised how shabby he must appear, after three days on the run. He rummaged in his purse, for his papers. Hold on, that was strange. He could not find them anywhere. He racked his brain for where they might be. Damnation.

"I must have left my documents in Ettrick Forest," he muttered to Turnbull. "Those hunters took them from me, and I forgot to get them back." The sentry rolled his eyes at this likely story. "Still, my ring will do. It bears the warden's mark." Antoine lifted his hand, but, to his horror, his finger was bare. How could this be? He had never taken off that ring, since Albany had given it to him. Could it have slipped off, with all the travelling they had done? It was impossible, surely. With a sinking heart, he realised that there was only one explanation. He grimaced.

"Baird must have stolen it when we shook hands at the old woman's."

Chapter 34

Turnbull looked at his master in disbelief but also with relief that it was not he who had been hoodwinked. Still, this was no time for point-scoring, they really needed to get through this gate. He wondered whether a Scots voice might help. "I have my own papers," he said, rummaging in his purse.

The sentry pushed his documents away. "I've had enough o' this. Now move away, so that others can get out."

"You don't understand. We must speak to the king and queen tonight. We have reason to believe that this plague is false. That it's been staged, to do them harm."

"Sweet Mary, I've heard it all now."

"We can pay you to let us in. Just name your price and we will pay it." Turnbull paused, for it occurred to him that they had barely a penny left. "Once we've been to the palace, of course. Just give us your name and we will make sure you're well rewarded."

The sentry laughed. "Ye must be mad. Or think I am. Now for the final time, be on your way and take your wild stories wi' ye. These gates are closing and ye're no' getting in."

He called to another guard, and they took one of the huge oak barriers each. Some of the rabble who were waiting to leave surged forwards, in fear of being locked inside the plague-ridden city. They pushed Antoine and Turnbull back, as the gates swung inwards. There were some final, frenzied arguments as families complained that they were being separated. Then the great portal closed, deadening all noise and light and movement from within, like a douter snuffing a candle.

"We're done for," said Antoine, looking up at the impregnable walls.

"I fear so," said Turnbull miserably. He thought of trying the other city gates, but no doubt they would have shut as well. There was no point looking for a gap in the defences either, for they had been strengthened after the last war. He was about to suggest heading down to Leith, to see whether they might find a way in through the port, when he heard a strange hissing noise.

Turnbull cast about to see if someone was trying to attract their attention, but there was nobody else nearby, the crowds having dispersed to find shelter for the night. The hissing sound came again, seeming to emanate from the wicket gate. He dismounted and walked towards it.

"I'm the other guard," said a reedy voice through the grille. "I heard ye tell my serjeant ye'd offer good money for some help?"

"Yes," said Turnbull excitedly. Perhaps their luck was about to turn.

"Well, I cannae open the gate. My master will be back soon and will flog me if I do. But in any case, I think the folk ye're after may have gone already. Ye talked o' the queen – sorry, the king's mother, I should say. She left for Tantallon a few days ago. Just after her husband went to Newark. They're a' fleeing, our lords and masters, leaving us wee folk to risk our lives as usual. Hamilton's gone to Craigmillar. Even the king may be moved, if he hasnae been already."

"What? The king has been moved?" Turnbull was horrified that the plot might already be in play.

"I didnae say that. I said he might have been. My brother's in the castle guards and telt me last week that they were making contingencies for His Grace. Then yesterday, some o' the lads were gossiping about a child leaving the city, in a carriage."

"Did they tell you who was with this child? Or where he was going?"

"No, it was just talk. Might no' even have been him. But if it was, I wager he'll have been sent to his mother. That's the natural place for a bairn to be, when times are troubled, after all."

Turnbull frowned. "His Grace is not a normal bairn. And his mother is the last person that the captain of the castle would assign him to."

"She is rich. Perhaps she paid him?"

"No, it is impossible," said Turnbull, although the words felt false in his mouth. Oh God, that was it. Falsehood. The queen might have rumbled her husband's false behaviour and resolved to take her destiny into her own hands.

"Tantallon's on the sea," continued the guard. "So mayhap she's persuaded the captain that His Grace should have some fresh air, until this pest blows over."

Or she plans to take him on a ship to England, thought Turnbull, as he slammed his hand against the gate and ignored the guard's pleas to return with money.

They wheeled the horses round and headed back to the main road, this time travelling in the same direction as the last few stragglers from the city. The sun had set, but they still had another hour before the dark descended. Was there anything they could do?

"I cannot believe that the queen has managed to remove her son from the castle," said Antoine, as they pulled up at a crossroads. "But if she has, we can hardly chase her to Tantallon. It's hours away, and she has a whole garrison at her disposal: the two of us will have no chance on our own. If we're to challenge her, we need to find a place for the night, then gather reinforcements in the morning."

"We'll be lucky to get a bed at this hour, with so many people on the road. As for reinforcements, where will we find them, if we cannot enter the city?"

Antoine thought about it. "The guard said Hamilton has fled to Craigmillar. That's only a couple of miles away. I hate to say it, but that arrogant man is our best hope."

Turnbull did not like the idea of placing their trust in Hamilton, but he could offer no better option. With that in mind, they retreated through the outlying steadings of Edinburgh, towards Craigmillar. Although it was after the curfew, no watchmen dared to venture out here, so groups of refugees idled around braziers, drinking and warming themselves against the chill night air. There was menace in these congregations, and Turnbull felt anxious, each time they passed one. The flames reminded him of the torching of Baird's hut that morning. He wondered when the Douglases had realised that the book and letter had not perished. More importantly, where were the attackers now?

Instinctively, he withdrew their precious cargo from his pannier and shoved it underneath his doublet. He hoped the action would make him feel more secure, but the ledger's thick leather cover only accentuated the rapid beating of his heart.

They were less than a mile away, but this last stretch was particularly dangerous. The Chapel of St John had recently been established as a hermitage for vagabonds and attracted all sorts, especially at this hour. Sure enough, as they passed the gates, a line of destitute wretches was queuing in the hope of a bed. A priest inspected them, holding a lantern to their faces. Some of them had been branded, just like the vagabond who had won the wager against Walkerburn.

"I had forgotten about our friend V-Face," said Turnbull, when they were safely past. "I'm not sure how he fits in with all this. Or whether he is of any import at all. As for finding him, that place shows it won't be easy. Such marks are not so rare in these troubled times – and the constables' irons will be busy in the next few days, no doubt. The pestilence brings their cruel streak out."

Antoine sighed. "It's a terrible thought, isn't it? That all this suffering might be for naught. Or rather to further some game of power. You know, that's the one place where we are on shaky ground."

"What do you mean?" said Turnbull.

"We have the book and letter, the brooch, the nosegay and a host of circumstantial evidence that points to Douglas. But this story about the plague is just an idea that the innkeeper planted this morning. We have no actual proof of it. Nor of the notion that someone – the queen or otherwise – aims to use it, to seize the king. For all we know, the child may still be tucked up nicely in his tower, safer than ever now that the city is under lock and key."

"Then what?" said Turnbull. He sensed that his master was hatching one of his plans and wished that he would make haste with it.

"I fear that we need proof of this false pestilence, before we go charging off to Hamilton."

Turnbull was stunned. "We're only half an hour from Craigmillar. Surely we bring him what we have tonight, then if he seeks more evidence, we search for it by daylight?"

"No, we need to be sure of ourselves first. Come with me. I have an idea that won't take long."

Turnbull shifted uneasily in his saddle but followed his master as he took a sharp right off the road and onto a wild heathland known as the Burgh Muir. It was not a safe place to linger at any time, let alone at this hour. The lad's discomfort was not helped when they passed a crude gallows, the smell of fresh wood suggesting that it had been erected recently. There was no body dangling from it yet, but the sight of the empty noose was still disturbing: Death was abroad, it seemed to say, and he could tighten his coil round anyone.

It was almost dark now, but the waning moon allowed them to reach the top of the Muir without too much trouble. Turnbull was still not sure what his master was up to but indulged him as he dismounted and prowled around on foot. An owl screeched to its mate, but otherwise, all was still. Presently, the Frenchman stopped.

"Well," he said. "What do you see?"

"Nothing," said Turnbull, peering through the gloaming.

"Exactly. This is where they normally bury the bodies, when the plague's in town. Always at night, as well. But the place is deserted. No pits have been dug. There are no carts about. None of those great cauldrons either, where the collectors boil their clothes afterwards. Why, come to think of it, isn't it strange that we didn't see a single corpse by the wayside – unless you count that dog on the midden wagon?"

Turnbull shuddered at the idea that he was currently standing atop an enormous graveyard, albeit one that had not been refilled recently. "That's true. But absence of evidence cannot be taken as proof, if I remember my legal studies. Do you think Hamilton will be convinced by this?"

"Who knows, but it has convinced me that we should go to him. If he doubts us, we can bring him back here in the morning and let him see with his own eyes. Now let's get out of this godawful place, before the ghosts rise up and take us."

Chapter 35

Antoine had been to Craigmillar before, as the court sometimes made use of its fine hunting grounds. It was an impressive fortress, surrounded by huge curtain walls. But at this hour it was almost invisible. As they waited outside the main gate for someone to answer their calls, Antoine felt like they were about to step into some great void, a chasm where their accusations might fall into the nothingness. He steeled himself, as the gate opened, only to be greeted by a familiar face.

"Pentland?"

"I see you are as surprised to see me as I am you," said Albany's secretary, drily. He was carrying a lantern on a stick. "But as you may have noticed, the city is in some disorder. So Lord Hamilton has kindly invited me to join his camp until things settle down."

Antoine thought it an unlikely act of generosity, but he had no time to question it. "Is Hamilton about?" he said. "We believe there is a risk of far greater upheaval but that we may prevent it, if we act quickly."

"What manner of upheaval?" said Pentland, eyeing them suspiciously.

"I can explain when we have His Lordship's ear. But we have evidence that Douglas and the queen are at odds with each other and that this plague has been staged by one of them, in order to seize the king."

The secretary frowned, then gave a thin smile. "Do you indeed? Well, come and tell us all about it. This should be entertaining."

Antoine bristled at the fellow's mocking tone, but he and Turnbull entered the castle, handed the horses to an ostler and followed the swaying glow of Pentland's light.

The keep's entrance was hidden around a corner, to impede would-be attackers. Half a dozen soldiers stood outside it, clad in Hamilton's galley-ship livery. They waved the visitors through the arched doorway, into a dimly lit passageway. The ceiling was low, the walls as narrow as a crypt's. There were murder holes in the roof, and the Frenchman thought he saw somebody through them, following their progress, but by the time they had climbed the spiral stairs to the first floor, there was nobody there.

They continued past the Great Hall, which was crammed with soldiers, settling down for the night, and up another flight of stairs, where yet more troops stood at a gallery. The foul smell of seal blubber hung in the air, suggesting that they had been polishing their weapons. This was a garrison in a state of readiness, then. Antoine hoped that he would be as well prepared for whatever was about to pass. He tensed as they came to a landing, and Pentland knocked on a low door.

"Well, well," said Hamilton as they entered. He was sitting at a desk in a gloomy little room, lit only by an inadequate sconce of beeswax candles. He folded some papers away. "I heard you lost that prisoner of yours. I assume you've come to beg forgiveness?"

Antoine cursed inwardly, at having to start on the back

foot. "Baird has gone, it's true. But he has brought us something of far greater import. Something I think you'll find very interesting."

"How intriguing," said Hamilton. He gave Pentland a meaningful look and bade them all sit down. Pentland took a jug of claret from the desk and poured them each a cup while Antoine explained how Baird's men had stolen the book and letter from Walkerburn's servant, prompting Lord Douglas's bloody quest to recover them. After some initial scepticism, Hamilton started to lean in. His eyes widened with each twist and turn of the tale, culminating in the attacks on Ravenscleugh, Baird's forest camp and the hut at Fala. At the end, he pushed his chair back, as if to take it all in.

"So Baird was connected with this after all?'

"Yes, although he only found out about the book and letter after he escaped. When he realised their significance, he did his best to come to us."

Antoine wondered why he found himself putting in a good word for Baird, even though the rogue had stolen his ring, but in any case, Hamilton was not interested. "Well, never mind him. Are you still in possession of these papers?"

Turnbull lifted up his doublet and produced the book and letter. He placed them on the desk, and Pentland joined his master on the other side to read them. Hamilton sipped his wine as he devoured the evidence. When he had finished, he licked his lips.

"These could split our enemies in two. Are you sure they're genuine?"

"The writing tallies with other papers we found in Walkerburn's study," said Turnbull.

"Then no wonder Douglas is so keen to seize them," Hamilton said, rubbing his hands. "The dalliance with Lady

Traquair is one thing – it is hardly a surprise for a man to have a mistress – but stealing his wife's rents to pay for the filly, that is something different."

"Margaret Tudor is a proud woman, she will not put up with it," agreed Pentland thoughtfully. He retook his chair and ran a finger round the edge of his glass. "On the other hand, we must be careful how we bring this to her. If His Lordship or I present it, she will reject it out of hand. If *you* show her it, de Lissieu, and explain how you came by it, she will be more inclined to trust it."

Antoine furrowed his brow. "I don't know about that. When we last spoke, at the palace, it was not on good terms."

"That was my fault," said Pentland, with uncharacteristic modesty. "I had just put her in a rage by keeping her from her son. But as a general rule, she likes you, does she not? Or at least she sees you as a man of honour, an opponent but not an enemy. That's why Albany chose you to escort her back from exile."

Antoine could not deny this, but he had an uncomfortable feeling that he was being set up here. As if he were being asked to carry all the risk of making such a momentous accusation about Douglas, leaving others to reap the rewards. "Perhaps. It is complicated though. There is another piece to this puzzle. One that we have only just discovered. It relates to the disorder in Edinburgh and—"

"De Lissieu believes that the pestilence has been staged," interjected Pentland. "And that Douglas or the queen might be using it to seize the king."

Antoine glowered at the secretary for blurting their news out that way, as if to undermine it. He spread his arms. "I know it sounds unlikely, but we received intelligence this morning, from a credible source. And we have just passed by

Burgh Muir tonight. There is nothing there: no graves, no carts, no huts. Just gallows to scare people away. Meanwhile, the city is in turmoil, and the castle guards talk of the king being moved."

"I see," said Hamilton. He cast another glance at Pentland. "And you believe Douglas is behind this too?"

"That was our original thought. But now we hear that the queen is at Tantallon, so we fear she may have heard of her husband's deceit and plans to make her own bid."

"She may already have taken her son," said Turnbull. "That's why we've come here at this hour."

Antoine waited for Hamilton to explode at his enemies' outrageous behaviour, but the aristocrat nodded calmly, over steepled fingers. When he finally spoke, his voice was measured.

"Have you told anybody else of your suspicion?"

"No, this has all unfolded today."

Hamilton nodded. "And could you have been followed here tonight?"

Antoine felt uneasy. "Nobody knows we're here."

"Well, this is all very unfortunate. Very unfortunate indeed. But you needn't worry that the queen has staged this fraud. Or Douglas, for that matter."

"How so?"

A smile flickered on Hamilton's lips. "Because it is all my doing."

Antoine could scarcely believe what he was hearing. He made to get up, but Hamilton stayed him.

"Calm yourself, de Lissieu. I said there's nothing to worry about. Quite the opposite. As you know, I have long suspected Douglas of meaning to seize the king. So when the queen returned and Pentland here raised fears about the pestilence, it gave me an idea. We could use these fears to put the city under measures and prevent *anybody* from reaching the castle – not just her."

Antoine looked at him, open-mouthed. "You have terrorised a whole city, on some foolish whim?"

"Scarcely on a whim," snapped Hamilton. "This whole country depends on the safety of that child. If a few beggars have to shift their lazy arses out of town awhile, or some merchants have to close their stores, so be it. The king is safe, that's all that counts. Even Douglas would not storm a city rife with plague."

"What if he is desperate?" said Antoine, his anger mounting. "This trouble with his wife might push him beyond reason."

"Or what if he realises it's all a fraud, as we did?" asked Turnbull. "He could walk into an empty city and take the castle at his leisure!"

"You idiots. You think we haven't thought of that? If he tries to storm the castle, he will find it full to the brim with my best men. And even if he gets past them, he will not find the king. Because he is not there."

"What? Where is he, then?"

Hamilton gave them a withering look. "Come with us and we will show you."

Antoine's mind whirred as Hamilton and Pentland led them up a further flight of stairs and then along a passageway to a strong, studded door. Could this precious child really be here at Craigmillar? Before he could ask, two guards knocked on the door and ushered them in. They entered a beautifully panelled chamber dominated by an enormous poster bed, by which knelt the king and a young female servant.

"My lord," said the woman, fearfully. She put her arm around the boy as they bowed and advanced. "What brings ye here at this hour? His Grace is about to say his prayers."

Hamilton made a calming gesture. "Do not fret, Ailsa. We simply bring two visitors, here to check His Grace is well. We won't be long." He turned to the child. "Your Grace, you remember Monsieur de Lissieu? And this is his friend, Master Turnbull. Pray, tell them how you like your time at Craigmillar."

"I like it very much," said the boy, puffing out his rosy cheeks. Antoine watched for any signs that he might be speaking under duress, but the child's enthusiasm seemed quite genuine.

"That is good to hear, Your Grace. What is it that appeals to you?"

"I'm not locked up all day. I can come and go about the courtyard, as long as my guards are with me. There are other bairns for me to play with." The boy beamed at Hamilton. "His Lordship says I may even ride a pony tomorrow."

Antoine could not help feeling that this was precisely the kind of regime that he had proposed in Edinburgh. Now Hamilton had appropriated it as his own, to curry favour with the boy. Still, it was good to see that the child was well and happy.

"We all of us wish the best for you, Your Grace. So, you do not want for anything?"

"Nothing, sir. Apart from my mother. But Cousin Hamilton says I will see her soon."

"Without Lord Douglas," added Hamilton. "That is your wish, is it not?"

The child scowled at the mention of his stepfather's name and nodded.

"Then I think we are all done here, unless you have any more questions, de Lissieu?"

Antoine had many more questions, but none that could be answered by a five-year-old boy, so he politely declined, and they left the king to his prayers.

Chapter 36

The keep was full of soldiers, so Antoine and Turnbull were given a private chamber in the East Range. It was cosy enough, but yesterday's deluge of news meant that they slept fitfully.

It was clear that Hamilton and Pentland had no appetite for confronting the queen with her husband's treachery. So should they visit her themselves? Antoine felt it was a risky idea for Douglas might be back at Tantallon by now, ready to intercept them. And even if they could reach Her Grace, she might direct her fury at the messengers, rather than the message. No, they needed to think of a way to catch her alone, at the right moment. Meanwhile, their best bet was to stay here, as there was surely no safer place right now, than within this ring of steel.

The castle's defences revealed themselves as even more impressive in the morning. Troops lined up in the courtyard, drilling to the bark of their serjeant. Men stood on the battlements too, assembling piles of rocks to be dropped through the machicolations. Others readied the cannons which poked out of the inverted keyhole loops. In the middle of it all was Hamilton, and beside him, the object of all this fuss, the king. He was wearing a purple bonnet, with peacock feathers sticking from the brim, and holding the cloth horse toy that he had clutched at Edinburgh Castle.

"Are you here to take me riding?" he asked Antoine and Turnbull as they approached.

"No," Hamilton answered for them. There was a weariness to his voice. "We went through this before, Your Grace. We do not have a pony suitable for you yet, so we will let you try some hawking instead."

The boy frowned. "You promised I could ride a pony."

"Yes, but then I found that our beasts are all too big. We should have a pony by the morn – or a mule if you prefer. Meanwhile, I am sure you will find the hawking to your taste. It is the sport of kings, after all."

Hamilton looked over the child's head and rolled his eyes at Antoine and Turnbull. "So, de Lissieu, I suppose you two will be off to Tantallon, to warn the king's mother?"

Antoine explained his fear of interception, and Hamilton shrugged. "A fair point. You must not let Douglas catch you." He curled his lip. "But do not tarry too long. It's not just the country that depends on that book and letter, you know. Your own lives are bound up with those pages."

Yes, it certainly feels like we've been stitched up, thought Antoine, but he passed over the implied threat. "Then help us reach the queen, at least. Help us discern when she might be without her husband. Lend us some men to visit her."

Hamilton stopped him with a hand. "If all goes well, she will soon be without her husband for good. But for now, I need every man I have, to protect His Grace. You look after your side of things, and I will look after mine."

With perfect timing, the serjeant shouted for the soldiers to split into two sides, causing the courtyard to part like the Red Sea. A burly man strode through the middle, bearing a hawk on his outstretched arm. The bird wore a beautiful leather hood, embellished with red and yellow beads.

"This is Master Fraser," said Hamilton, as the man gave a deep bow. The movement caused the bells on the bird's leg to jingle. "He has come to make a falconer of you, Your Grace."

The king tilted his head, to inspect the hawk. It was not much bigger than a blackbird, with grey-brown upper parts and a dark-streaked breast. "It's just a merlin," the boy protested.

"Not any merlin, Your Grace," said Fraser. "This is Circe. The finest hunter I've ever known. She'll make a fine friend for ye, I promise."

"Merlins are for lassies. A king should have a proper falcon."

"And so you shall have, one day," said Hamilton. "But a peregrine is hard to manage. Better to start with one of these. You know, falconry is all about biding your time, Your Grace. Master Fraser has tamed this bird over many weeks, played with her, eaten with her, even slept with her on his arm. He has sewn up her eyelids to make sure she trusts him, then unsewn them once she bends entirely to his will. Now you will have to show the same forbearance in learning how to fly her. It will be a good lesson for you. Those who wish power must have patience, as they say."

Antoine found the sentiment disturbing, from one as conniving as Hamilton. But it was surely better that the king went hawking, close to the castle, than charging around the countryside on a pony. He decided to lend his support. "Lord Hamilton is right, Your Grace. Indeed, I have a feeling that you will excel at this sport. Why don't we join you and you can show us?"

Hamilton seemed to have tired of his young charge and declared that he would watch from the battlements, so Antoine and Turnbull joined the king and the falconer outside. The approach to the gate bordered a wide, open heathland, which was full of small birds and rodents, so they began the lesson there. Fraser was a stickler for detail and insisted on issuing a lengthy series of warnings and precautions before they started, prompting yet more complaints from the king. The bird, in contrast, waited patiently until it was time for her to be transferred to the king's arm.

Antoine helped the child to put on a glove and move the merlin over. It was not an easy task, because the boy refused to surrender the cloth horse, which he held in his other hand. There was further advice about the importance of building trust with your bird. A lecture on the need to keep her hungry, not to reward her too readily. Antoine could see the king losing interest and began to think that he should offer a quick ride on the back of his horse after all. But eventually, once Fraser was satisfied that his pupil had paid his art sufficient respect, he took off the bird's hood, untied her jesses and helped the boy cast off.

For a while, Circe had them all under her spell. She cut through the mackerel sky like an enchanted arrow, soaring high, swooping low, causing the heathland to rustle with escaping prey. Even the king seemed to appreciate her elegance: perhaps he felt a fleeting kinship with this free spirit, who would soon be trussed up and returned to her dingy mews. He asked Fraser when the bird would bring them something, and the falconer said he would walk through the long grass to flush out some sparrows. But as he set off, a cart rolled up the castle path and startled Circe. She retreated to a nearby tree and turned her keen eyes on the vehicle.

"Who can this be?" said Fraser.

Antoine squinted at the cart. The driver was an old man, the load a pile of heather branches. No doubt they were intended for Hamilton's supposed cleaners, to burn around the city. The reminder of this fraud irked Antoine.

"You should ask your master that. But come, let's return to our sport, before we lose His Grace's mind again."

Fraser scowled at the notion that anyone could tire of this pursuit, but it was true; the little king had already retreated into a game with his cloth horse. The falconer took out a lure and began to whirl it around, to fetch his bird back in. Circe left her perch and shot towards the movement, but some shouting from the castle put her off and she pulled up abruptly, climbing into the heavens, before retreating to her tree again.

When Antoine turned to the castle to see what the problem was, he saw that the cart had become stuck in the gate. The sentries were shouting at the driver, but he did not seem able – or prepared – to budge. Antoine cursed the hubbub as yet another disruption caused in pursuit of Hamilton's great pretence. But hold on, His Lordship himself was waving from the battlements. It looked like he was beckoning.

With growing irritation, Antoine walked back to the castle, leaving Fraser and Turnbull to recapture the bird. Hamilton was leaning over the ramparts, his face like thunder.

"This idiot has got himself stuck in the gate," he called down. "He says you sent for him, so you can damn well get him out."

Antoine was bemused. "I've never seen this man in my life, let alone asked him to deliver anything."

"He says you asked him to bring the load here."

"No, I said the warden telt me," interjected the carter. "A Frenchman named Delishy or suchlike. He showed me his ring and telt me to wait at the gate for payment. But this wasnae the fellae."

Antoine gaped. There was only one person who could have impersonated him in this way: Baird. But why would he do such a thing, unless it was some kind of parting jest? He took a closer look into the back of the cart, lifted a couple of heather branches, but there was nothing vexing. The more Antoine tried to parse it, the less sense it made.

He called for Turnbull to come over, while he continued to quiz the carter. The old man confirmed that the "French fellae" who had ordered the delivery had been thirty or so, with long dark hair and striking blue eyes. He had wanted the heather branches to burn at Craigmillar, to ward off the pestilence. It had all sounded perfectly plausible, and the carter insisted that he would not be going anywhere until he had been paid.

Antoine sighed. The only way to check whether there was some hidden message in Baird's delivery was to unload the cart and search it properly. But first they would need to dislodge it from the gate and pull it into the courtyard. He climbed into the back and over the driver's seat, where he reassured the carter that he would get his coin in due course. This settled the man, and he took a nosebag to distract the horse while Antoine clambered down behind its back legs, to see how the cart was stuck. At the same time, Turnbull crawled through the wheels to get a look from below. They had just identified the problem – a jutting plank which had jarred against the gate's frame – when there was more shouting from above.

"Watch out!"

"Who's that?"

"For the love of God, protect the king!"

From his cramped position, Antoine could not see the cause of all this alarm, but it scared him, nonetheless. He scrambled back across the cart, Turnbull doing the same underneath. The horse stirred with the sudden noise and movement. As Antoine clambered over the pile of heather branches, the shouting built around him. He could see the king now, standing with his cloth toy, in the middle of the heath. The falconer had abandoned his bird and was running towards him. But from the opposite direction, a man was riding at full tilt.

As he got closer, Antoine realised that it was Baird. The horse seemed to slow, the shouting to die down, as the reiver came to the boy. God's blood, what was he up to? Antoine threw himself off the cart and ran towards the king. Turnbull was close behind him, the falconer racing from the other side. They were almost upon the child. Antoine watched the child's eyes open wide at the sight of the wild intruder. But he did not look afraid. Indeed, he seemed giddy with excitement.

"Your Grace, will ye ride?" called Baird, as he leant over his horse's flank, an arm outstretched. The boy nodded eagerly, and the reiver grabbed him by the elbow and tossed him up behind him. For a moment it looked like the child might slither off the other side, and Antoine lunged forwards, hoping he might yet save him.

But Baird reached around to steady him. And in an instant, they were off.

Chapter 37

Antoine watched in horror, as Baird and the king disappeared over the heath, the falconer flailing about behind them. He turned back to the castle, where Hamilton stood screaming from the battlements, and then to Turnbull's ashen face. The unfolding disaster reminded the Frenchman of the chaos that last night at Ravenscleugh, except this time, he had not lost a mere prisoner but a king. He wanted to be sick but forced his limbs into action. He ran back to the gate and tried to get the cart free.

"Should we fire a round?" shouted one of the gunners overhead.

"Don't be ridiculous," came Hamilton's voice. "You'll hit the king, you fool."

"Then what, my lord?"

"Hold on, I may have it," shouted Antoine from below. Pressing his boot against the cart's jutting plank, he snapped it off, and the driver was finally able to pass through into the courtyard. Now, all they needed to do was clear some space, to fetch their horses and give chase.

"Move back!" called Turnbull. The soldiers parted, and they both raced towards the stables, where the ostlers were desperately readying some horses. Hamilton had climbed down from his perch and was running about the courtyard.

"Is that who I think it was?" he snarled, as Antoine tried to catch an ostler's attention.

"I fear so, my lord. But we can still catch him if we're quick. We just need to get this cart out of the way and—"

"You just need to stay where you are, that's what *you* need to do. The rest of you, get moving, you lazy curs. And get the beacon lit. You know the plan. We have men stationed all the way along the coast. If that devil passes, they will fall on him, but meanwhile, get on his tail, for the love of Mary."

Antoine and Turnbull tried to push past to the stables, but the serjeant barred their way, as the ostlers helped a dozen soldiers to mount their horses and rush through the gate. On the battlements, someone lit a bale of hay in an iron basket. Hamilton raced about like a madman, his eyes wild, mouth jabbering wordlessly with rage and fear.

"I should have listened to the Widow Scrimgeour," he spat, as he clawed the air with frustration. "She warned me that you were too close to Baird."

"What do you mean?"

"You've clearly been duped by him – he's used whatever you told him, to follow you here. Perhaps you are even in league with him, working with Douglas to steal the king and bring this country down!"

Antoine shook his head at this latter claim but had a horrible feeling that there might be some truth to the first accusation. He remembered the intense interest with which Baird had listened to their conversation in Old Peggy's cottage. Had he heard something, that might advantage him? Was he still intent on winning himself a pardon? Surely he must know that kidnapping the king would simply guarantee his death?

"I am certainly not in league with Baird. And I am equally sure neither of us is working with Douglas. His Lordship tried to kill me at the tannery and then all of us at Ravenscleugh. He sent a man to murder Turnbull's mother, slaughtered Baird's friends in Ettrick Forest, sent a gang to burn him alive in that hut at Fala. We are none of us friends of his."

"So what's Baird up to? You think he's in the pay of Margaret Tudor?"

"If he was, he'd surely have taken her that book and letter himself."

"Then what's he up to? Where's he gone?"

"I don't know yet. But what I *do* know is that we're your best chance of finding out. By your own admission, nobody is closer to his ways than us."

Hamilton considered this for a moment, without responding. He took a few steps backwards so that he could shout up to the men on the battlements, to see whether any other beacons had been spotted. A sentry replied that there had been no such signals, adding the unnecessary rejoinder that there should have been by now.

Hamilton cursed under his breath. "Very well, you can go after Baird. Just mark you this: as things lie now, your head is on the block. Your young assistant's too. But I will not let you bring the axe upon *my* neck if this turns out wrong. I will make it clear to all who ask that I had secured His Grace and that it was you who plunged him into danger. I will bring witnesses that you took him out hunting this morning, while I stayed inside. I will speak of your friendship with Baird and get that carter to tell how the French warden ordered him to obstruct the gate. Do you understand what I am saying? You can save yourself if you can save the king – but otherwise, you are done."

"Oh, I understand all too well," said Antoine.

"Then get on that godforsaken road," said Hamilton. "And do not come back empty-handed."

Turnbull was glad to leave Craigmillar but churned up by Hamilton's threat. How had they managed to get themselves into such danger – and more importantly, how might they save themselves? He hoped his master might have a plan, but as they reached the end of the castle's path, he was alarmed to hear the despair in his voice.

"It's been at least half an hour since Baird got away. He could be anywhere by now."

Turnbull scratched his head. "Anywhere but the coastal road, otherwise we'd have seen one of Hamilton's beacons by now."

"So he's not headed to Tantallon. Or at least not by the obvious route. Which suggests he's not looking for Douglas or the queen. What can he be up to?"

Turnbull pondered this. "We need to remember what Stumpy Watt told us: climb into our quarry's head. What is Baird thinking right now? What would give him the greatest pleasure?"

"Us wasting time trying to fathom him," said Antoine miserably. He stroked his beard. "But failing that, remember that first night when he talked of there being no greater joy than a chase across the moors?"

Turnbull nodded. He recalled that moment perfectly, the first time they had glimpsed this sorcerer at work. He had spoken of the freedom of the hills, the open spaces, the smell of heather in the air.

"I think you're right, sir. Let's leave the coast to

Hamilton and head inland. It will still be like looking for a needle in a haystack, but it's our only hope."

"Our only hope," repeated the Frenchman thoughtfully. He tilted his head, as if mulling an alternative, but said nothing more. He jerked his reins, and they turned the horses in the direction of the Lammermuirs.

They had to take the main road for a while, weaving in and out of the townsfolk who were fleeing to the coast. The flow of refugees had slowed, for most people who could escape had already done so. The only ones who were left were a ragbag of older stragglers, hawkers and looters. Turnbull shuddered as they passed a group of bailiffs. They were kneeling on a thief's back, as they prepared to cut off his hand with a cleaver. Turnbull thought of intervening, only to remember that they must not tarry, otherwise Hamilton would subject them to an even crueller punishment. As he rode past, he tried to block out the crack of the blade as it split the man's bone, the screaming that broke the sweet summer air.

Presently they came to a drovers' path, leading off from the main road. If Baird were headed inland, as they hoped, this would have been the first route to present itself, so they followed it up a hill and along a ridge towards a grassy plateau. A shepherd was tending his flock, and they cantered over to speak to him. The sheep scattered, and the shepherd started to run back to his sheiling hut, so they came to a halt and called out that they meant no harm. As the shepherd eyed them nervously, they advanced more slowly and introduced themselves.

"We're looking for a man who may have passed this way a little earlier. He would be quite recognisable, for he had a boy on the back of his horse."

The shepherd held his crook tightly, as if he might wield it as a weapon if things got rough, but he seemed to relax at this enquiry.

"Aye, a fellae just like that came past an hour ago. He was headed over that way."

"Where exactly?" Antoine urged.

The shepherd shrugged. "Just over that brae, that's all I saw. He was going fast, like you were. So I kept oot o' his way."

Turnbull tossed the man the last of their coins, and they raced off in the direction he had given them. The brae was steep, and it took them a while to climb it. The ledger that Turnbull had stuffed up his doublet was an encumbrance, the stiff leather cover making it harder to ride at speed. He thought of stopping to put it back in his pannier, but his master urged him on to the crest of the hill. It was only once they reached the summit that the landscape opened, and the full scale of their task dawned on them: the track split into a myriad of even smaller trails, criss-crossing the hills from one valley to another.

"Jesu, this is impossible," said Antoine.

"He could have taken any of these," agreed Turnbull.

"Or ridden overland, for that matter. Never mind looking for a needle in a haystack; this is a whole hayfield, stretching on for miles. We'll never find him on our own."

"Then what do we do?"

"Give me a moment!" said Antoine tetchily. He put his hands to his temples and gave them a rub. Round and round his fingers went, the frown on his face intensifying with every turn. The action seemed to mimic the circles they were moving in, thought Turnbull. Then the Frenchman stopped. His eyes widened. He pointed towards a patch of cottongrass.

"Wait. Look over there."

Chapter 38

Antoine dismounted and walked over to a fork in the trail, his gaze fixed on the flash of purple and green that stood out against the drab scrub: a peacock feather. He picked it up and let it flutter in the breeze.

"There's only one way this could have got all the way up here."

Turnbull nodded. "From the king's bonnet. Looks like they took this fork, then headed yonder."

"We should follow this path to that rocky outcrop. Look, there's a natural line of travel."

"Then what?"

"We see if there is someone else to quiz." Antoine turned the quill in his palm and gave a hollow laugh. "You know, some say the flesh of these birds does not decay. That they represent immortality, life eternal." He stared into the eye of the feather. "Perhaps God sees our plight and is telling us that he will protect us."

"I hope so," said Turnbull. "Though others say these prideful beasts do the Devil's work." He shrugged, as his master let the feather fall and remounted his horse. "Well, I suppose we will find out who is right, before too long."

They continued on their chosen path, passing into another

valley. It looked identical to the last one: a great open space, dotted with sheep. Except this time, there was nobody to ask further directions. Indeed, there were no landmarks, no milestones, no signs of human life at all. In the absence of any other clues, they stuck to their trail until it gave way to another crude junction, scratched into the dirt. Antoine suggested tossing a coin to decide their next move, only for Turnbull to remind him that they had none left. Their task began to look impossible again, when the lad spotted another feather, snagged upon a gorse bush.

"Perhaps God is smiling on us after all," said Antoine.

"Yes, it's just past the crossroads," said Turnbull. "Like a finger pointing the way." He paused and creased his brow. "But perhaps this is not providence at play?"

"What do you mean?"

"I wonder whether the king is dropping these on purpose. Think about it, he's a bright boy. He must know that he's being pursued. Perhaps he's trying to tell us where he has been taken, without Baird knowing?"

"Sweet Mary, you could be right. But hold, he only had a small clutch of feathers in his bonnet. How many do you think: three or four at most? If we're to find him before his clues run out – or Baird spies his plan – we must hurry."

Turnbull nodded, and they galloped across the valley floor, then up an escarpment, which overlooked yet another wild dale. Once again, the trail branched off in a multitude of directions, and once again, a feather came to their assistance, this time sticking out of a marshy area to their left. It seemed to point downhill to a lonely, whitewashed cottage.

"That settles it," said Antoine. "This can be no accident. I'll wager Baird's taken His Grace to some kind of hide-out there – or at least passed through for some reason. If we make haste, we may yet catch him. But let's be careful, he may have others with him."

With that, they edged down the hill. As they advanced, Antoine remembered how Baird had used smoke and the cover of those rowan trees to escape the hut at Fala, and he was reassured to see that the cottage stood on its own. He was about to tell Turnbull to skirt round the back and check for hidden exits when a man came out the front door. He was setting up a bench outside a square serving hatch. It looked like this was a drovers' inn: a primitive hostelry, where cattlemen could stop for a drink outside or take a bed for the night, on their way to market in Edinburgh.

"Good morrow," called Turnbull, raising a hand.

The man put the bench down, without taking his eyes off the visitors. His face was weather-beaten and framed by a shaggy mess of dark hair. He waved back, but the action was slow and deliberate. It was only as they drew nearer that he relaxed, perhaps spotting the opportunity for some unexpected custom.

"Ye here for a drink, gentlemen? Or will ye be stopping the night?"

"Neither," said Turnbull. "We're looking for a man and a young boy, who may have ridden through earlier."

The innkeeper frowned. "I see. Well, I'm afraid I cannae help ye. As ye can imagine, we dinnae get many strangers round here, so we'd notice someone like that." He lightened again. "To be honest, we'd notice anybody at a'. Now can I no' tempt ye wi' a wee ale? It must be thirsty work riding these hills on a day like this."

"No, if you haven't seen them, we must be on our way."

"That's a shame. But wait," the man raised a finger. "We

have two other guests. Ye could ask them if they've seen anything."

Antoine looked at Turnbull and shrugged. "We may as well, while we are here."

"Then an ale it is," beamed the innkeeper. He called over his shoulder, and a girl arrived, his daughter by the look of her untamed dark curls. "Jess, these men wish to converse wi' our guests. Get them a drink while I fetch them."

The pair went inside, leaving the new arrivals to dismount and catch their breath. "Let's do this quickly," said Antoine. "I think the innkeeper is just trying to bully us into an ale. His interest will soon wane when he finds out we are penniless."

"True. He's right about this riding being thirsty work though. These nags must be parched. I'll see if there's a trough round the back."

Turnbull led the horses round the side of the cottage, while Antoine stretched his legs. As he looked about, he was struck by the desolation of this place and how preposterous it would be to find a king here. Indeed, what was he himself doing here: he who had once harboured fancies of a return to Paris? All those dreams were gone now, of course, his ambitions reduced to dust in these vast, wild hills. As he contemplated defeat, he heard Turnbull's voice, low but insistent, from round the corner.

"Sir, come quickly, we have a problem."

Antoine frowned but hurried to the back of the cottage. He was relieved to find that his young friend was safe – but immediately saw what was wrong. Standing beside Turnbull were their old horses, Carbonel and Fogo.

"What the hell is this?" he said.

"I don't know," said Turnbull. "But it's them all right.

Listen to the way they greet us. Which means those guests must be—"

The back door swung open, and two men appeared. One of them was the fellow with green teeth who had led the burning of the hut at Fala – the other a stocky man with a round, blotchy face. They were holding swords, and Antoine and Turnbull only just had enough time to draw their own before the pair advanced.

"Well done," said Green Teeth to the innkeeper, who lurked in the doorway, his daughter cowering behind him. "We'll pay ye well for this." He turned to Antoine and Turnbull. "As for you two, ye'll get what ye deserve as well."

He took another step forwards, his mean eyes fixed on them. Antoine tried to remember where he had first seen him – he was sure he had glimpsed him before the fire at Fala – but as he wracked his brain, Blotchy lunged at him, and their steel clashed. At the same time, Turnbull threw himself at Green Teeth, only to be repelled.

"You tricked us at the bothy," said the reiver, with a sickly smile. "But ye'll no' get away this time. We have men searching everywhere for ye."

"We'll see," said Turnbull, and he thrust again, only for Green Teeth to step to the side.

As his friend dodged the blow, Blotchy took the chance to make his own jab at Antoine's face. The Frenchman jerked his head back but felt a sting to his cheek, then a warm, salty trickle running down into his mouth. It felt like a flesh wound, but it was still a warning: these men would not be easily overcome. To make matters worse, the innkeeper had decided to join the fray. He was coming from the cottage with an axe. They needed to get out of here quickly.

Antoine edged towards the horses, which were now

getting restless by the trough. It would be impossible to mount them, unless he could distract their attackers somehow. Could he lift up the trough with his foot and kick it at them? No, it would be too heavy. There was a pitchfork, which might make it easier to hold them at bay, but he would have to stoop to pick it up, and he could not take the risk. If only Turnbull would come a bit closer, perhaps they could cover for each other.

Out of the corner of his eye, Antoine saw the innkeeper creep off to the right. He was giving them a wide berth, as if he meant to circle behind them. If he managed to do that, they would be done for. Turnbull seemed to spot the threat as well, for he took a couple of side steps towards his master. However, as the lad changed direction, he stumbled and fell to one knee. God's nails, he'd dropped his sword as well. He was now at Green Teeth's mercy. As he grasped desperately for his weapon, the reiver kicked it away and stepped over him. Then, as Antoine watched on with horror, Green Teeth raised his sword and plunged it into Turnbull's chest.

There was a strange silence. Antoine had seen many men die without uttering a sound and even more paralysed momentarily, before the shock wore off and the scream of pain took over. But this was different. Turnbull looked startled but otherwise unaffected by the blade sticking out of his chest. Green Teeth was confused as well. He gripped the hilt of his sword and tried to push it further in, but the weapon appeared to be quite stuck.

Antoine looked to the heavens in search of a divine explanation, but when none came, he resorted to more earthly wiles. Spotting that Blotchy was distracted, he swung his sword with all his might, so that he sliced through the reiver's quilted jack and deep into his flesh. Blotchy screamed and fell backwards, clutching his arm.

At the same time, Turnbull recovered his own sword and, from his prostrate position, swiped it through the back of Green Teeth's legs. He, too, crumpled to the ground, howling like an animal. This just left the innkeeper. But the fellow did not seem to fancy his chances anymore and backed off, his axe by his side.

Now the real test came. Antoine stepped over his attackers' writhing bodies and stood astride Turnbull. The lad was still pinned down by Green Teeth's sword. There was no blood around the hole. But perhaps the blade was wedged against a rib or stuck in an organ, so that the wound was plugged. Antoine knew that removing it might do more harm than good, but he surely had no choice.

He gripped the hilt and pulled gently. The shaft did not shift, so he gave it the slightest twist, hoping to God that this did not make things worse. Something gave way; there was a harsh sound, not the sucking noise that sometimes came from body wounds. Antoine gave another pull, and, ever so slowly, he eased the blade out.

For a moment, Turnbull lay on his back, his fingers moving towards the hole in his chest. He closed his eyes, and Antoine worried that he might be gone after all. Then the lad sighed, as he pulled out a piece of dark brown leather from underneath his doublet.

"Sweet Mary. It was the ledger. The book saved my life."

Chapter 39

Turnbull continued to finger the hole in his doublet, as they rode up the brae. They had reclaimed their old horses, and the familiar feel of Fogo underneath helped to steady his nerves as he contemplated his brush with death. Yet he could hardly relax, for the spectre of the executioner's block still loomed large ahead of them. Indeed, the axe had lowered with every minute they had wasted at that cursed cottage. And it kept falling as they paused on the brow of the next hill.

"Where do we go now, sir? Should we scout about for further feathers?"

His master frowned. "I've been thinking about them. I fear they might have been the Devil's work after all."

"What do you mean?"

"Would a five-year-old really have had the wits to mark the way like that? And even if he did, would the feathers present themselves so perfectly, if they had merely been dropped? No, I fear someone has laid them out on foot, stuck them in exactly the right places, secured them so that they would not blow away. Remember Stumpy Watt telling us that one of Baird's favourite tricks is to leave a false trail?"

"Oh God."

"Exactly. I worry that he may have done this to throw us off his scent."

"He led us to that cottage on purpose, knowing that those men were there?"

"Perhaps. Either way, he tricked us good and proper. Christ's wounds, he's probably miles away by now." The Frenchman used his sleeve to dab his own wound, on his cheek. "You know, I wish I could remember where I'd seen that fellow from the cottage before. That might help us learn what's going on."

Turnbull felt sick at the idea of explaining who Green Teeth was, and how he had unwittingly allowed him to storm Ravenscleugh. He tried to move the enquiry on. "We know he's one of the Douglases, that's all. But come, we must focus on Baird and the king. And quickly! Which way do we go? Left or right?"

The Frenchman cast his gaze about the Lammermuirs before looking Turnbull in the eye, with unusual directness. "Yes, we're at a crossroads, alright," he said at last. He looked grave, as if he were building up to something. "But the choice we face is greater than which path to take."

"What do you mean?" the lad said uneasily.

"Earlier you said that climbing into Baird's mind was our only hope – and I agreed. But what if there is another way? What if we decided to cut our losses and run? If we made that choice now, there is still a chance that we could find a ship – or scramble to safety somehow."

Turnbull could not believe what he was hearing. "You're saying we should give up our mission altogether? Leave the king to his fate?"

"I said 'we'," said Antoine slowly. "But in truth, Lord Albany addressed this mission to me alone. You have simply been obeying my orders – even when they have been flawed." He paused. "What I am saying is that I will stick at this task, until the bitter end. But if you would rather save your skin, while you can – well, I would not blame you."

Turnbull thought of the executioner's block again. How sweet it would be to dodge the axe and reinvent himself elsewhere. Yet he could not leave his master like this, not when he knew that he was partly responsible for their predicament. He shook his head. "No, we got into this together, and we must get out of it together."

His master gave a wan smile. "Then we must think harder. Where might Baird be headed? We will only have one chance at this, so we must make our guess a good one."

They went over the possibilities. Could he be heading back to Ettrick Forest? Unlikely, for he would meet Douglas's men on the way, and they clearly meant to kill him. The coast? Impossible, for Hamilton's ships were watching the sea. Tantallon to meet the queen, then? But no, there were beacons along that road and no signal had come back. Turnbull was starting to think he should have accepted his master's offer of an escape, when the Frenchman groaned.

"What is it, sir?"

Antoine wore a pained expression. "It may be nothing. But I have recalled something that Baird once said to us."

"Go on."

"He talked of the joy he felt, when out on the moors. The freedom of the hills, the open space, the smell of heather in the air. That's why we came this way, isn't it?" The lad nodded as Antoine continued. "But he mentioned one other thing, something quite specific that I'd forgotten until now. He spoke of the call of wolves."

Turnbull furrowed his brow. "True, but how does that help us?"

"Think about it: there are very few wolves in the Marches these days. In fact, I'd say there's only one place round here where you'd hear them in the night."

Turnbull thought about this, then his eyes opened wide. "Wolfsruther."

"The name rather gives it away, doesn't it? The marsh of the wolves. As wild a place as you'll ever find. We could reach it by nightfall, if we hurried."

"Why on earth would Baird have taken the king there?"

"To hide away, before he strikes out for his true destination. Christ's bones, he's like a wolf himself, creeping back to his favourite den until the hunt has passed him by."

Turnbull shuddered at the stories he had heard about this place. Folk said that the wolves there had such a taste for human flesh that they would gladly leave a sheep untouched if a shepherd were on offer. Some said the beasts could even steal men's voices and use them to turn hunters against each other in the night.

"Perhaps we should go to Black Rig first and get a band of men for the morn. It's not so far from there, and we could be more certain of catching him?"

"No," said Antoine firmly. "If we don't get him tonight, he will be gone. It's now or never." He paused. "Well, what do you think?"

Turnbull was not at all sure of his master's theory. And if they did go further inland, it would remove all hope of an escape for themselves. But he had no better plan. He squinted into the afternoon sun and pointed towards the southwest.

"I think we should stop talking and start listening for wolves."

The Dance of Vipers

They rode hard for the rest of the day, over the mosses and grasslands of the Lammermuirs, through summer pastures, across babbling burns and sikes. Occasionally, they would meet a peasant and ask them whether they had seen anybody come this way, but the response was always the same: a dull-eyed shake of the head. Antoine began to worry that he had taken them both on a fool's errand. But they were now deep into the hills. There was no going back. All they could do was put their heads down, while they still had heads at all.

By the time they reached Wolfsruther, it was getting dark. A wind had picked up, sending a chill through the air. The long grass seemed to whisper to them, perhaps warning them to go no further. As Antoine cast about the vast open moorlands, he felt Turnbull's eyes upon him, awaiting instruction. He felt touched by the lad's loyalty in following him here, but also deeply responsible for him. It was all very well to risk his own life, but he must not let the boy down.

Some lights appeared in the distance. Half a dozen of them, perhaps, like a cloud of glow worms over the swamps. Antoine and Turnbull braced themselves for more trouble, but as the lights bobbed and weaved through the gloaming, their dim glow revealed that their owners came on foot: a good sign. There was some barking too, and as the party got closer, it became clear that this was a group of hunters, bearing lanterns.

"Greetings, strangers," said the leader of the group. He was an old, sinewy man, dressed in animal skins, giving him the appearance of a satyr. By his side, he had an enormous hound, wearing a long-spiked collar: protection against the jaws of wolves. "What brings ye here, to a place like this?"

Antoine recalled Green Teeth's boast that their enemies

were "searching everywhere" for them – and reminded himself that the last hunters he had met, back in Ettrick Forest, had been working for the Douglases. But there was something about the old man's earthy nature that he trusted. And besides, they were desperate for help.

"We are looking for someone. A single rider with a boy."

The man gave a dry laugh. "We've been on this moor all day. There's naebody here but us. And if ye have any sense, ye'll leave wi' us as well."

"The wolves are on the prowl tonight," explained one of his companions. "They have new whelps to feed. Why, they were tracking us just now, and we could practically hear them lick their lips."

"The man we're after won't be put off by that. He's as cunning as a wolf himself and knows these moors from old. Tell me, where would a fellow like that go, if he didn't want to be found?"

The old man looked at Antoine with incredulity. "He would go through that pass," he said, pointing towards a narrow gap between two steep hills. "And then find a cave in the rocks beyond. But the approach is marshy and can suck a man under in an instant. The wolves also like to use the caves. We've dug pits all about, to try to catch them. Only a madman would venture there – and only a magician could come out in one piece."

Antoine nodded. "Well, our fellow is something of a magician, so if that makes us the madmen, so be it."

He bade the hunters farewell, and they headed towards the pass.

Night fell quickly on the moor. Antoine and Turnbull had

just enough time to squeeze through the rocky entrance to the next valley, before they were shrouded in black. As the hunter had warned them, the ground was marshy underfoot, and Antoine recalled a time last year, when Carbonel had almost led them to their deaths in such a bog. He hoped his horse had learnt his lesson since then, but without any light to guide them, beyond that of the crescent moon and a few stars, safe passage was doubly difficult. With every step, every squelch and gurgle, Antoine expected to be plunged into a treacherous morass, but whether by chance or God's mercy, they eventually reached firmer land.

On the far side of the valley, a campfire was burning. And by its light, two human shapes were just visible, one large, one small. Could it be Baird and the king? The thought was irresistible. But to reach them and find out, they would have to navigate another few hundred yards in the dark, without being detected. Worse, they would have to beware of the creatures with yellow eyes, which now watched them from the ridge.

"I think we'll have to leave the horses here," whispered Antoine. "Otherwise, Baird will hear us coming."

"But the wolves, sir?"

"I know. The horses will not like it, but I'm afraid we have no choice."

"I wasn't thinking of the horses..."

It was a good point, but Antoine just wanted to get this over. "Once we're near the fire, they'll stay away from us. Now let's hurry, before we give ourselves away."

They dismounted and soothed the horses before leaving them and creeping along the marshy valley floor. The ground was soggy, but easier to judge themselves, rather than through their horses' bodies. On Antoine's instructions, they kept their swords sheathed, lest they winked in the moonlight. Little by little, they advanced. They could hear voices – a man and a child. They seemed to be quite merry, in contrast to their bleak surroundings. Perhaps this wasn't Baird and the king after all? Except when they got to within fifty yards, the taller figure stood up, and the flames gave them a perfect view of his face.

"Will Baird!" Antoine called out instinctively. The reiver froze, his arms tense by his sides. Antoine watched him squint into the dark and realised that they had an advantage over him: the campfire meant that they could see him, but he could not see them. It felt good to be the one dishing out the surprises for a change.

"Who goes there?"

"Old friends," called Antoine, hurrying forwards. "Here to retrieve His Grace."

"Ah, de Lissieu – and Turnbull, I presume." Baird seemed to relax a little. "Ye've done well to find me here. I thought those feathers would deceive ye."

"They almost killed us. But enough of that. We're here now, so give us the king."

At this, the boy stood up and joined Baird by the side of the fire. He held his kidnapper's hand. "I don't want to go with them," he whined. "We are having fun!"

"Listen to that, de Lissieu. His Grace enjoys my company. Perhaps ye should leave us be?"

Antoine was tired of this. "Enough of this nonsense, Baird. We're coming forward now. Two of us against one. So put your hands on your head, where we can see them. Make one false move and we will strike you down."

Baird sighed but did as he was asked, causing the king to raise his hands as well. The reiver laughed indulgently at the boy's mimicry. And yet, as Antoine advanced, he found something profoundly sad in it: the idea of a king who was a prisoner in his own country, handed back and forth between great men as if he were a slave. Ruefully, he reflected that he was just the latest adult to take custody of him. And for what? To take him from a place where he was free and happy, so that he could be confined in some dingy castle.

He told himself to forget such silliness; his life – and that of his own young friend – depended on securing this child. Keeping his eyes firmly on Baird, as he stood by the flickering campfire, he quickened his pace.

But as he came forward, the ground gave way, and he plunged into a deep hole, with Turnbull on top of him.

Chapter 40

They lay in complete darkness for a moment, chests heaving, before Antoine untangled his limbs from Turnbull's and stood up. His knee ached, as he groped about for support. To his right, there was a long, hard structure, seemingly made of wood. He traced a hand along its rough bark surface, only to withdraw it abruptly, when it tapered to a sharp point. Turning to the other side, he found a cold, damp wall which extended just above his reach. Soil crumbled in his fingers. By Jesu, they had fallen into one of those wolf pits that the hunters had spoken of.

"Are ye alright?" said Baird, looming over the edge. He extended a torch, bathing them in an angry red light.

"It looks like it," said Turnbull, as he scrambled to his feet. "Not that you would care."

"I'm sorry, gentlemen, I kent about the pit, but no' the stake. I wish ye no harm, ye must ken that by now."

"There were Douglases at the cottage you pointed us towards," said Antoine. "I suppose you didn't know about them either?"

"By the Holy Ghost, I didnae. I simply wished ye off my trail." Baird paused. "Douglases, you say? That's no' a good sign for any o' us."

Antoine snorted. "Perhaps you could cut a deal with them? I wouldn't put anything past you now."

"Those wretches who have killed my friends? No, they'd be the last folk I'd parlay with."

"Then, what?"

A ghastly howl echoed round the hills.

"I will take the boy back to his mother," said Baird. "He should never have been ripped from her in the first place."

Antoine did a double take. "You're working for the queen?"

"No, but I'm sure she will appreciate my gift when I surprise her. At the very least, it should be enough to secure a pardon."

"You forget she's not in power these days."

"She may be if she possesses the king. As I told ye long ago, we live in times of change."

"How do you even propose to reach her? She's at Tantallon, surrounded by her husband's men. And you're headed in the wrong direction."

"No, it's you who's barking up the wrong tree, monsieur. All I need to do is get the lad to England. That's what – three hours' ride from here?"

Antoine's jaw dropped. It was true: if the king were taken over the border, he would be under the de facto control of Margaret Tudor, even if she took a while to join him.

Spotting his discomfort, the reiver gave an impish smile. "Ye ken, it was you who gave me the idea, monsieur. Back in Old Peggy's cottage, ye said that stealing the king was Douglas's only hope. So I thought the same might apply to me. But ye also said I'd have no rest in Scotland, so I cooked up this wee plan."

Antoine felt sick at the notion that he had been the

architect of his own downfall. He could think of little else to say, beyond proffering a feeble warning. "There are men stationed all along the frontier. They'll catch you before you get anywhere near it."

"Ah," said Baird, a note of mischief in his voice. "But they cannae catch what they cannae see. On which point, forgive me one last time. I must disappear."

He swiped the torch away, and they were plunged into darkness again. There was the sound of a child's laughter and a horse's hooves heading away. Then that terrible howling started up again, more vicious and insistent than before.

Antoine scrabbled about the walls of the pit, hoping that there might be some rock or root which they could use to clamber out, but it was impossible in the pitch black. He considered climbing along the stake, but the angle was too steep, the risk of falling and being impaled too great. In despair, he urged Turnbull to make a stirrup with his hands and tried to haul himself up. His knee throbbed when he pushed on it. His arms were weak, and he couldn't get purchase on the edge of the pit. He felt drained of all energy and hope, but Turnbull told him to keep going, and with one last heave, he managed to get his elbows over the side and pull himself to his feet.

Once on the surface, all Antoine could see was the glow of the fire – and, behind him, those yellow eyes. The wolves were closer and more numerous than before. Their howling had been replaced by a low, breathy growling. God's blood, the beasts would be upon him if he was not quick. He needed a burning log to ward them off and help Turnbull to escape somehow. Could they still catch Baird and the king? He did not care for now – all that mattered was getting out of here alive.

Antoine's heart pounded as he turned his back on the wolves and groped towards the campfire. He took each step carefully, lest he fell into another pit. The snarling got louder, and he half-expected to be pounced on at any moment, but as he felt the warmth of the flames upon him, he was relieved to hear the noise die away again. Now he just needed to make a torch. Kicking about the logs at the base of the fire, he found one that had not burnt out and was cool enough to pick up. He turned to go back to the lad, only to see that the yellow eyes had formed a circle: the wolves had surrounded the horses!

What was he to do now? Should he run to the nags' defence or continue trying to rescue Turnbull? He decided to prioritise the former, for without horses, they would surely be doomed. And in any case, the lad should be safe in the pit for now. But wait – he would get another torch, so that Turnbull might help himself. He found one and started making his way back, as briskly as his knee would allow. He waved the torches and shouted as he went, hoping to scare off the wolves, but it seemed to have no effect on them. Perhaps he had lost his mind: what was it the hunters had said about only madmen venturing here?

He reached the pit with the torches still burning and handed one down to Turnbull.

"What the hell's going on?" the lad said, as the growls mixed with whinnies in the night air.

"The wolves are at the horses. I'll need to see to them."

"What about me? I can't get out of here on my—"

"See if you can make some footholds in the wall, with your sword. Then join me as soon as you can."

With that, Antoine took out his own sword and ran towards the wolves. With the help of his torch, he could see that they were about a dozen strong, and were taking it in turns to press Carbonel and Fogo. The horses were putting up a good fight, rearing and kicking at their attackers, but they couldn't hold out forever against such numbers. Antoine waved the torch in wild swoops and shouted more loudly than ever, but the wolves were undeterred. As the hunters had said, the beasts were determined to fill their bellies.

He broke into the circle, just as one attacker leapt onto Carbonel's back and sank its fangs into his hackles. The horse shrieked and tossed his neck back and forth, but the wolf hung on as it was thrown this way and that. Its accomplices abandoned Fogo to focus on this stricken victim, snapping at the horse's forequarters in an attempt to get at his throat. Antoine caught one of the wolves with his sword, sending it spinning away with a whimper. He swiped another across the muzzle, causing a spray of blood to land across his face. This cleared the way for him to stab at the leader of the pack, still swinging about from Carbonel's neck. Furious at the plight of his beloved horse, he struck the wolf with such force that it fell lifeless to the ground. But as it dropped, so did Antoine, with a set of jaws clamped round his ankle.

The pain was excruciating, as if his bone were in a vice. He roared as he hacked at the wolf's hind legs, but the beast was moving with such a frenzy that he could not land a blow. More snarling muzzles appeared at his face. He pushed the torch into a golden eye, and its owner leapt back, but the others would not give in. As he felt his strength ebb away, there was an almighty roar, and his attackers scattered sideways. Turnbull appeared on Fogo, raining fire and steel down on the wolves, while his horse trampled on their fleeing bodies.

One by one, the hell-creatures slunk off into the gloom, leaving Antoine on his back, gasping for air. Turnbull dismounted to help him stagger to his feet and clamber onto Carbonel. Then, as he cursed bitterly at his suffering and their predicament, they returned through the pass and headed for their tower at Black Rig.

It was not far to their old stronghold, but the pain in Antoine's ankle and knee made the journey seem like an eternity. The whole left side of his body felt like it had been put through a meat grinder. Carbonel was sluggish too, his gait uneven, the wounds on his hackles slick to the touch. Even Turnbull and Fogo, while physically unharmed, were utterly shattered by their latest ordeal. When the serjeant of Black Rig opened the main gate to let them in, they all collapsed into the barmekin.

Anderson was a shaven-headed, battle-hardened soldier, who had seen all manner of things on the frontier, but even he declared himself astonished at the events that they recounted. Why, it was less than a month since he had waved them off, to escort the queen over the border. Now they were chasing after the king, in the opposite direction?

"I'm afraid so," said Antoine. "And if we cannot catch him, we'll be chased ourselves." He sighed and turned to his young aide. "I fear we've run out of road, Turnbull. I should have made you flee, when you had the chance."

The boy set his jaw. "I told you, sir. I will not leave you."

"But we have no idea where Baird is now – or how we might stop him."

"You will think of something; you always do."

"Look at the state of me, lad." Antoine felt his eyes

brimming, through a mixture of exhaustion, pain and emotion. "I can barely raise a hand, let alone make a plan."

"We'll patch ye up tonight," said Anderson. "Then we can take ye to Mistress Gray at daybreak. She'll have ye ready to go again in no time."

Ah, Catherine. Antoine had barely spared her a thought this last mad week, but how he wished that he could see her now.

Anderson took his arm and guided him towards the tower. A pair of sentries had come down from the wall-walk to see what all the fuss was about. Other soldiers emerged from the barracks and stared at their master's dishevelled state. Antoine wondered what would happen to them if Margaret Tudor came to power and Albany were deposed. As he climbed the spiral staircase and limped into his chamber, he thought of all of those who depended on him. He must stop his self-pity, put away his own desires.

"Visiting Mistress Gray will only slow us down. We must focus on Baird alone. We know he means to cross the border and will likely make an attempt in the morning."

"Not tonight?"

"No, even for him, it will be easier in the light."

"I don't know," said Turnbull. "He boasted that he could not be caught if he could not be seen. He talked of disappearing. Does that not point to him using darkness as a cloak?"

Antoine slumped on his bed and put his head in his hands. Perhaps the lad was right. For all they knew, Baird might be crossing the border right now. If so, they were already too late. And yet, there had been something strange about Baird's words and the way that he had delivered them. As if they were another of his childish riddles. Had he been trying to give them one last clue, or was he simply enjoying a private joke at their expense?

"Good Lord, I think I have it."

Turnbull gripped his shoulder and sat down beside him on the bed. "I knew you would. So what's he up to?"

But Antoine was too tired to go through it all right now. "I'll tell you in the morning, if my idea still makes any sense. Meanwhile, fetch some bandages, Anderson. And make sure everyone is ready at dawn. This day has been the longest of my life, but if I'm right, tomorrow may be even longer."

Chapter 41

Antoine had hoped that sleeping in a familiar bed might ease his nerves, but the pain caused him to lie awake, fretting over their precarious situation. Never mind those feathers, it was as if their whole journey this last month had been one long false trail, where every choice had been proved wrong, every path had brought them closer to their destruction. Now, as they stood on the brink of disaster, he was about to make one last leap on their behalf. But would it finally bring them to safety or send them hurtling into the abyss? When the umber light finally peeked through the shutters, it was time to find out.

Antoine took Turnbull's arm but gave little away as they went downstairs. He could tell the lad was itching to find out his plan, but he was too tired to explain it twice, so he suggested that they dispense with breakfast and go straight to the courtyard to meet Anderson. The serjeant had the whole garrison ready, in line with his orders. There were about thirty men, experienced fighters from the Marches. Antoine gave an approving nod, before taking Anderson and Turnbull aside.

"So, what's the plan, sir?"

Antoine took a deep breath. "A good question. We'll be going to Mistress Gray's house at Cheeklaw, after all."

Anderson looked crestfallen. "Were my bandages no' good enough, sir?"

"No, you've done a fine job as ever, serjeant."

"Then why visit Catherine?" said Turnbull. "I thought you said it would slow us down?"

"Because I supposed that Baird must plan to cross the border at first light. But what if I am not the only one who might wish to visit Mistress Gray?"

Turnbull gaped. "You think Baird's at Catherine's?"

"I do, insane though it might sound. They barely met at Ravenscleugh, but he was quite fascinated by something she spoke of there. Do you remember, when we had dinner together? She talked of collecting fern seeds at midnight, on Midsummer's Eve."

"Midnight at Midsummer?" said Anderson, his eyes wide. "Do such seeds no' render ye invisible?"

"So the story goes. The idea's as flimsy as a tinker's tent if you ask me, but Baird was transfixed by the notion. He said that he might have to visit Catherine one day, to see if her magic held good."

"A throwaway joke," said Turnbull. "He was flirting with her, as he tried to charm us all."

"Perhaps back then. But I feel the idea might have grown on him. He fancies himself as a sorcerer. He prizes his ability to escape any trap, no matter how tightly sprung. What could be more enjoyable for him, than to disappear with the king, only to reappear triumphant in another country?"

Turnbull clasped his head as he repeated Baird's words at Wolfsruther. "'They cannot catch me if they cannot see me. Forgive me, gentlemen, I must disappear.'"

"You see my point? Listen, I might be clutching at thin air here. Baird has tricked us so many times that I cannot tell anymore. But it makes more sense than charging about the whole length of the frontier, in the hope that we might find him. So unless you have a better idea, I suggest we head to Catherine's now, with every man we have."

Turnbull and Anderson assented to the plan, although they agreed that they should not alarm the men by telling them too much about their mission. After all, coming face to face with a powerful enemy was one thing, but battling an invisible one was quite another.

Cheeklaw was not far from Black Rig, so they were there within the hour. As they rode through the ancient oak forest which surrounded Catherine's cottage, they saw nothing to disturb them. All was quiet apart from the snorting of their horses, and the occasional clink of a soldier's armour. It was the same when they emerged into the clearing. They passed Blind Gibb's house: a tumbledown cottage made of strips of wood and earth. As usual, chickens pecked about in front of it. Next, they arrived at Catherine's place, a prettier affair, with whitewashed walls and a beautiful herb garden. Antoine breathed in the familiar mixture of lavender, rosemary and sage as they drew near.

Silently, he directed his men to dismount and form a ring around Catherine's cottage. Again, all seemed in order. The shutters were closed, but that was quite normal as Mistress Gray was a private person, who did not welcome the prying eyes of others. Anderson signalled from the side of the cottage that everybody was in position. Satisfied that it was safe to proceed, Antoine also dismounted, his wounds aching, as he slid down Carbonel's side. He began to creep up the path. But before he made it to the door, it creaked open.

"God's mercy!" exclaimed Catherine. She looked over his shoulder at the mass of troops and horses surrounding her house. "I thought that ye were Gibb, come to breakfast wi' me. What are ye doing back here, wi' a' these men?"

"It's a long story, Mistress Gray. But for now, all I need to know is whether our prisoner Will Baird has visited you this morning?"

"Will Baird? Of course not. Why would ye say such a thing?"

Antoine's heart sank. "It doesn't matter. I had a fancy, but it seems that I was wrong." He had a flash of inspiration – or, more truthfully, desperation. "He may have been in disguise – or maybe he used... a boy to do his bidding?"

She gave a blank look. "The sun is barely up. I havenae seen a soul."

"Ah, well. I'm sorry." What an understatement that was. Antoine had the crushing realisation that this might be the last time he saw Catherine. Should he use this moment to apologise for the way they had last parted? Or even to express the feelings he still had for her? But no, he had already humiliated himself quite enough. All he could do was say farewell with his eyes and hope that she, who saw so much that others missed, could detect his meaning.

"I'm sorry too," Catherine said softly. "But I wish ye well, wi' finding him." She paused and returned his stare. "Perhaps ye should ask Gibb if he has seen anything."

Antoine nodded, although he was sure their mission was over now, their fate quite sealed. There had only been one reason for Baird to come here – and it had not been to visit a blind man and his chickens. He signalled for his troops to stand down. But wait a moment. Catherine had encouraged him to ask Gibb whether he had *seen* anything. That was a strange word to use of a man that they both knew to be sightless. Was she trying to tell him something?

He tried to remain calm. "Should I ask Gibb to keep an eye on you, as well?"

"Aye, that would be much appreciated."

So she *was* trying to say something. It could only be because Baird was listening to her right now. He must be in the cottage. Unless – no, it was too mad even to think such a thing – he had taken that fern seed potion already and had rendered himself invisible? He was certain such talk was nonsense, but if he was wrong, Baird might even be standing beside them now, enjoying his deception!

Antoine motioned for his men to stay where they were. Then, keeping his eyes fixed on Catherine's, he spoke very deliberately. "You know, before I visit Gibb, why don't we go inside, to talk for old times' sake?"

Catherine hesitated, as if formulating another coded response. But Antoine did not have to wait for it, for the door creaked again, and Baird appeared beside her. He held a dagger in his right hand and placed the other around Catherine's waist. The king's rosy face peeped out from between their hips.

"Ye just willnae give up, will ye?" said the reiver.

Antoine's rigid face masked the rush of blood to his head. "This time it was *you* who gave *me* the idea, Baird. But enough talk. Hand over the king. You can see how many we are, there's no way out of here."

"None that ye can see, perhaps. But as ye must have guessed, I dinnae plan to be seen much longer."

"If you've taken Mistress Gray's potion, it clearly hasn't worked."

"No' yet, it hasnae. But I feel it coursing through my veins. His Grace reports the same. And very soon, we will be having the adventure of our lives, isn't that so, my little friend?"

The king nodded, but Antoine saw how nervously he eyed the soldiers. The men from Black Rig were not the well-groomed bodyguards the boy was used to; they were harder, fiercer, wilder.

"Let His Grace go, Baird. Then we can talk about your life."

"I have no life, if I give up the boy. Now tell your men to get back, afore somebody gets hurt." The reiver raised his dagger a fraction, so that it was on a level with Catherine's waist – and the king's throat. His eyes were red-rimmed, his face lined. Perhaps Antoine was not the only one on the brink.

"Come on, Baird, we both know you won't hurt either of them."

"Oh aye? How sure are ye o' that? How well do ye really ken me?"

Antoine had asked himself this many times these past few weeks and now found the answer more elusive than ever. He could not forget Baird's good qualities: his charm, kindness and playfulness. But he also saw the determination in the man's eyes, watched his grip tighten on the dagger. He nodded to Anderson, to get the soldiers to back off.

"That's better. Now someone bring me my horse." When nobody stirred, Baird moved his dagger another inch towards the king's throat, causing the boy's lip to tremble. "I said, someone bring my horse!"

It was the first time Antoine had ever heard the reiver raise his voice. Perhaps he was unravelling, after all. Or was it yet another act? Either way, the shouting had further upset the king, who had started to snivel. They needed to calm things down. Reluctantly, Antoine told Turnbull to fetch the horse. Then he searched his brain for some way to solve this, without provoking bloodshed.

Whatever the correct approach, it would surely require the kind of careful handling that he had learnt in his years as a diplomat, so he was alarmed when Catherine took over the negotiation.

"I dinnae claim to ken ye, sir. But afore these gentlemen arrived this morning, I saw how tender ye were, wi' His Grace. You spoke kindly to him, said ye'd bring him to his mother."

"Aye, that's where the boy belongs."

"Quite so. And what do ye think his mother would want ye to do right now?"

"I have no time for guessing games, mistress."

"Then what would *your* mother want ye to do?"

Baird's face darkened. "I barely knew my mother. I was orphaned in a raid."

Antoine worried that Catherine was fanning the man's flames, when they needed to douse his fire. He tried to flash her a look, but she seemed determined to proceed.

"Ye must remember something of her, though? I can hear it in your voice."

"God's nails, ye dinnae cease. But very well. I remember the look in her eyes as the reivers struck my father down. She shouted for me to run, so I escaped across the moors, and that was the last I saw or heard o' her."

"There, that's all ye need to ken," Catherine said, clasping her hands over his, upon the hilt of the dagger. Antoine moved forwards, terrified that she might have pushed the reiver too far, but she would not be stopped. "She wanted ye to be safe, no' to die at her side. Just like this boy's mother would rather ye left him safe wi' us, than bring him to her deid. There will be soldiers, everywhere on the border. Think how many dangers ye'll expose him to."

Baird prised her fingers off the dagger. "If your potion does its job, we will have no worries."

"If it was going to work, it would have worked by now. It's time to run. Make yerself safe but make this boy safe as well." She paused. "Think o' this child's mother. But if not, think o' yer ain."

Turnbull came back with the horse, to find the group frozen, as if in a spell. Antoine mused that, though Catherine was not a witch as some said, she possessed her own kind of magic, a rare ability to read others' minds, find the darkest corners of their hearts.

Still glowering, Baird lifted the king onto the front of the saddle and then climbed on behind. But there was a heaviness to his movement, that was quite unlike the fluidity that Antoine had come to associate with him. He still held the child tightly with his left arm, but his dagger hand hung limp by his side.

"What do ye say, de Lissieu? If I leave the king wi' you, what will happen to me?"

Antoine knew he should clap this rogue in irons and take him back to Edinburgh. But the thought of guarding him filled him with dread. As did the idea of keeping him anywhere near the king. He decided that giving him up would be a price well worth paying, for recovering His Grace.

"A man like you does not need a potion to disappear. You can still make it to England on your own and create a new life for yourself."

"What kind of life?"

"You'll find something. Or something will find you. As

Mistress Gray says, we will see that the king is reunited with his mother, under the proper conditions. And I will do my utmost to make sure nobody comes after you."

"There's no chance of a pardon, then?"

"Even less chance than before."

Baird smiled, that twinkle in his eye returned. "Aye. It was a long shot. But long shots are always worth a try, are they no'?" He ruffled the king's hair. "Well, I enjoyed our adventure, little man. But these folk are right: it's time for me to go."

With that, the reiver scooped up the boy and tossed him down to Turnbull. Antoine rushed forward, throwing one arm around the child and the other around Catherine. Baird spurred his horse, and the soldiers turned to their master for permission to give chase.

But Antoine was too engulfed in a wave of relief to bother with vengeance. As he watched Baird race off into the forest, he thought the words at the same time that the king shouted them: "Let him go!"

Chapter 42

Two hours later, Antoine sat at the window of his chamber at Black Rig. Catherine had refreshed his body dressings and was applying some old wine to his final wound: the cut to his cheek. As she dabbed away, he gazed down on the courtyard, where the king was playing with Anderson. The serjeant had stuck a wooden pole in the ground, and they were taking it in turns to throw horseshoes at it. The old soldier was letting the boy win, causing him to let out peals of high-pitched laughter.

"Children recover quickly, don't they?" said Antoine, with a smile.

"Or they learn to hide their pain," said Catherine. "Now hold still, I'm almost done."

There was an edge to her voice, and he realised that he still had work to do, to win back her favour.

"At any rate, it is good to see His Grace is safe and well. We have you to thank for that," he said.

"I hardly think so."

"No, it's true. You saw something in Baird that I missed."

"I listened, that is all."

"Yes, you listened, and I did not. I had oft noted his childish disposition, his sense of mischief, his love of play and magic. I saw how he loved that urchin Fleabite and his tenderness towards the king. But I did not relate any of it to his own hard beginnings. He never had a childhood, did he?"

Catherine gave his cheek a final dab with a muslin cloth. "I believe that's why he craves adventure now." She paused to put her equipment away. "As for me, I want a quiet life, where men dinnae turn up on my doorstep wi' daggers and the king is just a face upon my coin."

Antoine nodded sheepishly. "I'm sorry that I have been a poor friend these past few weeks. I should never have dragged you into this in the first place – or ignored your counsel when you gave it. Today you've proved your worth yet again. Without you, we'd be dead men."

She laid her hand on his, her voice softening. "Aye, well Death has a habit of coming back when he thinks he has been cheated. So while I may have chased him from your door today, make sure you dinnae open it for him again the morn."

Antoine spent the afternoon at rest, while the others prepared for the journey back to Craigmillar the next day. That was still the safest haven for the king, for now: if they took the whole garrison from Black Rig with them, they could escort him safely back to Hamilton, then press His Lordship to abandon this nonsense with the false plague and let the boy see his mother. With a little more goodwill on all sides, the child could be restored to Edinburgh, and by the time Governor Albany returned, it would be as if nothing had ever happened.

Turnbull stood in the yard, overseeing the arrangements. Anderson had procured a covered wagon from a local miller that, while hardly fitting for a king, would allow them to transport him with the minimum of attention. The tower's cook had prepared a batch of meat pies that they could eat upon the hoof. The stable boys washed down the horses, paying particular attention to the wounds that Carbonel had suffered from the wolves.

It was late afternoon when Turnbull appeared at Antoine's door, holding a sheaf of papers.

"They found these in Fogo's saddle bag, when they were cleaning him," he said. "They must have belonged to the Douglases."

Antoine saw that something was troubling the lad, so he beckoned him forwards and took the papers from his hand. The first two pieces of parchment made him jerk his head back. They were crude sketches of him and Turnbull, labelled with their names, in case there were any doubt.

After his initial shock, he tried to make light of them. "Not the most flattering of likenesses, but they'd do for showing round the taverns."

"Yes, it explains how that innkeeper recognised us at the drovers' inn. But look at the others, sir."

Antoine turned to the next two sheets. One was another portrait, this time of a rough-looking fellow, with a brand upon his forehead: although the picture was accompanied by a question mark, there could be little doubt that it represented the man they had been calling V-Face. The other parchment showed a map of Craigmillar Castle.

"Interesting," said Antoine. "The Douglases must have been searching for that vagabond as well. And it looks like they might have heard about the king being moved too."

"Do you think we should be worried?"

Antoine creased his brow as he stared at the sketches. "Their interest in Master V-Face does not concern me greatly. Like us, they must have heard that he had won a wager against Walkerburn and suspected that he had taken that book and letter as payment. But we now know that it was the servant who stole them and Baird's men who robbed him in turn. The map is more troubling though. Look, someone has marked points of weakness in the walls and hiding places in the hunting grounds."

"Douglas must be planning an attack of his own."

"Well, he'll get a surprise if he tries that now: we've got His Grace, and Craigmillar is full of Hamilton's men." Antoine paused as he examined the map. "But let us think this through. Perhaps we should not take the king straight back there. We can't stay here too long, of course, otherwise Hamilton's rage with us will only increase. But if we delay our departure for just a day, it will give us time to send a scout ahead, warn the garrison there and report back with the lie of the land."

Turnbull nodded. "A good idea. I'll ask Anderson for our swiftest rider. If we send someone now and they change horses at Craigmillar, they should be back by tomorrow afternoon. Better safe than sorry, eh?"

Yes, thought Antoine, remembering Catherine's counsel. And better alive than dead.

The king was delighted to hear that he would spend another day at Black Rig: while he wanted to see his mother, he was enjoying the relative freedom of the tower. The soldiers told him stories from the battlefield and taught him fencing moves. He, in turn, amused them with impersonations of Hamilton and Douglas. The good cheer that came from having a child in their midst seemed to spread through everyone. Antoine was pleased to find that Catherine was in better humour with him and that she and Turnbull had put aside any ill feelings of their own, from Ravenscleugh.

That night, they retired to their chamber exhausted – but also suffused with that strange euphoria which comes from narrowly avoiding a common peril: the warm glow of survival. Naturally, the king took the bed, while the three friends slept on the floor, to keep him company. As Antoine watched this precious child nod off, clutching his cloth horse, he wondered what the boy would dream about and hoped that his own nightmare might finally be over.

But that hope was shattered by a frenzy of shouting, in the early hours of the morning.

Chapter 43

Antoine leapt up and ran to the window, just as Anderson appeared at the door.

"What's going on? Surely the scout cannot be back already?"

"He is," said the serjeant. "But I'm afraid he's no' alone. Look."

Anderson opened the shutters, as Turnbull scrambled to their side. The sun was just starting to rise, but its creeping light was joined by a multitude of flames, pin-pricking the surrounding land. They looked like embers, spilled from heaven's hearth, but Antoine immediately understood they were the torches of an army, moving slowly towards the tower.

"The Douglases," explained the serjeant, ruefully. "They captured our scout last night and beat our news from him."

"God's blood. There's hundreds of them. Have they set out their demands?"

"Aye, their man's at the gate right now. They want the king, o' course. The book and letter. And both o' you." Anderson paused. "They say they'll burn the tower and kill everyone inside, if they arenae satisfied within the hour."

There was a cry behind him, and Antoine turned round to see Catherine comforting the king. "I do not want to go to my stepfather," wailed the boy. "Tell his men to go away!"

"Alas, we may have little choice," said Antoine, as he made for the stairs, as fast as his aching body would let him. On the way to the basement, his head spun at this reversal. The only thing in their favour was the king's presence: the threat to burn the tower was surely a bluff, as Douglas needed his stepson alive. So more likely, they were looking at a siege. But that would simply delay their fate by a matter of days. They were doomed, he thought, as Anderson guided him through the teeming mass of soldiers in the courtyard, towards the outer gate.

A sentry moved aside to give Antoine the grille. Through the mesh, he could see a thick-set man, with beetling brows and a tightly pursed mouth.

"You've heard my master's terms?" said the fellow, without so much as an introduction or acknowledgement of Antoine's higher station. His impertinence rankled with the Frenchman. Perhaps he would not give in so easily after all.

"I have, but I will not meet them."

"Then ye ken what we will do. On your own heid be it."

"No, what I know is that you cannot torch this place, while the king is with us. So let us start afresh. I will come with you, if that is what you want, and will gladly converse with Lord Douglas. But you must leave the tower – and everyone within it – while we parlay."

Turnbull began to protest over his shoulder, but Antoine waved him silent. An idea was forming that if he could distract the besiegers somehow, the others might find a way to alert Hamilton, perhaps even reach the queen and tell her of her husband's treachery.

"Impossible," said the messenger. "My master is at Tantallon and is impatient for what's rightfully his. He has forbidden me frae bargaining."

Antoine set his jaw. "At the very least, there should be no need to hand over my assistant."

Again, Turnbull remonstrated, but in any case, the messenger was having none of it.

"Lord Douglas was quite specific. He wants the two o' ye. Plus the king. And the book and letter."

"And if we refuse? We have already established that you cannot simply burn the place."

A wicked smile came upon the man's tight lips. "Forgive me, sir. I fear I've no' relayed my master's instructions in full. In an hour, we will strangle your scout, within full sight o' ye all. For every hour hence, we'll do the same to someone frae the local village. Then when we have captured the tower – which ye ken fine we will do – we will wring the necks o' anyone still living, afore burning it to the ground. Once we have rescued His Grace, o' course."

Antoine took a moment to process the sheer evil of the proposal. Was there no end to these people's lust for power? He could not countenance the slaughter of all those innocents, even if saving them sent him to his own death. The sticking point was Turnbull – but when he looked at the lad, he nodded sadly, as if he, too, accepted the need for sacrifice.

"Very well," said Antoine. "We will be out within the hour. But if you touch a soul within this tower, just know that there will be far worse waiting for you in Hell than anything you've described."

Antoine and Turnbull spent the hour saying farewell to their comrades, while spurning their offers to fight to the last. They saved their most heartfelt goodbyes for Catherine, thanking her for all she had done to help them and urging her to pray for them. She blinked back her tears as she told them to stay strong and God would protect them. Then they gathered up the king, and, despite his moans of protest, they accompanied him through the gate and walked towards the Douglases.

"Good," said the man from the grille, who was now at the front of the group. The soldiers had put out their torches, but in the morning light, they seemed even more numerous than before. As they formed a circle round their captives, they reminded Antoine of the wolves who had attacked them, just two days ago. An old fellow with a wattle chin pulled a false smile at the king.

"Your Grace, you come wi' me. I've got a pony ye can ride."

The boy paused his sobbing at the mention of such a treat and looked to Antoine for his approval. The Frenchman grimaced at the shameless bribery of these wretches, but gestured for him to go, so off the lad trotted, still clutching his beloved cloth horse.

"Now the book and letter," said the group's leader. Antoine shook his head in despair but handed over the ledger which had saved Turnbull's life. The fellow opened it and flicked through the first few pages to check that it was what they were looking for. He then gave a cursory glance at the folded parchment letter inside the book's front cover and gave a nasty smile of victory.

"Finally, the rest o' your possessions. Put your hands against this cart, so that we can see what else ye've got."

Antoine and Turnbull walked over to an old hayrick and spread their arms and legs, so that the fellow could search their bodies. He took their purses, swords and daggers first. Next, he made them take off their doublets and shirts, to check they weren't concealing anything. The final indignity came when he told them to remove their hose and boots. The soldiers jeered as they stood naked on the heath, covering their privy parts. Antoine saw that his own men were watching too, from the battlements of Black Rig. And was that Catherine with them? He burnt with shame and anger.

Only after further questioning, clearly designed to increase their humiliation, were they allowed to put their clothes back on. Their hands were tied. They were forced onto the hayrick, four guards in with them so that they could not discuss their plight. The army closed in behind them, and they rattled off, over the moors.

It took eight hours of painful progress, in the fierce sunshine, without food or water, and with the mockery of their captors ever in their ears, before Tantallon rose from the ocean. Antoine recalled their last visit, a few weeks ago. Then they had travelled with hope in their hearts. Now, they arrived only with despair: another cruel turn of time's great wheel.

Once the army had passed over the drawbridge, the portcullis and gates clanged shut behind them. Yet more troops emerged from the battlements, so that they were engulfed in a noisy, hostile throng. Antoine saw the king being escorted to the North Tower, by a group of ladies-in-waiting. One of them tried to take the boy's toy horse from him, but he hugged it tight, catching Antoine's eye in the process. The Frenchman tried his best to smile, but a soldier heaved him to his feet and threw him from the cart.

He landed on his knees, to the laughter of his captors. As another soldier prodded him with a stick, he felt like a pig on its way to market. Indeed, his wounds caused him such pain that he felt like he'd already been flayed. He began to wish the Douglases would just finish them off in the courtyard, but when a steward arrived to tell them they were to be taken for interrogation, he realised their agony was to be prolonged.

The steward carried a staff in one hand, while guarding a satchel with the other. He pushed them into the keep, and they climbed the stairs to the Great Hall. Dusk was falling, and the torches had not yet been lit, leaving the room gloomy except for a low, crackling fire. In front of it, at a long table, sat Lord Douglas, wearing a look of sickening self-satisfaction.

"It's good to see you both again," he said.

"I wish I could say the same," said Antoine, as the steward brought them forward into the flickering orange light. "We know all about your cheating of the queen. And your plan to kidnap the king from Craigmillar."

Douglas laughed. "I don't know what you mean about the queen. As for the king, it was you and your friend Baird who stole him from Craigmillar. Thank God my men found His Grace and we are once more united as a family."

"That is a base falsehood, as you know. We have evidence to prove your guilt."

"On the contrary, I have all the evidence now. And once I've finished with it, it's you it will condemn."

Douglas jerked his head to the steward, who reached into his satchel and produced the items which had been confiscated at Black Rig. He laid them on the table, and Douglas ran a finger over them. He gave a little chuckle, as he came to the portraits which they had found in Fogo's saddle bag.

"How vain to carry pictures of yourselves. Well, nobody else will want the likeness of two traitors, after you are gone, so I think we can dispose of these." He tossed the pieces of parchment on the fire and watched as their faces were consumed by the flames. "The same goes for this vagabond. We never did find out who he was, but it scarcely matters now."

He added the sketch of V-Face to the hearth, then picked up the ledger. "This book, on the other hand, looks fascinating." He opened up the leather tome and read some of the entries to himself, his countenance one of ecstasy, as if he were accessing some sacred text. When he had drunk his fill of it, he closed his eyes and calmed himself. "Ah, no. I am mistaken. It is some boring rental book. Nobody will care about this either."

Douglas flung the book on the fire, as Turnbull railed against his treachery. The acrid smell of burning leather began to swirl about the room. It reminded Antoine of the stench of the tannery. He tried to banish the memory of their attack as Douglas turned to the parchment envelope.

"As for this letter, I gather it contains the ravings of some local bailie, who took his own life, in a fit of madness. So I cannot imagine it will help us."

Still smirking at his contortion of the facts, he began to unfold the paper, only for Antoine to lunge forward and try to snatch it from him.

"Enough of this deceit! You know what's in this letter. It proves that you've been stealing your wife's rental incomes, to pay for your mistress!"

The steward restrained him, allowing Douglas to jerk his hand back and dangle the letter over the fire. His cruel smile hardened.

"It seems the bailie's madness was contagious. I had better destroy this too, lest others are afflicted."

Antoine made one last attempt to grab the letter, but Douglas let it drop and together, they watched it blacken, curl, disintegrate.

"There, I'm glad we've got rid of all that rubbish," said Douglas. "It means we can concentrate on the real evidence tomorrow." Turning back to the table, he stacked the remaining objects in a pile: their original orders from Albany, the map of Craigmillar, the slander sheet from Walkerburn's house, the two pieces of brooch and the nosegay from The Boar's Head. Antoine stared at him, trying to fathom what he meant, but Douglas did not elaborate.

"You will be held fast tonight, gentlemen. Then you will face trial in the morning. Lord Hamilton and that wretched scribbler Pentland have been summoned to face charges of their own." He inspected his nails. "They will resist the call, at first, of course. But when they realise I have the king, they will see they have no choice."

Ah, thought Antoine. The villain sees a chance to bring his great rival down with us: they were all to be cooked in the same pot, then. He grasped about for some glimmer of salvation.

"The queen would not approve of this. Will she be present at our proceedings?"

"No," said Douglas. "My wife is blissfully happy with her son, no thanks to you and your conspirators. I will not disrupt their sweet reunion. But do not worry, I will tell Her Grace all about your perfidy, once your sentence has been carried out."

Chapter 44

The steward took Antoine and Turnbull back through the keep and out through a side gate, where they were met by half a dozen guards, carrying lanterns. Walking round the main wall, they came to a barred window slit, which Antoine took to be the dungeon. But there was no external door. He paused, confused, only for the steward to move him on.

"Too good for traitors like you," he grunted. "You're going to the rock."

The Bass Rock? Antoine's heart sank as he cast his eyes again on that awful crag. He recalled what Turnbull had once said, about its fearful reputation. But there was no point protesting, and besides, their stay would not be long. The steward prodded him onwards and it was all he could do to avoid slipping as they edged down a steep staircase, cut into the cliffs, and along a wooden jetty. There, they were shoved onto a long rowing boat, and they set off into the black.

The sea was eerily calm, but in the dark, and knowing their grim destination, the journey felt as if they were being ferried across the River Styx itself. Every stroke of the oars took them closer to their own Hades: the stench of guano filling their nostrils, like the fumes of sulphur that the priests warned of on All Souls' Day. Antoine's stomach churned, not just from the assault on his senses, but from the dread realisation that if they were executed tomorrow, they would die unshriven, without having made a confession.

"I am so sorry," he said to Turnbull. But the lad seemed to be tormented by his own thoughts and did not answer.

Eventually, they reached the rock. A wall of harsh noise greeted them: the screeching of thousands of gannets, gulls and puffins, settling down for the night. Another party of guards took over the task of marching the prisoners uphill to the gaol. The men handled them roughly, and Antoine was made dizzy by their constant jostling, together with the birds' shrieking, the stink, the darkness and his own desperation. He was glad when they reached a tiny block, all on its own, and were flung inside.

The door slammed, and then the hatch pulled back, almost immediately. A goggle-eyed man leered in, his face lit by a lantern. "If ye're quiet and give me no trouble, I'll bring ye some ale in an hour. If no', I'll give it to your axeman, so he fouls his blow tomorrow. It's up to you."

So much for a fair trial, thought Antoine. He groped about the room and found a stone bench, with a straw mattress. He lay on it, and Turnbull did the same, his continued silence gnawing at Antoine's conscience. If only he had insisted that the lad went when he had the chance. Or better still, if he had not taken him on this mission in the first place. The boy had been like a son to him, and it pained him that he had failed him so.

"I'm sorry," he said again.

There was a long pause, before Turnbull whispered his reply. "No, I am sorry, sir. So much of this has been my fault."

They were lying so close that Antoine could feel the lad's

breath upon his cheek. "Don't say that. You have been at my side throughout. I could not have wished for better."

"If only that was true," said the boy, his voice cracking. He made a guttural noise, as if he might be sick. "I've been keeping something from you. Something I must get off my chest, before we are... dealt with."

"What kind of thing?"

"You remember that fellow with the green teeth, who burnt the hut at Fala and then attacked us at the drovers' inn? You said you remembered him from somewhere but couldn't recall where. Well, I know who he was. I have always known. He was the man speaking to me outside the provisioner's shop that time."

"Ah, so that was it. Well, no harm done. Wait, are you saying he was an acquaintance?"

"Far from it, he was pestering me. Not for money, as I told you though. He was one of the brawlers, whose horses we took on Midsummer's Eve. He demanded that we give the horses back. Or he would harm my mother." Turnbull's voice had dried up, almost to a croak. He cleared his throat. "He kept badgering me when you were not about. So eventually, I agreed to his demand, if he could find me some intelligence in return. It was he who told me that Baird planned to escape on the full moon – only to turn up with an army of his own, the night before."

Antoine gasped. "He led the Douglases' attack on Ravenscleugh?"

"Yes," groaned Turnbull. "He turned up for the nags, as we had arranged. But when I realised he meant us harm, I did not let him in, I swear. It was the only time I have been false with you, and I have regretted it ever since."

Antoine was stunned that the boy had kept such a secret

from him. But there was no point in berating him now. "It was a stupid mistake, that's true. But in truth, it cost us little. That fellow would have attacked Ravenscleugh, with your encouragement or not. And it was you who got him in the end, at the drovers' inn."

He hesitated, thought again about the dire fact that they would die unshriven. While confiding in a friend was hardly the same as confessing to a priest, perhaps this would count for something, when he was called to reckoning. "I have something I've been keeping from you too," he whispered. "Not a mistake, as such, although God knows I have made enough of those. A secret."

Turnbull drew his breath. "Go on."

"When we began this mission, I had in my mind that it would be my last here. That once Albany was returned, I would take his ship back to France. I had been meaning to tell you but never found the moment. Then, as things unravelled, of course I saw the chance was gone."

Turnbull sighed. "I had suspected something of the kind. I was surprised you stayed on last year, when you had the opportunity to go."

"That's testimony to you. I found fulfilment in our work together. Then perhaps my head swelled, and I entertained thoughts of bigger things. Now look where my pride has brought us both."

"Was that what you and Catherine were talking about, that night at Ravenscleugh?"

"Yes, she was vexed that I had not told you of my plan. The fault for that was mine, not hers."

"Then our consciences are clear. Let us hope that God looks kindly on that."

There was another long silence, filled only by the

heaving of the sea and the last calls of the birds. All at once, Turnbull began to intone the Lord's Prayer: quietly at first, then more forcefully. Antoine was used to reciting this with the lad each evening, but the words carried far more meaning in this grim cell. He remembered a time, in his previous life, when he had been incarcerated in a Venetian prison, in a similar state of despair. That time, his prayers had been answered. Could the Almighty spare him again?

Antoine found himself joining in, the two of them enunciating each word with greater passion than the last, until the last plea rang out: "Deliver us from evil."

The hatch slid back, and the gaoler reappeared, his goggle eyes fixing them accusingly. "I was just coming wi' your ales," he said, holding two wooden cups to the hole. "But if ye keep up that din, ye can whistle for them."

Antoine sat up. "No, please, let us have them. We were just saying our prayers."

"It's a bit too late for those," scoffed the gaoler. "I fear God doesnae smile on would-be child killers."

Antoine was so startled by the accusation that, at first, he did not understand its meaning. Then he realised this was what Douglas planned to charge them with in the morning: kidnapping the king, so that they could murder him. He shook his head at the outrageous calumny of it. To be executed was bad enough, but to have one's good name destroyed for all time was too much to bear.

"If you mean His Grace, we'd never harm that boy."

"A likely tale. I hear the proof is damning."

"You wouldn't say that if you knew aught of our story. Come, if you let us have our ale, we'll tell you everything. Then you can judge whether we're the villains your master makes out – or whether it is he who is the knave."

Antoine watched as the gaoler weighed the need to get on with his duties against the opportunity for some gossip. He hoped that the temptation for tidbits might prove too much for a man confined on this desolate rock. Of course, telling this lowly turnkey anything would not help them at their trial tomorrow, but at least it would let them rehearse things for their day of judgement in the next world. He was pleased when the man nodded and pushed the cups through.

In between gulps of ale – the first fluids they'd had all day – Antoine and Turnbull took it in turns to describe their journey of the last few weeks. How they had stumbled on Lord Douglas's deception of his wife, fought off his murderous attempts to conceal the truth, uncovered his plot to kidnap the king, and rescued the boy from the hands of an outlaw, at great risk to themselves. They spared no detail, and when they were finished, they could see their listener was quite transformed, his leering expression replaced by one of concern.

"If what ye say is true, then you will suffer a grave injustice," he said earnestly.

"Not if you could pass our story on?" said Turnbull.

"Who to? As ye've already said, my master willnae want to hear it."

"Then help us to escape. Never mind your Lord Douglas. Our master is Lord Albany. And if you help us get out of here, he'll see you are well rewarded."

Ah, that was the Turnbull that Antoine loved: the lad was never one to give up, no matter how grim their situation. Of course, the gaoler could not possibly agree to such a wild proposal, but it had been worth a try. He waited for the hatch to close again, but instead, the turnkey's leering expression returned.

"How much are we talking, and how certain are ye that I'll get it?"

Antoine took over, his heart thumping at the idea that they might yet avoid the axeman. "Enough to see you never have to work on this stinking island again. And as certain as the sun will rise tomorrow."

The man scratched his nose. "Then just afore that sun comes up, I will knock on the hatch three times. Me and my son will land ye down the coast, then we'll a' have to make our own escapes. Ye'll have to help with wi' the rowing too."

"Of course, of course," said Antoine. He was about to add that they would need some swords as well, but the hatch closed, and they heard the gaoler bustle off.

They were plunged into darkness again, but hope's candle now burnt in their breasts, and the thought of tomorrow's first rays of sun was seared onto their brains. That night they offered further prayers, but this time to thank God for smiling on them. And to their unlikely saviour angel.

Chapter 45

Antoine and Turnbull had been awake for hours, when the faintest glow appeared around the edge of the door's hatch. The birds were already screeching outside, so they had to strain for any sound of their rescuer. At times, they were deceived by a gust of wind or the clatter of the sea on the rocks. But presently, they heard the crunch of footsteps on the path. A whispered conversation. The jingle of keys. Some more hushed words. Three knocks followed, just as they had been promised.

The men stood up, as the grille opened and the gaoler appeared. Antoine felt a wave of excitement swell within him. But just as quickly, his hopes were dashed, as the turnkey stepped aside and Lord Douglas pushed his face to the hatch.

"I hear you tried to bribe my man," he sneered. "Luckily, Master Inglis is a loyal servant and came straight to me, with lots of juicy details which we did not have before."

God's teeth, so they had been betrayed. Worse, they had provided their enemies with further sticks to beat them with. Antoine tried to protest, but the door swung open, and they were bundled out of the cell, into the blinding light. Within minutes, a team of surly oarsmen was propelling them to their doom, under Douglas's steady gaze.

Antoine saw Turnbull's lips move in silent prayer. But

that treacherous turnkey had been right, it was too late for that, unless a miracle intervened.

Upon reaching the castle, they were taken to the Great Hall. As Douglas had predicted, Hamilton and Pentland were already there, sitting at two chairs in the far corner. Antoine tried to catch their eye, but they looked straight ahead, their faces drawn. Douglas resumed his place at the centre of the top table and told Antoine and Turnbull to stand in front.

As they shuffled forwards, their hands still tied, a cadaverous fellow in a black cap and gown entered the room. With his sunken cheeks and tombstone teeth, he could have been Death himself, but Douglas introduced him as his clerk.

"I have not been able to find any lawyers at short notice, so I will prosecute the case myself. Master Sandlin here will take notes."

The clerk sat beside his master and unfolded a bundle of papers and other objects, including the items which had been confiscated at Black Rig. When he had everything in place, Douglas cleared his throat.

"Very well, let us begin. Hamilton and Pentland, I will come to you later. But first, I will deal with de Lissieu and Turnbull, as befits the gravity of their crimes." The clerk passed him a piece of paper, and Douglas flashed them a wolfish smile, before reading from it in a low monotone. "Antoine D'Arcy de Lissieu and George 'Dod' Turnbull, you are brought before this court today to be charged with high treason against the king and his mother the queen, culminating in the kidnap of His Grace with intention to murder him; the murder of the queen's equerry Fortingale and sundry others; collusion with a notorious outlaw; and various other offences including fraud, theft and obstruction of the law, which while lesser, are still punishable by death." He fixed them in a piercing gaze. "How do you plead?"

"Not guilty, to every charge," said Antoine.

"Not that it will make any difference," added Turnbull.

"Unrepentant to the last, I see. Then let me surmise your vile conspiracy. Master Sandlin, pass me the first set of papers." The clerk nodded and slid a letter across the table. Douglas licked his lips. "Your orders from Lord Albany. I presume you recognise the seal?" He held it up, and Antoine nodded. "As we all know, your master is not content with being our governor; he wishes to wear the crown himself. But while he grasps for it, he knows he cannot be caught red-handed. So some months ago, he concocted a plan to seize control, while he was out of the country. You were to be his instrument."

Antoine rolled his eyes in disbelief. "My master is in France, signing a treaty which will benefit all of us. If this is how you mean to conduct the trial, we may as well stop right now."

"Oh, there will be no stopping until I say so," snarled Douglas. He waved the letter again. "These papers show that your master instructed you to inspect the king's quarters at Edinburgh Castle, then report immediately to the notorious reiver Will Baird, at Ravenscleugh. Knowing what we do now, I think we can all guess why."

"That is a ridiculous interpretation. We were to check that the king was happy, and then – quite separately – we were to guard Baird, not report to him."

"There should be a page in there about the queen as well," said Turnbull. "How we were to welcome her and make sure she was treated well."

Douglas gave an exaggerated frown and pretended to search about the table. "How strange, that page is missing." He persisted with the jest a little longer, before resuming his grave countenance. "In any case, you did no such service to my wife. Instead, you enticed her over the border with promises that she would be allowed to see her beloved son – only to renege on these promises days later. According to Master Inglis, you even created some false pestilence to cover your trail?"

That damned gaoler, contorting their words. "That was not our doing," said Antoine sourly. He glanced at Hamilton and Pentland for help, but they offered him no succour. So that was how they aimed to play this, the knaves.

Douglas smiled, as if he understood. "Perhaps we should come back to that. But either way, you accompanied me to the castle, where I recall you taking a great interest in the defences. You seemed to count every guard, make a note of every passageway. And once you had seen how securely His Grace was kept, you recommended that his restrictions be loosened, no doubt to make plucking him all the easier."

"I was concerned for your stepson's happiness, an idea you seem to find quite alien."

Douglas ignored the jibe. "You left early the next day, eager to share your intelligence with Baird. But you were almost foiled from the start, for the queen's loyal equerry suspected you. Fortingale followed you to The Boar's Head tavern, a known den of malcontents, and heard you discuss your plot."

"That's an outright lie."

"Not so." Douglas snapped his fingers, and the clerk held up the plague bags from the tavern. "These nosegays prove that you were there. You knew he'd listened at the window – when we visited the place, the innkeeper confirmed it. Indeed, he told us that you came back later and ordered him to destroy the records. No wonder, because by that time, you had hunted down Fortingale and murdered him."

Antoine shook his head at the shameless way Douglas bent the truth. He prayed again for that miracle, but time was running out as their prosecutor picked up his pace.

"You proceeded to the tower and made contact with Baird, as agreed. Together, you hatched a plan – for him to snatch the king, in return for his freedom – and even formed a perverse friendship with him."

"I warned de Lissieu not to get too close," Hamilton interjected. Antoine spun round at the double-dealing wretch. He clearly meant to save his skin, even if it meant selling everyone else's. "The keeper told me these two even dined with Baird, as if he were their toping partner."

"Shut your crooked mouth for now," snapped Douglas. "We will have plenty of time later to discuss why you visited Ravenscleugh – and had your own converses with Baird. What is clear – cosy dinners or not – is that, from this point, your foul plot took shape. No doubt it was Baird who counselled you to distract me, with a plot against the queen. But if you were truly concerned by that, why not send a warning to Her Grace, in Edinburgh?"

"Because I thought she was with you, at Newark. Of course, that was your fancy woman, wasn't it?"

Douglas curled his lip, as the clerk passed him another piece of paper. "You also found pamphlets like this in Lauder, alleging that your master wished to kill the queen. But you did not bring them forth. Instead, you ordered them to be concealed."

"Destroyed, not concealed. Because they were quite obviously false. I came straight to you, with a more general warning though."

"Only so you could present yourself as an ally. And like a fool, I believed you. But the more I thought of it, the more your story did not chime. Then suddenly I had it. I saw what you and Baird were up to and sent my men to Ravenscleugh to foil your plot."

"To kill us all, more like," said Turnbull.

"This is where you began to show your true colours. You helped Baird escape, using some secret passage. Now your game was in play, but again we were on to you. I sent a man after you, but you slaughtered him in cold blood. Here is the brooch which you held on to, like some infernal keepsake."

Turnbull began to protest that the brooch had been taken from someone who had tried to kill his mother, but Antoine stopped him, lest he incriminated her.

"Then you disappeared, and we lost you for a while. But your confession to the gaoler has helped us fill the gaps. We tracked Baird to a hut at Fala, but it seems you helped him escape and met at some old crone's cottage, to finalise your plan. Afterwards, you raced to Edinburgh and tried to breach the city gates but heard that the king was at Craigmillar – Hamilton, we will deal with that later – so turned your evil attentions there. You had a map drawn up, to enable an attack." The clerk passed him the sketch. "See, it details all the castle's weak points."

Hamilton let out a cry of outrage. "So, de Lissieu was in on it, as I suspected! My Lord Douglas, he tricked us all. He bribed a carter to block the gate. I can find you the man; he said he was briefed by a Frenchman named de Lissieu, who showed him his warden's ring!"

"That was Baird," spluttered Antoine. "He stole it from me!"

"Or you gave him it. Then you insisted on going hawking with the king so you could guide Baird in!"

"Silence!" shouted Douglas, thumping his fist on the table. "Hamilton, you will pay for your lax security later, but for now, let us stick to the facts."

A fat chance, thought Antoine, as Douglas rattled off further charges.

"Baird stole the king, and you followed him, under pretence of chasing him. Two of my men almost captured you at some drovers' inn, but you murdered them and stole their horses."

Antoine shook his head. "They attacked us. And the horses were ours."

"You then arranged to meet Baird again, at Wolfsruther of all places. Somewhere no honest man would ever venture. Then, yet another time, at some witch's house in Cheeklaw. I hear your friend the sorceress even gave Baird a secret potion, that he might evade us." Douglas turned to the clerk. "Sandlin, make a note. We should pay that hag a visit."

This was too much for Antoine. "Leave her out of it," he exclaimed. "She has nothing to do with this."

"We shall see," replied Douglas, his eyes narrowing. "But finally, we come to the most damning fact, and one which you cannot possibly deny. Which is that you let Baird go and took possession of the king, secreting him at your tower. No doubt you thought you'd got away with it and could kill him, without eyes on you or your master. But luckily, my men found you, before you could have your evil way."

Douglas pushed his chair back and spread his arms, as if

to say that the case was inarguable. And so it was, in this pathetic excuse for a court.

Antoine shook his head. "Your account is but a parody of what has been going on. Your cheating of the queen. The countless attacks on us and others. Your own designs on the king. But be careful how you tread, my lord. These charges strike at our master, not just us, and Lord Albany is still this country's governor."

"Not for much longer," said Douglas, gathering up the pieces of evidence. "Not when these foul crimes of his are known."

"We have many witnesses to what you have done. You cannot simply exclude their voices today."

"No, but I can silence them, with a little time."

Antoine felt his bile rise at the young man's wickedness. He strained at the rope around his wrists, but there was not a bit of slack. In any case, there was no way out of the hall, let alone the castle. It was over, then.

Douglas steepled his fingers and creased his bow, as if he were giving the evidence serious consideration. He turned to the clerk, and they traded whispered thoughts in a further pretence of deliberation. Then the young aristocrat nodded gravely.

"Very well. After hearing all the evidence, this court finds you both guilty of all charges. You will therefore be taken from this room immediately, and your heads will be removed in the courtyard." His face brightened. "Normally, we would stick them on the battlements to rot. But if you prefer, de Lissieu, we could send yours back to France? And perhaps yours to your mother, Turnbull?"

Douglas laughed as the prisoners were dragged away. Antoine cursed the notion that the wretch's chuckle might be the last thing he heard, save the whistle of the axe. But the men had barely reached the door when they were brought to a halt by a powerful voice.

"Go no further. My lord, your scheme has been uncovered."

Chapter 46

The queen swept in, causing all to bow. She was resplendent in a gold dress and pearl necklace, that radiated majesty. But her eyes were blazing, her lips tightly pursed. She carried her son's cloth horse in one hand, and in her other, she held a letter. Good God, thought Antoine as he shuffled back to the centre of the room, perhaps my prayers have been answered after all.

"We are in the middle of important matters, Your Grace,' said Douglas, frowning. "Cannot this wait until we're done?"

"I come here on those matters," she replied icily. "For I have chanced upon something that casts a very different light on the murky business you're discussing."

Douglas shifted in his seat. "Oh yes, and what might that be?"

"A letter from the king. Or rather a letter which the king has given me, from the pocket of this toy. It was penned by a man named Walkerburn."

Turnbull gasped. "But I thought—"

"No," said Antoine wearily. "In our last hour at Black Rig, I placed another parchment in the ledger and hid the real one in His Grace's plaything. I asked him to give it to his mother, when he had the chance. Nobody spotted the fake when we were first searched – they were too busy with the ledger – and when His Lordship questioned us, I pressed him to put it on the fire before reading it, by trying to snatch it from him."

"So it is quite real?" said the queen, her cheeks burning.

"Absolutely, Your Grace. We've been trying to find a way to bring it to you."

"You mean trying to trick her," spat Douglas, before turning to his wife. He looked rattled but put a hand across his heart. "The whole thing is made up by Albany, my love. To drive a wedge between us."

"Then how do you explain it?"

"As a forgery. Cooked up by these two, when they knew they had been caught."

The queen gave Antoine and Turnbull a penetrating look. "Well, do you have anything to prove the script is true?"

The two looked at each other, but their blank faces betrayed their empty minds.

"There, I told you so," said Douglas. "They cannot prove a thing."

"But I may be able to," said a voice from the side. Antoine was surprised to see Pentland sticking up for them – indeed the secretary's hand-wringing suggested he too was unsure of his change of sides. "I-I think I may have another letter from this Walkerburn in my baggage. Just one of many I have received from local bailies these past few months, in relation to financial matters. If you give me a moment, I could look for it?"

Douglas spluttered that this would be a gross distraction, but the queen ordered Pentland to go. A vein throbbed on her husband's forehead as she took another look at the letter in her hand.

"We will soon see what Pentland comes back with. But if this letter is true, it shows that you have deceived me, in more ways than one. It is beneath me, as a queen, to discuss the bawdier allegations it contains, but the milking of my estates is another matter. I will not tolerate it, do you understand?"

"Calm yourself," said Douglas sharply. "I will get Sandlin here to explain the numbers."

"Do not dare to calm a queen! And do not imagine that you can gull me like some silly girl, either. For this letter tallies with my own investigations." The men sat openmouthed as the queen jabbed a finger at her husband. "Yes, I, too, have been busy this past month. I have long been vexed by the creaming of my rents, so I tasked my loyal Fortingale with it. He established that the problem centred on my lands at Ettrick Forest, so he went to make enquiries. He reported that these two seemed to have naught to do with it, but that some dead bailie named Walkerburn might. Then he himself was killed, before he could find out more."

Douglas waved her away. "De Lissieu killed Fortingale. We have already established that."

"Not true, Your Grace," said Turnbull. "Your husband let us present no evidence. If he had, I would have explained how I spoke to the fellow who found Fortingale. A mercer named Barty Veitch. According to him, your man's last words were to pass a warning to you."

"Tell me where this Veitch lives and I will visit him," said Douglas through gritted teeth.

"No need," said his wife. "Veitch is well-known to my people and has already passed his story on. I gather that de Lissieu tried to send word to me too, through some provisioner in Lauder. Then, hearing I was at Newark, he raced there – only to discover you were with your so-called sister." The queen said these last words as if she were spitting poison. "That puzzled me, for, as you know, your sister has been in St Andrews the whole time. But now I understand."

Douglas reddened as he struggled for an alternative explanation. Eventually, Sandlin came to his rescue. He bowed his wizened head. "With the greatest of respect, Your Grace, I fear you leap to false conclusions. Surely the word of your husband should count for more than the letter of a madman and the gossip of some peasants."

"Not when his word can be so easily disproven, you ghoulish churl."

"Now you grow over-wrought," said Douglas.

"No, I grow impatient for the truth."

"The truth is staring you in the face, woman!" said Douglas, slamming his fist on the table. "These two kidnapped your son and meant to kill him. And if you're not careful, you will be next on their master's list!"

He picked up the pamphlet containing the slander about Albany and threw it across the table. It hit the queen's gown and fell to the floor. Not even deigning to look down at it, she kicked it to the side so that it skimmed across the flagstones and landed at the feet of the newly returned Pentland.

"I have found that other letter," he said awkwardly, as he entered the room and scanned the array of angry faces. He stepped over the pamphlet and placed a small piece of parchment on the table. It contained only a few lines, relating to some unpaid burgh tithes, but the spidery handwriting was a perfect match for Walkerburn's death note. The queen put the two documents side by side and raised her eyebrows at her husband.

He fiddled with one of his rings. "Very well, the letter

may be genuine. And suppose this bailie wasn't entirely mad. None of this changes the fact that you are my wife. Your lands and incomes are mine, according to the law."

"Not according to the terms of my dower, which supersedes the common law."

In the corner, Hamilton stirred. "You are right, Your Grace. And I for one would support you in any action to recover the monies owed." O-ho, thought Antoine, the fox had picked his moment to pounce. The balance of power in the room had shifted, and the slippery devil was making sure he was on the right side of it. Douglas flashed him a venomous look.

"I trust it will not come to that," said the queen. "But enough of this spectacle; we should deal with this in privy. Meanwhile, these men must be set free. Someone must pay recompense for any crimes committed. And above all, my access to my son must be reaffirmed. Are we all agreed?"

The men nodded meekly, and the queen turned her back on her husband's pathetic attempts at reconciliation and bustled from the hall.

"By Jesu, that was close," Antoine said to Turnbull as they stood on the battlements that evening. They were both utterly exhausted and had to lean on the walls, just to avoid collapsing.

"Aye, Baird would have been proud of your deception," laughed the boy.

"In truth, I was more minded of that trick that Crichton played at Ravenscleugh, throwing the wrong key in the furnace."

"Well, whatever gave you the notion, it came good."

Antoine stared at their former prison on the Bass Rock. "Yes, I suppose it did. We're free anyway, and our heads stay on our shoulders."

"So what do you think will happen next?"

"It depends on when our master returns. Hopefully soon, in which case, he can handle Douglas. I doubt he will stand trial, for there's so much of this he can deny, and, for all her rage, the queen may not wish to cut him loose just yet."

"And if Albany is further delayed?"

Antoine sighed. "More of this nonsense."

For a while, they said nothing. Antoine felt his wounds sting and his bones ache. He thought of all that they'd been through, all the bodies they'd had to leave along the way. Had the pain and bloodshed been worth it? His head throbbed with the politicking that they'd witnessed, and he tried to piece together what it all meant for them, for the country, for life itself. But he was too weary to find any such profundity. All he could think of was his bed.

He laid an arm on Turnbull's shoulder, and they trudged to the far end of the battlements. They had been given their old quarters in the East Tower, one storey down, on the fourth floor. It would be a fine change from last night's cell, but in truth, any resting place would do. A few more steps and they would be there. And yet, just as they rounded the corner, they saw a hooded man creeping along the landing on the floor below.

What was this now? Would this thing never end? They pressed themselves against the central column of the staircase, so that the stalker did not see them, but they got a glimpse of him as he paused and removed his hood.

The flickering wall torch was just enough to reveal that he was an ugly brute of a man, with a V burnt into his forehead.

Chapter 47

They waited until the man had disappeared down the corridor, before peeling themselves from the wall. Antoine felt his head pound afresh.

"That was V-Face, surely?"

"Why else would a vagabond be creeping about the castle?"

"Then he was one of Douglas's men, after all. But what's he up to now?"

For a moment, Antoine had a terrible fear that the man might be hunting for the king, but the child was with his mother, in the other tower.

Turnbull grabbed his elbow. "Hamilton and Pentland are the only ones on this floor," he whispered. "Perhaps Douglas has sent him to exact revenge."

Antoine sighed at the thought of yet more bloodshed. Given their treachery in the Great Hall, he was half-minded to let Hamilton and Pentland fend for themselves. But this shadowy figure was the final piece of their puzzle. They couldn't just let him slip through their fingers. So, summoning what little strength he still had, Antoine ignored the lure of his chamber and led the lad downstairs.

They arrived at the landing and checked that V-Face was not there. There was only one door, so he must already be in the room. Damn. As they crept along the short passageway and took a position either side of the door, Antoine wondered whether they were too late. But there were no sounds of fighting from within. Perhaps Hamilton and Pentland were not there, and V-Face had entered to lie in wait for them? If so, they must be stealthy too.

He turned the handle and was relieved when the door opened easily. Carefully, he pulled it ajar and peeped round the corner. Hamilton and Pentland were there after all, albeit with their backs to him, looking out to sea. They were conversing light-heartedly. But unbeknownst to them, a shadow was passing across the wall, behind them. V-Face now came into view – and in his hand, he held a knife.

"Stop right there!" called Antoine, throwing the door open, his sword in hand. Turnbull charged in behind him, as the other three men swung round.

"What's going on?" said Hamilton, alarmed.

"This man, he's here to kill you," said Antoine. He turned to V-Face. "Now, put that dagger down, sir."

There was a tense moment, while the men sized each other up. Antoine hoped that Hamilton and Pentland had their weapons handy as, if so, it would be four against one. But even if they didn't, the intruder would hopefully know that he was caught. Sure enough, V-Face held up his knife and put it on a nearby table, which had been laid out with food and wine. But as he did so, he allowed himself a smirk.

He opened his other hand, to show an apple. "Should I put this down as well? I was just cutting it for His Lordship, but mayhap ye think I might throw it at him."

Antoine frowned and waited for Hamilton to respond, only for him to turn away and exchange some muttered words with Pentland.

"I'm afraid there's been a misunderstanding," said the secretary, when they had finished conferring. He bade the new arrivals in. "Pull up a chair and we'll try to explain. Perhaps I should begin by introducing you to Master Kinnart."

V-Face gave a mocking bow and swaggered to the table. As he went, Antoine got his first proper view of the burnt flesh on his forehead and imagined what kind of pain the man must have experienced in receiving it. No doubt he was a hard fellow, whoever he was. Still bewildered, Antoine and Turnbull replaced their weapons and took their seats beside the ruffian, while Pentland poured them all some wine.

"Master Kinnart is a former inmate of the Chapel of St John," the secretary continued. "The vagabonds' hermitage, near Craigmillar. Perhaps you passed it when you visited us?"

Antoine nodded, although their ride from Edinburgh seemed like an eternity ago.

"Kinnart has been helping us. So there's no need to fear him. He's on our side."

"What side is that?" said Antoine coldly. He remembered how readily Hamilton and Pentland had deserted them at their trial.

"Why, Albany's, of course. We've all been trying to do his work, while he's away. It's just our methods that have differed. So be at ease. You're amongst friends."

The words jarred with Antoine, but he took a cup of wine and gestured for Pentland to go on.

"As you know, Lord Albany is currently delayed in your country. But have you heard the problem? The English, meddling as usual. They press your people not to sign a treaty with us, without a change of governor."

"King Henry's doing, I suppose."

"Of course. Albany had hoped that inviting Margaret Tudor back might ease her brother's loathing for him. But alas, Henry is pig-headed. So we are left with a stalemate, with the governor stuck in France and the country prone to mischief – as we have already seen."

Antoine nodded, but still he was bemused. "So what's Master Kinnart's part in this?"

"I'll come to that," said Pentland, taking a sip of wine. "The point is, we're still hopeful that Henry will back down. Or that your king will simply defy him. But the longer Albany is delayed, the more nervous the lords of council will grow. Before long, they'll seek a deputy, at least, to steer the ship of state until he's back. It is imperative that this is not Douglas. So a while ago, we decided to make sure of it."

"Make sure?" said Antoine.

"Give the truth a helpful hand," said Hamilton.

"That's right," said Pentland. "We had heard of Douglas's deception of his wife, long before you brought us those papers. We saw how it might split their faction and even bring her to our side. But we feared she would not believe us, if we brought her the news directly. It needed to come from a source she trusted."

Antoine creased his brow, causing Hamilton to laugh. "He means you, you fool. That woman trusts you, for some reason. So we came up with a little scheme to make sure that you stumbled on the news."

Now Antoine really didn't understand. He glanced at Turnbull, but it seemed the lad was none the wiser.

"We heard that Bailie Walkerburn kept certain ledgers that would prove Douglas's deception. But our sources said he was loyal to his master and could not be bought. So we decided to take more direct action."

The secretary pursed his lips, as if he did not wish to elaborate. It caused Hamilton to tut impatiently, before taking over.

"What Pentland means is we sent Kinnart to sort it out. As you may imagine, our friend is not a man to be trifled with. He paid off Walkerburn's servant, Dewar. Together, they drugged the bailie and strung him up, as if he'd done it to himself. Then they left the ledger out, where you would find it. For separately, we'd sent you down to Lauder and told you to visit the town on your first day."

Antoine gasped. So this whole mission had been a fraud? And Turnbull had been right about the bailie's death, after all? He reeled at the way they had been tricked.

"What about the letter? It was forged, then?"

Pentland held up his ink-stained hands. "I'm afraid so, as was the one I produced today. I may be an odious little scribbler, as Douglas told me at the palace, but I am a rather good one."

"And the story of the card game?" said Turnbull.

"A little ruse to support our story. Master Kinnart is a striking figure, shall we say, so we got him to buy drinks for the tavern and brag about his win, so that folk would remember him."

"Walkerburn was a gambler, that bit was true," said Kinnart, as if it justified his actions.

"Everything about this was true," said Hamilton forcefully. "As I say, we were just helping the facts see the light of day."

Antoine shook his head. Perhaps Hamilton was not quite as bad as Douglas, but the way he wrapped himself in virtue was nauseating. He felt his anger rise. "Then why not be open with us, in the first place?"

"Would you have helped us, if we'd told you?"

"Of course not, the thing's depraved."

"Then there's your answer. And save your holy outrage, for it was not our fault that things went astray."

"Aye," said Kinnart, through a mouthful of apple. "The wife must have found the book and letter while Dewar was fetching ye. She suspected something was amiss, so hid them, only for Dewar to force it out o' her when ye'd gone. Then the knave obviously thought he might make some more coin, by taking it to Douglas."

"That was his mistake and the start of all our problems," said Pentland. "For, of course, Baird's gang robbed him on the way."

"Aye," said Kinnart. "But at the time, I didnae ken that. When I heard the wife was deid and the servant gone, I kent something had gone awry, so I got some men to dress as cleaners and search the house. They found nothing, but I heard Dewar had made off to Ettrick Forest, so I followed him, only to find he was already deid. At that point, I kent our game was up, and I returned to Edinburgh."

"Yes, I must say, this was not the news I had been hoping for," said Hamilton. "And when you sent your own message from Ravenscleugh, I decided to take a look for myself. I feared that Baird was to blame, but when I spoke to him in privy, I was reassured that he knew nothing. In fact, I assumed Douglas must have destroyed the goods. That meant it was time to double down on him."

Pentland shrugged. "There were already rumours that the queen had brought the plague with her, we did not make them up. But Kinnart's story of the cleaners sparked an idea for something bigger."

"The fake pestilence," said Antoine with disgust.

"Exactly. The cleaners allowed us to put the whole city in a state of alarm and move His Grace to Craigmillar. You know that part already. But not the crucial part! When you visited us, we told you that the king's presence was a great secret, as it should have been in normal circumstances. But in fact, Master Kinnart had spread the news in certain taverns, so that the Douglases would hear of it."

"That's why they were carrying that picture of him. And the map of Craigmillar," said Hamilton. "We wanted them to make an attempt on the king, so that we could catch them in the act. We practically invited them. Safe in the knowledge that we were armed to the teeth and had troops stationed all the way here."

This was a deception too far for Antoine. He leapt to his feet. "You used the king to bait a trap? This is treason, however you dress it up!"

Kinnart gripped his arm and locked him in a menacing stare. "Pray, do not lose your temper, sir."

"And be careful with your language," snapped Hamilton. "This was a well-thought plan, to *protect* the king from treason. And it was all working until you and your friend Baird crashed in."

Antoine was too weak to resist the force of Kinnart on his arm, so he slumped back in his seat. But he was still simmering with rage. "I wonder whether the queen would see it like that? Her beloved son used like a worm upon a hook."

"The queen will never hear of this, as it's in nobody's interest to tell her, not least yours. Listen. We have got what we all want, de Lissieu. Douglas is defeated. The queen is split from him. The king is safe, thank God. You should be thanking me, not preaching from your pulpit."

Antoine noted how Hamilton ordered his priorities. And yet, perhaps he was right that the ends justified the means. They lived in difficult times, where it was not always possible to achieve good things in a good way. Was it wrong to sacrifice a few lives, in order to save far more? He took another draught of wine and felt his bones call for sleep again.

"So what happens next?" he said quietly.

"As I say, hopefully, Albany will return soon and see that we have kept the land in good order. But if he is further delayed, the lords will choose a deputy to oversee the king, and we will all need to get behind them."

Hamilton did not need to spell out his own ambitions for such a role: the smug expression on his face told Antoine everything he needed to know.

"You know, I could use a pair like you," said Hamilton, before quickly correcting himself. "If I am chosen for higher office, of course."

Antoine looked at Turnbull and was glad to see the look of horror matched his own.

"I will consider that a no," said Hamilton, his voice hardening. "But do not think you can go back to your old life straight away. Douglas has it in for you. So if you do not want my patronage, you will have to lie low until Albany's back."

"And what does that mean?"

"Give up your role as warden and find a new master for a while. Just make sure whoever it is can protect you though. For as I told you back at Ravenscleugh, we live in dangerous times."

Antoine was about to reply that this was a contemptible reward for everything that he had done, but he realised that he no longer cared for the baubles of success. A few hours ago, he had expected to lose his head, so losing a job did not seem so bad.

He got up and put an arm around Turnbull's shoulders. "Don't worry about that. We'll be gone in the morning."

Epilogue

SEPTEMBER 1517 – TWO MONTHS LATER

It felt strange to be back in Lauder. But then again, it had been a very strange summer.

Albany had finally signed his treaty in August, but there was still no sign of him coming home. Some said that he might be back by Christmas, others that King Henry would never relent on the matter. Either way, the delay had prompted the lords of council to appoint Hamilton as his deputy, just as the scoundrel had hoped. Antoine shuddered at the thought of his smug face, as he strutted about the palace.

Meanwhile, the queen had begun legal action to recover the monies stolen from her. Thanks to the evidence that Antoine had provided, the case was crystal clear. However, the move had proved unpopular with the lords, fearful that their own wives might try something similar. Antoine suspected that Hamilton had encouraged her to press her suit, knowing full well that it would damage her. If so, it was a great shame because, based on her showing at Tantallon, she would have made a better leader than any of the men.

As for Douglas, he was now excluded from council, and

his brother put under lock and key, to prevent further trouble. So, while he still made threatening noises from afar, there was little he could do to harm Antoine and Turnbull, as long as they stayed out of his way.

To that end, they had spent the summer staying with various Albany loyalists. At first, they had welcomed the chance to rest, the opportunity to heal their bodies and give their minds some peace. But as time went on, and there was still no sign of their master returning, they began to get itchy feet. Was this all that life held for them now? To hide away like rabbits in a burrow?

They talked often of the little king, and how they risked the same fate: being passed from one gloomy castle to another. They longed to be out in the world again, before the leaves were off the trees. So when one of Mungo Bell's messengers brought them the wedding invitation, they jumped at the chance to go.

"Here come the happy couple now," said Turnbull, as Crichton and Elspeth made their way out of the church and joined them on the common, where a long table had been set up.

As the pair weaved through the small gathering of townsfolk, Antoine mused that the last time he had seen them, they had been covered in shit and fleeing from a gang of killers. He was cheered to see how happy they looked now, despite that inauspicious start. He was glad, too, to hear the joyful peals of Lauder's bells, which had once tolled for the Walkerburns.

"Congratulations," he said, rising from the table. "And thank you for inviting us to your special day."

"It is we who should thank you," said Elspeth. "God rest

my dear mother, but she would have been quite content if we all perished in that tower."

"I don't think so. She loved you in her own way. And she saved all of our lives."

"Aye, but it was you who set us free."

"We have full lives in front o' us now," said Crichton, shaking Antoine's hand. "I am back at the smithy, and Elspeth serves at The Red Lion. God willing, we will have bairns afore too long."

Antoine saw the love in their eyes, despite all that they had been through. Or was it because of that? He thought again of their escape from the cesspit. Perhaps that was all true love was: wading through shit but finding someone to hold your hand as you ran. He wouldn't know, of course.

"Talking of bairns, look at this young man," said Stumpy Watt, as he wandered over with Fleabite. The feral child that they had rescued from Ettrick Forest was now dressed in a good set of woollens, plain but respectable enough for an occasion such as this. Turnbull had found Stumpy and him jobs on his mother's farmstead, providing the help that she had so often asked him for. But as she joined them, Antoine saw that she had gained more than two hard workers from the arrangement.

"All my boys together," she exclaimed, with a pinch of Fleabite's cheek. "Just like the old days. Except now I have lassies as well." She gestured across the common, where Stumpy's wife was playing merrily with her daughters. One of the girls had pulled her bonnet over her face and was staggering about like a drunkard, to shrieks of laughter from the others.

"So much for the quiet life," said Turnbull to Stumpy, with a wry smile.

"Aye, but this noise is good. I feel alive again. My wife kens I'll no' go back to my old ways, and if I'm ever tempted, this wee man will put me right."

Fleabite shrugged and looked at his feet. Antoine wondered whether the boy had recovered from the massacre he had witnessed. What had Catherine said about children learning how to hide their pain? He thought of asking the lad how he was getting on, but Fleabite was already tugging his adoptive father's arm, and they ran off to join the fun.

Turnbull's mother watched them fondly. "Thank ye for sending me them," she said to her son. "And thank you, too, monsieur. When we last met, I telt ye to make your mission count. It sounds like that's what ye did."

"I hope so," said Antoine, although he avoided her eyes. "Your son was like a rock, you know."

"Well, we certainly ended up on a rock," laughed Turnbull, without elaborating. Antoine thought that was just as well: his mother would not be so friendly if she knew how close to death they'd come. As it was, it was good to have her blessing at last. She embraced her son, before joining her newfound family on the other side of the common, where some minstrels were unpacking their instruments.

Now Antoine and Turnbull were alone.

"So what do you really think, lad?"

"Of what?"

"Whether our work counted for aught. Yes, we may have saved the king, but the country is still divided. Villains still wait to pounce. And nobody will face trial for the crimes that we uncovered. I fear we ran hard, just to end up where Albany left us."

Turnbull shrugged. "We kept the peace, as we were

ordered. And we're still alive, aren't we? It could have been a lot worse."

They fell into a silence for a while, each lost in their own thoughts. It was a beautiful day, perhaps the last of the season. The corn had been harvested, but the trees and bushes still hung with berries. Next week it would be Michaelmas, the feast to mark the Archangel's great victory over Satan. After that, the dark and cold would creep in, and the Marches would be terrorised by nightly raids. But for now, the small crowd was bathed in a golden light, smiling, laughing, chattering. The minstrels were clearing a space for dancing. Antoine should enjoy this moment, so why did he feel empty?

A hand touched his shoulder, and he swung round. "Catherine!"

"We weren't expecting you," said Turnbull, with obvious delight.

"It's a long way for me to come on my own, but I wanted to see ye both. To make sure ye were well."

She sat down and took a cup of ale. Antoine felt his spirits rise a little, just from being in her presence. But he saw she was unsettled. He reminded himself that she, too, had been through a lot this summer – and that he had brought the trouble to her door. Fumbling in her haversack, she brought out a little cloth parcel and placed it on the table, between Antoine and Turnbull.

"I received word frae Baird," she said, to their surprise. "Nothing much. A short letter, begging forgiveness for his rough treatment o' me and saying that it was all a ruse: he would never have hurt me or the king. I believe him, don't you?"

Antoine and Turnbull nodded. They had spoken of this already.

"He said the potion didnae work either, but he escaped over the border and has formed a new gang in Redesdale."

It made sense. "A man like him will never be short of work," said Antoine.

"He asked me to thank you too. And look, there's something else."

Catherine gestured to the cloth parcel and told him to open it. Inside was the warden's ring that Baird had stolen at Old Peggy's cottage: a symbol of Albany's favour but also a trinket which had almost cost Antoine his head. He turned it over in his palm.

"So the reiver who did not kill was also a thief who did not steal. He truly was a riddle, that fellow. Still, I'll have little use for this now."

Catherine frowned. "Ye should keep it for when Albany returns and restores ye to your post."

"I am beginning to doubt that will ever happen. And even if it does, I'm not sure I would want the job."

"Then, what?"

Antoine shrugged. "All I know is that I never want to mix with the likes of Douglas and Hamilton again." He caught Turnbull's eye. "Or their equivalents in France. Once, that was my ambition; I hoped that the ranks of others would enhance my own. But I now see that playing with such mighty creatures only covers you in their mighty filth."

He looked across the common where the minstrels were encouraging folk to form a circle. Crichton lifted Elspeth in his arms, as the townsfolk kicked up a halloo. Stumpy and his wife chivvied their girls into line and forced them to hold hands. Turnbull's mother took Fleabite and hugged him to her side.

"Ye've made all these people happy," said Catherine softly. "Perhaps there is a clue for you in that?"

"What do you mean?"

"There are folk like this, all over the Marches, that need someone like you. Ye seem to enjoy helping them as well."

Antoine sighed. "It is fulfilling. But I fear there's no living in it."

"I don't know," said Turnbull, as if his imagination had been sparked. "The land is full of folk who will pay for justice, without embroiling us in treason. We will find something, I know we will."

Catherine smiled. "As ye said o' Baird, a man like you will never be short o' work."

Antoine did not answer her, but, not for the first time, he felt the power of her truth. He looked at the ring again. "I should get Crichton to melt this in his forge. It will provide him and Elspeth with some coin and leave some for Stumpy's family too."

"That's a beautiful thought," said Catherine. "Now let us see to your happiness as well."

She stood up and nodded to the dancers, who were just about to start. Antoine scanned the wedding guests and was comforted by their ordinariness: old folk, young couples, craftsmen, milkmaids, farm lads, apprentices and children. Not a lord or lady amongst them. Yes, he would be quite happy to live amongst such people and do what he could to improve their lot.

He was done with the dance of vipers. Done with its wearying twists and turns. His two friends extended their hands and pulled him to his feet, as the minstrels began to play.

Thank you

Thank you so much for reading this book. It would be wonderful if you could take a minute to leave a review on one of the usual platforms.

And if you'd like to learn more about the locations mentioned in this story, you can get a free behind-the-crime-scenes guide when you visit www.AKNairn.com

Historical Note

As with the first book in this series, *The Trail of Blood*, this is a work of fiction – but one with some firm historical underpinnings.

I based my hero on a real-life French diplomat, Antoine de la Bastie, who was made Warden of Scotland's Eastern Marches in 1516. A good man, who sought to bring peace to the troubled region, he was murdered in September 1517, just as *The Dance of Vipers* ends. However, I'll be giving my Antoine a much longer life.

The real Antoine's last mission was to welcome Margaret Tudor back to Scotland (she eventually arrived on the 15th of June 1517, after overcoming her fears of walking into a trap). He was then charged with looking after King James V at Craigmillar, because of an outbreak of the plague. I was attracted to the drama of these two historical events, and Antoine's role within them, so used them to bookend my story, while playing with the surrounding narrative.

While the king wasn't abducted from Craigmillar in 1517, he was the subject of many other kidnap attempts as a child. Most notably, there were concerted bids at Stirling (1515), Melrose (1526) and Linlithgow (also 1526), during which hundreds of people died. The king eventually escaped captivity in 1528, under the cover of a hunting expedition:

another element which I adapted. In fact, two of James' namesakes (James III and VI) were abducted while hunting, while James I was taken by pirates and held hostage in England for 18 years, so this was something of an occupational hazard for Stewart children!

Lord Albany had a short temper, but he tried his best to unite the factions ripping the country apart, and his motives in inviting Margaret Tudor back from exile were good. However, he was dogged by groundless rumours – that he intended to bed the queen, kill her, or murder the king – and Henry VIII's hatred of him kept him detained in France for several years, at great cost to Scotland's stability.

Margaret Tudor found out about her husband's betrayals a little later than I have suggested and probably did not confront him as publicly as I have depicted (although many historical accounts include such scenes). In the last few years, several historians have even questioned the story of his relationship with Lady Jane Stewart, which was hitherto accepted as fact. What is not disputed is Douglas's appropriation of his wife's finances and his generally awful behaviour towards her – or the fact that she spent the next ten years fighting him in the courts (and even in battle), before obtaining a divorce in 1527. Overall, I've tried to reflect contemporary (and often misogynous) criticism that Margaret was prone to complain, while acknowledging the tenacity and leadership she showed in a man's world.

When it comes to Lords Douglas and Hamilton, one stylistic confession is that I've adapted their titles: while these names are technically correct, they were more commonly known as the Earls of Angus and Arran, respectively, which I feared might be confusing. More importantly, I've invented their various misdeeds. But as they were both serial conspirators, I don't think I've done them an injustice. Indeed, it's almost impossible to list the sheer number of plots and counter-plots these two were involved with during this period.

Will Baird is a fictional creation. But again, I've used research to bring him to life. For instance, there was a notorious reiver called Adam Scott, who operated out of Ettrick Forest around this time and rejoiced in the title 'King of Thieves' (as opposed to my 'thief of kings'). Meanwhile, the equally infamous Richie Graham managed to escape from Carlisle Castle by jumping from the privy. And another rogue, named Jock o' the Peartree, kidnapped a sheriff's child, by scooping him onto his horse, with the words "Master, will ye ride?"

The Douglases' threat to strangle the locals in front of Black Rig was inspired by two grisly events two centuries earlier. In 1333, English forces exerted pressure on the defenders of Berwick by hanging hostages – including the Scottish governor's son – in front of the town's walls. And in 1346, Scottish soldiers forced an English commander in Cumbria to watch his sons being strangled, before he too was executed.

Finally, even the wolves were real. Or at least they could have been. The last documented report of these creatures in the Marches comes from 1458 (when ten were caught at Cockburnspath). But observers were still complaining that they were 'everywhere' in 1528. And what better place for them to lurk than Wolfsruther ('the swamp of the wolves'), now better known as Westruther.

In short, this was an extremely dangerous time and place to be alive – especially as a five-year-old king. And even if I've imagined some of the traitors' twists and turns, *The Dance of Vipers* was very real.

Acknowledgements

First and foremost, I am hugely grateful to my wife and kids for putting up with any viperous behaviour from me, while writing this book.

Thanks also to Craig Hillsley for taking time out of editing Booker Prize nominees to put my humble story through its paces; to Lynne Walker for her expert proofreading (not proof reading); and to Lorna Reid for the stunning interior design of the book. Great appreciation also goes to Kari Brownlie for another amazing front cover – and to the supremely talented Alex Kidd for the wonderful map.

In terms of reading, I cited a number of general texts on the reivers in *The Trail of Blood*, so I won't repeat them here. However, I must highlight a few books which informed the specific storyline of *The Dance of Vipers*. In particular, the following were invaluable: *The Minority of James V* by Ken Emond (2021); *Margaret Tudor: The Life of Henry VIII's Sister* by Melanie Clegg (2018); and *The Thistle and The Rose* by Linda Porter (2024).

I also consulted *The Last Wolf in Scotland* by John G. Harrison (2020), *The Eleven Plagues of Scotland* by W. J. MacLennan (2001), and *An Elephant Crossed the Valley* by Mary W. Craig (2021) for specific information on wolves, the plague and the Sanctuary at Stow, respectively.

As ever, any mistakes or creative re-interpretations are mine – but I console myself that any such crimes will be minor compared to those committed by my characters, both historical and fictional.

Printed in Dunstable, United Kingdom